Journey Of Revenge

To E. J. McCormick Jr., The best Lawyer / Legal expert on The planet! I hope you enjoy The book.

Thanks!

David Z. Price

David Z. Price

Library of Congress Control Number: 2010906664

ISBN:	Hardcover	978-1-4500-8338-6
	Softcover	978-1-4500-8337-9
	E-book	978-1-4500-8339-3

This is a work of fiction. Names, characters, places and incidents either are the product of the author's imagination or are used fictitiously, and any resemblance to any actual persons, living or dead, events, or locales is entirely coincidental.

This book was printed in the United States of America.

To order additional copies of this book, contact:
Xlibris Corporation
1-888-795-4274
www.Xlibris.com
Orders@Xlibris.com
76891

To my wife, Terry, and my friend Mike Rozich. It would be impossible to travel the straight road in life if it were not for individuals such as these. I will always be indebted to them for the trust and confidence that they displayed toward me even when the times were the darkest. I can only hope that I can continue to make them proud of me as a person, friend, and companion.

Special Thanks

I would like to thank Sonja Moline for her editing expertise. Her help was invaluable during the writing and completion of this novel.

Chapter 1

As I sit here in this pathetic cage, I can only wonder how I chose to be the person I am. What made me do the things I have done? Who drove me to be the animal that I am today? I believe that I have the answers to these questions, but do I? I am a person who really and truly has no compassion for others, no real values in life, and no value at all for human life. I lost the ability to love long ago. It seems so distant, so long ago, since I really cared about anything or anyone. This is probably the reason why I never married. No, I surely didn't need anyone in my life, especially a woman.

It's amazing how the brain controls everything that one does and the memories it chooses to store. Much like a computer, the brain stores bits of information at random, pulling them to the forefront whenever you desire. Fortunately, with a computer you can erase the bits of information that you don't need. It's not the same with your trusty brain, no, not at all. It keeps all of the information whether it's good, bad, or evil. The bad memories that you want to erase are always pulled to the forefront at the most inopportune times. Many, many sleepless nights are spent with these memories racing through my brain. Memories that others would not be able to comprehend, memories that are so filled with terror that most would rather lie awake than succumb to dreams as horrific as mine. Ah, but the brain is an impossible device to control. It lays in wait to cause me more pain than I can bear. It possesses an infernal ability to recall the evil that has been inflicted on me throughout my life. Evil that I can only hope few others have endured; as life should not be about evil, but about fun, laughter, and friends. These are vacant in my life, and my only friend has become the dark side of life and the evil that comes with it.

I look out at the prison yard upon this cloudy, gloomy, cold miserable afternoon. I never go to the yard with the other inmates. I have requested solitary confinement. I know all too well that I have no control of the anger that lies within me. I am the evil that comes to you in your worst nightmare; I am the person in the dark alley who waits to lunge at you just when you least expect it. Yep, that guy is within me and has been for almost as long as I can remember. It's not something that I'm proud of—it's how I was made; it's how I locked in my values at a young age. You see, people like me are not born evil. They are made evil by the training they receive when they are raised into adulthood.

I watch now as the inmates begin to gather in the yard and make their drug deals, swap cigarettes, tell lies, and determine the fate of their enemies. They come from all walks of life, from doctors who kill their wives, to street bums who kill to live. Not really different, are they? No, not really. All of them have chosen their destiny as I have, some just a little different way than others. One thing we have in common is that we are all pathetic, destined to live the life of an animal in a cage, destined to breathe the stench of filth in this crappy facility, and most of all, destined to die in this hole we now call home. Yeah, I chose the wrong path, but it's difficult to make the right decisions when the only way you view the world is through negative eyes. Once your life slides to the dark side, it's impossible to get back. Imagine never being able to think positively, never trusting anyone, never sharing your feelings with loved ones, because in reality, no one is ever loved. That's just how it is. Not that I wanted it that way; that's the way I was brought into this world, and that's the way I'll go out. As everyone knows, we all start the dying process the day we're born. For some it just takes a little longer than others. For me, it's been too long already, but the verdict should be in any time now, so my pain will soon be over. I wish no appeals, no deals—just end it, as I'm ready.

It all seems so very stupid to me; I sit here and wait for a verdict from what they call a jury of my peers. How could they possibly be my peers? They have no clue what makes me the way I am. They can't determine my true fate if they don't know me, but the folks running the show say this is fair. How is that possible? I can't explain it just as I can't explain why I kill. Is it a matter of desire to destroy the enemy, or is it because I am just an evil person, as I have always been led to believe? I don't know. I can't sort it out at this point, but I know that the desire to kill has lived within me for almost as long as I can remember. I have never feared dying, or for that matter, I have never feared anyone. Even the biggest and meanest person I've known during my life was easy to take down. It only takes one well-placed shot to drop an elephant. Even a poorly placed shot will drop a life-form as fragile as a human.

Now the rain starts. It's a perfect way to drop the daylight hours into darkness. The gloominess of these days only makes my disposition worse. Why should this day be any different from any other? Day after day, I spend thinking of the bad times that I have endured. You see, it's difficult to think of the good times when you have had none. I was trained not to have fun; I was trained not to trust people, and I was trained not to love. I envy the people who have fond memories of family and friends, as they are truly blessed. My only memories are painful ones, memories that should be forgotten but never will be.

Chapter 2

I was born in the small town of Monroe, Michigan. The year was 1949. My first memories from childhood began with my parents and me arriving at my grandparent's home on my grandfather's seventy-sixth birthday. I was just three and a half years old at the time. It's really hard for me to believe that my mind allows me to remember back that far into my childhood.

As soon as we entered the door, my grandfather came into the room. "Hey, Zeke's here!" he shouted. "Marie, give Zeke to me so I can hold him for a while."

My mother handed me to my grandfather, and a huge smile crossed his face. I was named after my grandfather's favorite uncle, and right from the start, he was very happy to see me. We walked to the living room of the old home, and my grandfather sat on the couch. He placed me on his lap very gently. I sat very still. It was as if I could feel the kindness radiate from him and surround me. Charles held me on his lap almost the entire time we were there. He spoke with my mother, never taking his eyes off me, and told her how happy he was that I was born. Charles told her that he had always wanted a grandson to carry on the family name. You see, I was a late-life baby as my father, James, was forty and my mother, Marie, was thirty-four. This was Marie's first pregnancy and, as things worked out, her last pregnancy. I guess he was worried that a grandson was not in the cards for him, and my mother's pregnancy with me was his last chance to have his wish. Charles seemed to be genuinely proud of me and very happy when he held me close to him. I really did like him and was drawn to him like a magnet whenever he was around.

Now, here I am standing in my grandfather's bedroom. I'm standing at the end of a huge four-post canopy bed watching my grandfather die. His name was Charles Baker. He was my father's father, the seventh son of a seventh son. Not a big man but a kind man. He was a gentle person who people were drawn to, as he seemed to radiate peace and kindness. He was stricken by a stroke two weeks after his seventy-sixth birthday. He didn't really have a prayer, as strokes were always fatal in the early '50s; no one could have really expected anything different than his death.

My grandfather passed a few hours later. I remember my parents trying to get me out of the room so he could be taken to the funeral home for preparation.

I didn't want to leave because I had no understanding of death, but I was fascinated by the fact that the old man just went to sleep and couldn't wake up.

I was very saddened by his passing because I realized that I could no longer see him, be held by him, or listen to him. He was just gone—no longer would he smile upon me. As hard as it is to believe, I have full and total recall of all events from this age forward.

All the relatives and friends came out in force to the funeral. I didn't quite understand, but it seemed as if some only came to enjoy the smoking room in the basement of the establishment and not to pay their respects to my grandfather. Still, many people did seem as if they were saddened by the death of the kind old gentleman. I, however, was very bored at the funeral. I just sat and stared at my grandfather as if I were expecting his eyes to open any minute.

I got mad when people interrupted my thoughts by picking me up and saying, oh, what a cute little boy. There was an endless stream of people bothering me, and I was not happy! Luckily for me, the days of the funeral passed very quickly. I traveled with my mother and father to the cemetery in a limousine provided by the funeral parlor. I watched as they lowered my grandfather into the dark cold earth. The minister was a gravel-voiced

Southern gentleman who was a Baptist. He made sure that not a dry eye remained in the crowd, sure that we all knew death was upon us, sure that we all knew there was a very distinctive difference between heaven and hell. By the time he was done speaking of devils and the demons within hell, I was sure that was a place I didn't want to experience!

When the sermon was finished, my father wanted to stay until the grave was totally covered. He had buried his father with his pocket watch and rings, and trust in the funeral director was something he didn't have.

Shovel after shovel, I watched as the dirt was thrown on top of the coffin. I imagined being inside and not being able to get out. What if he were really still alive in there? God, what a horrible thought! Finally my grandfather was buried, and we got in the car for the journey home. From this point forward, things began to change. The kind old gentleman was gone, and my father seemed to be really affected by this change in his life.

The days after the funeral were brutal for me. It seemed as though I was being treated differently.

My parents were making me stay on the living room couch for hours at a time, not letting me play with toys or do anything but sit there and stare at the wall. My father could not afford the luxury of a television. TVs were new to the market and more expensive than he could justify on his meager salary. So there I sat, my every movement watched as if I were a person who was not to be trusted. How could this be? Just a few weeks before, I was the center of attention; now I was being treated as if I were of little or no importance. I began to make up things in my mind to keep me occupied during these times of confinement. I made up imaginary friends, convinced myself that they liked me, and convinced myself that my parents would soon be good to me again. I really could not have been farther from the truth on the last topic.

I finally convinced my mother to buy me a few coloring books so I had something to do. That was a mistake, as she would watch me color and continually yell at me if I got outside the lines of the picture.

It progressed to the point where she would smack me on the hand with a foot-long ruler if I did not keep the crayon within the lines of the picture. Believe me, this was no gentle rap. This was a hard smack with the intent to inflict pain. Many times, my hand wore a bruise; many times, that bruise was smacked again with agonizing pain. Within a few weeks, I chose not to color anything anymore because it had become far too painful for me, and I was afraid that her anger toward me would worsen.

Chapter 3

I was not able to leave my confinement within my home from age 3 ½ until I started school at age five. We did not go for a drive in the country, to a park, or a restaurant. To me, the world outside my home was nonexistent. It appeared that my parents were either ashamed of me or they feared that disaster awaited me if I ventured into the world outside. To me, the why did not matter, but my resentment toward them began to grow. I wasn't having any fun, and I didn't want them to either.

School! Lots of other kids my age! This was great for me—a way to get out of my total confinement and a way to meet friends. I was quick to learn that school came with more rules. No talking in the classroom, assigned learning activities, and of all things, coloring projects. What were they trying to do, get me killed?

I was somewhat hyper, and therefore I made the mistake of talking to one of my classmates when the teacher was addressing the class. The teacher was Ms. Jackson, a leather-faced woman approximately sixty years old. She had never been married and had very little patience with disobedient students. I was very afraid of her because she seemed very angry most of the time. So what did I get on my second day at school? I got a whack on the hand with a foot-long ruler. I was really getting tired of this routine. I tried not to make any more mistakes, but once again, I crossed the line with the angry Ms. Jackson. This time I was assigned a chair facing the corner of the room staring at the wall. Just like the days on the couch, I was back in hell again.

At the end of the day, Ms. Jackson handed me a note to give to my parents. I couldn't read, but somehow I knew this was not a good thing. My mother waited outside the school yard for me, since I was not allowed to walk the three blocks to and from school by myself. I could not be trusted. About halfway home, I handed the note to my mother.

"What's this?"

"A note Ms. Jackson gave me for you."

She opened the note, and I saw an immediate frown come across her face.

"So you decided to be evil in class today?"

"I am sorry, but it was hard to remember all the rules."

"We'll see what your father has to say about this!"

I was very scared at this point because I had little contact with my father.

He worked sixteen hours per day, seven days per week, and he seemed particularly mean when he worked first shift. Unfortunately for me, this was the shift he was on this week. I walked very slowly toward my house, as I did not look forward to facing my father.

I entered the house very quietly.

"James!"

My father was sleeping, trying to get the rest he needed prior to going to work at midnight. But my mother's yell was very loud, and he awoke very quickly and was immediately in a bad mood.

"What?" he snapped.

"Your son has been evil in school, and he needs to be taken care of now!"

"Come in here, boy!" he boomed.

I slowly walked into the bedroom where I saw him removing his belt from his pants that were hanging on a closet door. I stood very still, petrified.

“I told you to come here, boy, now come here!”

I went over to my father, and he proceeded to beat me across my bottom with the belt so hard that the pain was unbearable. Finally he stopped and said, “Let’s see if you can learn to behave now.” I was in great pain, and I immediately retreated to my room and lay down in bed.

The next day in school was an embarrassment to me since it was so painful to sit at my desk that it was noticeable to the evil Ms. Jackson. She called me to the front of the class.

“What’s wrong with you?”

“What do you mean?” I was hoping she would just leave me alone.

“Well, it’s obvious that you have trouble sitting. Did my note to your parents get you spanked?”

When I confirmed her suspicion, she said, “Well, finally parents who will punish a child for being bad.”

“I don’t think I’m bad.”

“You talk back to me one more time, and I’ll send another note home to your parents!”

I surely did not want this to happen, so I said nothing more and returned to my seat.

Two weeks later, Ms. Jackson assigned coloring projects to the class. I was not very good at this, but since she assigned it, I had to do the coloring project. It did not turn out too bad—at least I thought it was fairly good. Ms. Jackson looked at all the projects done by the class, and then she announced that she wanted us to take the project home for our parents to see. Then she said something that made me cringe. She said that she wanted our parents to sign the coloring project and for us to bring it back to class so she would know that they had viewed the work. I was horrified. The work would never please my mother, and I did not want to be whacked with a ruler again. I had no alternative, so I took the work home to my mother for her viewing and signing. She was brutal to me.

"What, are you stupid? This is terrible. Can't you get anything right? How difficult can it be to color a simple picture? It's just impossible for you to do anything right, isn't it?"

The next move for her was to reach for the ruler; only this time, she hit me about the head, neck, and arms very hard—hard enough to make bruises. I again retreated to my room for the evening and did not come out for dinner. I really didn't want to be humiliated for my lack of coloring skill any more.

Much as with my parents, I was never able to please Ms. Jackson. She continued to give me work to take home, and I continued to be told how stupid I was with the end result being a beating. Sometimes with a hand, others with a ruler, others with a belt. It didn't matter; they all hurt, and they all left permanent mental scars that would never heal.

Chapter 4

It was Sunday morning and summer vacation from school, so I didn't fear the evil Ms. Jackson anymore. God, I hated Sunday!

My parents were dedicated Baptists, so we went to church every Sunday.

The kids in my Sunday school class's ages were from five to thirteen years old. My parents always took me to the classroom thirty minutes early because they did not want to be late for their Sunday school class. As soon as all adults left the room, the older kids would turn out the lights and pound the little kids. They all knew the teacher would not be there until minutes before the class would start. This was horrible! I would just cover my head, and they would hit me all over my body. No need telling my parents—they would be convinced that it was my fault, as always.

This Sunday turned out to be an especially bad day for me. My parents dropped me off at the classroom and left for theirs thirty minutes early, as usual. Immediately the older kids turned out the lights and started the pounding routine. I escaped and hid underneath one of the front pews in the room after receiving a pretty good pounding and kicking. The pounding stopped, and the lights went on as normal, but I was afraid to come out of hiding. The Sunday school teacher, Mr. Snyder, arrived shortly thereafter and came to the front of the room. He immediately noticed me under the pew and told me to come out. Reluctantly, I obeyed his command. My suit was all dirty from the floor, and I was pretty much a mess. He frowned at me and said, “Haven’t you been taught better than this, and what are you doing under there anyway?”

“I just want to be alone.”

“Well, if it’s alone you want to be, then go sit in the corner.”

How unfair! I was the victim, yet I was being treated as if I were the problem. I went to the corner and sat staring at the wall for the entire class period. I was really getting pissed at the older kids for getting me into trouble.

Unfortunately, the Sunday school teacher informed my parents that I was misbehaving in his classroom. I listened as he spoke to my parents, and fear came over me because they looked especially agitated as he spoke. It seems that my father was very good friends with this person, and he found it embarrassing that I caused this individual trouble. It was a very silent trip home, which caused me to be even more afraid of the consequences in store for me.

That was my first memory of wanting to die, as dying would be easier than the beating that was in store for me. After all, it seemed easy to die. Like my grandfather, just simply go to sleep and never wake up again.

My parents and I changed clothes, and I sat down on the couch in the living room. I heard them talking in the other room, but I really couldn’t understand what they were saying. When they came into the living room, it was clear they were angry. My mother looked at me and said, “So you’re just going to be evil no matter where you are, aren’t you?”

“I’m not trying to be evil. I just don’t want to be bothered by anyone.”

“No, some kids are just evil, and you’re one of them.”

The next words out of her mouth horrified me.

“In Sunday school class, you have learned about the devil and hell, haven’t you?”

“Yes,” I replied.

"Well, don't you know that the devil comes in the night and takes little evil boys like you away to hell and they are never seen again?"

God, I was scared. I remembered the speech of the Baptist minister at my grandfather's funeral and how horrific the devil and hell sounded. This was certainly something that I did not want to face.

I sat on the couch and watched out the window as my father cut a branch from a willow tree in our yard. He methodically began to peel the bark from the limb.

"Mom, what's Dad doing?"

"You'll see very soon."

When my father completed the task of peeling the bark from the limb, he came into the house with the limb in his hand. This would be my first, but not the last, experience of being beaten by a willow branch on my bare bottom. The pain and welts would last for weeks, and the mental anguish, forever. My penalty was very severe for my "antics" in the Sunday school classroom. I retreated to my bedroom and just lay on the bed, and as it tuned out, I was not allowed outside for the next two weeks. I lay there thinking of my mother's words to me. I pictured in my mind what the devil looked like remembering him from my Sunday school lessons. I got so very afraid that I made myself sick and threw up on my bed. This only resulted in another beating as I again had inconvenienced my mother. Of course, I was exiled to the couch again. I was getting tired of being the whipping boy, but I had no other choice than to take it because to complain just made things worse.

When nightfall came, I did not want to go to bed. This may be the night that the devil chooses to come for me, I thought. My mother came into the room and saw me sitting on the couch.

"You know it's your bedtime, so get to bed."

I walked very slowly down the hall to my bedroom. I flicked on the light switch upon reaching the door, and I immediately looked under the bed to see if the devil lay in wait for me. I was relieved to see that the area under my bed was clear of demons. I undressed and put on my pajamas and lay across my bed with the light still on. I had no intentions of turning it off. It was not very long before I heard my mother's footsteps coming down the hall. She entered my bedroom glaring at me.

"What's this light doing on?"

"I want it on while I sleep tonight."

"We don't have money to waste on electricity!"

She flicked off the light and left the room. I now lay awake in total darkness. I curled up in a tight ball with my feet tucked as close to my body as possible. For hours that night, I listened to every sound inside and outside, since I just knew he would come for me. This scenario took place night after night for several years, and many times, I became physically ill due to the anxiety that lay within me.

I became more and more irritable because of exhaustion more than anything else. I was getting used to the beatings now; sometimes they were administered for a reason, sometimes not. It didn't matter. I was evil, and I came to know it. Why would I question my parents anyway? They were the adults, they were the ones who controlled me, and yeah, that's right, they were the parents, weren't they?

Chapter 5

Here I sit at the dinner table looking at food that I do not wish to eat. I guess it must be good because my father and mother seem to like it. But I think it's terrible. I know what's coming very soon. My mother looks over at me.

"What's your problem?"

"What do you mean?"

"You're not eating your food."

"I don't like it."

"That's okay. You'll sit at the table until you finish, even if it means you don't sleep tonight."

I looked away and just stared at my food. I kind of laughed inside at her comment. You see, two years have passed since my mother's comment about the devil, and I'm really not getting any sleep anyway. To sit at this table all night would really not be a punishment. Unfortunately, I knew that if I didn't eat the food, another beating would be the outcome, so I wolfed down the food trying not to taste it. This scenario took place almost every evening until I just decided to eat everything in front of me with no argument, no matter how good or bad it was.

Another school year was upon me. The only contact I had with other children was at school. At home I was never allowed to play with the neighborhood children. I was not even allowed to go outside our yard. It appeared that my parents did not want the evil child playing with other children. I worked very hard to be the kind of son my parents wanted, but I just could not do anything right.

I walked to school every day by myself now. I was either at least trusted to do that alone, or maybe my mother just got tired of the three-block walk every day. I don't know, but I was happy to get the time alone. The only restriction to my daily walk was the homeward journey from school. I had only five minutes to make the walk home or there was hell to pay.

My new teacher was Mrs. Moore. She was very nice and, for some reason, really liked me. I stayed a few minutes extra one night to help Mrs. Moore clean the chalkboard, which she really appreciated. That was a mistake. I arrived home exactly eleven minutes late. Marie was waiting for me at the door.

"You are late, where have you been?"

"Mrs. Moore likes me, and I was helping her clean the chalkboard so she could post tomorrow's lessons."

"Why would she want you to help her? I don't believe you."

"You can ask her yourself. I was just trying to be helpful."

"Get on the couch. Your father will be home soon."

Great, I don't understand why every time I try to do something good, it turns out bad. It was not long before my father was home. He was working day shift, so I hoped he was in a better mood. I could hear Marie and James talking in the kitchen. James seemed to be actually defending me, which made me happy. Unfortunately, Marie did not let him take my side at all. She continued to tell him that I needed to be disciplined for my late arrival until he had no choice but to agree. I can hear Marie walking toward the living room now.

"Zeke, look out the window please."

I went to the window and saw my father getting another willow branch out of the tree. I turned back toward the couch to sit down, and Marie grabbed me.

"No, look out the window, and watch your father."

"Why?"

"You need to see the pleasure he takes when he cuts the limb and peels the bark for your spanking."

"No, I don't want to!"

Marie held my head toward the window. I tried to fight, but she was too strong. I looked at my father as he was peeling the bark from the limb. He did not look happy at all. It appeared to me that he seemed somewhat disgusted with what he was doing. This made me feel better, but I knew what was in store for me.

The beating was less severe than my first one. Unfortunately, the end result was still very painful. I knew that my father did not enjoy the task of beating me. He appeared to just do what he was commanded to do by my mother. It was probably easier for him to do what Marie said rather than listen to her yell at him for not disciplining me. I actually felt sorry for my father. It must have been very difficult for him to work all the time and then deal with Marie when he arrived home. Maybe that's why he worked as much as he could. I really don't know, but I do know that he was not home much at all.

School was going well for me now. I liked Mrs. Moore, and the other kids in my class were really friendly. About the middle of the school year, we began to learn how to print our name and print the alphabet on wide-lined paper. This was difficult for me. I did not have the coordination to print very well, and much like coloring, I always went outside the lines on the paper. Mrs. Moore helped me quite a bit to improve my ability to print my name and the alphabet. She was very proud of the improvement that I was making. I was very happy that she cared enough to help me.

About a month after we were doing printing exercises, Mrs. Moore told us of an upcoming parent-teacher conference. We were all given notes to take home so our parents could schedule a time for the day of the conference. I obediently took the note home and gave it to my mother.

"What's this?" Marie snapped before she opened the note.

"It is a note from Mrs. Moore about a parent-teacher conference."

"Why does she need to talk to me? Have you been bad?"

"No, everyone had to take the same note home."

"Okay, but I better not find out you're being evil or doing your lessons wrong."

"I'm not being evil or doing my lessons wrong. Mrs. Moore likes me, and she thinks I'm doing really well."

"We'll see after I talk with her."

I was very worried by my mother's comments. I knew that she might be unhappy with my printing assignment, but I felt that Mrs. Moore would convince her I was doing well.

God! I didn't know the students had to go with their parents to the conference. What a nightmare for me. I was already having trouble getting any sleep, and now the thought of my being with Mrs. Moore and my mother had me terrified. Finally the day came for the conference. Marie and I walked to school together. My mother did not say a word to me on the way to school. We arrived at Mrs. Moore's classroom precisely on time. Mrs. Moore greeted us with a big smile.

"Hi, Zeke. Hello, Mrs. Baker, how are you?"

"I'm fine. How's Zeke doing with his studies?"

"Zeke is doing very well. He has been working hard at learning his printing and alphabet. I'll show you some of his work."

I was horrified. My work would never live up to my mother's standards. This was only going to be hell for me, and I knew it.

Mrs. Moore handed my class work to my mother. She very slowly went from page to page reviewing my work. I could feel the beads of sweat begin to form on my body. You could see by my mother's facial expressions that she was not happy.

"Well, Zeke," she said. "This is not very good, is it? I don't understand why you can't do anything the right way."

"I am trying very hard to do it the way Mrs. Moore shows me".

Mrs. Moore looked very surprised at my mother's comments.

"Mrs. Baker, Zeke's work is well within the limited abilities of his age-group. His work will get better as he progresses through the year."

You could see that my mother was angered by her comments.

"No! Zeke continues to do poorly on his assignments and never takes the time to do things properly. He will be punished for his lack of ability to do his work correctly. I will make sure that he does not continue to be a problem for you."

"Zeke is no problem. He is a very nice boy and enjoys school."

"He only enjoys playing at school. He's not smart enough to understand the benefit of learning. We're done here! Let's go, Zeke."

Marie grabbed me by the arm and walked, almost ran to the door with me in tow.

My God, am I really too stupid to do things right? I guess I am because I'm always being told that I am.

The walk home was set at a very fast pace, and again, my mother spoke no words to me. I knew I was in trouble, and I knew I would be punished. If I were as stupid and evil as I have been told, then I needed to be punished.

My father would not be home from work for at least two hours, so I felt safe for the present time. My mother looked at me very sternly with a scowl on her face.

“Get into your bedroom, Zeke!”

Reluctantly I went to my room. It was not very long before Marie entered my door with a broom in her hand. She laid the broom on the floor next to my bed.

“Come over here, Zeke,” she commanded.

Slowly I walked to her.

“What?” I asked.

“I want you to kneel down on the broom handle until I tell you to get up.”

“No, that will hurt!”

“Do it, and do it now!”

Slowly I descended onto the broom handle.

“Don’t let me see you get up until I tell you!”

After only minutes, the pain was unbearable. My legs went numb, and my kneecaps throbbed with excruciating pain.

“Mom, can I get up now?”

“No! I’ll tell you when it’s time to get up. Don’t ask again or you will stay there longer.”

I was crying uncontrollably now. It was just too much pain. Why can’t I be good? Why can’t I do the right thing just once in my life? I heard her footsteps coming down the hall, and I hoped that my time on the broom handle would soon be over.

"Well, it's been thirty minutes on the broom handle now. Is that enough for you?"

"Yes!"

"Have you learned your lesson?"

"Yes!"

At this point, she came behind me and pushed down on my shoulders with all her weight.

I almost passed out from the pain, and I screamed very loudly. She smacked me across the head very hard.

"Be quiet, the neighbors will think I'm killing you."

"Okay. Please let me get up now."

At this point, she allowed me to get up and sit on my bed. My knees still hurt so bad that I kept crying uncontrollably. My mother shook her head.

"What a baby. You can't take a little pain, can you? Well, just remember, keep being stupid and evil, and more pain will come your way." She laughed and walked out of my room toward the living room.

I was very angry inside, but I knew better than to let my mother know. I was getting punished almost daily for any reason that came into my mother's mind.

My legs were very sore for my walk to school the next day. Mrs. Moore smiled at me when I walked into the classroom.

"Hi, Zeke, come over here. I want to talk to you."

The other kids were still out in the hall playing. We still had another ten minutes before the class started, but I needed to sit down as my knees still hurt from the previous day. I slowly walked over to Mrs. Moore.

"Hi, Mrs. Moore, how are you today?"

"I'm fine, Zeke. I need to know if your mother punished you because of your lessons that I showed her at the conference."

"Yes."

"That's not right, Zeke. Your school lessons are fine. I'll talk to her and let her know that I'm not happy about your punishment."

"No! Please don't do that. It will only be worse for me. Just let me go sit down."

"Okay, Zeke. I just want you to know that I think you're a good boy and a fine student."

Funny, she thinks I'm a good boy and a fine student, and she's the teacher. My mother thinks just the opposite, and nothing I do will change her opinion. I did notice a change in Mrs. Moore from this point forward for the remainder of the school year. She remained close to me, and every printing lesson that I did received an A, no matter how poorly I actually did the printing assignment. She was really a good teacher and a good person. Mrs. Moore was killed in a car accident the next school year. I was at school when the principal announced her death to the students. I was very sad. When I got home, I went in the living room to tell my mother.

"Mom, Mrs. Moore was killed in a traffic accident."

"I know, I read it in the newspaper this morning."

"Mom, could we go to her funeral? I really liked her."

"Why?"

"She was a good teacher."

"Look, she's dead, and going to the funeral is not going to change that. So the answer is no, we're not going to the funeral."

I was very saddened by her comments. Mrs. Moore was a good individual, and there were many times I wished she were my mother instead of Marie.

Chapter 6

It is now a week prior to my eighth birthday. I'm sitting on my bed dreading the task of asking my mother for a birthday present. I finally get up the nerve to go out into the kitchen to face her with my request.

"Mom, can I have a birthday cake, baseball mitt, and a baseball for my birthday?"

"No! You can either have the cake or the baseball mitt and baseball, not both!"

I really wanted the cake, but if I had to choose, it would be the baseball mitt and baseball.

"Okay, I want the baseball mitt and baseball. Forget the cake."

I thought back to last year when I made the mistake of asking for my present early. This angered my mother. I remember her comments to me.

"You are really a very greedy little boy, aren't you?"

"I'm sorry, but it's the morning of my birthday, and I wanted to see what you got me."

"Well, now you will have to wait for your present. I might not even give you one!"

I was devastated. I ran to my room to be alone. It was a full week later before she gave me my present.

I wasn't going to make that same mistake this year. So on the day of my birthday, I sat at the breakfast table and said nothing of my birthday. It was now lunchtime, and still no mention of my birthday. I was sitting at the kitchen table looking at more food that I didn't want to eat when my mother entered the room.

"Zeke, here's your birthday present."

"Thanks, Mom!"

I opened the present immediately. It was a Nellie Fox baseball mitt with a baseball placed in the web. It was not the one that I wanted, but I was happy anyway.

My mother watched me as I looked at my present.

"Well, Zeke, do you like your present?"

"Yes, I like it very much. Thanks!"

I went outside in the yard to play catch by throwing the ball up in the air and catching it.

I was happy to get older because I could only escape my house of horrors if I were old enough to leave home forever. I was receiving punishment often, and it was now always my mother who administered the beatings. My father continued to work all the time. The only contact I had with him was when he came home to go to bed. I had trouble understanding why he worked so much.

I really wanted him to play catch with me in the yard today, so I waited patiently for him to come home. I was happy to see his car pull in the driveway.

"Hi, Dad!"

"Hi, Zeke, how's your birthday going?"

"Mom gave me this baseball and mitt for my birthday."

"It looks like a nice ball and mitt, Zeke. Throw me the ball."

I threw the ball to him. He looked at it, threw it back to me, but I dropped it.

"Looks like you need practice, Zeke."

"Yeah, will you play catch with me?"

"No, Zeke. I'm tired, and I need to go to bed."

My father never had time to play catch or do anything else with me. Since I was not allowed to have friends, I just stayed in the yard and threw the ball into the air and caught it over and over again. Over time I actually became very good at catching the ball.

Another school year was upon me with more assignments, far more difficult than last year. My teacher was Mrs. Douglas. She was a pretty lady in her late thirties with dark brown hair. She always seemed happy and friendly to everyone. We were going to learn how to write in cursive this year. (No, not a writing project!) I was terrible at printing; how could I ever learn to write?

Mrs. Douglas went to the blackboard and used a device that held four pieces of chalk to draw lines across the blackboard.

"Okay, class, we are going to take turns writing letters of the alphabet on the blackboard. Each student will write two letters of their choice."

One at a time, we were called upon to go in front of the class to write our letters. It was especially hard for me to do this assignment. I was so afraid of not doing it perfectly that my hand actually shook when I went to write. Mrs. Douglas noticed my hand shaking, and she came over to me.

"What's wrong, Zeke?"

"Nothing is wrong, Mrs. Douglas."

"Then why is your hand shaking so much?"

"I'm nervous because I want my letters to be perfect."

"Zeke, no one is perfect. Just write the letters the best that you can, that's all I ask."

I felt better now, so I began to write the letters the best I could. They were really not very good, but they were better than I expected.

After a month of practicing letters of the alphabet at school, we were given homework assignments, which consisted of writing words on wide-lined paper. Great—another thing for my mother to find fault with, another thing that will result in a beating. I really didn't want to take the assignment home, but I had no choice.

When I arrived home, my mother was at the door waiting for me as usual. I supposed she was watching the clock to see if I could get another beating for being late. You see, I never knew if it would be a beating, the broom, the ruler, the willow branch, the hand, or just another day of screaming at me and telling me that I'm evil and stupid. It didn't matter; I was getting used to it by now.

"What are you carrying under your arm, Zeke?"

"It's writing homework for school that I need to do at home tonight."

"Okay, make sure you start it right after dinner."

I went to my bedroom to do my writing assignment after Marie and I finished dinner. I did not want her to see my writing or, for that matter, bother me while I was doing it. Oh no! I hear her coming down the hall.

"Zeke, bring your homework assignment out to the dining table to do it. You will be more comfortable writing on the dining table rather than on your bed."

"No, I'm okay in here."

"Don't make me smack you. Do what I tell you!"

"Okay."

I was terrified. I was a better printer than a writer, and my printing got the crap beaten out of me. I had no idea how I was going to please Marie with my poor writing skills.

I laid my papers on the table and began to write the words that Mrs. Douglas had assigned. It was not long before Marie came over to the table.

"Zeke, you need to stay within the lines and make your letters better. What you have done so far is terrible."

"Okay, I'll try harder."

My hand started to shake again. I remembered what Mrs. Douglas said about doing the best I could, so I settled down. I very slowly moved the pencil across the paper, creating the words of the assignment. I wrote each word ten times as we were told to do by Mrs. Douglas. I looked at my work, and I was pleased. Pleased not only to finish the assignment, but pleased because it looked good. I started to get up from the table when I heard Marie coming into the room.

"Are you done with your assignment, Zeke?"

"Yes. I'm going to put it in my bedroom so I won't forget to take it to school on Monday."

"No, you're not going to put it away! I need to look at it to make sure it's done properly."

God, I didn't want her to look at it. This could only mean trouble. But what else could I do but hand her the paper?

I could immediately tell by her facial expression that she was angry.

"Zeke, this is terrible. Why is it so difficult for you to do things right?"

"I don't know, I do the best I can. I am really trying."

She looked disgusted with me and began tearing my homework into pieces.

"Don't, Mom! I need to take it to school for Mrs. Douglas to grade on Monday."

"No, Zeke, you'll do it over and over again until you get it right. Now get back at the table and start over."

I went to the table, got out another piece of paper, and began to write. Marie was standing over me making me very nervous. My hand began to tremble again. No way was I going to be able to do better than before. I wrote the first two words ten times each when Marie grabbed the paper and ripped it to pieces.

"You will learn to do it right, even if it takes all night and the rest of the weekend."

"Mom, please don't keep tearing up my homework. I'm trying to do it right, it's just hard for me to do it perfect."

"You can do better, and you will!"

I went through more than thirty pages of wide-lined paper that night and still did not complete the assignment. Marie tore up my last attempt at about midnight. She looked at me with disgust.

"Get to bed! You'll start again in the morning!"

I went to bed and lay awake thinking about my mother's anger toward me. I began to hate her for treating me as if I were stupid. She would always call me stupid and evil when she was mad. I could never please her no matter how hard I tried. I finally drifted off to sleep.

I was awakened in the morning by a smack to the head with a ruler. Marie was leaning over me.

"Get up, boy! It's time to start your homework again!"

"Don't hit me anymore. It hurts."

Marie delivered another painful whack with the ruler.

"Don't tell me what to do, boy. I'm your mother, and I'll do whatever I want to you."

I got up out of bed and got dressed. It was only 5:00 AM, no wonder I was still tired.

"Mom, where's Dad?"

"He's working doubles this week, so he won't be home until late tonight. Now quit talking and get to the table and do your homework."

I went to the table, and the whole process from the night before began again. I would get to various stages of completion, and Marie would tear it up saying I was stupid and my work was terrible. I was holding the pencil so tight now that my hand would cramp, and it was very painful. The homework process went through Sunday evening before she finally let me finish the assignment. She picked up the final paper and looked at it.

"Well, this is still not good, but it will have to do. You are terrible at everything you do. I never thought a son of mine could be this stupid."

"Mom, do you really think I'm stupid and I will never get any smarter?"

"Yes, Zeke. Unfortunately, you're going to grow up to be one of those people who will never be good at anything."

I wanted so badly to be smart. I wanted to please my mother and father. I wanted them to be proud of me. This was never to be. Never would I hear praise from them; never would I feel love from them; never would I feel the happiness that other families feel together.

Chapter 7

I managed to survive another school year, another birthday, another year of mental and physical abuse, and another year of just plain being an unhappy kid. I had learned to become aggressive with other kids at school who chose to give me a hard time. I decided I wasn't going to take any crap from anyone other than the misery I lived with at home. My parents decided that I could venture out of our yard this summer. I don't know why they decided to allow me more freedom, but it was okay with me. I was still somewhat restricted, as I was not allowed to leave the area of the city block where we lived. I was also not allowed to cross any street within the area. It made me a little happier to have more freedom, and it gave me the opportunity to meet a friend. His name was Tony, and we were the same age. I did not meet him at school. He went to a private school in the area, and I attended a public school. I had noticed him as he passed our house going to the corner store during the previous years of my yard confinement. For some reason, he never stopped and talked to me. He was a good kid and enjoyed the same kid things that I enjoyed. It was fun to spend time with Tony.

Unfortunately, both of his parents worked; and he, along with his sister, had numerous household chores to complete each day. Tony's sister, Polly, was older than Tony and I. She had just turned twelve years old. She was very pretty, with somewhat of an upturned nose, deep green eyes, and long flowing blond hair. Her body was perfect, and I can remember that looking at her aroused me sexually. Of course, I had no idea what that was all about, but I remember it as a good thing. She treated Tony and me very well, always making us good snacks and playing games with us whenever time was available.

Most of the time I spent with Tony was helping him and his sister do the daily household chores. Polly was a good cook and was depended upon to have supper on the table each day when her parents arrived home from work. Tony always seemed sad. One day I looked at him and said, "Why are you so unhappy most of the time?"

Tony paused for a moment and said, "I never have time to play with anyone or just be a kid. I'm always working at our house doing chores."

"But, Tony, we always have at least a little time at the end of the day to play baseball or basketball, don't we?"

"Yeah, I know, but it's always for an hour or less, then you have to go home, and I'm stuck here doing the dishes after dinner, then it's off to bed."

Tony's problem was much different from mine. He was never beaten by his parents and never mentally abused in any way. But he was used as a slave to do the chores his parents either did not want to do or they had no time to do. His inability to have time for himself was really a burden to him at an early age. I could tell his sister felt the same way. This saddened me, and I tried to help them every day as much as I could.

Tony was not allowed to play at all after the new school year started. I had no friends other than Tony. The neighborhood was an old neighborhood consisting of many elderly people without children. Without Tony, I was alone again.

The beginning of the new school year was a bore for me. I didn't want to be in school, and I didn't want to be at home. I was really lost without my friend, Tony, during the school year. I became even more aggressive due to my treatment at home. I was turning into the evil person that I have so long been told lives within me. My aggression caused me to be sent to the principal's office on numerous occasions, and I had become known as a problem child. Being sent to the principal's office had little or no effect on me. After all, I was left alone to sit by myself, and that was fine with me. Unfortunately, on one occasion during the middle of the school year, I was involved in a fight with a classmate that resulted in my opponent receiving a broken nose. I was again exiled to the principal's office for discipline. The principal, Mr. Schultz, awaited me with paddle in hand. I had not experienced a paddling by a teacher or a principal prior to this. Mr. Schultz looked at me and said, "Well, Mr. Baker, you've proven to me that you need discipline. I've spoken to you on numerous occasions before about your behavior. I've taken your recess time, I've made you do school chores, I've even put you alone in a room for hours. None of these disciplinary actions have improved your behavior, so it's time for drastic measures."

I looked at Mr. Schultz and thought, here's an old guy who thinks he can change me by beating me with a paddle. What a joke; I have beatings all the time, and I doubt whether he can hurt me any worse than I've already been hurt. So I looked Mr. Schultz in the eyes and said, "Okay, what do you want me to do?"

Mr. Schultz replied, "Bend over, and put your hands on my desk."

I somewhat reluctantly obeyed him and bent over and placed my hands on his desk. At this point, he administered five whacks with the paddle, which pretty much lifted me off the floor. The pain was excruciating, but I was not going to cry for him or anyone else. I just stood there and took it. When he was finished, he looked at me and said, "Now, have you learned your lesson?"

I looked him directly in the eyes and paused for a moment just to gaze into his eyes. To my surprise, I saw a concerned look on his face when his eyes met mine. There was actually a hint of fear in his eyes, like he was uncertain of his safety. I replied, "Yes, sir." But I was intrigued by the thought that Mr. Schultz appeared to be somewhat disturbed by what he saw in my eyes. It really fascinated me.

A moment later, I heard Mr. Schultz on the phone with my mother asking her to come to school so he could discuss my behavior with her. At this point, I really didn't care about the outcome of their conversation. It really didn't matter to me at all.

My mother arrived at Mr. Schultz's office a short while later. Mr. Schultz greeted her with, "What are we going to do with this boy, Mrs. Baker?" She looked at Mr. Schultz and said, "What did he do now?"

“He got into a fight in the school yard and broke another boy’s nose. His family just took him to the doctor, and there will be medical bills to pay.”

“I’m sorry for what happened to the other boy, Mr. Schultz. Zeke is a problem child and has been right from the start. We discipline him for his evil ways, but it has little or no effect on him.”

“Unfortunately, Mrs. Baker, I had to give Zeke five hard whacks with the paddle today, and I’m sure he does not wish to experience that again.”

“Well, Mr. Schultz, if you gave him five hard whacks with a paddle, I’m sure his father will want to do the same. Please tell the other boy’s parents that we will take care of the medical bills for the injuries inflicted by Zeke. Thank you for putting up with Zeke. I can only hope he changes his evil ways. I will take Zeke home now so his father can decide his punishment.”

“Thank you for understanding, Mrs. Baker. I will pass along your message to the injured boy’s family.”

With that we were out of the office and down the hall to the door. Not a word was said on the way home. Kind of unusual; normally she’d be telling me how stupid I was or just yelling and screaming at me all the way. But not today, so that was okay with me.

We arrived home, and I went into the bathroom. I pulled down my pants and assessed my injuries. I was really bruised from the paddling, and I knew that the punishment from my father would inflict terrible pain on my already-bruised bottom. I could hear my father and mother talking through the door, and I heard the back door slam hard. I walked out into the kitchen and asked my mother, “Where’s Dad?”

“He went to the hardware store.”

“Why?”

“It’s really none of your business, Zeke.”

I looked into my mother's eyes as I had to Mr. Schultz. To my amazement, I saw the same concern come across her face, the same hint of fear as I had seen earlier with Mr. Schultz. I was pleased to see that she too felt uneasy with my gaze.

It wasn't long before my father arrived home from the hardware. When he came into the house, he was carrying a three-foot-long, one-half-inch dowel rod.

He looked at me and said, "Get into your bedroom, Zeke!" At this point, I walked to my bedroom unsure what the dowel rod had to do with my punishment.

My father walked into the room behind me and said, "Well, son, Mr. Schultz gave you five whacks with a paddle, now I'm going to give you five more with this dowel rod. Now, bend over, and place your hands on the edge of the bed." I realized what was coming. I bent over and slowly placed my hands on the edge of the bed. I knew the pain from this beating would be unbearable. He hit me four times, and on the fifth hit, the dowel rod broke in half with a piece of it flying across the room and sticking into the wall. The pain was so great that I almost passed out. My body trembled, and tremors of pain racked my entire body. How much more could I take? How much more would I allow?

The remainder of the school year was not much different. The other kids knew by now not to press their luck with me. They knew the outcome would be painful, but I also knew the outcome would be painful for me. I still got into minor scrapes, but nothing to equal the broken nose of my classmate earlier. I still sat mostly by myself and watched the other kids from afar. I didn't need them, and they surely didn't need me.

Chapter 8

Another year has now passed, and I am ten years old. I have grown quite a bit, and few at my age choose to challenge me. I am known to have a quick temper and ready to fight at any opportunity. I still get abused at home, as I live the life of an evil problem child in the eyes of my parents.

Tony and I have grown closer over the last couple of years. He still is unhappy about not having time to do the things he wants to do, and I still try to help him and his sister with their daily chores. But it's summer now, so we all work together to get things done as quickly as possible. Tony is really a good kid, and for some reason, we seem to be happy together. His sister continues to develop as a lady. She's now thirteen years old and seems to be happy even though she works at home all the time.

Tony and I were playing catch one day, and we took a break to have a Coke. He seemed especially unhappy, and it bothered me deeply. I looked at him, and I could feel his sadness. I asked him again, as I have in the past, about his sadness. He replied, "I don't know, but sometimes I just want to be dead. I only have fun when you and I can be together, Zeke. Summer is coming to an end soon, and I won't be able to play with you again until next summer."

"Don't worry, Tony, the school year will pass fast, and we'll be together again."

"Yeah, I know, but it's hard for me when I can't even talk to you, Zeke. You're my only real friend."

"I feel the same way, Tony, but we can't let our parents continue to make our lives miserable."

"I know, Zeke, but we have no way out until we grow up and leave home, and that seems like such a long time to me."

"Yeah, you're right, Tony. But we will make it, and then we can leave home and have our own lives without the interference of our parents."

"That would be great, Zeke, but I don't know how much more I can take."

"I know, Tony, but we have good times together. We can at least look forward to that, right?"

"Yeah, I guess so."

At this point, I saw a distant look come over Tony's eyes that I had never seen before. It seemed as if he was very far away and was lost, unable to find his way. It was very scary to me, yet I could somehow relate to the place his thoughts took him. I didn't know how to feel about Tony's sadness, nor did I know how to fix it. I was very bothered, as he was my only friend, and I wanted him to be happy. It's kind of funny; we never fought, we were always happy together—really out of character for me.

The school year started, and I was back at being me, the problem child, the kid who just didn't care. Not like Tony, I looked for trouble, and it was normally easy to find. Most of the teachers had heard of me by now and watched me closely. I got in several problems during the first part of the school year, but none that were as bad as the prior year. Detention from recess, extra homework, lectures by teachers and the principal, notes to my parents that got me more beatings. That was pretty much the extent of it.

On one Saturday, I was lying in bed, and I remember looking at the clock to see that it was exactly 8:00 AM. I got out of bed. I could hear my mother in the kitchen cooking breakfast. I got dressed and went into the dining room and sat down at the table so I could have breakfast. I was looking out the window toward the street when I saw Tony's mother walking up the sidewalk to our house. It appeared she was crying, and I wondered if she was hurt or what was wrong. She knocked on the door, and I answered it. She looked at me, choking back the tears, and said, "Hi, Zeke, is your mother home?" I said, "Yes, Mrs. Evans, she's in the kitchen, I'll get her for you."

I was very nervous. I went into the kitchen and told my mother that Mrs. Evans was here to see her and that she was crying. Marie looked at me and said, "What did you do now, Zeke?"

"Nothing, Mom, I really didn't do anything."

At this point, my mother went into the living room to talk with Mrs. Evans, and I followed. Mrs. Evans stood there with tears streaming down her face. She looked at me and said, "Zeke, I have some bad news for you."

"What is it, Mrs. Evans?"

"Tony climbed the electrical tower at the river on the way home from school yesterday and jumped off."

"Is he okay, Mrs. Evans? Did he get hurt?"

"He's dead, Zeke."

I stood there unable to speak. My best and only friend was dead. Dead, gone, no longer could I run and play with him; no longer could we share conversations together, have fun, or do chores. I was stunned beyond belief. I looked at Mrs. Evans and said, "Why, why did Tony do this? We were friends!"

"Zeke, I found this note on Tony's bed, and I want you to read it."

I took the note from her hand, and it read,

> Mom and Dad,

> I'm sorry I just can't take it anymore. I am never happy. I don't have time for myself, and I never have time to play with my friend, Zeke. I just don't want to go on living and being unhappy. At least I won't feel the pain of sadness anymore. Tell Zeke that he really was my best friend.

I broke down into tears after reading Tony's note. I couldn't believe that I let Tony down. I should have been able to help him and make him understand that things would get better. When I lost Tony, I lost the only friend I ever had. My mother told Mrs. Evans that she was sorry. They hugged each other, and Mrs. Evans left for home still sobbing uncontrollably. I went to my room. I was no longer hungry for breakfast. I just wanted to be alone to think about Tony.

I lay across my bed and cried until I could no longer cry. I should have talked to Tony more about his sadness, and maybe this would never have happened.

It seems that much like my grandfather, anybody who I had feelings for ceased to exist. It seemed as though I was the one who was always involved in pain and agony. Maybe, just maybe, my mother was right. I was an evil person, and bad and evil things followed me. I replayed the last discussion I had with Tony over and over in my mind. I can still see the emptiness of his eyes as though they were floating pools of blue water with a depth unknown. There was an eerie calmness about them that seemed to reach his inner soul. He was truly lost within himself, and I was not able to reach his inner thoughts. I was not able to save him from himself. I made a vow never to make friends with anyone else again. Why would I want to endanger the life of another good person? It was clear to me that I was the problem, and my solution was to be a loner. After all, I had lived half my life in solitude already—confined, controlled, and abused.

I decided not to go to Tony's funeral. I wanted to remember Tony as the kid down the street who I had fun with because I would never allow fun to enter my life again. I really missed Tony. He was the only person I felt safe talking with, and I think he felt the same way.

I would occasionally go and help Tony's sister, Polly, with her daily chores during the summer. She was alone now to handle all the housework and cooking. I could tell that she was not only sad because of Tony, she was also sad because her household chores were now doubled. She had turned from the happy person always laughing and joking to a very quiet, reserved individual. That pretty smile that was always on her face was now gone and appeared very seldom in the future.

I thought about Tony every day. I just couldn't get him out of my mind. I needed to be alone, I needed to think, and I needed to be out of sight and out of mind. I walked into our garage to just sit and be by myself. Marie collected everything in the world, and they were all stashed in the garage. There sat our old junk dining table with a furnace box on top of it.

The box was approximately four feet wide, six feet long, and three feet high. I got up on the table and peered inside. The box was empty, kind of unusual for Marie; she always stuffed empty boxes inside of empty boxes.

It seemed as though she thought the world would run out of boxes, so she wanted to make sure she had enough.

Finally a place where I can hide, a place where I can be alone, a place I can be at peace. I climbed into the box and sat down for a moment. It was a great place! I decided to go into the house and get a few things like my drawing set, View-Master, and a couple of books to read. I went back into the garage and again entered the box. I sat for hours and read my books. I took breaks to draw pictures that only I see, that only I determine if they were good or bad. I even started printing some notes to myself in a tablet. I just decided to describe my feelings as each day passed. It was very hard for me to do anything but print my notes because my hand always began to tremble when I would try to write in cursive. You see, the destruction of my writing skills at the hands of Marie had continued, and it wasn't getting any better. I was in the box every day for the next two weeks. It was so great not to be bothered by anyone. Kind of the out-of-sight, out-of-mind thing was working for me.

On the first day of the third week in the box, I could hear my mother calling for me. I totally ignored her because she probably just wanted to blame something on me so I could be either beaten or told how evil I had been. Either way, I had no plans to give up my solitude! I heard her calling and calling my name as she walked down the street. I even heard her when she was directly behind me as she circled the city block where we lived. I knew that it was now safe for me to come out of the box and enter the yard from the garage. I grabbed my baseball mitt and baseball and began playing catch by myself, throwing the ball into the air and catching it. I had grown so accustomed to this routine that I could almost catch the ball with my eyes closed. I now heard her coming down the sidewalk near our house calling my name. She finally came within sight of me and glared angrily at me. She looked into my eyes and said, "Zeke, where have you been?"

"I was down the street next to Tony's house, and I heard you calling, so I came home."

"I don't believe you. I looked down the street before I went around the block, and I didn't see you!"

"But I was there, Mom."

"You'd better not be lying to me, you little evil brat, because I'll find out, and there will be hell to pay!"

"I know, Mom, I'm not lying."

At this point, she left me and went into the house. Funny, she didn't even say what she wanted. So I waited until I felt it was safe and reentered the garage to get back in the box.

I thought of Tony all the time when I was in the box. I had let him down. He was trying to tell me he needed my help, and I had not understood his problem. It was my fault Tony was gone. Was it my fault because my grandfather was gone? The thought of this raced through my mind. Yes, it probably was my fault. He liked me, he touched me, and he died just like Tony died. The thought of this was killing me inside, and many times, I was sick over it. I sat in the box day after day thinking about Tony, my grandfather, and how really evil I had become. Many, many times over the next two years, I received beatings because my mother could not find me during my stays in the box. But I never revealed to anyone my sacred place, my place of solitude, my place of peace.

Chapter 9

I have just entered the eighth grade in junior high school, and my thirteenth birthday is rapidly approaching. I still frequent the box when it is necessary for me to find solitude. It's remarkable how great I feel alone, hidden from interference from the outside world. A world consisting of one person, a world where I make the rules and my opinion is the only one that matters. My life has not changed much over the years. I'm still stupid and evil. I'm the kid who just can't get anything right. The kid destined for a lifetime of failure. I woke this morning to Marie screaming my name.

"Zeke, get out of bed, it's time for school."

I had become accustomed to her screams, and for some reason, my fear of her was dwindling. Yeah, she still beat me and screamed at me, but it just didn't bother me as much now. I have become a person without fear.

I got out of bed and began to dress for school. I was beginning to like going to school. It was kind of fun for me. Kids who wanted other kids hurt would come and find old Zeke, and for the right money, I would take care of their problem. I was the most feared person in school. The teachers knew it, and all my classmates knew it. After finishing breakfast, I left my house for school. The walk to the junior high school was only about one-half mile, and the weather was good, so I normally enjoyed the walk. As I approached the school yard, I noticed one of my classmates approaching me. His name was Tommy. I had little contact with him, but he was known to be a so-called tough guy. As he approached me, I said, "What's on your mind, Tommy?"

"Nothing, Zeke, I just wondered if you could help me get the chain back on my bike. It came off when I was riding it to school."

"Sure, Tommy, I'll give you a hand. Where is it?"

"It's in the alley behind the Adams home."

I followed Tommy into the alley. When we arrived at his bike, I looked at him and said, "What's the matter with you, Tommy? The chain is on the sprocket, and the bike looks fine."

Tommy looked at me and said, "Well, Zeke, that's not exactly why we're here."

As I looked up, I saw three more of my classmates come out from behind the Adams garage. John, Gary, and Bob were three other so-called tough guys at my school. John was younger than I, and Gary and Bob were six months older.

Trouble was on the way, and I knew it. I thought about turning and running, but that really was not my style. I stood my ground and said, "What do you guys want?"

John was obviously the spokesperson for the group, and he looked at me and said, "We have some problems with the way you handle yourself, Zeke."

"Really," I said.

"Yeah, really," John replied.

"What do you plan to do about it?"

"Well, Zeke, we plan to teach you a lesson that you'll never forget."

With that, all four jumped on me and began pounding me. I fought back the best I could. I knocked Tommy down right away, and I know that I broke Gary's nose before I was knocked to the ground. That's when the kicking started in my rib area. I grabbed John's foot and gave it a twist that resulted in a loud scream from him as he fell to the ground. Unfortunately, it was hopeless for me, as there were just too many of them for me to take all at once. I finally curled up into the fetal position, and they continued to kick me until Mr. Adams came behind the garage and yelled at them, making them scatter. I noticed that John limped away and appeared to be in great pain. This pleased me.

Mr. Adams helped me up from the ground and brushed me off. He looked at me and said, "What's the problem here, young man?"

"I don't know. These guys just jumped me."

"Why don't you let me take you home so you can clean up?"

"No, I'll be okay. I'll clean up at school."

"Don't be foolish. Your eye needs attention, and you're bleeding from your nose."

"It's not a problem, I've been in fights before. I'll be all right. Don't worry about me."

"Well, okay, but if you need anyone to tell your parents what happened, you can call on me."

"Okay, Mr. Adams, I'll keep that in mind. Thanks for your help."

At this point, I continued my journey to school. I went into the restroom and attended to my injuries. I really did look a mess, and my ribs really hurt. I pulled up my shirt and saw bruises beginning to form along my rib cage. I was really pissed at those dopes, and I had no intention of letting them get away with what they had done to me. No way could I hide my facial injuries from my parents, and no way did I intend to let them know who did this to me.

I proceeded to my first class for the day. Not a person asked what happened to me; not a person really cared what happened to me. Remember, I was the toughest, meanest person who existed in this crappy school, and my classmates did not want to risk getting me angry by asking stupid questions.

I made the walk home after classes had ended for the day. I knew that more trouble awaited me at home. In reality, I really didn't care. I walked into the house, and Marie looked at me with disgust and said, "What the hell happened to you?"

"I got into an argument with some kids at school."

"Well, it looks like you finally met your match, didn't you?"

At this point, I didn't want to get into a word exchange with Marie, so I said, "Yeah, I guess you could say that."

She looked at me with those angry eyes of hers and said, "Well, you know what your father thinks of fighting, so you know he's going to punish you for being stupid enough to be dragged into a fight again."

I just shrugged my shoulders and walked into my bedroom to lie down. Wow, my ribs were killing me. I ran my hand down my ribs on the right side, and the real pain began three ribs up from the bottom. I was sure they were broken, but I was not going to tell anyone. I didn't want anyone to know that I was in pain. I began thinking about what happened today. Four dopes had the nerve to jump me and beat the crap out of me. Had it not been for Mr. Adams, my beating would have been even more severe. What would my plan be to pay them back? I gave it some thought, and I decided that I would single them out individually and see how tough they would be when they were alone—alone, facing me, one-on-one. Yep, that's the best way to solve this problem. I had no intention of letting them think they had beaten me at my own game.

Great, I hear my father's car pull into the driveway. Well, hell is now about to start all over again. James walked into the house, and Marie was immediately on him about how he had to do something with me. The same old thing: I was evil, and I had to be dealt with appropriately. I could hear my father's footsteps come down the hall, and he entered my room.

"Zeke, why can't you behave like the other kids in your class?"

"I don't know, Dad. I guess I'm just not as smart as the rest of them."

"You know, Zeke, I always wanted a son. But now that I have one, I wish I had never wanted one in the first place. You are not a child I am proud of, and you never will be. You're not even smart enough to know right from wrong. I wish you were never born."

My father's comments cut through me like a knife.

How could he speak to me this way? I thought parents were supposed to love their children. But I guess when you are a bad seed, you need to be treated as one.

My father rose from my bed and said, "Zeke, look at me."

I looked up at my father, and he immediately hit me with a backhand across my face that sent me to the floor of my bedroom. At this point, he just left the room without saying another word.

I got up from the floor and just lay in bed the rest of the night thinking, actually plotting against my four newest enemies.

Over the next few months, I managed to catch each one of them alone so I could make them pay for their attack against me. All of them left with various levels of pain. I had learned over the years how to inflict pain very well. I intentionally left Tommy for last. He had betrayed me, and his error in judgment cost him dearly. By the time I finished with Tommy, he knew never to cross paths with me again. They all knew not to mess with Zeke again. The consequences were just far too painful.

Chapter 10

Summer! What a great time of the year! My last year at junior high is coming in September, and I'll be glad when it's over. My fourteenth birthday is rapidly approaching, and in my eyes, I'm much nearer to my goal of leaving my life of hell behind me forever. The clampdown on my life by my mother is more and more unbearable. The physical and verbal pain and torture that is put on me has become a fact of life. I am very unhappy most of the time, but the summer months give me some relief. I can at least get out of the house and wander the neighborhood. I have no friends except for Polly, nor do I intend to have any. Almost everyone in school lives in fear of me, and the ones who don't are just too stupid to show fear.

My mother is in the kitchen this morning making breakfast. She bursts into my room and screams, "Zeke, get out of bed, and get dressed for breakfast!"

"All right, Mom, I'll get up and get dressed."

I don't have much in the way of clothes, just blue jeans and faded shirts. No shorts allowed due to my parents' religious beliefs.

So the hot summer days are just a little hotter for a kid like me. I sat down at the dining table and awaited my breakfast. Crap, oatmeal again! I just stared at the bowl. I know the routine all too well by now, either eat the crap or sit at the table all day. I wolfed it down trying very hard not to puke. My God, this stuff is terrible. Her oatmeal is always a bland, sticky bowl of mush that sticks to the roof of my mouth like glue. No taste other than a pastelike taste. Well, at least I finished it without choking to death. Marie walked into the room and stared at me and looked at my empty bowl.

"Done already, Zeke?"

"Yes, I'm finished."

"You must really like my oatmeal!"

I choked back the laughter and said, "Oh yes, it's very good!"

With that I pushed my chair away from the table to get up. Marie looked at me and said, "Where are you going, Zeke?"

"Just outside to ride my bike."

"Okay, but I want you back here by lunchtime."

"I'll be back, don't worry."

"Yeah, you'll be back because you know what will happen if you're not!"

I know that she will make good on her threat, so I always make sure I return home on time.

I really just want to get out of the house and get away from Marie. That's all that really matters, as I have no plans for the day. I don't have anything to do other than my normal routine of wandering through the neighborhood.

It's a very warm summer day, and the early-morning sunshine feels great. I look ahead of me as I ride my bike down the sidewalk. In the distance, I see the vagrant Whitey walking toward me with a burlap bag of bottles to return to the corner store. His normal routine is to collect bottles that people toss in the streets and ditches, so he has enough money to purchase the usual daily bottle of Mogan David wine. He is a dirty, smelly man with brown teeth and gray-black hair. Always unshaven, always with the same tattered jacket, pants, and shirt that bear the stench of a lifetime of wear. He constantly mumbles to himself, and not one word from his mouth makes any sense. He is a living waste of flesh. I dislike him. I turn into Polly's driveway to avoid him. I watch as he passes. His face turns to me, and he stops, mumbles something that I can't understand, then turns and walks on. I'm really glad he didn't come toward me, as I want nothing to do with him.

I wait in the driveway for a few minutes until I'm sure he's gone. I am just getting ready to ride off when Polly comes out the side door and says, "Hi, Zeke!"

"Hi, Polly, what are you up to?"

"You know the routine, Zeke, I'm cleaning house and trying to figure out what to make for dinner."

I looked at her for a moment. God, she was beautiful. She was sixteen years old now with the body of a twenty-year-old.

Her green eyes seemed to have the ability to penetrate deep into me. Her long blond hair was gathered in a ponytail that dropped to the middle of her back.

"Yeah, I guess I wasn't thinking. I know that you're always busy during the day."

"Yeah, I don't have any time for myself since Tony's been gone."

My thoughts went to Tony for a moment. How had I let Tony die? He was the only person I trusted, the only person I could call a friend. God, I missed him.

"Zeke, do you have time to come inside for a couple of hours and help me with my chores?"

"Sure, Polly, I'll be glad to help you."

I entered the side door of her home and followed her to the main level of the house. "What would you like me to do, Polly?" I asked.

"Well, you know how much I hate mopping the kitchen floor, don't you?"

"Yes, I remember. Is that what you would like me to do?"

"Yes, if you don't mind."

"No, I don't mind, Polly. I'd be happy to do it for you."

With that being decided, I went to the basement to get the mop, bucket, and soap. Polly followed me downstairs because she planned to clean the recreation room that was in the basement.

I returned to the kitchen and began to sweep the floor prior to the mopping routine.

It was a very large kitchen, and her parents were always very critical of how the kitchen was cleaned. It was a real pain to sweep and mop the floor, and I knew that if I screwed it up, Polly would end up getting blamed. So I very painstakingly took my time and did the best job possible.

I was about halfway done when Polly emerged from her duties in the basement of the home. She looked tired, but she always had a smile for me. It made me feel good to see her smile. I looked at her and said, "Well, are you finally done for the day?"

"Are you kidding, Zeke? Not even close! I have to go upstairs now and vacuum and make the beds."

"Okay, I'll be awhile here. No need to worry about the kitchen. I'll have it spotless by the time I'm done."

"Okay, Zeke, thanks for your help!"

Polly went around the corner and upstairs to start cleaning the bedrooms. She was really a good person in a bad situation. I was glad that she did not have to endure the beatings and verbal abuse that I did. I was also glad that she enjoyed my company. I kind of saw bits of Tony in her personality, and that brought me a level of happiness.

I worked hard for about another hour and finally finished the floor. I looked around the kitchen very closely, and everything looked perfect. I was glad to finish the job, and I took the mop and bucket back to the basement.

I came back upstairs to the main level of the home and yelled upstairs to Polly so she would know I was leaving. "Hey, Polly, I'm leaving now."

She yelled back, "Wait, Zeke, can you please help me for a little while longer?"

"Okay, Polly, I'll be right up."

I got to the top of the stairway where the hall area extended to four different bedrooms and one bathroom. Polly's home was really a huge home when compared to other homes in the neighborhood. I yelled, "Okay, where are you?"

"I'm in my bedroom, Zeke."

I headed to her room and wondered why the door was closed. I opened the door to find Polly completely naked on her bed. I stopped and started to back out of the room.

"I'm sorry Polly, I didn't . . ."

"No, Zeke, it's okay. Please come into my room and close the door."

I slowly reopened the door, and I gazed at her naked on the bed. She had closed the curtains, and the lamp on her nightstand was on low. The light from the lamp seemed to dance across her skin. My God, she was absolutely beautiful. Every inch of her body was perfect; her face, her breasts, her legs were all magnificent. I was speechless and a little afraid.

"Zeke, please come over and sit on the edge of my bed."

I thought to myself, *I am never going to be able to do that.* I already had an incredible erection from just looking at this beautiful young woman. Somehow, Polly seemed to sense my problem.

"Zeke, please come over here."

I walked over to the edge of the bed and stood in front of her still mesmerized by her total beauty. She reached up and began to undo my belt. My God, I was trembling now.

When she had my belt open, she unsnapped my pants and began to pull my zipper down. She seemed totally taken by the task at hand. My pants were now down around my ankles. She looked up at me and said, "Zeke, please take your shirt off."

I obeyed her like a child would a parent. She reached up and began to pull my briefs down.

My mind was racing with anxiety. There I stood completely naked in front of a beautiful young woman, who appeared to want me as much as I wanted her. I kicked my pants and briefs out of the way, and now I stood in front of her totally naked with an erection that was screaming for attention.

Polly reached up and began to stroke my penis. It was not long before I exploded in her hand and across her stomach.

"I'm sorry, Polly. I just couldn't control myself."

"Don't worry, Zeke, I can get you to want me again, maybe even more than you did before."

Polly got off the bed and came back almost immediately with a towel to clean up the mess that I made. She cleaned herself up, and then she cleaned me off very gently. When she was finished, she looked at me with her beautiful eyes and said, "Please lie on the bed now, Zeke."

I lay down immediately. I was not nearly as nervous as I had been earlier. Polly stood above me just staring at me with a gaze of excitement.

"Zeke, I want you to lay still and enjoy what I am about to do to you."

My mind raced through thoughts like lightning across the sky. I thought of the pleasure that she had just given me, the excitement that was again filling my body, and the anxiety of what lay ahead. I had no idea what Polly planned to do to me, but I knew I wanted her to enjoy me as much as I enjoyed her. Polly slowly caressed my penis with her hand, and then she began to kiss me on my inner thighs and lower abdomen. She slowly worked her way to my penis and inserted it in her mouth, licking and slightly sucking during the process. The feeling was unbelievable.

It was only a short time before I was ready to go again. I didn't really fully understand what Polly wanted as I was fully erect again, but she seemed to enjoy what she was doing. Remembering what she said prior, I just lay there and enjoyed her like she wanted.

Just as I was ready to climax again, she pulled away and moved up and kissed me full on the lips with her tongue entering my mouth slightly.

This was the first time I had ever kissed a girl, and the feeling was terrific. She moved her body over me and leaned down with her breasts in my face and said, "Zeke, please suck my nipples." I obediently followed her command and began licking and gently sucking her nipples. I could feel the excitement race through her body, and she began to tremble.

After a few moments, she placed one leg on each side of me and began to slide down my body, gently placing my penis inside her. Then she began to move up and down on me. The feeling was incredible. I reached up and caressed her breast and nipples with my hands. The excitement between us began to build with fiery passion. My hands moved from her breast to her beautiful ass as I helped her increase the speed of her up-and-down motion. Soon she began to moan uncontrollably, her mouth gaped open, and she gave a slight scream, which immediately made me explode again. She collapsed on me and began to kiss my neck and ear. We lay there, glued together for at least fifteen minutes before she rolled off and collected a towel for both of us. I didn't know what to say for a moment, and then I turned to her and said, "You were terrific, Polly!"

"No, Zeke, you were terrific. I'm still trembling from the orgasm I had. I can't believe how good you were, Zeke. I'm really glad that we had sex, and I hope we can continue to share this for a long time. I never would have guessed that you would be so good since you are so young and inexperienced."

"You will get no argument from me, Polly. I've never felt like this before, and I don't want the feelings to stop. All you need to do is let me know when I can come over to see you. We'll do the chores for the day and spend the rest of the time in bed enjoying each other."

"Don't worry, Zeke. We can be together at least during the rest of this summer, and I will be sure to have you over as much as possible."

"Yeah, I know, then it's back to school, and your parents will be there when you get home from school. It really will be a drag during the school year without seeing you and touching you."

"I know, Zeke. I feel the same way. Please do not let anyone know about us, Zeke. You know my parents are very strict and would never let me see you again if they knew we were having sex."

"I know, Polly. I will never tell anyone about us. You can trust me."

"Thanks for understanding, Zeke."

Polly and I began to get dressed. When we were dressed, she walked me to the door and again kissed me. This time the kiss seemed to last minutes. She was incredible. I looked at her and said, "Thank you, Polly, for caring about me."

"Zeke, I've always cared about you. You were Tony's only friend, and he cared deeply about you. Don't worry, Zeke. We have lots of time to enjoy each other. You'll see."

"I believe you, Polly. Please make sure you wash the towels we used so your parents don't find them."

"Don't worry, Zeke, I'll get everything cleaned up, and they'll never know that anything happened between you and me."

"Good-bye, Polly, and thanks again. See you soon!"

"Bye, Zeke."

I walked out the door and headed down the sidewalk on my bike toward home. My mind went back to Polly as I rode toward home. I wondered if she loved me. No, that's impossible. My own parents don't even love me, why would anyone else? The thought of love completely dropped out of my mind.

I never considered that I would ever have sex with someone as beautiful as her. I really never thought that I would have sex with anyone. Why would anyone want me, the evil kid, the kid who wasn't very smart, and the kid who could never do anything right? Great, I just had my first sex, and it was incredible.

But most of my pleasure seemed to drain out of my body as I headed up the sidewalk toward our house. I was about to enter hell again, and I knew that only pain and punishment awaited me.

Chapter 11

Well, the summer is over, and my time with Polly was unbelievable! The sex just got better and better during the summer. It's almost impossible to get her off my mind. I will miss her during the fall, winter, and spring months of the school year. Yep, that's right, back to school again; fourteen years old, ninth grade, and I hate this almost as much as I hate home. It is difficult for me to stay away from trouble. It's as if it follows me everywhere I go. I have learned to go to a place in my mind where everything is good and no evil is ever present. Kind of hard to explain, but in this place in my mind, everything is perfect. I imagine a dog that I can never have in real life, friends who I won't allow in a real life, parents who care about me, and even Tony lives in the place I visit in my mind. I find myself going to this place more and more lately. I am consumed with the happiness that I feel when I allow myself to drift off to this special place.

I am supposed to be doing a reading assignment in class. Mr. Gwen has just assigned us the chapter to read. We are supposed to write a short essay about the chapter by the end of the class for evening review by Mr. Gwen. I opened the book, just another thing I hate doing, reading and trying to figure out what to write. I began to turn the pages to the assigned chapter. I immediately drifted off to the place where I really want to be. The perfect life, filled with the good and happy things in life. I don't really know how long I was locked within my mind, but it must have been a long time because I was snapped out of my trance by the whacking sound of Mr. Gwen's pointer hitting my desk. I look up at him, and he remarks, "Well, Mr. Baker, are you having a good daydream?"

With this the classroom roared with laughter, as apparently everyone had been watching Mr. Gwen approach my desk.

I gazed at him for a moment, a gaze that unnerved him as it had Mr. Schultz and my mother when I was younger. I was happy to see him uncertain of himself. I was happy that I could present that kind of fear by just gazing at him. He backed away from my desk a couple of steps. The laughter ceased, an eerie calm came over the classroom.

Without ever stopping my gaze, I said, "What's the problem, Mr. Gwen? I have my book opened to my reading assignment!"

"Well, it doesn't appear that you're reading it, does it, Mr. Baker?"

"You'll have your essay by the end of the class, so don't worry about it."

"Okay, Mr. Baker, let's see what you can do during the remainder of the class period."

I flew through the pages of the chapter and wrote a quick, short essay about what I read. I knew it wasn't very good, but I really didn't care.

I thought about the incident in the classroom on my way home and decided that someone had to pay for my humiliation by Mr. Gwen. That someone had to be Mr. Gwen because he was fully responsible for my humiliation. I had decided long ago that I would never let anyone get away with humiliating me. Mr. Gwen would be no exception.

The next day, I hid and waited near the teachers parking area for Mr. Gwen to arrive. He was a small man in stature, approximately forty years old, slightly balding. After about fifteen minutes of waiting, Mr. Gwen pulled into the parking lot. His car was a blue-and-white 1960 Chevy Impala. I watched as he walked into the back entrance of the school. When he was gone, I looked around to see if anyone was watching or near the area. Just as I started to come out of my hiding place, another teacher, Mr. James, pulled into the lot. I again waited for him to enter the school through the back entrance. Once I felt it was safe again, I entered the teachers parking lot and ducked between the cars, looking through the car windows to assure I was not being watched. I finally made my way to Mr. Gwen's car. I carried with me an old ice pick that was among my father's tools. I went from tire to tire piercing the sidewalls of the tires in at least two places with the ice pick. The air slowly hissed out of the tires as I slid back to the front of the lot carefully watching to assure I was not seen by anyone. I laughed to myself as I thought about Mr. Gwen arriving to his car that night to find four flat tires. He deserved what he got. He should have thought twice before messing with Zeke!

I arrived home that night at my normal time. I slipped into the garage and put the ice pick safely back in the toolbox exactly in the place where it was before I took it.

My mother was on the phone, so I just went to my room and sat on the edge of the bed staring at the wall.

It was not long before Marie flung the door open and looked at me with her angry eyes. I just looked back and waited. She then said, "Well, boy, have you got anything to tell me?"

"No, why should I?"

"Well, that was the school on the phone, and one of your teachers, Mr. Gwen, said his car was damaged today."

"So why would you think that I would know anything about it?"

"Because of the way you are, Zeke. You're no good and never have been. If you did this, your father will have to pay for the damage, and he won't be happy."

I knew that she purposely left out the part about what damage was done to the car. She was sure that I would say something stupid about the tires, and then she would know it was me. So I just looked at her and said, "Why would they call here?"

"The principal is calling everyone who is in Mr. Gwen's class."

"Okay, I guess that makes sense."

"I know it was you, boy. I can feel it."

"It wasn't me, I had nothing to do with it."

"I don't believe you, but the principal will find the one who is responsible! For your sake, I hope it was not you."

With that Marie turned and walked out the door slamming it behind her. I thought for a moment that I should have kept the ice pick and used it on her.

I was tired of her and the hate that she always displayed toward me. I deserved better. I was never the evil person until she pounded that word in me so deep that you couldn't carve it out with the sharpest knife.

The night passed quickly with no more discussion from Marie on the topic. I walked slowly to school the next day. I knew that the principal, Mr. Morgan, would suspect me as a prime candidate for the damage to Mr. Gwen's tires. I was not in my first class for five minutes before Mr. Morgan called me to his office. There Mr. Morgan sat with Mr. Gwen looking at me as I walked through the door.

"Hi, Mr. Morgan, you wanted to see me?"

"Yes, Zeke. Are you aware of the damage that was done to Mr. Gwen's car?"

"Yes, my mother told me you called our house last night and talked with her about it."

"That's right, I called everyone in Mr. Gwen's class. I also received some calls back from parents that discussed the damage with their children. Do you know what these parents told me, Zeke?"

"No, I have no idea."

"They told me that their children told them that you were the only one they knew who possessed the ability to do something like this."

"Why would they say that? I have never damaged anything that belonged to someone else!"

"Well, Mr. Baker, we have turned this matter over to the police, and I'm sure they will be questioning you. You can go back to class now. I think we both know who did this, don't we?"

I just turned and walked out the door without answering his question. I finished the rest of the day at school without anything further being said about Mr. Gwen's car.

I arrived home at my normal time again only to find a police car in our driveway. Great, more people to ask me dumb questions. They must really think I'm stupid. What do they expect me to do, rat myself out?

I walked into the house and was greeted by Sergeant Murray, who was seated on our sofa drinking a cup of freshly brewed coffee.

"Hi, Zeke," he said.

"Hi."

"I guess you know why I'm here, don't you?"

"Yes, Mr. Morgan said that the police would be investigating the damage that was done to Mr. Gwen's car."

"That's right, Zeke. What can you tell me about the damage?"

"Nothing, I have no idea what happened to Mr. Gwen's car or who did it."

With that Marie chimed in and said, "You'd better tell him the truth boy, we don't want any trouble with the police!"

"I am telling the truth!"

Sergeant Murray looked at me and said, "Look, Zeke, we are going to be investigating the damage to Mr. Gwen's car, and it would be a lot easier on you and the police department if you told us what you know."

"I did tell you what I know, I have no idea who could have damaged Mr. Gwen's car."

“Okay, Zeke, but remember, if you’re not telling the truth, the punishment will be harder on you. I’m just giving you the opportunity to tell what you know.”

Sergeant Murray got up and handed my mother the empty coffee cup and walked to the front door.

He looked back at me and said, “I hope you’re telling the truth, because if you’re not, juvenile hall is in your future, and then jail if you don’t start making smart decisions.”

I watched as Sergeant Murray walked to his patrol car. I thought about his parting comment: if you’re not telling the truth, the punishment will be harder on you. What a joke! How could my life get any worse? The punishment I endure daily was far worse than sitting at juvenile hall or in a jail cell somewhere reading a book. Or in reality, juvenile hall or a jail cell would probably serve as my box, my tranquil place where I could sit and go to that place in my mind where happiness truly exists.

Just as my thoughts were coming back to reality, a whack came across the back of my head. I turned to face Marie; I felt the cold stare come into my eyes as I looked into Marie’s eyes. I again saw fear come across her face. I really don’t know what came over me, but I advanced toward Marie, and she backed up into the kitchen. My left hand grabbed her by the throat and pushed her up against the refrigerator; my right hand clenched a fist and jabbed her in the stomach. She let out a groan followed by a gasp of air and slid down the refrigerator to the floor. Marie grabbed her stomach and started to say something, but I stopped her. I crouched down to her level and again gazed at her with that same cold stare. She tried to look away, but I wouldn’t let her. Much like when she forced me to watch my father cut the willow branch from a tree years prior, I forced her to look at me. Once I had her attention, I told her with great force and authority in my voice, “Don’t even think about telling my father about this or you’ll regret it for the rest of your life. Do you understand me?” Marie looked at me and said, “I can’t believe that I raised a son as mean and evil as you.” A slight grin came across my face, and I said, “Yeah, I can’t believe that I have a mother as evil as you either. Now, are you going to tell my father anything about this?”

"No, Zeke, I won't tell James anything. It wouldn't change the way you are anyway. It wouldn't make you the son I wish I had, it would probably only make you meaner than you already are."

I slowly stood up from Marie and walked into my room. I could hear her get up from the floor after several minutes.

I know she was hurt because the punch in the stomach was delivered with great force. I didn't care; she deserved what she got, and I felt good about it.

The police investigated the case for months, yet they never found any evidence that linked me or anyone else to the crime. I learned that I was good at lying when I needed to be. I also learned that I was good at laying in wait to cause misery to my enemies. Mr. Gwen never challenged me the rest of the school year. In fact, he gave me a higher grade than I deserved for the class. Funny, I cause pain to the enemy, and the enemy gives me a gift. That would prove to be a valuable lesson for me in the future.

Marie kept her word and never breathed a word to James about our little encounter in the kitchen. She too had learned a valuable lesson, a lesson delivered by me, a lesson that she would never challenge again.

Chapter 12

Well, it's my favorite time of the year again, summer! I'm free from homework and all the dopes at school. I can't wait to have the opportunity to see Polly again. I just finished cutting the grass and cleaning the lawn mower. As I put the mower in the garage, I heard Marie call my name. As usual, a chill comes across my body every time I hear her call my name, even though I know I now have some control over her. I walked to the house and climbed the stairs of the back porch to see what she wanted.

"What do you want, Mom?" I asked as I entered the kitchen.

"I need you to go to the corner store and pick up some milk for dinner."

"How much do you want?"

"Two quarts will be enough."

"Okay."

Marie handed me the money for the milk, and I head toward the corner store. The store is an old brown cinder brick building that has been in existence as a grocery store for fifty years. It has two apartments above the store, and a cellar where full cases of pop and canned goods are stored to replenish what is sold daily at the store. The cellar also houses the empty cases of both pop and milk bottles to be returned to the distributors for refund. I am very familiar with the basement of the store. I have helped the owner, Stan, transfer empty pop and milk bottles to the basement from the main level, and full bottles of pop and canned goods to the main level from the basement. On the main level of the store are the basic needs any family would require for meeting daily food requirements. At the back of the main level is a large meat-cutting area where the owner labors at cutting top-quality choice cuts of meat. People who desire quality meat travel for miles to purchase meat from this small neighborhood store.

As I turn the handle of the door, I can smell the stench of the vagrant Whitey. I have no idea why, but Stan has always been a friend to Whitey.

Whitey always brings his daily find of returnable bottles to this store to exchange for cash and the liquid that keeps him alive, Mogan David wine. I open the door, and Whitey turns and stares at me. He has a constant smirk on his face and continually mumbles to himself. It appears that Stan has the ability to fully understand everything that Whitey mumbles, where I, on the other hand, can't understand a thing he says.

They both watch me as I approach the cooler that stores the milk, butter, and cream. I guess Stan wants to make sure that I don't pocket anything without paying for it. As for Whitey, I guess he just wants to make me feel uncomfortable. I picked up two quarts of milk and approached the counter. Whitey jumped at me as I passed by him. I jumped away from him as the smell alone was killing me. I looked at him and said, "Keep away from me, you creep!"

Stan shouted at me, "Watch your mouth. Whitey is a friend of mine, and he means you no harm."

"Well, tell him to keep away from me. I don't like him, and I don't want him to touch me."

"Look, Zeke, Whitey has special needs, and he is not a danger to you."

With that Stan handed Whitey two bottles of Mogan David wine, a pack of cigarettes, and a pack of wrapped meat along with a couple of dollars in change. Whitey grabbed his items and headed toward the door mumbling all the way to and out the door.

I placed the milk on the counter and handed Stan the money to pay for it. Stan gave me my change, and I went out the door without saying another word to him.

Whitey was outside the store sitting on the stairs that led up to the apartments above the store. He had already started to drain one of the bottles of Mogan David into his body. He was drinking it so fast that some of the wine was streaming down his face and onto his shirt. He glared at me as I walked past him to go home.

Just as I was even with him, he started yelling at me in some gibberish that I could not understand. I just kept walking without even looking in his direction.

When I got home, I put the milk in the refrigerator and handed the change to my mother. I was uneasy about asking to leave the house to ride the neighborhood on my bike, but I had nothing to lose, so I asked Marie if I could go for a bike ride. Without hesitation she said okay, so I was off.

I immediately went to Polly's house. I wanted her, and I wanted her bad!

I knocked on the door, and it seemed forever before she answered.

I smiled at her and said, "Hi, Polly, it's great to see you!"

"Hi, Zeke, how are you?"

"I'm great! Can I come inside?"

"Yes, Zeke, come inside, but we need to talk."

I went inside and sat down on the couch in the living room.

"Okay, Polly, what do you want to talk about?"

"Well, Zeke, it's something really hard to talk about. I like you very much, and I have always enjoyed having you around the house with me. But I have a boyfriend now who I really love, so you and I can't have sex anymore. It just wouldn't be right."

I was in total shock. I thought that Polly loved me as much as I loved her. I looked at her in disbelief and said, “Polly, what happened to us? I don’t understand.”

“Look, Zeke, I met Scott at school, and I fell deeply in love with him. He is a great guy, and I want to marry him when I graduate next year.”

My shock turned to anger. I looked at Polly, and my hands began to tremble.

I wanted to hurt her; I wanted her to feel the pain I was feeling. It would be easy to hurt her; I could snap her like a twig. But I just couldn’t hurt someone who I cared so much about. I looked at her and said, “Good-bye, Polly. I’ve had a great time with you over the years. I hope that you and Scott are happy together. I won’t bother you anymore.”

Polly began to cry. She looked up at me as I stood up and said, “Please don’t hate me, Zeke. I really like you.”

“I don’t hate you, Polly. I just don’t like you very much anymore.”

I walked to the door. I could hear her sobbing all the way to the door. I just opened the door and walked out of the house and out of her life forever.

God, I was hurt. The pain inside me was unbelievable, far worse than any physical pain that I had experienced. I felt sick, really sick, like I was going to vomit. The deep, empty feeling that came over me totally engulfed my body. I was again totally alone in the world, alone because a girl named Polly didn’t want me anymore.

I decided to go down to the river just to sit and think and watch the water race past me. The River Raisin flows through Monroe County, directly through the city of Monroe, and ends at Lake Erie. I rode my bike to the Macomb Street Bridge and hid it in the bushes next to the riverbank. There are far too many creeps in this area to leave my bike visible for anyone to steal or destroy. The Macomb Street Bridge was one of my favorite places to visit on the river. Traffic was light on the bridge, and there was no river traffic. Even fishermen did not frequent the area; they tended to stay downriver toward the lake. The fishing was much better downriver from the bridge. That made this a secluded area, and few people bothered to come here. This was great for me. I really didn't want to be bothered. I went down the steep riverbank and walked under the bridge. It was always ten to fifteen degrees cooler under the bridge, and the coolness felt good to me. I sat down on the layered stones under the bridge near the water's edge. The river was higher than normal for this time of year, and the water raced past me wildly with a loud whoosh and gurgle. I could not even hear the cars pass overhead.

This lulled me into a sense of calmness, and I began to think of what had just happened with Polly. Why would I be stupid enough to think that someone as beautiful and nice as Polly would care about the evil no-good kid named Zeke? What a joke; I should have known better. I didn't deserve anyone like her. I wasn't good enough for her. Otherwise she would have never fallen in love with Scott. My calmness immediately turned to anger. Why would I ever trust a female anyway? They always hurt me—my mother, Polly, the evil Ms. Jackson at school. My only contact with a female who seemed to care about me was Mrs. Moore, and she's dead. She probably didn't really care either; she was just like the others, lying to me just to win my confidence so she could use me. Well, it wasn't going to work anymore. I will never trust a female again. I will use them as they used me. They will pay for the pain they have inflicted on me!

I sat in the same place for hours thinking, lulled into a trance by the racing water and the coolness that the shelter of the bridge provided. Suddenly I was aware of someone around me. Unfortunately for me, the wind was in my face, so I didn't pick up the stench of the vagrant Whitey. He grabbed me from behind, around the neck with one hand; and with the other hand, he grabbed my crotch and squeezed hard. The pain was horrendous, and I yelled out. He put his filthy hand over my mouth and lessened his grip on my crotch. He was surprisingly strong, and I was helpless to escape his grip. He began laughing and mumbling as normal for this piece of filth. Finally he said something I fully understood. He looked directly into my eyes and said, "Give me your money or I'll separate you from your balls, boy!"

I was horrified by his comment. I tried again to escape his grip. It was impossible; he was just too strong. This seemed to anger him, and to my amazement, he released his grip on my crotch as he placed his forearm around my throat. His grip with his arm was tight, and when I tried to wiggle away again, I began to choke and gasp for air. Again he laughed and said, "Go ahead, boy, choke yourself to death, I don't care if you live or die. I'll get your money either way."

I sat very still. He was now very much in command of the situation.

He reached into his pocket and produced a knife with about a four-inch blade. He flicked it open with one hand and said, "Well, boy, are you gonna give me your money, or do I separate you from your balls? It's your choice!"

Again horror raced through my body. It was bad enough being held by this piece of crap. His stench was being absorbed by my clothing, and his skin contact to my skin was making me sick. Luckily for me, I had five dollars in my pocket. Five dollars meant a lot to me. I had saved my allowance of five cents per week for almost two years to get five dollars in my pocket. I was saving for a Daisy BB gun that I wanted, and I knew my parents would never buy for me. I had no choice but to give it to him. I was still gasping for air, and I struggled to say, "Okay, I'll give you the money I have. Just let me go!"

Again he laughed and said, "I'll let you go when I have your money in my hand."

I reached in my pocket and handed him the five one-dollar bills that I had folded in a large paper clip. He grabbed it out of my hand and backed away from me keeping the knife pointed in my direction. I stood up and faced him. The thought crossed my mind to just rush him and take my chances, that I could overpower him and get the knife out of his hand. Then I remembered how strong he was when he held me captive. I knew better than to take the chance. He could easily stab me with the knife and then leave me for dead. I slowly backed away from Whitey. I looked him in the eye and told him, "This is not over. I'll get even with you when you least expect it."

This time he erupted in laughter. When he was able to talk, he said, "You're just a kid. I'm not afraid of you. You'd better get your ass home before I decide to cut you."

I said nothing more to Whitey. I climbed the steep riverbank back to where I hid my bike. I looked back at Whitey from the top of the riverbank and yelled down, "It's not over!"

More laughter erupted from the piece of trash who had robbed me. I was so mad that I couldn't even think straight.

I was so extremely mad that I rode my bike directly in the path of a car when I entered into the street from the Macomb Street parking lot. The car screeched to a halt with its tires smoking. The front bumper of the car actually touched my leg, and I tumbled to the pavement. I wasn't hurt, just shook-up. I knew I could have been killed easily. Funny, I could have been killed minutes before too. I guess it was my day to beat death, my day to survive. The driver of the car raced to my side and yelled, "What the hell were you thinking about? You could have been killed!"

"I'm sorry, sir, I just wasn't watching what I was doing. Don't worry, I'm not hurt at all. I just lost my balance."

"Are you sure you're okay?"

"Yes, I'm sure."

I lifted myself and my bike off the pavement and rode off toward home. My thoughts went back to the events of the day. My spirits at the beginning of the day were very good, very happy. In just a short while, my spirits went from very happy to very sad. What a terrible day; my only love dumped me, and I was almost killed twice within a span of a few minutes.

As I approached the street I lived on, I thought to myself, a normal child would tell his parents about the robbery. But I didn't have normal parents. I didn't dare say anything about the robbery to them; it would again be something that was my fault because everything was my fault. My thoughts turned to the vagrant, Whitey. He was a problem, and I needed to deal with him. He needed to pay for what he did to me. It really wasn't the money that angered me as much as the fact that he held me captive. He controlled me, only for a short period of time, but still, I was controlled. Nobody holds me down! Nobody controls me! Yep, Whitey would get my full attention. Whitey would know pain and agony when I had finished with him. He would know never to cross paths with Zeke again.

Chapter 13

Whitey, my mind is obsessed with him. I hate him more than anything. He is the scum of the earth and the latest person to be added to my list of enemies. The school year is almost upon me now, and I still have not had the opportunity to get my revenge for the incident with him at the Macomb Street Bridge. Every time I see him and try to follow him, something gets in my way to stop me. He has the uncanny ability to know when I follow him. He will abruptly turn around and give me the finger and burst out with his stupid laugh. At other times, I can't get away from the house because Marie continues to hound me with chores.

I am growing very tired of her verbal abuse. She continues to tell me how stupid and worthless I am and, of course, how evil I have been all my short life. She at least knows now not to hit me. She knows what I am capable of, and she fears me when James is not around. Lucky for me, James is almost never around. He always works double shifts seven days per week and is normally sleeping when he is home. We almost never have dinner together unless it's a holiday. He is consumed with work, and I believe that he works to stay as far away from Marie as he can. He's not happy when he's home, and it's very obvious to me. I can't blame him; Marie is almost as ruthless with him as she is with me. He has no peace when he's at home for a day, just grief and agony much like me.

Well, time is getting short to be able to settle the score with Whitey this year. I plan to try and track him today, as I have completed my chores for the day. It's Friday, and I know that Whitey always stumbles along the street

I live on to visit Stan at the store so he can cash his bottles, get his crappy wine, smokes, and junk food. There is a vacant cement block garage with a flat roof that sits on a brushy lot directly next to the corner store. I rode up to the garage on my bike and kicked open the side door. There is no lock on this building. The only light that comes into the garage is through the open door. The building has no windows. The floor is dirt, and the garage is completely empty. I place my bike inside the garage so it's out of sight. I look around the perimeter of the building and find a large tree with a branch hanging over the roof of the garage.

The tree is very close to the garage, and I can use the side of the garage and the tree to climb up to the limb that hangs over the roof. I finally reach the level of the roof and climb onto the limb that extends over the roof. I carefully climb out on the limb and lower myself to the cement blocks that extend above the flat roof. I need to be really careful here. The roof is in very bad shape, and I could be through the roof and on the dirt floor inside the garage if I don't watch where I step. I walk the blocks around the roof until I find a safe spot in the corner of the garage nearest to the store.

I crouch down so that just the very top of my head and my eyes are above the blocks that extend a couple of feet above the flat roof. I look at my watch; it's now 12:30 PM, and I lie in wait for my enemy. God, it seems as if the time is crawling at a snail's pace. My legs are starting to ache. The crouched position that I am in is not very comfortable. But I know I can't risk being seen by anyone. Finally at about 1:30 PM, I see Whitey coming down the street. I immediately become irritated just by the sight of this scum. I watch as he stumbles along the street carrying his burlap bag of bottles toward the corner store. Just as Whitey gets to a point on the sidewalk across from the garage, he stops and turns directly toward the garage. I immediately duck down, flat on my stomach, behind the block wall. I lay in wait careful not to expose myself to the enemy. After about five minutes, I inch my way back up the block wall until I can see the street and sidewalk below. Whitey is nowhere to be seen. I can only assume that he is now in the store. Another waiting game begins as I know that Stan will keep Whitey entertained for at least an hour. I continue to watch. I see neighbors who I know enter and leave the store, still no Whitey. Finally, he exits the store, crosses the street to the other side, and starts heading south toward the river. I wait until he is completely out of sight before I climb down the tree and retrieve my bike from the garage.

Just as I emerge from the garage door, I hear Stan yelling at me. He owns this vacant garage as well as the property on which it sits. As my luck would have it, he was taking empty boxes out of the store to the trash container when I came out of the garage. I have no time to deal with him, so I just ignore him and ride off down the sidewalk on the opposite side of the street where I last saw Whitey.

I'm pedaling very hard because I know I need to get in sight of Whitey. I finally see him in the distance ahead of me. He is probably a hundred yards in front of me on the opposite side of the street. I back off a little as we approach Elm Avenue. I know that it will take time for him to cross Elm Avenue because the traffic is normally heavy this time of day. To my amazement, he elects to stay on the same side of the street and heads east on Elm away from downtown. I figured he would cross the street and head west toward downtown. This is really going to be difficult now because I don't have near as many trees to cover my presence on this road. I stay back now nearly two hundred yards. I know I can get closer once he crosses the railroad tracks near the Consolidated Paper Company. The tracks are located at the top of a steep incline, so once his head disappears on the other side of the tracks, I can zoom up to the bottom of the incline without being noticed. I also need to be very careful when I pass the paper company because my father works there and many of his friends know me. They tend to sit outside and smoke when they are on break or when they just plain decide to walk off the job for a while. Luckily for me, I have never seen my father when I pass on the Elm Avenue side of the factory. I look ahead and see Whitey's head disappear on the other side of the tracks. I pedaled as fast as I can to get to the bottom of the incline on this side of the tracks. I turn my head away from the paper-mill toward the road so that I may not be recognized by my father's friends. I now stop and inch up the incline until I can see Whitey waiting to cross the street near the Winchester Street Bridge. I watch as he crosses the street and heads toward the bank of the River Raisin. When he reaches the bank of the river, he stops and looks around him on all sides. He does not see me because only my head appears above the tracks, and I'm about two hundred yards away from him. After he is confident that he is not being watched, he continues to walk down the bank of the river toward the water. The riverbank is steep near the bridge, and soon he is out of sight.

Now I'm really confused. Where could he be going? How was I going to follow him when I have no idea whether he would head upstream or downstream?

Moments passed before I thought of what to do. It was simple. A railroad trestle spanned the river just west of the Winchester Street Bridge.

I crossed Elm Avenue, stashed my bike in the brush on the side of the riverbank, and walked over to the railroad bridge. I watched closely as I walked down the railroad track toward one of the cement pillars supporting the bridge. I did not see any sign of Whitey. Crap, I hope I didn't lose him again. I almost think he has the ability to become invisible. I reached the first pillar and climbed down the steel beams of the bridge until I was safely on top of the pillar. The pillar is approximately thirty feet long and fifteen feet wide, so I have plenty of room to move about. I leaned out from the steel beams connected to the pillar and looked downriver toward the Winchester Street Bridge. There he was, under the bridge, drinking his cache of wine that he got from Stan. I need to be careful because the railroad trestle is only about a hundred yards from the bridge, and it would be easy for him to see me if I were out in the open on the pillar.

Something caught my eye about ten feet above Whitey on the cement-and-stone base of the bridge. It was a bedroll with clothes scattered next to it. This must be the place where Whitey sleeps. What a find; I actually had followed my prey to its lair. I watched for some time as Whitey ate his junk food and drank his wine. I knew that I would not have any opportunity to settle the score this day, but at least now I know where he spends his nights.

I slowly made my way back down the railroad track to my bike. It's now 4:00 PM and time for me to get home before I've been missed for too long.

I jump on my bike and head down Elm Avenue toward home. However, I made a fatal error; I forgot about the gathering of workers at the paper-mill. Unfortunately for me, this would be the only time that James was with the other guys outside the factory. My eyes met his as I came across the railroad tracks toward home. He waved me over to him. Great, just another time that I will be in trouble with my parents, probably a beating or grounding awaited me. I rode over to where my father was standing with the other workers. Without saying a word, he walked with me away from the other workers. When we were out of earshot, he looked at me and said, "Well, boy, why are you at this end of town?"

I knew he was going to be mad because this was the most unsavory part of the city. Most of the low-income people lived here, and most of the crime happened within a couple of mile radius of where we stood.

I looked up at my father and said, “I was just over at the river seeing if anyone was fishing.”

“Well, was anyone fishing?”

“No, I didn’t see anyone at all along the riverbank. There were a couple of people fishing across the river near the water filtration plant, but they were the only ones on the river.”

“You know that I don’t like you around the river, don’t you?”

“Yes, I know, but I just like to watch the people catch fish.”

“I know, Zeke. I was the same way when I was your age. I always went down to the river to either fish or watch people fish. I really liked talking with the folks fishing. Most of them are very good people.”

“You’re not mad at me about being down at this end of town?”

“No, son, I’m not mad at all. I’m just a little concerned for your safety when you’re in this part of town. You see, I know that Marie is hard on you, and I know that you don’t have near the fun that a boy your age should. I want you to have time to enjoy being a kid. Well, I guess you’re not really a kid anymore. You’re a young man now, far too old to be called a kid.”

“So you’re not going to tell Mom about my being out of the neighborhood?”

“No, son, this will be our secret and our secret alone. I don’t want you to say anything to your mother either about your being here or about our conversation.”

“Don’t worry, Dad, I won’t say a word.”

“Just be careful when you come down to this end of town, son, a lot of bad people frequent this area. Some of them wouldn’t think twice of beating you and taking your bike.”

“I know, Dad, I will be careful when I come here again.”

“Okay, son, good-bye, and please be careful on your way home.”

“Okay, Dad, thanks for not being mad at me. I’m really just trying to have a good time when I can.”

“I know, son, see you at supper tonight. I decided not to work a double today. Marie is making meat loaf for dinner tonight. I told her to make it for me, but I know it’s your favorite.”

“Great! Thanks, Dad!”

I again mounted my bike and headed for home. I thought about our conversation on the way home. He was as much a victim as I. Marie controlled him just as she controlled me. I could always see the pain on his face when Marie scolded me for nothing, or when she forced James to punish me for no reason. He was never happy at home; he was never allowed to be. I really believe that James felt as worthless as I did because of Marie’s wrath. Fortunately for him, he had the ability to be away from her most of the time. I, on the other hand, in the past, had to suffer her physical and verbal abuse. At least now it was only her verbal tirades that I had to contend with. She knew better than to hit me again. She knew that Zeke would never tolerate her hands on him again.

As I turned onto our street, I thought back to Whitey. I now know where he spent his time when he wasn’t scrounging for bottles, digging through trash, or bumming the streets. Most importantly, I knew where he slept. That was most important to me. The day of the week to strike him would be Friday. He always went to Stan’s store every Friday, and he always left with the same things—wine, smokes, and junk food. He would surely be drunk and pass out around nightfall each Friday night. Too bad, Whitey, I now know exactly where you eat, drink, live, and sleep. I now have a plan for my revenge.

All I need to do now is to slip out of the house when Marie is asleep and make you pay for what you did to me. Believe me, pay you will.

Chapter 14

My fifteenth birthday was a couple of days ago. Birthdays really haven't meant much to me for a while. Marie always screwed with me about my birthday. It was a game to her; make the kid beg for a gift, make the kid beg for a cake. She had really turned me off to birthdays, and I let them come and go without really caring.

Two months have now passed since I tracked Whitey to his lair. I have not yet had a chance to slip away unnoticed. It is really difficult to try to give Marie the slip. She has the ears of a cat and the ability to read me like a book. She always seems to know when I'm up to something, especially when it's something evil. On three separate occasions, I had almost made it to the back door when I heard Marie scream, "Zeke, what are you doing up?"

Each time I would yell back, "Just getting a snack out of the fridge, Mom." Of course, the response from her would be, "Get back in bed! You know the rules, no snacks at bedtime!" I would retreat back to my room and not dare risk being heard again that evening.

I have thought everything through in my mind about my upcoming night with Whitey. I knew where my father kept an old hunting knife that he had in his possession for years. I could get this knife easily and put it back in exactly the same spot before anyone would know that it was missing. I did not plan to use the knife on Whitey, but I did plan to protect myself from him if it were necessary. My plan was to catch Whitey drunk and either passed out or asleep; it really didn't matter to me. I planned to carry a souvenir miniature Louisville Slugger with me to use as a weapon against Whitey. I found the bat in the alley behind our house a couple of years ago, and only I knew I had it. It had been stashed in my box since the day I found it. I knew that it would come in handy someday. It will work perfectly for my revenge with Whitey, easy to carry and easy to conceal. If my plan worked out right, Whitey would never know what hit him until he woke up with a cracked head that hurt like hell.

It's Friday, and I have to try again to escape my piece of hell so I can get my revenge against Whitey. My father was working the night shift, so I didn't need to worry about him. All I needed to do was slip away without Marie having a clue I was gone.

I lay awake in my bed waiting, listening for Marie to go to bed. It was nearing eleven o'clock. I was getting tired. I struggled to stay awake; I could visualize Whitey lying in his cardboard lair, in a drunken stupor, unable to protect himself from my attack. It would be so easy to inflict pain on my enemy, so easy that I almost laughed out loud. Lucky for me, I managed to choke the laughter down and remain quiet as a mouse.

Finally, at 11:15 PM, I hear Marie walk to her room and close the door. I decided to wait until midnight before I would try to slip out of the house. My plan was different tonight; I had worked on my bedroom window over the past several weeks so it would open very, very quietly. The windows in our home were old wood-framed windows that swelled with humid weather, so I used a small wood chisel to trim some of the layers of paint from the slide rails so the window would open as quietly as possible. It took me weeks to do this because I could only work on the window rails when Marie was either at the corner store or out working in the yard. I got lucky one evening. Marie spent at least two hours in the front yard talking with a neighbor who lives across the street from us. This provided me with the time necessary to finish the rails to perfection.

I watched the clock next to my bed like a hawk for the final tick to midnight. No sounds are emitting from Marie's room. It was stone quiet in the house; I needed to be very careful not to make a sound. I slid out of bed and put on my clothes. I chose to wear the darkest clothes that I owned that night in order to stay fully concealed in the darkness. I placed a small flashlight in my pocket and the knife on my belt. I used great caution when I opened the window, not a creak, not a scrape, not a sound came from opening the window. I placed a small wooden rod in the window to keep it open during my absence. I lowered myself to the ground and looked around for any neighbors who may be outside. I could not see or hear anyone. I walked behind the house to our unattached garage, where I could retrieve the miniature Louisville Slugger from my box and my bike for the ride to the river. Again, as I emerged from the garage, I looked and listened for anyone in the area. Luck was with me; not a soul was within eyesight or earshot. I slid on my bike and began my trip to the river.

It was a cool, damp night, not a rainy night, just a cool dampness in the air. I chose to ride on the sidewalk, not in the street where I might be detected easily by oncoming traffic. Traffic was almost nonexistent that evening. Whenever a car entered the street, I moved into the yard of nearby houses and stayed concealed close to the structure of the home. I eased up to Elm Avenue in complete and total darkness. My luck was holding; no cars were in sight. Just as I placed my foot on the pedal to begin crossing the street, I heard a sound. It was laughter from down the street I was going to cross. I peered down the street toward the light cast by a streetlight a hundred yards away. There I saw a couple walking hand in hand toward me. They were not yet aware of my presence, so I moved silently away from the street behind the hedges of a nearby home. I lay down with my bike and waited for them to pass. They stopped at the corner where I lay and chatted for a while. Then they turned down Michigan Avenue and walked away in the direction of my house. As soon as they were out of sight, I again went to my previous position on the corner in order to cross Elm Avenue. I crossed the street without any further problems.

I could not risk going past the paper-mill where my father worked. The place is lit up like a Christmas tree at night, and it would be easy to spot me. He would not be nearly as forgiving if he caught me here after midnight. I rode up within sight of the mill and turned toward the riverbank between the houses. When I reached the riverbank, I stowed my bike in the brush, just beneath the top of the bank. This is where my small flashlight would be necessary. The riverbank was very steep and very hard to walk in the daylight, so it would be much more difficult at night. I eased down the riverbank to the edge of the water. I now turned on my flashlight. I would be concealed from the houses and people traveling on Elm Avenue. I didn't worry about the other side of the river. The Monroe Water Works and vacant land covered most of the area. I would have been concerned about this place in the summertime as local toughs gathered here to drink and party with women. It was far too cold for them to be here tonight.

I finally reached the place I was most concerned about crossing, the paper-mill pump house. The pump house spilled wastewater from the paper-mill into the river in front of me.

It was necessary for me to place the flashlight in my mouth and attempt to walk the web flange of the steel beams that supported the pump-house structure. This was not an easy task because I had to cling to the vertical beams as I walked the web of the horizontal beams. I slowly inched my way across the face of the pump-house structure toward the water's edge at the other side. I finally reached the bank and continued my treacherous walk toward the Winchester Street Bridge.

My next task was to climb the bank at the railroad trestle, cross the tracks, and descend back to the river's edge. There was no possible way to cross the base of the railroad trestle because the first cement pillar of the trestle began at the riverbank and extended into the water. About halfway up the bank, I turned off my flashlight so I would stay concealed from the paper-mill workers and the people traveling on Elm Avenue. I reached the top of the riverbank and slipped across the tracks without being detected by anyone. I began my descent down the riverbank to the water's edge when I stepped on some loose soil, lost my footing, and slid out of control down the bank toward the water. I managed to gain control of my footing just prior to splashing into the water. I was very unnerved at this point, so I stood in silence for at least ten minutes to calm myself.

Once I regained control of myself, I continued my journey toward the Winchester Street Bridge and Whitey's lair. I decided to travel the last one hundred yards by moonlight. The moon was almost full tonight, and the sky was crystal clear. I knew this would be a risk because I could easily stumble and fall into the water. I could never explain wet, muddy clothes to Marie, and no way could I throw them away. She knew every piece of clothing I had, and I would have to account for anything missing.

I carefully approached the bridge. I strained my eyes to see if I could see Whitey lying under the bridge. It was impossible to see under the bridge; it was just too dark. I approached the bridge with great caution. I am now just thirty feet from the edge of the bridge. I catch the sound of a moan from under the bridge. I freeze with excitement; my prey is here! He is within striking distance. I am motionless now.

I listen for any further sounds emitting from the piece of filth I know as Whitey. I laughed quietly as I heard him mumble in his sleep. This is really funny. When he's awake, it's impossible to understand his mumbles; in his sleep, I can understand every word. He's dreaming about a woman. What woman would even think about being with this piece of trash? Again I laugh quietly. I move toward him very slowly, careful not to make any noise that would wake him from his drunken dreamland. Something strikes my foot. I looked down to see a stone that has separated from the mortar that held it in position in the seawall. The seawall was built by county workers to keep the riverbank from eroding during times of high water. The stone was approximately twelve inches long, six inches wide, and six inches thick. I touched the miniature Louisville Slugger lashed to my side and looked down again at the stone. I thought briefly and picked up the stone. I figured the stone weighed approximately ten pounds. I tossed the stone up and down, just letting the stone ever so slightly leave my hands.

My mind went back to the incident at the Macomb Street Bridge just months before. Whitey showed no pity on me; he did not care at all when he inflicted pain on my body. He did not care that he controlled me and held me captive. I would show him the same respect; I would show him pain, pain that would make him understand not to mess with Zeke again.

I held the stone in my hand and advanced toward the sound and now the stench of Whitey. I moved closer, but I still could not see him. It was far too dark under the bridge. There was nothing else I could do but turn on my flashlight to see exactly where Whitey was lying. I shined the flashlight toward the water so I could see the area under the bridge in the perimeter of the light. On my second pass with the light, I picked up the outline of Whitey lying on a makeshift bed of cardboard and an old tattered sleeping bag. I moved toward him with the stone in my right hand and my flashlight now in my mouth again. I kept my left hand ready for my knife if I needed it. I am now directly above him. He is totally out, either in dreamland or drunken land. Either way, I really didn't care. He was lying on his back facing up toward the underside of the bridge. I took the stone in both hands, raised it above my head, and crashed it down on Whitey's forehead.

It sounded like the whack of a baseball bat striking a baseball when the stone hit him. I waited for a response, but all I heard was a gurgling sound coming from Whitey. I shined the flashlight directly on Whitey's face. His eyes were open, but they were glazed. It looked as if his eyes were staring into nowhere, not really fixed on anything, just a cold, empty, unfocused stare. He was bleeding from a deep gash on his forehead. The blood was flowing freely from the gash in his head. His body was trembling and jumping uncontrollably. I wanted him to stop jumping. I wanted him to close his eyes. I couldn't stand the cold, glazed stare anymore. I raised the stone again and struck another blow to his forehead. This time there was no crack of a baseball hitting a bat. There was a thud as if you had crashed the stone into a watermelon. I knew then that Whitey's life was over. I knew then that I had taken a human life. I waited and listened as he thrashed about in front of me. I finally heard him take his last gasp of air and leave this life forever. I stood over him for several minutes before I thought about what I had done. A slight chill came over my body, and I trembled for a brief moment. But I felt absolutely no remorse at all for what I had done. Whitey was an evil person who had wronged me, and I didn't care that his life was over. In fact I was happy that I would never have to look over my shoulder again in fear of Whitey.

I sat by the edge of the water for several minutes. Then it hit me, fingerprints. I looked at the stone still in my hands; I stood up and threw the stone out into the water as far as I could throw it. It hit the water with a resounding splash. I sat back down on the riverbank and thought. My God, was there any blood on me? I quickly looked over my clothing with the flashlight. I could detect no blood on any of my clothing. Sweat began to bead out on my forehead. I needed to make sure that nothing could link me to the area. I looked around with my flashlight, making slow circles around Whitey's body. Nothing, I mean nothing could link me to this crime unless someone saw me on the way back home. I held the flashlight on Whitey's eyes for a moment. They were still open, gazing up at the bridge. The same cold, glazed stare came from his eyes. It was somewhat unnerving for me. Not that I was scared; I don't scare easily. I turned off my flashlight and stood listening to the sounds of the night.

It was time to make my journey home. I turned on my flashlight and looked at my watch. It was now 1:30 AM, and I knew that it would take me at least forty-five minutes to get home, return the knife, my bike, and the miniature Louisville Slugger to their proper places, plus return unnoticed to my room. I began my trip back upriver to the location of my bike. I was tired, and I really needed to focus on making my return trip without being detected by anyone or falling in the river. I reached my bike without being detected and headed toward Elm Avenue and home. I moved quietly down Michigan Avenue toward home. The streets were empty, and I did not need to hide or stop along the way.

I reached home, and to my horror, our porch light was on. I stopped my bike near a neighbor's house and looked toward my house. Marie was not in the yard or on the porch; she was nowhere to be seen. I headed around the block in the opposite direction of my home. It was the only way that I could get to the garage side of our home without being seen in the porch light. The garage was thirty feet from our house, so I could get into the garage undetected from the north side of the property. I put the knife back into my father's tool chest, the miniature Louisville Slugger in my box, and my bike in its normal place next to the workbench. I exited the garage moving slowly and quietly around the back of the house to my bedroom window. I waited outside my bedroom window and listened for any sounds coming from the house. Then I heard it, James's voice coming from the kitchen. He must have come home early tonight, tonight of all nights. I couldn't wait any longer; I lifted myself as quietly as possible up the side of the house and into my already-open window. I stepped into my bedroom, eased the window shut, and turned the lock on the top of the window casement. I could still hear James talking to Marie. It seems there was a problem with an electrical transformer at the paper-mill tonight, and management had sent everyone home early. I silently took my clothes off and went to bed. I thought about the events of the evening and the chances that I took to eliminate my enemy. It was worth it to me. It was worth the risk to kill the piece of crap who had dared try to hurt and control Zeke. People like him must pay for their evil ways; they must learn that people they hurt will get revenge. Revenge so fiercely administered that more often than not, will be extremely painful for them, or even fatal to their existence on this earth. You see, it's really their choice.

Chapter 15

Things were pretty uneventful for the next week after Whitey's demise. I'm beginning to wonder if he's dead or not. Nothing in the local paper about his murder or of anyone finding him hurt. I'm starting to get a little nervous about the whole thing. I've had a couple of dreams where I can see Whitey's face, the cold stare of his dead, glazed eyes. At times I even think I hear his insane mumbling or his jeering laughter. I keep looking around me when I walk to school to see if he is lurking about. I must be going crazy. I know he's dead. I looked into those eyes; all the life was drained out of him. Or was it? Today is Friday, his day to travel to the corner store; I'll watch to see if he passes after I get home from school. I get home from school at 3:00 PM, and he always passes our house between 3:00 PM and 3:30 PM every Friday to return to his lair.

I arrived home from school at exactly 3:00 PM. Marie was in the kitchen cooking dinner. I went past her and put my books in my room; she said nothing to me. I again walked past her and went outside; again she said nothing. Kind of unusual for her, but I didn't care. I was glad she said nothing; it would only have been something that I didn't want to hear.

Our garage was built three feet from the neighbor's garage, so it was a perfect place to position myself so I would be as secluded as possible. I sat on the ground and gazed out toward the sidewalk and street. I needed to watch the sidewalks on both sides of the street and the street itself as Whitey had used them all in the past to walk to and from the corner store. My mind raced back to the night only one week ago. The night at the river, the night that Zeke settled the score with Whitey. I waited until 3:30 PM, and still no Whitey. I left my hiding spot and walked to the corner store to see if Whitey had arrived at the store prior to my arrival home from school. I walked into the store and looked around. The floor of the store was made out of wood and always creaked with every step you took. Not a soul was in the store. Stan came out from behind the meat counter and said, "What do you need, Zeke?"

"Hi, Stan, I just came down to get a couple of packs of baseball cards."

"You know where they are, help yourself."

I went around the bread counter and thumbed through the baseball cards in the box. This is normal for me. I always try to figure out which pack had the cards I needed in my collection. Kind of an impossible feat as the packs were sealed, and it was really not possible to tell what cards lay inside. I picked two packs out that I liked and gave two cents to Stan for payment. Stan looked at me for a moment and said, "Wait, Zeke."

I turned back from the door and looked at Stan, "What do you want, Stan?"

Stan handed back the money that I had given him.

"What's this for, Stan?"

"Ah, Zeke, you help me a lot with the storeroom, and I think it's time I gave you something extra for the help."

"Thanks, Stan! Let me know when you need help again."

"Okay, Zeke, have a good night."

"Okay, Stan, thanks again!"

With that I went out the door and walked down the street toward home. Of course, when I got there, Marie was boiling mad. She looked at me and said, "Where the hell have you been?"

"I was just down at the store getting some baseball cards and talking to Stan."

"Well, you're late for dinner, and you know I don't like it when you're late!"

"Yeah, I know."

I went to the table and looked at the crap I had to eat. It was boiled pork hocks and beans. Great, why doesn't she just feed me dog food? It would probably taste a lot better than this crap. I just shut my mind down and stuffed the crap down my throat.

As I finished my food and my mind came out of its shutdown mode, I saw the evening paper lying next to the table. The front page read, LOCAL HOMELESS MAN FOUND MURDERED NEAR WINCHESTER STREET BRIDGE. I was in a trance, totally focused on the caption of the story. I picked up the paper and began to read the article. Local fishermen had stumbled onto his body while they were wading the river fishing for late-season pike. The cops didn't go into too much detail with the reporters. I guess they didn't want to let anyone know the details of the murder. It just said that he was murdered near the edge of the river and that there were no known suspects. Nothing was said about how he was murdered, just that he was murdered. I read further into the article. It seems that the man known as Whitey had a real name, Thomas L. Johnston. I guess I really didn't even think about him as a person with a real name. The final sentence in the article stated that the case was being turned over to the homicide detectives for investigation. I re-thought my steps of the previous Friday; did I forget something? Would the detectives be able to tie me to the murder? No! I had covered my tracks well, very well. I was in the clear, and if questioned, as long as I kept my head, I would never be linked to the crime.

I pushed the paper aside as my mother entered the room. She picked the paper up and started to read the front page. Only moments passed and, she said, "It's really sad that someone killed that old homeless man everyone knew as Whitey."

"Why do you care about him?"

"Well, he was just a guy down on his luck, trying to get by on whatever money he could scrounge up from bottles or odd jobs. He was not so different from us, he just wasn't smart enough to hold down a good job. Much like you, Zeke, just not smart enough."

"What do you mean? My grades in school are okay. I'm as smart as any other kid in school."

"You may be smart in some ways, but not book smart. You don't have the intelligence to make it in this world. You will struggle to survive; you'll probably be just like Whitey. Living on the streets alone, wandering around begging people for food and money. You'll be sleeping in cardboard boxes, under bridges, living in filth. You will waste your life like so many others do. There is no hope for you or anyone else like you."

"I will be all right. I can get a job and make the money I need to survive. You'll see, I'm not stupid, I'll show you that I can make it on my own."

Marie erupted in laughter. She finally gained control of herself and said, "You're right, Zeke. I can't wait to see what a failure you will be."

I pushed my chair away from the table and walked outside. I really needed to get away from her. She never got tired of abusing me. It really didn't matter if it was physical abuse or verbal abuse. The pain was the same. Her words cut me as bad as a switch or a belt. The pain just all ran together. I had become used to it all.

I need to go back to the river. I don't know why, but I have this deep-burning desire to go back to where I ended Whitey's life. I grabbed my bike and began to ride toward the river. I'm nearing the Winchester Street Bridge; I see one marked sheriff vehicle and one unmarked detective vehicle. I really didn't expect them to still be at the bridge. I stopped at the Standard Gas Station near the bridge and checked my bike tires for air. I kept gazing in the area of the bridge to see if any deputies came up from the river. Just as I was about to leave, Bill, the station owner, came out and walked toward me. I knew Bill pretty well because he always patched my bike tires for free when I had a flat. One time he even gave me a new tube for my tire at no charge. I looked up at him and said, "Hi, Bill."

"Hi, Zeke, what can I do for you today?"

"Nothing, Bill, I was just getting some air for my tires."

"Okay, Zeke, let me know if you need anything else."

At this point, I decided to play stupid with Bill. As I got on my bike, I said, "Hey, Bill, what are all the cops doing at the bridge?"

"That's where they found Whitey's body yesterday. Someone had beaten him up pretty good, good enough to kill him."

"Do they know who killed him?"

"No. They had the dogs down there yesterday, pretty much all over the riverbank. It's really just a matter of time before they find out who killed him. These local cops are very good at their job."

I thought for a moment. Dogs, I never thought about the dogs. They could track me; they could follow me right to my house. Then I remembered the rain; the rain fell for two days straight after I killed Whitey. Luck was still with me. I quickly went back to the conversation with Bill.

"I hope they find the guy who killed him. Just won't be the same without Whitey around picking up bottles and taking them to the store."

"Yeah, he kind of kept the streets clean of bottles and anything else of value."

"Yep, he sure did. See you later, Bill, thanks for the air."

"Anytime, Zeke, have a good day, and be careful when you ride in the streets. There are lots of crazy drivers out there."

"I'll be careful."

I rode off in the direction of the bridge. I became very nervous as I neared the structure. Cops were all over the place. More sheriff cars were parked on the other side of the bridge. I stopped my bike on the bridge. The structure was very old and decaying. The sidewalk that crossed the bridge was crumbling, and the small cement pillars in the bridge railing were also crumbling. Many small pieces of the pillars were strewn about on the sidewalk. I peered over the railing toward the river.

Two cops were sifting through what was left of Whitey's stuff. Two more cops were looking closely at the rocks that lay at the riverside and along the river's steep bank. I knew what they were looking for, and I also knew they would never find it. The rock they wanted lay at least twenty feet out in the river.

My mind drifted off from reality. I thought about how clever I was to chuck that rock into the river. I wasn't stupid like Marie said; I was smart. Maybe my wisdom was only used to cover my tracks and to outwit my enemies, but at least I used my brain for something. I had planned to outwit Whitey, and I did just that. In fact, I did it with such wisdom that it would be impossible to pin anything on me. Just as I was drifting off further from reality, I was brought right back by a harsh, raspy voice that snapped, "What are you doing here, kid?"

I looked up right into the face of Officer Fairchild. At least that's what it said on his name tag. Again he snapped, "Are you deaf? I said what are you doing here, kid?"

The sound of his raspy voice sent a chill through my body. I didn't like his tone, and the sound of his voice was creepy. It was as if he had something stuck in his throat that was trying to stop the words from getting to his mouth. I looked up and said, "I was just riding by, and I saw you guys, so I stopped to see what you were doing."

"Well, just keep riding. We don't need your help. We have enough problems without having to deal with kids like you."

"Okay, I just wanted to see what was going on."

I turned my bike around and headed back down Elm Avenue toward home. At least that's what Officer Fairchild thought. When I was out of Officer Fairchild's view, I turned between the houses back to the river. I put my bike in the same spot where I had left it the night I killed Whitey. I eased along the riverbank again just like that fatal night. When I reached the pump house, I went to the top of the bank and looked toward the paper-mill. No paper-mill workers were outside in their usual hangout. I walked across the top of the steel frame that supported the pump house to the other side.

Once there, I moved very cautiously toward three large willow trees, keeping the trees between me and the cops near the bridge. They were totally unaware that they were being watched. I leaned against one of the trees and looked through a small opening between the trees toward the bridge. It was fun to watch them sift through the area. I got a rush that flowed through my body. I relived the night one week earlier, the night of Whitey's demise. I relived the anger that flowed through me that night. The feeling of my being in control. Finally, for once, I was the controller, not the one controlled. The feeling was unbelievable; it was better than anything, better than the sex with Polly. What a rush!

After about thirty minutes, I moved away from the trees and back up the river toward my bike. The cops didn't worry me; I had already outsmarted them once before. Sergeant Murray was no match for me when I destroyed Mr. Gwen's tires. These cops would be no different. They could sift, dig, and scratch all they wanted. They would find nothing, nothing that would lead them to me or anyone else. I would win this one like the last one. I was becoming better and better at outsmarting my enemies and the cops who pursued justice. Justice, what the hell is justice anyway? I have never known justice; I've only known misery. I was fast becoming the judge, jury, and executioner. Zeke was finally getting back at the people who wronged him. Zeke was finally winning the game.

Chapter 16

My dreams have been horrific over the past eight months since the demise of Whitey. Not really because I killed this piece of trash, but more because of all the pain inflicted on me during my childhood. The verbal and physical abuse has left permanent scars etched in my mind. The only thing that continues to haunt me about Whitey is the look of his death face and the cold, glazed stare of his dead eyes. I just can't get that image out of my mind.

It's now the middle of June. I am now sixteen years old and managed to pass the tenth grade. I will move on to the eleventh grade in the fall. Not much longer will I have to endure the pain of living with Marie; not much longer will I take verbal abuse from her! I plan to leave home immediately upon graduating high school. I will be free; no one will ever control me again! No one will ever abuse me again!

I lie here in bed; it's 7:30 AM. Friday morning, and it's time for me to get up, get dressed, and have breakfast. I exit my bedroom and walk to the kitchen where Marie is cooking.

"Well, you're up early, Zeke."

"Yep, I was awake, so I decided to get up for breakfast."

"Breakfast won't be ready for another forty-five minutes. But you can take the trash to the road and sweep the sidewalks while you wait."

"Okay. What's for breakfast this morning?"

"Something that's really good and good for you, cornmeal mush."

I wanted to puke. Why do I even ask these questions? I might just as well be surprised. Cornmeal mush is absolutely terrible. Good for me? How could that crap be good for anyone? I walked outside and took the trash can to the road for the Friday pickup by the city. Now for the task of sweeping the sidewalk, another duty that I never really understood. Marie insisted the sidewalk from our porch to the city sidewalk and back required sweeping every day in the summer. Why, I don't know. It's just another one of her stupid ideas. Just another way to make sure that she had some type of power over me, another way to control me.

I grabbed the broom from the garage and began sweeping the sidewalk. It was sunny and warm this morning. It would be a great day for me to take a ride on my bike and enjoy myself. I always preferred to be alone. I don't like people, and most people who know me don't like me. I'm good with that. I don't care what people think of me.

Well, the sweeping job is finally done. I place the broom in the corner of the garage and go into the house for just another crappy breakfast. As is normal for me, I wolf down the food without complaining. Marie looks at me as I place my dishes in the sink.

"What are your plans today, Zeke?"

"I think I'll go for a bike ride around the neighborhood."

"Okay, but I want you home no later than five o'clock. Your father will be home for dinner today, so you need to make sure you're here."

"All right, I'll be home by five o'clock."

I hopped on my bike and rode down to the Macomb Street Bridge. I walked to the same place where Whitey had grabbed me and inflicted pain on me months ago. This was the first time that I had ventured back to this place since that day. I sat at the same spot where I was sitting when he grabbed me, held me down, and robbed me. My mind flashed back to the time when Whitey briefly controlled me. My thoughts immediately filled with rage. I completely blacked out with anger. Even though the water was rushing by, I did not hear it. Even though the traffic on the road above raced by, I did not hear it. I was in a trance, a trance filled with anger and rage. I went back in my mind to the night I killed Whitey. He deserved what he got, and I knew it. I also knew that I would never allow anyone to inflict physical or mental pain on me again. I sat there for two hours, and many thoughts of my past blew through my mind. I was done with this spot now.

I would never come here again. I decided that I would never stay in a place where pain was inflicted on me. Just like my home, when I'm done there, I don't plan to return. Only a couple of years left now before I leave that house forever.

I climbed up the riverbank and hopped back on my bike and traveled toward home. When I reached our street, I decided to continue down Noble Avenue toward North Dixie Highway. For some reason, the thought hit me to go to the north quarry off Dixie Highway and spend some time alone there. Much caution is required to get to the north quarry as you must pass the south quarry on the way. The north quarry is a fishing quarry, and the south quarry is a swimming quarry. They are approximately a half mile apart with brushy woods between them. Normally, during the summer months, many locals age nineteen to twenty-five hang out and cause trouble at the south quarry. I remember reading in the newspaper about a seventeen-year-old kid named Nick who went to this quarry with his girlfriend just one year ago. It seems that some of the tough guys hanging out there liked his girlfriend and thought it would be fun to grab him and throw him in the water. Every time Nick would climb out of the water, the jerks would throw him in again. The last time they threw him in, Nick never made it back to the surface. Not one of these jerks jumped in to save him. These jerks just laughed when he didn't resurface. They all went to jail for manslaughter, not murder. It seemed that they ruled it manslaughter because these jerks were drunk and supposedly didn't know what they were doing. What a joke!

With this in mind, I decided to circle back to the Mason Run area. The Mason Run is a drainage ditch that travels from the north side of the city making its way south to the River Raisin. A dirt lane runs north and south along the ditch approximately thirty yards from the bank. After the first mile, the road takes a turn east toward the quarry. Weeds are very high along the road, and once you travel the first quarter mile, it is impossible to see anyone on the lane unless you are also on the lane. I entered the lane and headed north toward the quarry. I like this lane because you are very secluded and alone. It kind of reminded me of the box, only you're outdoors in the sunshine. The lane does not go all the way to the quarry. It would be necessary to walk about one-half mile to reach the north quarry.

I stashed my bike in the brush and began my walk through a brushy wooded area west of the quarry. The walk through the brush is easy, and I reached the quarry with no problem.

I'm standing on the edge of the bank peering down at the water. It is crystal clear, and you can see jagged rocks jutting out from the bank into the water that are about fifteen feet below the surface of the water. The silence is broken by yells from the drunken jerks at the south quarry. A half mile away, and you can hear them like they are standing next to you. I look across the quarry at some old broken-down equipment that was left there when the original quarry owners went bankrupt and fled the area several years ago. The weather had decayed the equipment, and rust was abundant on the blade of the old dozer and the bucket of the backhoe. Behind the dozer and the backhoe sat an old dump truck mostly covered with trees and brush that had grown around it. It was really kind of interesting how the trees and brush wove through the equipment. Very much like when grapevines grow intertwined on a fence.

I begin looking around for a comfortable place to sit where I can see the water and the ducks swimming on the quarry surface. A perfect spot to relax! A large rock extends out over the water's edge about halfway between where I'm standing and the old equipment. The rock is about five feet above the surface of the water and has a hollowed out part that will make a perfect seat. I take a moment to look around the quarry to make sure that I am alone. I do not wish to be bothered, and I still have a vivid memory of Whitey grabbing me while I relaxed at the Macomb Street Bridge. Whitey was gone, but there are many other creeps out there to take his place.

Great, I am alone. Not a soul wanders here today but me! It's time for me to relax and enjoy the great weather today. I walk over to the rock and sit in the perfect saddle. Almost as if Mother Nature intended this rock to be a perfect seat. The ducks scatter as I make my way onto the rock. I sit down and lean back on the rock and relax looking across the quarry. I sat there for about an hour watching the ducks work their way back in my direction. It was really peaceful and relaxing.

I notice a movement toward the area of the equipment. Someone is in the cab of the old dump truck. The cab is in a very shaded area, but I saw what appeared to be a cigarette being lit.

I moved from my position on the rock and walked back into the brush as if I were going back to my bike. Once I entered the brush and walked in out of sight, I went north past the north edge of the quarry and then east toward the old dump truck. I eased up to the edge of the truck and looked directly into the rearview mirror. Staring back at me was this beautiful image of a young girl about my age. She stuck her head out the window and said, “You’re not very good at sneaking up on people!”

“Maybe not, but I was pretty close before you saw me.”

“Yeah, but I saw you, didn’t I?”

“Yep, you did. Come on out of the truck so we can talk and don’t have to yell to each other.”

“No, I like it here. Why don’t you come in here with me? I have an extra Coke if you want it.”

“Okay.”

With that I walked to the passenger side of the truck and opened the door. The door opened with a loud creak. The hinges were rusted, and the grease that kept them lubricated was long since gone.

I was amazed when I entered the truck; she looked just like Polly. This beauty has the same blond hair, the same green eyes, the same beautiful body, the same beautiful smile.

She gazed at me for a moment and, without saying a word, handed me a Coke out of a small cooler. It was ice-cold and nice to have on a hot summer day. I opened the can and took a sip. I looked at her for a moment, thanked her, and then I asked, "What's your name?"

She smiled and said, "My name is Nicole, what's yours?"

"My name is Zeke."

"So, Zeke, what's your story?"

"I don't have a story. I live a couple of miles from here, and I find the quarry to be a quiet place where I can be alone. I don't like people very much, and I'm happy when I am alone. What's your story, Nicole?"

"Well, I'm from Inkster."

"Inkster? That's got to be thirty miles from here. How in the heck did you get here?"

"I ran away from home at the end of the school year. My life at home was not very good. I have a stepfather who liked to touch me, and if I didn't let him touch me, he beat me. I don't want him to touch me anymore, so I left home, and I never plan to go back."

"Did you tell your mother about this?"

"No, I didn't. She wouldn't listen anyway. She is completely controlled by him and would never believe me."

"I kind of know how you feel. My mother has treated me very badly all my life. She has beaten me for no reason, screamed at me for no reason, and continues to tell me how evil and worthless I am. The older I get, the more I believe the evil and worthless part."

"Yeah, parents can make you feel pretty bad when they want to. I know that my stepfather treats me like crap. The only time that he is good to me is when I let him touch me. He doesn't care about me, he just uses me to satisfy his needs. God, I hate it when he touches me."

"Where have you been staying since you left home?"

"I have slept under bridges, at parks, and for the last week, I have used this old truck as my home. Not too bad. I wash my clothes in the quarry, take a bath in the quarry, and use the old outhouse that the quarry contractors built here years ago. It's a pretty good life right now."

"What about money for food?"

"I took five hundred dollars from a stash of money that my stepfather kept at the house. The money will provide me with food for a long time. I plan on being somewhere warm before winter sets in, and I can find work there. It seems only fair that he pays for touching me and making my life miserable."

I remained silent for a moment. Her comments about her stepfather and her life have sickened me inside. This beautiful person in front of me hates her life much like I hate mine.

"I'm sorry that you had to leave home, Nicole. It doesn't seem right that a person who is not even related to you can make you so miserable that you run away from your own home."

"I know, Zeke, but I am far better off on my own."

I envied her in a way. She had the courage to leave a bad situation to be on her own. By herself, much like I wanted to be by myself. She was free of her situation. She had enough money for food to last her for some time. Living in the truck was not that bad. Probably the worst thing was mosquitoes at night and the risk of having some undesirable finding her new home and abusing her further. A risk worth taking!

"Hey! Are you in a trance or something?"

"Kind of. I was just thinking, that's all."

"Well, quit thinking, and let's quit talking and go for a swim."

“I don’t have a swimsuit with me.”

“Who needs a swimsuit? Look out the window, we’re alone. We don’t need a swimsuit. Just take off your clothes, and let’s swim.”

Wow! What a great idea. If I take my clothes off, she’ll be taking hers off too! She’s beautiful! I can’t wait to see her naked!

“Okay, let’s go!”

I immediately start undressing while she begins to unbutton her blouse. She reaches back with one hand and unclasps her bra. I watch as it falls off her shoulders and into her lap. God, her breasts were beautiful. She looks over at me and smiles.

“What are you looking at, Zeke?”

“Well, uh . . . just . . . just you.”

“Well, Zeke, do you like what you see?”

“Yeah, I do, Nicole. You are beautiful.”

“Thanks, Zeke. Now quit wasting time, and let’s get in the water.”

We both throw the doors open and jump out of the truck at the same time. We race to the water’s edge and carefully slip into the quarry, avoiding the ever-present jagged rocks along the edge. I swim out to a submerged flat rock, one of many that jut out from the quarry’s edge. The water is cool and feels great as it consumes my body. I reach the flat rock, stand, and walk along the rock until the water is chest deep. I watch as Nicole swims out into the quarry. She is a great swimmer, and I continue to watch as this beauty swims along gracefully. After a few moments, she turns and swims toward me. She reaches me and stands up directly in front of me and gently places her arms around me. God, her touch feels good. I lean my head down to her and kiss her gently on the lips. She responds by grabbing the back of my head and pressing her lips harder to mine. Her tongue enters my mouth, and mine enters hers. We continue to kiss and hold each other tightly. I become aroused almost immediately. She reaches down and starts to stroke me slowly. Her touch is unbelievable! She grabs my shoulders and wraps her legs around me so that I can enter her. The sensation is incredible! We continue to kiss and make love. Memories of Polly returned to my head even though I tried to keep them out of my mind. Nicole began to moan, and tremors came across her body. Her moans became louder, and it turned me on so much that I exploded inside her. She grinned at me and said, "I'm glad you liked it too, Zeke."

"Yeah, it was really good, Nicole. I hope you liked it too."

"Yes, I liked it. I think you could tell by the sounds I made."

We both laughed together and agreed it was good for both of us.

We sat at the water's edge on another submerged rock. We looked out over the water and watched ducks swim past. I turned my head to look at her, and our eyes met. She stares directly at me and says, "Zeke, do you think that life will get better for both of us soon?"

"I don't know about soon, but I know that it will for me after I graduate from high school and leave my living hell behind me."

"Well, Zeke, I really hope that things work out for both of us."

We continued to play in the water and laugh together. What a great time. I realized that it was getting late, and I needed to return home. We went back to the old truck and got dressed. I held her for a while longer in silence. I leaned down and gave her one last kiss.

"Zeke, will I see you again?"

"Yes, I will come back to see you on Monday. I can't come any sooner because my mother will think I'm actually enjoying myself and make me stay home to do meaningless work. I must leave now or it will be hell when I get home."

"Okay, Zeke. I had a great time with you, I'll see you on Monday. Try to come early so we have more time together. I only leave here to go to the local party store for Coke, food, and smokes. It's about a two-mile walk, so wait for me, I won't stop anywhere along the way so I won't be gone long."

"Okay, Nicole, I'll see you Monday, don't forget."

"Don't worry, Zeke. I won't forget!"

I began my walk back through the brush to my bike. What a great time I had with Nicole. I hope that we can continue to see each other often during the rest of the summer.

Chapter 17

"Baker, Baker!" I'm startled back to reality by the shouts from cell-block guard Sullivan. He's just another guy who thinks he's the toughest guy around.

"What?"

"Get yourself to the back of the cell so we can cuff you and take you to the visitation area."

Sullivan is accompanied by two other guards, Burgess and Peters. He always comes with two other guards to assist him. Inside he knows not to face me alone. He knows that I can take him, and he lives in fear of me.

"Who the hell is here to see me?"

"Keith Welch, your court-appointed lawyer."

"What the hell does he want?"

"I don't know. You'll have to ask him yourself. Now get to the back of the cell as I told you or me and the boys here will have to use the nightsticks on you. Frankly, I wish you would make just one mistake and give us that opportunity."

I turned and faced Sullivan. My face was like stone, and my eyes were fixed on his. I saw again what I had seen on so many faces in the past. I saw the fear come to his eyes, tiny droplets of sweat began to bead out on his forehead, the corner of his mouth began to twitch.

"Okay, tough guy, we'll do this a different way. Peters, hold your gun on him, and if he tries anything, shoot him. Now, tough guy, back up to the bars, and I'll cuff you from the outside so we don't have to hurt you."

Hurt me? What a joke. It's impossible to hurt someone who has already absorbed more pain than the body can withstand. I turned my back toward him and slowly inched my way to the bars with my hands behind me.

I waited as the ever-clumsy Sullivan struggled with the handcuffs. Finally he was able to cinch the last cuff closed with an extra click just to inflict a little pain so he could feel in control. Little did he know that if I were given the opportunity, I would kill him just like I did the others. After all, I have nothing to lose.

Peters holsters his gun and begins fumbling with the keys to open the cell door. I watch and laugh as they drop to the floor. What an idiot! He bends down and retrieves the keys from the floor. He is now so nervous that it is impossible for him to get the key in the lock. Sullivan quickly grabs the keys from his hands and unlocks the cell. I stare out into the aisle totally motionless. Sullivan makes the mistake of grabbing me by the arm to move me. I turn quickly and slam him into the bars. Both Peters and Burgess draw their guns.

"Oh, sorry, Sullivan, are you all right? Maybe next time you won't give that extra click on the cuffs!"

He grimaces in pain. But he has the good sense not to retaliate.

"No, I'm okay. Put your guns away, boys. He's not going anywhere."

We begin the long walk to the visitation area. We get to the main level of the prison where a long block of cells houses the majority of the general population of the prisoners. These guys all knew of me, they read the papers, they followed the case. When we passed the first cell, the inmates along the way all began to chant "Zeke, Zeke, Zeke" as we passed. This makes Burgess, Peters, and Sullivan even more nervous. I, on the other hand, felt like a Roman gladiator going to the arena for battle. Imagine, these guys actually were on my side, something I seldom experienced during my life.

We finally arrive at the visitation room where Keith Welch awaits me. Keith is in his late fifties and stands slightly over six feet tall. He's in great shape for a guy who spends most of his time at a desk or in the courtroom.

"Hi, Zeke, how are you?"

"I'm fine, Keith. It's just another day in paradise at this fine government facility."

Keith turns toward Sullivan and says, "I would like to talk with my client in private."

"The only way you can do that is if we take him to the holding pen behind the visitation area so we can cuff him to the cage."

Keith looks at me and says, "Is that okay with you, Zeke?"

"Yep," I replied.

We walked toward the back where the holding cage is located. Sullivan unlocked the cage, and both Peters and Burgess drew their guns as Sullivan unlocked the cuffs and quickly locked them to the wire mesh of the holding pen.

Sullivan looked at Keith and said, "We'll be at the door to the visitation area if you need us, Mr. Welch. Don't get too close to this animal. He's like a rabid dog."

I lunged at Sullivan, but he was just out of my reach. He laughed and said, "That's right, you animal. You're at the end of your chain, aren't you?"

This irritated Keith, and he quickly responded with, "Quit harassing my client or I'll turn you in to the corrections review board!"

With that Sullivan, Burgess, and Peters left the room and closed the door to the visitation area behind them.

Keith pulled a chair up next to me and said, "Sit down, Zeke."

I looked at Keith and thought to myself, here's another guy who wants to give me orders. Orders don't work with Zeke. But all throughout the trial, Keith worked hard to defend me. Not that I cared, but it was obvious that he did. It was kind of fun to watch him in action.

His posture in the courtroom was perfect; his actions commanded respect from both his colleagues and judges. He is a true legal artist.

"Okay, Keith, I'll sit down and relax. What's on your mind anyway?"

"Well, Zeke, as you know, the jury has been out for three days now and still has not come to a verdict. They have recently asked for transcripts of the trial and the case file from the homicide detectives."

"What's that mean to me, Keith?"

"The case may be headed toward a hung jury."

"A hung jury, how can that be? They know that I'm guilty."

"Yeah, they know, but they also know you had it rough during your childhood, and I believe that some of the jurors can relate to your situation."

I thought for a moment. It was hard for me to believe that some of the jurors may have had a similar childhood as mine. I had actually forgotten that Keith had played that up to the jury during the trial. He was good at capturing the full attention of the jury and appealing to their compassionate side. Keith had also presented testimony from a psychiatrist who submitted that the reason I killed was that by age twelve, my values were locked in, and I had no way to escape my destiny. He even went on to say that if I had been taken under psychiatric care during my very early teens, my life would have been totally different. He blamed my parents for not recognizing my problematic conditions and for not getting me the help I needed. I wondered for a brief moment, would that have really made a difference? I doubt it. By my teen years, I was pretty hardened to everything both physically and emotionally. I don't really think that anything could have been done to change me from the person I am.

"What happens if the jury can't reach a verdict?"

"The state will call for a new trial, appoint a new judge, and we'll begin the process to select a new jury."

"How long will that take?"

"Probably another six to twelve months before the state can select a new judge, and we can begin jury selection."

"Unbelievable, they know I did it, yet they can't come to a verdict."

"Zeke, there's one other thing that I want to mention. It is possible that the jury will find you not guilty by reason of insanity."

Even though I told Keith in the beginning that I was guilty of murder, he believed that it was his job to get me a not-guilty verdict. He and I had discussed my entire life at length early on when he was handed the case. During our initial meetings, he told me that it would be impossible for him to sleep at night if he did not focus all his effort on getting me freed. So for his sake, I decided to let him handle the case the way he wanted. It seemed as if he had this overwhelming desire to see the wrongs that were handed me in the past righted. I know that Keith spent a great deal of time and effort focused on my case.

I looked up at Keith and asked, "What would happen then?"

"You would be required to enter a state-run institution where you would receive psychiatric treatment until the facility deemed you sane so you could return to a normal active life in the general population."

"Look, Keith, I know you have done everything that you can do to get me released. You worked countless hours to prepare for the trial. It was easy for everyone to see that you knew me better than I know myself. There is nothing else you can do. I just want you to know that you have been the only person in my life who cared enough about me to try and protect me. I know that I will never be able to pay you for the service that you have done for me. I do appreciate it, and I really believe that if we had met under different circumstances, we could have been friends."

"Thanks Zeke. I'm not going to give up on this case or you. You have been wronged all throughout your life, and I hope I can have a positive effect on your future."

Keith takes a moment to gather his thoughts and looks down at his watch.

"Zeke, I have to go now. I have another trial in an hour, and I want to make sure I'm on time for my client. I'll keep you posted on the progress of the jury."

"Thanks, Keith."

Keith grabs his briefcase and heads toward the door.

I turned toward the door and yelled, "Guard, guard!"

The door swung open, and Sullivan appeared with a stupid smirk on his face. Keith passed him on his way out and again warned him about harassing me. Sullivan turned toward him and said, "I treat him no different from the other prisoners. They are all in cages because they're all animals!"

Keith continued through the door and out of sight. As he walked down the corridor, he continually shook his head in disgust at Sullivan's comment.

Sullivan turned and came into the room along with Peters and Burgess. He looked at me and said, "Are you ready to go back to your cage, animal?"

"Yeah, I'm ready. Too bad you can't spend some quality time with me so we can get to know each other better. I'd like to have the opportunity to scramble your brains a little. But maybe I'm too late for that, you already seem pretty stupid."

"One day I'm going to forget that I'm supposed to guard you and show you how animals like you should be treated."

"Yeah, I'd like that, Sullivan, just you and me, no guards, no guns. That would be great!"

"Peters, Burgess, hold your guns on this animal so I can take him off the cage."

They obediently pulled their revolvers and pointed them at me. I never really liked looking down the barrel of a gun, but I was getting used to it now.

Sullivan unlocked the cuffs from the cage and again locked the cuffs on my wrists. We began the walk back to my cell. Actually I didn't mind the cell at all. I was alone in the cell, and that's the way I've been most of my life. For me being alone is a good thing.

When we reached the cell, Sullivan said, "Get in and back up to the bars so I can remove the handcuffs."

I stood in place at the door of the cell with my back to the open door. Sullivan was on the left side of me as I faced the cell.

"What the hell, are you deaf, Baker? I told you to get in the cell, now get in the cell."

With that he grabbed my left arm and pushed me into the cell. Unfortunately for Sullivan, my right hand firmly gripped a single bar on the cell door, and his forceful push slammed his wrist between the cell door and the door frame. You could hear the bones crack above his painful scream.

"I'll get you for this, you goddamned animal! I'll get you!"

"You'll need to stand in line behind everyone else who wants a piece of me!"

Peters slammed the door on the cell and locked it immediately. Burgess quickly removed the handcuffs from me through the protection of the cell bars.

I looked at Sullivan as Peters and Burgess ran to his aid. The pain must have been as tremendous as the joy was for me.

Peters and Burgess helped him down the hallway, and I'm sure toward the medical facility. Just another person who thought he could get the upper hand on Zeke.

Yep, Sullivan was just another person who suffered pain and agony at my hands, another person who had learned a valuable lesson. A lesson administered by Zeke.

Chapter 18

I sat in my cell for only moments before my mind drifted back to my childhood.

I had only met Nicole yesterday, but I already wanted to see her again. She fascinates me. She is on her own, alone against the world. I envy her. She does not have to answer to anyone. She can do exactly what she wants. It was the life that I so very badly wanted more and more every day. I lay in bed that night thinking about Nicole and wondering if she was thinking about me. I hoped that she was all right and that she kept herself secluded from the evil trash that hung around the south quarry. I decided that I wanted to leave home forever and travel with Nicole. That would be terrific! I will go to the north quarry tomorrow, Sunday, and talk with Nicole about my plan. I'm sure she will be as excited as I am.

I tossed and turned in bed most of the night dreaming about Nicole. I was dreaming about being with her and finally being able to enjoy life. I couldn't get her out of my mind. It's finally morning. I hear Marie banging pots and pans around the kitchen as normal. How am I going to get away from the house today without her bitching at me and ruining my good mood? I decided to try and trick her by offering to do some work around the house before she began ordering me to do countless hours of chores. I walked out into the kitchen where she stood over the stove cooking.

She looked around at me and said, "Well, Zeke, do you want some breakfast this morning?"

"Yeah, I'd like something to eat. I noticed that the grass is pretty long. I'll get the lawn mower out and cut it when I have finished eating."

"Well, that's a good idea, Zeke. Your father will appreciate it."

I sat down at the table with a glass of orange juice and waited for breakfast to be ready. It wasn't long before Marie came into the dining room and set breakfast on the table.

She must be in a good mood because she cooked eggs, bacon, and toast this morning, something that she rarely does. We sat and ate in silence. Marie does not speak to me very much these days. I guess she feels the silent treatment will get to me sooner or later. I can tell you, she won't hurt my feelings if she never speaks to me again. I finished breakfast and headed to the garage to get the lawn mower out so I could cut the lawn. It takes about an hour to cut our lawn, as we have a very large city lot, and I was in a hurry. I needed to get to the quarry so I could again be with Nicole. I pulled the mower out on the driveway, gassed it up, and pulled the starter cord to start the engine. I pulled and I pulled, but the engine would not start. Great, just when I need to get something done quickly, something happens to slow me down. I stopped to get my breath for a moment. Pulling the cord so many times was very tiring. Then it hit me; I remembered James had the same problem a month ago. He just pulled the spark plug out, dried it off, cleaned it with a wire brush, and then put it back in the engine. I asked him why he did this, and he told me that sometimes the engine gets flooded with fuel, and the plug fouls, needs to be dried, and then cleaned with a wire brush for better spark. I also remembered that when he did this, the engine started on the first pull. I went into the garage, got the toolbox, and removed the plug. I did exactly what James had done last month to clean the plug and then put it back in the engine. I grabbed the pull start cord and yanked it with all my strength. The engine immediately started as it had for James. Luck was with me today! I finished the lawn in a little over an hour because I decided to get the grass clippers out and trim around my father's rosebushes. James had taken these rosebushes from his father's yard after he died. It seems that his father loved roses and had raised these particular bushes for fifty years before his death. James took great pride with these roses and spent a great deal of time tending to them. I thought it would be good if I tried to keep the area around them looking nice for him. Finally finished! Now it was time to go and face Marie.

I walked into the house, and she was sitting on the couch shaking her head and reading the paper.

"What's wrong, Mom?"

"Well, another young man was killed at the south quarry."

Great, just what I needed to hear.

"How did it happen?"

"Well, it says that he was swimming with a couple of friends from his local neighborhood when four men, twenty to twenty-four years, old approached them and told them to leave. They refused to leave, and a fight broke out, and the young man who died was stabbed in the throat by one of the men."

"How old was the guy who died?"

"Eighteen years old, and he goes to your high school."

"What was his name?"

"It says here that his name is Gary Adams. Do you know him?"

I thought for a moment. "I don't really know him, but I know he's a senior this year, and he's the captain of the football team."

"Zeke, I want you to stay away from those quarries. The police are always being called out there for fights or to control drunks. I know that you think you're tough and will fight anyone, but these guys gang up on teenagers, and the outcome is not good. It's a very bad place, and I know that James would not be happy if you went there."

"I know it's a bad place, and I know to stay away. I can handle myself, but these guys don't seem to fight fair."

She turned her eyes back to the paper.

"I'm going for a ride on my bike now. I'll be back later."

She looked over at the clock and then me and said, "It's ten o'clock now, and I want you back here no later than two o'clock."

"Okay, I'll be back by two o'clock."

I turn quickly and head for the door. My bike is already sitting next to the house, so I grab it up and head for the lane behind the Mason Run. The tough guys at the south quarry didn't bother me. They would never travel through the brush to get to the north quarry; there was no reason for them to do that. They had everything they needed at the south quarry. I enter the lane and head north toward the quarry. Again the lane is clear, and I ride as fast as the dirt road will allow. I turn east toward the quarry and notice a farmer riding a tractor, cultivating the corn that is planted in the field nearest the quarry. This could be a problem because the farmer probably doesn't want me crossing his field. I really don't want to get close enough to the farmer to be recognized anyway. I continued north on the lane to the far north end of the cornfield where the lane turns east. I rode up to the brush at the northeast corner of the cornfield. Unfortunately, this put me at least a mile from the quarry. There was nothing else I could do but hide my bike in the brush at the northeast corner of the farmer's field and hope it wouldn't be found. The farmer was headed south in the field, and I knew that he could not look around to watch me and risk letting his cultivators cut into the rows of corn. That would be costly for him. He was at the far end of the field about to make his turn north when I entered the brush.

It was now ten twenty, and it would take at least twenty minutes to cut through the brush and reach Nicole. That would only give me about 2 ½ hours alone with her.

I walked through the brush as quickly as the thick vine-entangled undergrowth would allow. I finally reached the edge of the brush just before the quarry. I am again very cautious. I want to make sure that Nicole and I are alone. I hear voices coming from the other side of the quarry. I know that one is Nicole, but I don't recognize the other voice. I moved across the brush south, staying concealed until I reached a point where I could see down in the quarry at the east bank. There Nicole stood with a guy talking. I couldn't get a look at his face, and I had no idea who he was or why he was there. The clock was running, and I needed to talk with Nicole about my plan.

Then it happened. Nicole pulled her blouse over her head and dropped the straps on her bra as she had done with me.

I watched as she put her arms around this guy and kissed him like she kissed me. Now she dropped her pants, and he immediately shed his clothes, and they dove in the quarry. They both swam toward the west edge of the quarry, and when they got about halfway across, I recognized the guy. His name was Rich Wagner. He lived about five blocks away from my house. He was a sophomore at the high school I attended. Nicole said something to him, and they abruptly turned and swam toward the east side of the quarry. I wondered if she saw me and wanted to get away. Then I realized what she was doing. She swam directly to the submerged rock where we made love. She stood up on the rock and began kissing Rich. Within seconds, she was on him, making love to him. I completely blacked out with anger. I slumped to the ground holding my head because I thought it was going to explode. Just like Polly, Nicole had betrayed me. Just like Polly, the pain swept through my body. I would have rather taken a beating than feel the internal pain that I felt now. How in the hell could she do this to me? Why would she do this to me? I sat on the ground now shaking with anger. I could hear her moan and scream now as she had done with me. I wanted to go over to the old truck, wait for them, and kill them both for causing me pain. But that could not be done now. I didn't have a weapon or the time to kill them, dispose of their bodies, and return home on time. I knew that Marie would be watching the clock, and besides, I was not prepared to kill them now. I needed a plan. A plan to kill them would take time to think through, and time was too short now. I watched them as they lay back on the very rock that only two days before we had lain on together. My anger increased, my head was pounding, and I ached inside.

I could not stay and watch any longer. I began to work my way back to my bike through the brush. I reached my bike and headed down the lane toward home. The farmer was still busy at work in the field, but I didn't care about him anymore. I was focused on Nicole and Rich now. Soon they would both get what they deserved. Soon they would feel the pain that Zeke felt when he watched them today.

I will not rest until they are both destroyed. I will spend all my time planning to deal with them as I did with Whitey.

Chapter 19

It was early the next day when I got out of bed. I stood in the living room looking across the vacant lot in front of our house toward the straw stack fields that lay beyond. I remember my father telling me that the field consisted of two hundred acres of fenced land. He also told me the straw stacks that stood within the fenced area were ninety feet wide, ninety feet long, and ninety feet high. The stacks were made up of bales of straw that were purchased by the paper company from farmers all over the country. My father worked at the paper company where the straw was used to make paper. He said the straw was brought inside the plant and placed into cookers, cooked at a certain temperature for several hours, then blended by machines that he called beaters until it was the right consistency to make paper. I remembered seeing the beaters when the plant had an open house for employees and their families.

I decided that I would go over to the straw stack field today and look it over. I knew the watchman for the paper company carried a clock to punch with a key that was attached to different shacks within the field. These shacks housed fire hydrants and hoses in case a fire broke out. I also knew that he was in charge of weighing trucks leaving the paper company with loads to assure they were within the legal weight limit for road travel. The watchman's rounds were supposed to be every two hours, but I knew that they would often miss a round due to heavy truck volumes at the weigh scale they tended.

I went outside to the garage after breakfast. I was just about to take my bike outside when I noticed a pair of wire cutters lying on my father's toolbox. I remembered that he had used them a couple of days ago to cut wire stakes to support new roses that he had planted. I picked up the wire cutters and put them in my pocket. These would be useful to gain access to the straw fields rather than risk being seen by climbing the fence.

It was easy to get to the field. All I had to do was travel the same lane toward the quarry. It passed within thirty feet of the fence that guarded the straw field. I went to the northwest corner of the fence and laid my bike in the tall weeds on the east side of the lane.

I was completely concealed from sight of my house and the rest of the houses that were built along the west side of Mason Run.

The tall weeds and brush were just too thick to see through. I walked over to the fence and peered into the field. The fence is almost completely covered with wild grapevines, making it difficult for anyone who is on the outside to be detected by someone on the inside. I caught sight of the paper company watchman as he made his rounds. It's ten o'clock, and he's right on schedule. The shack nearest to my position was probably 150 yards away. I dropped to my stomach on the ground as he neared my position. The field is mostly overgrown with weeds, making it difficult for him to see me even if I remained standing. But I wasn't taking any chances on being spotted. My father knew every watchman who worked at the paper company, and I wasn't going to risk being detected. The watchman passed and continued his route throughout the field and back toward the weigh scale approximately three quarters of a mile away from my position.

I looked up and down the fence looking for the best place to cut the wire mesh so I can enter the field. I found an area in the fence about three feet square that was nearly one hundred yards away from the nearest shack in the field. I could cut the fence here, leaving the wild grapevines in place. I could then spread the grapevines and slip through the fence. I began clipping the wires of the chain-link fence. It was only minutes before I completely removed a three-by-three section of the fence. I spread the grapevines with my hands and forced my body through the opening. After I passed through the vines and stood up, I looked back at the opening. The grapevines had snapped back to their original position, and from twenty yards away, you could not even see that a section of fence had been removed.

I walked over to a straw stack that was in the second row of the field. I looked both ways and determined that the field consisted of fifteen rows north to south and fifteen rows east to west for a total of 225 straw stacks. The bales in the stacks were bound with two strands of twine from the baling machines that the farmers used. One of the bales in the middle of the stack three bales up from the bottom had one of the strands of twine broken.

This edge of the stack faced the fence where I had entered the field. Part of the straw had fallen out of the bale on the ground next to the stack.

I went over and began pulling more straw off the bale and spreading it on the ground near the base of the stack. When I had removed the entire bale, I looked at the pattern in which the bales were stacked. I decided that I could remove another bale, then another to build a makeshift tunnel into the stack. Luckily I brought my pocketknife along so I could cut the twine that compressed the bales. I cut the twine on the next bale, but it was very difficult to pull the straw out due to the force on the bale by the others holding it in place. I searched the area for something to help me dig the bale from its position. Ten wooden pallets lay next to the stack. These would be of no use to me for freeing the bale. I looked across toward the nearest shack and wondered if there was anything inside that I could use. It would be risky to go that far out in the field. I may be detected if workers came to this end of the field to get straw. I knew that they were working on the southeast corner of the field now, at least three quarters of a mile from my position. They always used a certain pattern to retrieve straw so they got the oldest stack in the field first working their way to the newest stack in the field last. It would be months before they got to the stack where I stood.

I approached the shack with caution. There was a lock on the hasp, but it was only locked to the hasp itself and not to the hinged plate that was connected to the door. I opened the door, which resulted in a loud creak from the rusty hinges that secured the door to the building frame. Inside the building lay a pitchfork and a shovel. Great, just what I need to get the job done! I grabbed them and ran back to the straw stack. I worked for a couple of hours and was only able to get four more bales removed from the stack. It was hard work! The tunnel was taking shape, but much more work needed to be done. It was time to head for home now.

I lay in bed that evening thinking about Nicole and Rich together. My hatred for both of them grew and grew. I couldn't wait to get my revenge, but wait I must. Because I needed a plan, a plan that would assure I would not be caught. I would need to think everything through before I struck.

Morning came quickly. It was Monday, the day I was supposed to be with Nicole. Well, that wouldn't happen, not today.

I had work to do on something that was now important to me. I would not see Nicole until I had completed my work in the straw fields. Besides, I had not yet figured out the best way to deal with the ever-growing pain and anger inside me.

I did several chores that Marie demanded be complete before I would be allowed to leave.

When I was done, I hopped on my bike and was off to the straw stack fields to continue my work. I entered the lane and immediately noticed a Detroit Edison line crew working on the power lines. The power lines ran directly above the west fence of the field that contained the straw stacks. I went to the north end of the fence and sat next to the vine-covered opening waiting for the crew to get done with their work on the power lines. It was forty-five minutes before they finished and left. I entered the field through the grapevines to continue work on my tunnel. When I got to the straw stack, I noticed that part of the straw bale that was immediately above the last bale I removed had broken and fallen. Loose straw clogged the area of the tunnel. I removed it with the pitchfork and slid into the opening in the stack so I could see if any more bales were going to break. Everything looked good, but I had a bad feeling about the stack collapsing on me, so I decided to use the old pallets to support areas where I removed bales. I didn't have a hammer, so I decided to go back to the shack where I got the shovel and pitchfork and search for other tools.

I entered the shack to look for the tools when I heard the sound of voices. I looked down at my watch; damn, it was ten o'clock. How stupid am I! It was time for the watchman to make his rounds. How could I have forgotten about him? It was surely the watchman coming, and someone was with him. I eased the door closed carefully, not moving it too quickly. I could not risk the creak of the hinges when he was this close. There were no windows in the shack, so I now stood in total darkness waiting. I could hear their footsteps getting closer. They stopped at the shack to punch the clock. The watchman explained to the other person that he had to be to this key within ten minutes of punching the clock at the last key.

That was proof that he was patrolling the area in a timely manner. The person with the watchman asked several questions about the route within the field of straw stacks.

It appeared that the watchman was training this person to perform the rounds; maybe he was just hired for the job. I didn't know, but I did know that sweat was beginning to pour off me now. It was hot in the shack, but I was also extremely nervous and very afraid that I would be discovered in the shack. I'm sure that it was only a minute that passed, but it seemed like thirty. Finally they moved away from the shack toward the next punch-key location.

I eased the door open, and it was good to feel the fresh air rush in the building. In the corner of the building, above the fire hydrant, a small toolbox lay on a shelf. I stood on top of the fire hydrant and lifted the toolbox off the shelf and placed it on the ground. I was amazed when I opened the lid to find a keyhole saw, flat-blade screwdrivers, pliers, hacksaw, tape measure, and a hammer. I looked around the shack further to see if there was anything else that I could use for my project. Hanging on the wall was an old kerosene lantern. Above the lantern on a shelf lay a box of Ohio Blue Tip matches. Great, it was very dark inside the tunnel, and I could use the lantern. It would give me more than enough light. I would have to be very careful with the lantern. One false move and I would have the entire straw field on fire. I now had everything I needed to work on my project. I went out the door of the shack and placed the toolbox on the ground. I very carefully eased the door closed. I stopped for a moment and looked around the area to assure that the watchman and his friend were out of sight. I picked up the toolbox in my right hand and headed back to the straw stack to continue my work.

I worked hard for the next seven hours dismantling the pallets and putting wooden planks and four-by-four supports in place to assure the bales above my tunnel would stay in place. I only halted my work when the watchman made his rounds in the field. My tunnel was on the backside of the stack away from the nearest shack. But I still lay quietly during his rounds so I would not be detected.

I was ten feet into the straw stack from my work the prior day. I decided it was time to build a chamber at the end of the tunnel where I could sit. It would be much like the box. I could sit or lie inside and be alone. Not a single person would have a clue that I was there.

I pulled eight more bales out of the interior of the stack to build the hideout. It made it much easier to remove the bales by using the claw end of the hammer to pull the bales apart.

I was very careful to continue to support the straw overhead with wood from the pallets.

Finally I was done. I went outside to scatter all the straw that I removed around the base of the stack on the side facing the fence where I entered the field. It was important that I do this so the straw was not easily visible next to the stack. When I finished spreading the straw, I went back into the tunnel to my hideout.

I sat in my hideout with the lantern and relaxed for a few moments. I watched as shadows from the flame danced across the straw walls of my hideout. It was really nice inside. It was cool because the heat from the outside was insulated by the straw surrounding me. What a great place for me to escape and be alone!

I looked down at my watch. It was five ten in the afternoon. I knew that I had better get home by five thirty or Marie would go nuts on me.

I exited the hideout and placed the shovel, pitchfork, lantern, and toolbox inside the tunnel. I started back to the opening in the fence and gave one last look toward the straw stack. There was a gaping hole where I had removed the first bale of straw. It was easy for someone to spot when walking the perimeter of the fenced property. I went back to the straw stack and gathered up some of the loose straw that I had spread around the stack on the ground. I took a couple of strands of twine and cinched the bundle of loose straw tight together. I then placed the bundle within the tunnel opening in the straw stack. I went back over to the fence and looked back at the straw stack. It was now impossible to tell that a tunnel existed. Perfect!

I slipped back through the fence and headed down the dirt lane toward home. My thoughts drifted back to Nicole and Rich. Again my body filled with anger, and my head began to pound. I needed to deal with them, and I needed to do it soon!

I arrived home at 5:30 PM and immediately went into the bathroom to wash my hands for dinner.

James was home for dinner, which was unusual because he continued to work all the time and was never home except to sleep.

I sat down for dinner with James and Marie at six o'clock. Nothing was said about my whereabouts during the day. That was good for me because I didn't wish to be interrogated about today's activities.

James talked with Marie about his work schedule for the next week. Again he would work the night shift sixteen hours every day, including Saturday and Sunday. I agreed with his logic. If I could work sixteen hours per day and sleep the rest of the time to be away from Marie, I would do it in a heartbeat. I had heard her brutalize him verbally on numerous occasions.

In her eyes, neither James nor I could do anything right. We were either too stupid or lazy to live up to her standards.

I remember one of Marie's most recent tirades on James. I was in my bedroom trying to go to sleep when I overheard her screaming at him in the living room. Marie screamed that she wished they were never married. She wished that she had never met James. She went on to say that James was the one who wanted a child, not her. But she was the one stuck with the job of taking care of me because James worked all the time. I never heard James say a word back to her. I think that he just sat there and took the abuse.

I went to bed earlier than normal. I was exhausted both mentally and physically. I lay and thought about Nicole. I decided that I would go see her tomorrow. I really didn't have a plan, but I wanted to see her and talk with her. I didn't know what I would say to her, but it was time that I faced the situation.

Chapter 20

Tuesday morning came quickly. I had breakfast with Marie in silence again. She was actually getting good at this silent treatment thing she had developed. I pushed away from the table and put my dishes in the kitchen sink.

"Zeke!" she yelled.

"What?" I responded.

"You've been pretty quiet lately. What have you been up to?"

"Nothing, I've just been riding around on my bike by myself. Why?"

"Normally when you're quiet, I get a call from a neighbor or the school that you've been fighting or causing problems with other kids."

"I only fight when someone challenges me. I have not caused any problems at all, and I'm tired of being accused of things that I don't do."

I felt the anger building up inside me. Marie was always accusing me of things I didn't do. I was growing very tired of her and her controlling ways. Maybe I needed to teach her another lesson.

"Well, Zeke, you know that your father and I have been talking about sending you away to military school if you continue to be a problem child. I told him that would probably be the best for you because at least you could learn discipline. Who knows? Maybe when you get out of military school, you might enlist in the army or navy. At least you'd have a paying job. I don't see you getting a job any other way. You just don't have the smarts to succeed in the job market."

God, I was pissed inside. I was ready to explode at her, but I knew that I had other business to deal with today.

"I'll be able to get a job when I get out of school. I need to get a job because I don't intend to stay here after I graduate."

"Good luck with that, Zeke! I really don't see it happening!"

"You'll see. I'll do it!"

With that I flung open the door and headed to the garage to get my bike. Marie screamed something at me as I rode away down the street. I don't know what she said, and I didn't care. She had me pissed off enough, and I needed to clear my mind so I could think.

I entered the lane and headed north toward the quarry. No electrical crews today, and no farmer. Good, I didn't need anybody to get in my way today. It was a bright sunny day, and the temperature was already in the midseventies. The sun felt good as I rode down the lane.

I reached the edge of the brush prior to the quarry and stashed my bike there. I started my walk through the tangled undergrowth. I again stopped short of the quarry, peering out at the area of the quarry to see if anyone was around. I saw Nicole sitting on a rock on the far side of the quarry drinking a Coke. She was facing away from me in the direction of the old truck. I did not see anyone else. I decided to sneak through the brush around to her side of the quarry trying not to make a sound. I was about fifty yards from her when I heard her say, "Okay, Zeke, quit sneaking around and come out of the brush."

Damn, she must have ears like a cat. I came out of the brush and walked over to Nicole.

"Hi, Nicole, how have you been?"

"I'm good. I thought you were coming to see me on Monday?"

"Yeah, that was the plan, but I had things that I had to do at home."

"Were the things you were doing at home more important to you than being with me?"

"No, Nicole. I had work around home to do, and I couldn't get away."

"What have you been doing the last couple of days, Nicole?"

"Nothing, I've just been here alone, swimming and enjoying the sunshine. It has really been warm the last few days, and swimming has been great."

I thought to myself, *Yeah, swimming has been great with Rich, not by yourself.* But I didn't want Nicole to know that I knew about Rich and her. I didn't want anyone to know about Nicole and me either. That would link me to her, and if something happened to Nicole, I would surely be a suspect. I looked down at Nicole as she lit a cigarette. The smoke floated up around her face and through her hair.

"Can I have a cigarette, Nicole?"

"Sure, but I didn't think you smoked."

"I don't, or at least I never have. I would like to try one to see if it's something that I like."

"Okay, here."

Nicole flips me the pack of cigarettes. The matches are stuffed between the cigarette package and the cellophane that keeps the cigarettes fresh while they're on the shelf in the store. I look at the pack in my hand, Marlboros. I pull one of the cigarettes out of the pack, put it in my mouth, and strike a match. I inhale slowly on the cigarette while holding the match to the tobacco protruding from the end. The smoke enters my throat and lungs. A slight burning sensation traveled along my mouth and throat. It was not really as bad as I suspected. I handed the pack of cigarettes and matches back to Nicole and continued to puff on the cigarette.

"Well, Zeke, what do you think of your first smoke?"

"Not bad, I actually kind of like how it makes me feel. It seems to relax me."

"Yeah, smoking has helped me get through some pretty rough times with my stepfather. Cigarettes seemed to make me relax and kind of help me forget the pain of him touching and abusing me."

I thought to myself, *Yeah, right! You probably wanted it! Just like with Rich and whoever else has been at this quarry with you.*

My blood began to boil when I thought about Rich and Nicole. But I worked very hard to hide my emotions.

"What are your plans, Nicole?"

"What are you talking about?"

"Well, you told me that you were going to stay here for the summer and travel to a warm climate before winter. I just wondered where you were going and when you planned on leaving the area."

"My plans are to leave for Florida around the beginning of September. I'll take my backpack loaded with everything I can carry and walk to I-75. I'll walk south on I-75, put my thumb out, and hitchhike to Florida where it will be warm and sunny. I don't think I'll have any problem getting a ride."

"No, Nicole. You are beautiful, and I'm sure someone will give you a ride wherever you want to go. But aren't you afraid that the wrong person will pick you up and hurt you?"

"I thought about that too. But I'll just have to take my chances. Besides, what other choice do I have?"

"I guess you have no other choice. It would be too cold for you to stay here at the quarry during the winter months. The only other place you could go is back to Inkster."

"Well, I'm not going back to Inkster and have that bastard touch me again. I just can't stand the thought of him touching me."

"Have you spoken with your mother lately?"

"No, I haven't spoken with my mother or my stepfather since I left home. I don't ever intend to speak to them again."

I finished my cigarette, threw it on the ground, and crushed it into the dirt with my foot. I was glad that she hadn't spoken with her stepfather or mother. I didn't want to take a chance on them knowing about me. The only person she may have mentioned me to was Rich. But I really doubted that she would talk about me while she was with him.

I stood in silence while many of the bad times of my childhood raced through my mind. My mood inside was shifting to total anger and rage.

"There you go again, Zeke. Your mind is out in space somewhere.
What the hell are you thinking about anyway?"

"Not really anything, Nicole. I was just thinking about the pain that I have gone through during my life. It's hard for me to forget about the things that have happened to me."

"Why don't we go for a swim? Maybe seeing me naked again will help you forget about the past for a while."

"Okay, let's go. Maybe you're right, I hope it makes both of us feel better."

We stripped off our clothes and dove into the water. We swam around the quarry for a few minutes before Nicole swam up to me and said, "Let's go back over to the rock and do it again."

I was now furious inside. Back over to the rock, the same rock where we first made love. It was only two days ago when she and Rich made love in the same spot. No, that was not going to happen. I will never make love to her again! It was time for me to handle the problem. It was time for me to show Nicole that hurting Zeke was a mistake, a fatal mistake.

"Sure, Nicole, let's go!"

I started swimming as fast as I could toward the rock, and Nicole was just behind me. Soon we both stood on the submerged rock just as we had days before.

She faced me, grabbed my shoulders, and started to put her legs around me when I stopped her.

"What's wrong, Zeke?"

"I want to do it different today."

"Different, how do you want to do it?"

"Turn around, and I'll show you."

Nicole turned with her back toward me, and I put my arms around her. I put my lips on her neck and kissed her gently and said, "Okay, are you ready?"

"I'm ready, Zeke!"

I moved my arms up from her waist, caressing her breasts. Then I made my move. I quickly put my arm around her throat and my other hand over her mouth to stop any screams. I was choking her down, and she was fighting violently for her life. The water was exploding, and her legs were kicking violently. But she could not escape. I was too strong, and she was no match for me. I whispered in her ear, "This is because of your friend, Rich."

It was over very quickly. She went limp in my arms, and I slowly let her down into the water. I held her head under the water for a couple of minutes just to make sure she was dead. I again felt the rush that I had felt when I killed

Whitey. It was incredible! Zeke was in control! Anyone who chose to control Zeke, or cause Zeke pain, would not live to talk about it.

What do I do now? I can't just leave her body lie in the water. I can't have her found. The farmer had seen me the other day; the line crew had also spotted me. If a body were found here, they may ask people in the area, and both the line crew and the farmer would surely mention me. They didn't know who I was, but the cops would surely go door-to-door questioning people. I couldn't risk it. I just couldn't risk being caught. I pulled her lifeless body up to the rocky shoreline out of the water.

I dried off with one of Nicole's towels and placed it over her face. I quickly put my clothes back on in case I had to leave quickly.

I now began to scan the area for some way to hide the body. I climbed up in the cab of the old bulldozer that sat in a rusted heap alongside of the old dump truck that Nicole had used as her home. Inside, folded up on the seat, was a heavy old canvas tarp. It would be perfect to roll around Nicole's body. I took the tarp down to the water's edge where Nicole lay motionless. I spread the tarp out and dragged Nicole's body up and laid it on one end of the tarp. I then grabbed the edge of the tarp and began to roll Nicole up in it. The tarp was big enough to make several laps around Nicole's body. Now what do I do? I remembered seeing some log chains lying near the rear of the old dump truck.

I walked over to the truck and found three log chains about ten feet in length with hooks on both ends. I took them back over to Nicole's body and thought for a moment. The best way to hide her body was to submerge it in the water. I knew the quarry was a hundred feet deep because James had mentioned it to me a few years ago. I rolled the tarp backward until Nicole's body was visible again. I placed three heavy rocks in the tarp with her. I went back to the truck and gathered Nicole's belongings. I placed Nicole's clothes and everything that she had within the truck in the tarp with her. I again rolled the tarp up with Nicole inside. I then cinched a chain tight at each end of the tarp and one in the middle. The hooks were clamped tightly to the links on the chain. It would be impossible for the tarp to unroll now. I took my pants, shoes, and socks off and walked out onto the submerged rock dragging the tarp with Nicole inside. I reached the furthest edge of the rock with Nicole in tow. I looked down in the water. The quarry had very clear water, and you could see about twenty feet down. I watched as fish swam past about ten feet below. After a moment, I pushed the tarp over the edge and said, "Good-bye, Nicole."

I watched as the tarp slowly swayed from side to side and sank into the water out of sight. I was at ease now. I slipped my pants, socks, and shoes back on.

Nothing was left that could be linked to Nicole, or was there? I went back and searched the truck again to assure that I had not missed anything.

I couldn't find anything in or around the truck. I walked the area around the edge of the quarry looking for anything that may put Nicole in this area. Nothing was to be found.

I then went back to the edge of the quarry near the submerged rock where I had dumped Nicole's body. I looked down into the water and said, "Too bad, Nicole, we could have had fun together. Good-bye."

I began the journey back to my bike. My mind was blank; I was numb all over. I had again taken another human life. But it was necessary. I would never let anyone hurt me or control me again. If they chose to, their lives would end like Whitey and Nicole. It was really not my choice to kill them. They forced me to kill them. I had no other way out. I needed the revenge. I needed to feel the rush that came over me when I was in charge. When I controlled a person and I determined whether they lived or died.

It was now time to focus my thoughts on Rich. He would be my next target of revenge.

Chapter 21

A week has now passed since I took Nicole's life. Many nightmares have come and gone since then. Visions of my childhood continue to haunt me during my sleep. Whitey's death face jumps out at me during my dreams. Those cold dead eyes have seemed to burn their way into my mind. Visions of Nicole's lifeless body lying on the tarp drift in and out of my dreams. I even hear Whitey's crazy laughter as if he were in the same room with me. Maybe I'm losing my mind; I don't really know. I do know that I fear nothing human. My dreams have a way to frighten the inner me. It's like another person inside me realizes fear and responds to it. I never show fear to anyone, and I never feel sorry for anything that I have done. I am a true loner, and I will stay that way.

I need to go over to my straw stack hideout and think through my plans for Rich. I need complete silence so I can plan his demise.

Marie is sitting on the couch this morning reading the newspaper. It's getting harder and harder to get away from home for more than a couple of hours. I need time away, and I need it today. I decided to leave the house through the back door and go to the garage and get my bike. Just as I exit the garage, Marie screams my name. Great, I'll never get the time alone that I need. I laid my bike on the ground and walked to the house to see what she wanted. I know that I need to be nice so I can get away from this house for a while. I stepped onto the porch and stood in front of the screen door looking directly at her. I really didn't know how to approach her. I was not very good at being nice to her, nor did I want to be nice. I finally got the nerve to say, "What do you want, Mom?"

"Where are you going now?"

"I'm just going for a ride on my bike. I might go downtown to the hobby store, or I may go down to the river. I haven't really decided yet."

"Why would you go to the hobby store?"

"Well, the guy who owns the store built a nice slot car track and holds races there every day from eleven o'clock to four o'clock.

It costs five cents to race, and the track holds eight cars across. The winner of each race gets twenty-five cents, and the store owner gets fifteen cents for holding each race. He gives free popcorn to all the racers and the people watching the race."

"I didn't know that you had a slot car that you could race."

"I don't have one yet, but they sell them there. I don't even know if I want one or not, but I think it would be fun to watch the races."

"Okay, go to the hobby shop or to the river, but I want you home for supper at five o'clock.

"Okay, I'll be home by five o'clock."

I went out the door, grabbed my bike, and headed toward the downtown district. When I was out of sight of everyone in the neighborhood, I circled back east on Elm Avenue toward the lane that headed to the Mason Run and the straw fields that lay beyond. When I crossed Noble Avenue, I saw the paper-mill watchman crossing Noble from his office toward the straw fields. I looked down at my watch to check the time. Funny, it was 10:30 AM. This is not a normal round for him. He must have missed his scheduled 10:00 AM round. I wasn't sure, so I decided to get to the far corner of the fence where I had cut the access hole to the straw fields. There I would lie in wait to see exactly what the watchman was really doing. I slipped inside the fence and lay in the weeds where I could see the punch key on the nearest fire shack. At least fifteen minutes went by before

I caught sight of the watchman. He was walking between the straw stacks three rows over from me. It appeared he was looking for something. He turned and was now coming directly at me. Great, I have nowhere to go; and if he comes any closer, he will surely spot me. I broke out in a cold sweat. I could never explain this to my parents. Suddenly the watchman stopped and bent down to pick something up. When he stood back up, he was facing directly toward me, and I could tell it was the watchman nicknamed Curly, a very close friend of my father. I noticed that he now had a pitchfork in his hand that he had obviously picked up off the ground.

He looked in my direction for a moment and then turned and headed back toward his office. When he was out of sight, I ran toward the row of straw stacks where I last saw him. I edged my head around the corner of the stack and watched him walk down the row toward his office. He then turned left toward the back of the straw stack fields. My curiosity got the best of me, and I ran down the row until I reached where he had turned. I again peered down the row of stacks, and I saw him walk to a wagon where paper-mill workers were loading straw to take inside the mill for stocking the cookers. When he got up to the wagon, he handed one of the workers the pitchfork. He spoke with the workers for a moment and then turned back in the direction of his office.

Whew! I'm a nervous wreck now; sweat is pouring off me. I turned and went back to my straw stack hideout. I really needed to relax alone now. I didn't need any more excitement today.

I arrived at my straw stack, removed the half bale that hides the opening, and slid into the tunnel. I brought my flashlight with me this time, and I turned it on so I could see into my hideout. It was cool inside the straw stack because the straw acted as insulation to keep the heat out and the coolness inside. Good, none of the straw had caved in this time. Everything was just as I had left it.

I needed to relax now and think about how to handle Rich. I turned the flashlight off and sat quietly in the darkness. I could actually put my hand in front of my face and not even see it at all. I was sitting in total and absolute darkness.

My thoughts drifted back to Tony and the great times we had together. I felt a tear trickle down my cheek. Funny, I had not shed a tear in many years.

I had become numb to physical and emotional pain, but not where Tony was involved. His death still torments me, and I believe that it always will. I feel completely responsible for his death. I should have helped him when he needed it. I was no friend to him. A friend would have listened to him and helped him through his pain.

I'm almost in a trance as my thoughts go back to Polly. She was my first and only love. But just as the others, she hurt me and betrayed me. Whitey hurt me and tried to control me; Nicole hurt me by betraying me. I blacked out again with anger, uncontrollable anger.

My head begins to pound. Sweat again begins to pour off my body; I start to shake uncontrollably. Why do people choose to betray me? Don't they know that Zeke will make them pay for their deception? Don't they know that Zeke will take their life for the pain they have inflicted on him?

My mind quickly switches to Rich. He needs to pay for the pain I suffered while I watched him and Nicole together. Oh, he will pay, but I must think of a way to make him feel pain as I felt.

I reach down and turn the flashlight on so I can look at my watch. Unbelievable, two hours have flashed past as I sat in my straw hideout racing through my thoughts from the past.

I feel somewhat unsettled inside about the north quarry. I don't know what it is, but I just don't feel right about it. I must go back to the quarry; maybe I missed something when I wrapped Nicole up with all her belongings. Impossible, I checked everywhere, didn't I? I must go back and look around again.

I exit my straw hideout and replace the half bale hiding the entrance. I slip back through the opening in the vines and hop on my bike and head for the north quarry.

It's two o'clock when I arrive at the edge of the brush line surrounding the quarry. I carefully check the area from the brush to assure that it's clear of people. It is clear, not even a breeze exists to ripple the water on the quarry; it is dead calm and silent. I slip out of the brush to the edge of the quarry. I look down into the crystal clear water and say, "Hi, Nicole, I hope you're happy."

I began to walk around the edge of the quarry toward the truck that Nicole called home. I looked at everything along the way to make sure that no signs of Nicole were left behind. When I reached the truck, I opened the door. The loud creak of the door hinges startled me due to the total silence in the area.

The dopes that frequent the south quarry must be sleeping it off as I could hear no sounds coming from that direction. I slipped into the driver's seat of the old truck and eased the door closed. I sat and looked directly at the spot where I had ended Nicole's life. Funny, I didn't feel any sadness for her. I didn't even feel any regret for killing her. After all, she really killed herself; she just used me to do it for her.

I'm snapped back to reality by a movement off to my right in the direction of the south quarry. Was it one of the tough guys from the south quarry coming my way? I was motionless staring toward the intruder. Just a few more steps and he would clear the brush line, and I would be able to see who was heading in my direction. It was only seconds before I realized that it was Rich. He was probably coming to see Nicole so he could have her again. Well, he was in for a big surprise.

Rich stopped and looked across the quarry and all around the area much as I do when I come here. He finally headed toward the old dump truck. I knew that he couldn't see me; the windshield on the driver's side was cracked like a spider web, and the sun was reflecting off the windshield directly in his face. He again stopped and shouted, "Nicole, Nicole."

What an idiot; if anyone was here, they would hear his call. This area was loaded with bad guys, and he would be no match for them. I opened the door of the truck quickly, and the screech of the hinges made him jump. He was only twenty feet away from me now. I maintained eye contact with him as I exited the truck. He looked very nervous. He knew me from school, and he knew my reputation.

"What are you doing here, Zeke?"

"Nothing, I'm just looking around the quarry to see if anything of value is here. What are you doing here?"

"Well, I met a girl here named Nicole, and I was coming to see her."

"Nicole? What does she look like? Maybe I've seen her."

"You wouldn't believe it, Zeke. She's beautiful, long blond hair, a terrific body, and a beautiful face."

"Well, I can't say that I've seen her, but we can look around to see if we can find her."

Rich and I searched for any sign of Nicole. Of course, we found no sign that Nicole or anyone else had been here.

Rich sat down on a rock at the edge of the quarry staring at the water. He put his head in his hands and said, "She's gone."

"Why was she here anyway, Rich?"

"She was a runaway. Her family life was awful, and she left home so she could be by herself."

"Well, maybe she went to another town, or maybe she decided to go back home."

"You're probably right, Zeke. She probably went on to Florida. That's where she wanted to be for the winter."

"That's probably where she went."

Rich got up from the rock where he was sitting and started to walk away in the direction of the south quarry. I had to stop him.

"Hey, Rich, do you want to see something cool?"

"What is it?"

"I built a hideout, and it's really a great place to go and relax. It's a place where nobody can find you unless you want to be found."

"Sounds like fun, is it far from here?"

"No, not far at all, just follow me."

"Okay, let's go."

Rich went back to get his bike and rode it over to where I stood next to the thick brush at the edge of the quarry. We began the walk back through the brush to where I had stashed my bike. It was a difficult walk as Rich's bike kept getting tangled in the brush along the way. We finally reached my bike; I picked it up, and we both hopped on our bikes and began to ride toward the straw stack fields. We rode side by side down the lane. Rich looked over at me and said, "Zeke, do you think somebody took Nicole?"

"Maybe, but I doubt it. I mean it would be difficult for someone to come across her at the north quarry. Very few people go there, just a few old guys who go there to fish a couple of times a year."

"Why were you there, Zeke?"

"I just went there to get away from home. I don't like staying around home very much."

"Why don't you like being home, Zeke?"

"I don't like my mother, and I'd just rather be alone."

"That's too bad, Zeke. Everybody tells me that you're a tough guy and not to trust you."

"Yeah, I know. I don't care about anybody anyway, so it really doesn't matter to me what they say."

"Well, you seem okay to me."

"Good, I'm glad you see it that way."

We finally arrive at the opening in the fence. I slip through the opening between the vines, and Rich follows behind me. We walk over to the straw stack, and I remove the half bale that hides the opening.

"Wait here, Rich, until I get the flashlight and get inside so I can light the way for you."

I went inside, grabbed the light, and turned it on to light up the tunnel.

"Come on in, Rich."

Rich climbed into the tunnel and followed me into my straw hideout.

"Wow, Zeke, this is great in here. It's cool, dry, and it's actually soft to lie on the straw. What a great place."

"Be careful not to knock down any of the supports that hold up the bales. If one of them gets knocked loose, the whole stack may fall on us."

"Okay, Zeke, I'll be careful."

"Hold the flashlight while I light the lantern."

Rich held the flashlight so I could see to light the match for the lantern.

"I need to be real careful here, Rich, one false move with this match and the whole stack will catch fire."

"I know, Zeke, please be careful."

The lantern mantle flickered for a moment, then it got brighter and brighter. The lantern's brightness cast shadows across the straw walls of the hideout. The area inside the hideout was now bright with light. I was surprised just how bright the lantern made the hideout. It was like immediate daylight from total darkness.

Rich and I sat down, and I listened while he talked about Nicole. I really only half listened to what he had to say; I really didn't care to listen to him. My brain was tuned in to destroying him, not to caring about him. I looked at my watch and realized that it was time for me to get home.

"Hey, Rich, I really had a good time talking with you today, but I need to go home now. It's getting close to dinnertime."

“Okay, Zeke, I had a great time today.”

“Great, let’s come back here on Saturday morning around eleven o’clock. Ride your bike here, and stash it in the thick brush next to the opening in the fence. I’ll wait for you at the opening in the fence. Don’t go inside without me.”

“Okay, Zeke, I’ll be here.”

“One more thing, Rich, don’t tell anyone about my hideout. I don’t need anyone coming over here screwing around with my stuff.”

“Don’t worry, Zeke. I won’t tell anyone.”

I turned out the lantern, and we both left the straw hideout. I laid my flashlight just inside the tunnel entrance. I then replaced the half bale in the tunnel opening so it would again be invisible. We exited through the fence and grabbed our bikes for the ride home.

“See you Saturday, Zeke.”

“I’ll be here. Don’t be late.”

I turned down Michigan Avenue toward home, and Rich went straight down Noble Avenue toward his home on Hollywood Drive.

It was hard playing the nice guy with Rich today. All the time I was with him, I wanted to choke him down the way that I did Nicole. He never suspected that his next meeting with Zeke would be his last. He never suspected the pain that Zeke would inflict upon him. He would pay the price for the time he spent with Nicole. He would pay with his life.

Chapter 22

I tossed and turned in bed most of the night. It was difficult to get Rich out of my mind. I was constantly thinking of ways to kill him. Finally an idea struck me out of the blue. Don't kill him immediately, make it slow and painful. Make him know real pain before he dies. How would I do that? Where would I do that? That's what I needed to figure out. Well, I wasn't going to get it figured out lying in bed. Not with Marie out in the kitchen banging pots and pans around.

I got out of bed, got dressed, and went out into the kitchen. Marie looked around and glared at me.

"You're going to do some work around this place today, boy. No running around for you!"

"What do you want me to do?"

"I want the lawn mowed, the hedges and rosebushes trimmed, and the sidewalks swept. I want you to start on it right after breakfast."

I looked at the kitchen stove and saw that she was cooking mush again. I hated mush, and she knew it. It was just her way of digging at me without saying a word.

"I'm not hungry this morning. It's still damp outside from the dew, so I'll trim the hedges and rosebushes first, then I'll cut the grass and sweep the sidewalks."

"Okay, but I want a good job done or you'll be grounded for a week."

Great, her idea of a good job and mine were two different things. I could not screw this up if I wanted to get my revenge on Rich. I couldn't risk another week going by without taking care of him. The more time I let pass was more time that he had to run his mouth about my straw stack.

The work she had laid out for me was going to take at least four hours to complete. I went out to the garage and grabbed the hedge clippers and a trash can so I would have somewhere to put the clippings.

I had only just started trimming the hedges when Rich rode up on his bike and said, "Hey, Zeke, what are you doing today?"

This is not good for me. I did not want to have anyone see me with Rich. If something happened to Rich, I would surely be questioned by police. It was far too risky a situation.

"I'm working around the house today, and I don't have time to talk with you."

Marie immediately yelled out the kitchen window, "I told you no goofing around today! Now get that kid out of here and do your work!"

"Well, Rich, you see what I have to put up with, so you'd better leave now before she brings a board out here to whack us both."

"Okay, I'll see you Saturday at eleven."

"Great, I'll see you then. Oh, by the way, keep your mouth shut about my hideout. I don't need anyone to know where I go and what I do."

"Don't worry, Zeke. I won't tell anyone. It will be our secret."

"Okay, see you Saturday."

Rich rode off toward Noble Avenue and out of sight. I continued to trim the hedges and the rosebushes. It took me from nine o'clock in the morning until two o'clock in the afternoon before the yard was ready for inspection by Marie. She looked over the hedges, rosebushes, and yard very closely.

"Well, Zeke, it looks like you've done a pretty good job here. It could be better, but I know it's difficult for you to do anything perfect. You're just not talented like other young people."

God, she pisses me off when she says I'm not as good as other young people. She tells me this all the time, over and over again. Why does she hate me so much? I just can't understand her constant anger toward me.

"I did the best I could, Mom."

"Yeah, I know, I just wish you could be good at something. You're getting older now, and it won't be long before you graduate from high school. I only hope that you can get a job to support yourself because your father and I want you to leave home immediately after you graduate."

The anger builds inside me. My father would never want me to leave home. I know that he cares about me. I know that he would never tell me to leave. It was all Marie's idea. She controlled his every move. He lived in fear of her, and I knew it.

"Don't worry. I'll be ready to leave home when I graduate. I don't like staying here now, so I know I'll be ready to leave by graduation."

"Good, that will be the best thing for all of us."

I just turned away from her as she only continued to anger me more. I put the mower, garbage can, and the hedge trimmers back in the garage. I grabbed my bike and rode off toward the straw stack fields. I heard Marie screaming my name as I rode away, but I really didn't care. I just kept riding away.

I dropped my bike to the ground when I reached the opening in the fence. I looked out into the straw fields to make sure no workers or watchmen were around. The field was clear of people, so I slipped through the fence and quickly into the straw tunnel that lead to my hideout. I turned on my flashlight so I could see my way into my hideout. This time I decided to put the half bale of straw back in place so it would be impossible for anyone to detect that I was there. The opening to the tunnel was now completely invisible from the outside. I knew that my oxygen supply would be limited, but I was sure that there would be enough for my stay.

I turned off the flashlight and sat in total darkness. How could I make Rich suffer the most? How could I make him feel the pain that he deserves? I must think. I must make this foolproof. I can't afford to make a mistake. I can't leave any loose ends, and nothing can track his death to me.

I sat there thinking for over an hour, and then it hit me. He was coming here on Saturday to see me. I would get him into the hideout and knock him unconscious. But how would I knock him out? I guess I could put a rock in the hideout and use it to hit him in the head. That's not a good idea. I could hit him in the head too hard and kill him instantly. That's not what I wanted. Then I remembered some starting fluid that my father had in the garage. He used it to spray in the carburetor of the car this past winter when the car was having a problem starting. I noticed that it contained ether, and my father told me that if a person breathed too much of this stuff, they would likely pass out. This would be perfect. My bike had a small saddlebag on the back of the seat that would fit the can of starting fluid and a rag, plus a few other items if I needed them. I would saturate the rag with the starting fluid and then put it over Rich's mouth and nose after he entered the hideout. He would then pass out, but for how long? How would I contain him after he woke up? I thought about this for a while, but I could not come up with any easy solution other than to tie him up while he was unconscious.

What's that noise? Something is in the hideout with me. I quickly turn on the flashlight and shine it in the direction of the sound. It's a large rat running around on the bales. He quickly exits down the tunnel when the light hits him. Funny, I had not seen any rats in here before. I knew that many rats lived around the straw fields, but I never had seen one in my hideout. They probably like it because they can run around without having to burrow through the straw.

Well, I have spent enough time here. It's nearing four o'clock, and the watchman will be coming soon. I must leave now so I will not be seen. I slipped through the fence and hopped on my bike and headed for home.

It's only a short ride from the straw fields to home, so I arrive quickly. I put my bike in the garage and start looking for the starting fluid. Marie has a bag of rags hanging on a nail on the wall. I took two rags from the bag, one to soak with starting fluid and one to use as a gag on Rich so he could not be heard.

For some reason, I can't seem to find the starting fluid, and I know it's here. I look through all the cabinets, the workbench, and toolboxes. It's nowhere to be found.

Just as I'm about to give up, I look up above the back window of the garage, and there it is on top of the two-by-four beam that is just above the window. I reached up and grabbed the can. It was about half full, more than enough for what I needed. I put the can and rags in the saddlebag on my bike. I now started to look around the garage for some rope that I could use to tie Rich up while he was unconscious. I noticed a small army backpack that my uncle had given me when I was about eight years old. I opened the backpack and pulled out a canteen, bullet pouches, parachute cord, and a pair of handcuffs with keys. I had forgotten that he was an MP in the Korean War, and he had brought back his handcuffs and given them to me along with everything else. The handcuffs and the parachute cord would be perfect for keeping Rich contained in the hideout. I slipped them into my saddlebag also.

I thought my plan through for a moment. Even if I handcuffed Rich and tied his feet together, it was possible for him to crawl out of the hideout and stand up to get the watchman's attention. I needed to make sure that didn't happen. I picked up two screws and two large flat washers along with a Phillips screwdriver from my father's toolbox. I would screw the chain of the handcuffs to the center four-by-four post that held the center ceiling boards in place within the hideout. If Rich pulled the four-by-four out of position, the ceiling would surely collapse on him, killing him instantly. Either way, he was going to die; I guess the choice was his. I was happy now; I had everything that I needed for the job. I couldn't wait for Saturday to come. I would finally make Rich pay for the pain I have suffered because of him and Nicole.

Chapter 23

It's finally Saturday morning. I have been working hard all week to keep Marie happy so I can get to my hideout on time. I sit down at the breakfast table to a miracle. Marie has made one of my favorite breakfasts. She finally made something good to eat—biscuits, sausage gravy with scrambled eggs and milk. This is too good to be true. I wonder what she wants from me.

"Looks like a good breakfast, Mom."

"Well, Zeke, you have been working hard around the house this week, so I thought I'd make you a breakfast that I knew you would like. But don't get used to it. Eggs and sausage are expensive, and we don't have money to waste."

"I know, but thanks for making it."

Marie went back into the kitchen, and I sat in silence eating my breakfast. When I finished, I went into the kitchen to rinse off my plate. Marie was busy cleaning the kitchen stove. She looked over at me as I was rinsing my plate off.

"Well, Zeke, what are your plans for today?"

"Nothing special, I might go down to the river and see if anyone is catching fish. I don't really have anything planned."

"Okay, Zeke, but you know the rules, be back here no later than five o'clock."

"Don't worry. I'll be home by five o'clock."

I went out the back door of the house and walked to the garage to get my bike. I rechecked my saddlebag to make sure everything that I needed was inside. Yep, everything was just as I left it a few days ago. Now I needed to hurry so I could get to the straw stack field ahead of Rich. It was ten o'clock, and I needed to make sure that I had the starting fluid, rags, handcuffs, screws, washers, and screwdriver inside the hideout before he arrived.

I got to the opening in the fence at 10:10 AM. I sat in the tall weeds and looked toward the fire shack that was closest to my hideout. This fire shack is the second punch-clock stop in the field for the watchman. It wasn't long before I saw him making his way to the fire shack so he could punch the clock with the key that was hanging there. He punched the clock, then he turned around and started walking back toward his office. When he was out of sight, I grabbed my stuff and headed through the fence toward my hideout.

Once inside I dug some of the straw out of one corner of the hideout and put all the things I needed inside with the starting fluid and one rag on top. I then covered everything up with straw so it would not be noticeable.

I quickly put the half bale back in the opening and went through the fence and sat down next to my bike to wait for Rich. It was now 10:45 AM, and no sign of Rich. Maybe he wouldn't come today. He may have thought twice about hanging around with Zeke. It's early. I'll wait until at least 11:15 AM before I worry too much about Rich not coming.

At exactly eleven o'clock, I saw Rich riding down the lane on his bike toward me. He was alone. That was good. I was afraid that he would be stupid and bring one of his friends along.

"Hey, Rich, you're right on time."

"Yeah, I thought I was going to be late. I had to go to the store and pick up some things for my mother."

"Well, let's go inside and relax. I have some chips and soda inside the hideout for a snack, and best of all, a couple of copies of *Playboy* magazine for us to enjoy. After we're done in the hideout, we can go to the quarry for a swim. I have some cigarettes in my saddlebags for us to smoke at the quarry. We can't smoke inside the straw stack. We might start the whole stack on fire."

"Sounds good, Zeke, let's go inside."

We went through the fence, and I led the way into the tunnel. I needed to be in the lead so I had time to soak the rag with starting fluid.

"Hey, Rich, wait outside here until I get the lantern lit. My flashlight battery is getting low, and the light from the lantern will be needed so you will be able to see your way into the hideout."

I remembered what my father had told me during the winter about starting fluid. He said, "Always read the warning label on everything you use, it may save your life someday. Look at the warning label on this starting fluid. It says it's highly flammable and causes drowsiness if inhaled."

Highly flammable—I'd better be careful when I light the lantern. I'll put it at the far side of the hideout, away from where I will open the starting fluid. I lit the lantern and crawled over to the other side of the hideout. I set the lantern down on a piece of pallet board about two feet from the farthest wall. I didn't want to get the lantern too close to the straw because I was afraid of the entire stack going up in flames.

"Can I come in now, Zeke?"

"Not yet, just give me another minute."

I crawled back to the corner where the starting fluid was stashed. I grabbed the can and the rag. I turned my back to the lantern and opened the can slowly, hoping the vapors would stay on my side of the hideout. I soaked the rag with the starting fluid. Wow, I needed to be careful. I was getting drowsy just from the fumes in the air.

"Okay, Rich, you can come in now."

Rich entered the tunnel and came into the hideout.

"What's that smell, Zeke?"

"I spilled some of the lantern fuel."

I had purposely left the flashlight toward the entrance of the hideout. I did that so I could ask Rich to get it for me, and when he turned his back, I would grab him and put the soaked rag over his mouth and nose.

"Hey, Rich, can you get me the flashlight. I left it at the entrance to the hideout."

"Okay, I'll get it."

When Rich turned his back to me, I grabbed him around the neck and put the starting-fluid-soaked rag over his mouth and nose. He struggled only slightly before he was overcome by the ether in the starting fluid. I took the rag away from his face and released my grip on him. He dropped facedown into the straw. Was he dead? I hope not; I didn't want it to be that easy for him. I turned him over and checked to see if he was breathing. Yeah, he was breathing, but he was breathing very slowly. I moved him out to the tunnel because the ether fumes in the hideout were very strong. I tossed the starting-fluid-soaked rag outside the straw stack on the ground. I then sat next to Rich for a few minutes to make sure he kept breathing.

I went back into the hideout to get the screwdriver, screws, washers, and handcuffs. I started screwing the handcuffs to the center four-by-four post. This was a tough job. The four-by-four post was made of oak, and it was extremely difficult to turn the screw into the wood. I managed to get the screws in place and secured the handcuffs tightly to the four-by-four post.

I grabbed the parachute cord and went back to Rich to tie his feet together. He seemed to be breathing better now, and I hurried to tie his feet securely. After his feet were tied together, I sat next to him for twenty minutes. I needed to let the fumes clear out of the hideout before I put Rich back in to handcuff him to the post.

I went back inside to see if the fumes had cleared. The air in the hideout was good now, so I went back to the tunnel to get Rich. He was moving slightly now, so I dragged him back into the hideout and clipped the handcuffs closed around his wrists. I sat and waited for him to wake up.

Another hour passed before he opened his eyes. I smacked him hard across the face to get his attention.

"Don't hit me, Zeke! What's wrong with you? Why did you do this to me?"

"You can blame your little girlfriend, Nicole, for this. She's the one that brought this on you."

"Nicole, you knew Nicole?"

"That's right, Rich. I knew Nicole. She was mine. She was going to leave with me until you came along. You ruined everything, Rich. Now you are going to pay for it."

"What are you going to do to me, Zeke?"

"Well, first of all, I want to let you know that if you try to get away, the center post that you're handcuffed to will surely be pulled loose, and the entire straw stack will collapse on you. So if I were you, I would be very careful how much I moved around. At this point, I'm not really sure what I will do with you. You're lucky that you're alive. I could have killed you easily when you were unconscious."

"Zeke, you're not going to leave me here, are you?"

"Yep, I plan to leave you here until I decide what to do with you."

"Please don't leave me here, Zeke. I'm sorry about Nicole. I didn't know that you were going to leave with her. Anyway, she's gone now, so why does it matter?"

"Nicole is gone because I made her go away, you dope. She's dead. She lies at the bottom of the quarry. Nicole deserved what she got, and I'm glad she's dead."

"God, Zeke, you killed her? What the hell is wrong with you? Why would you do that?"

"I guess you just don't understand. Nobody, I mean nobody hurts Zeke and gets away with it. You and Nicole hurt me, and now you both will pay!"

"Zeke, you're not going to kill me, are you?"

"I don't know, Rich. What do you think?"

"Oh my god, you're going to kill me. I know you are. I can tell by the look on your face. Your eyes, what the hell is wrong with your eyes?"

"My eyes are focused on the hatred that I have for you, Rich. It's a hatred that I can't control. Enough talk, Rich. I'm going to put a gag on you now so you won't be able to call for help. Pull the center post down after I leave if you want. It'll make everything easier for me."

I went back to the corner where I had stashed the rag for the gag. I put the gag on Rich very tightly. I put the starting fluid back in the corner under the straw because I knew I may need it again, depending what I decided to do with Rich. I put the screwdriver in my pocket so I could return it to my father's toolbox. I then grabbed my flashlight and turned the lantern off. The hideout fell into total darkness. I clicked the flashlight on and put the beam in Rich's eyes. I could tell that he was horrified, but I really didn't care.

"See you soon, Rich. I hope you have a good night."

He mumbled something through the gag, but I couldn't understand a word of what he was trying to say.

I crawled out the tunnel and replaced the half bale sideways so that approximately four inches of space was between the half bale and the side of the tunnel opening. This would provide enough space for fresh air to get through so Rich wouldn't suffocate. I looked down and saw the rag that I had used with the starting fluid lying on the ground at the tunnel entrance.

I grabbed the rag and noticed that the starting fluid had totally evaporated from the rag and it was dry now. I put it in my pocket and slipped back through the opening in the fence to the place where the bikes were hidden in the weeds.

When I reached the bikes, I put the rag and screwdriver in my saddlebag, just in case I needed them again. I really had not considered what I would do with Rich's bike. I didn't take that into consideration in my original plan. It was kind of bad planning on my part. I thought for a moment and decided the appropriate place for the bike would be with Nicole. I got on Rich's bike and rode toward the north quarry. When I arrived at the brush just before the quarry, I got off the bike and began dragging it through the brush toward the quarry.

I again waited in the brush just before the quarry to make sure that it was clear of people. I walked out of the brush toward the edge of the quarry with the bike. When I was sure that nobody was there, I grabbed the bike by the back tire, and I began to swing it in a circle until I reached what I felt was the right speed. I then let go of the bike, and it plunged into the quarry approximately twenty-five feet from the shore. I watched it sink into the depths of the quarry until it drifted down out of sight.

No reason to stay here any longer. I began my long walk back to my bike. I looked down at my watch; it was now four o'clock. It would take me about twenty minutes to walk to my bike and about another ten minutes to get home from there. I would be home easily before five o'clock. I managed to get everything done in time just as planned. I walked up to my bike, hopped on, and began the ride home. I didn't feel sad about anything that I had done. I felt a sense of peace within me. I can't and I won't let anybody hurt me or control me anymore. Those who chose to do these things to me will die. I don't want to kill anyone. They chose to kill themselves using me as a tool of death.

Chapter 24

Sunday morning could not come quickly enough for me. God, I had horrible dreams during the night. I saw Whitey's death face float through the air around me as I was standing alone in total darkness. I heard his insane laughter. I could smell the disgusting stench of him in my nostrils. The most horrid vision of them all was Nicole, her hair flowing around her face as she drifted up from the bottom of the quarry. Her eyes were open, fixed on me as she rose to the surface. Her mouth did not open, but I continued to hear her say over and over again, "Why, Zeke, why?" She reached out for me. I was frozen in place, and I could not move a muscle. Her fingers touched my face, and they were as cold as ice. She caressed my face with her hands and leaned toward me to kiss me. Water poured out of her mouth and across my face when she opened her lips to meet mine. The smell of death was all around me. It was a sickening and disgusting smell. The odors of death made me begin to choke and gag in my sleep. I awoke suddenly from my nightmare. My body and my pajamas were saturated with a cold sweat. I was trembling. Zeke trembling! Was I actually in fear of something?

I stared up at the ceiling and watched a spider crawl along its way. Much like my enemies, I could crush this spider in an instant. But why would I do that? The spider had not harmed me. The spider had not tried to control me. The spider, in its own way, was much better than people. Sure, some people are deathly afraid of them; but then again, those people live in fear of everything. I, on the other hand, live in fear of nothing. I watched as the spider started to descend from the ceiling on a thread of web. He was dropping directly toward my right arm, which lay motionless on the blankets. He slowly descended and dropped directly on my arm. He began to crawl up my arm toward my shoulder. I continued to lie motionless as I watched him crawl along my arm. He stopped near the top of my shoulder and appeared to look me directly in the eyes. His mouth appeared to consist of two very tiny fangs that opened and closed continually as if he were trying to say something to me. After a few moments, the spider crawled off my shoulder, onto the bedding, and then down to the floor where he crawled away under the bed. Funny, I actually enjoyed watching his journey. I kind of envied him. Nobody was around to bother him. He was alone and did the things he wanted; nobody controlled him, and nobody hurt him.

It was time for me to get out of bed. I went out to the kitchen, and to my amazement, Marie was not cooking breakfast. I walked into the living room where Marie was reading the morning paper. She looked up at me and said, "Get dressed for church, Zeke."

"I don't want to go to church."

"Well, that's too bad. You're going to church with your father and me, and that's final."

"I thought Dad was working today?"

"No, he decided to go to church with me today and not work. He will be off work until Monday, when he starts working twelve hours per day on afternoon shift."

"What time will he start his shift?"

"His shift starts at 4:00 PM, and he gets off work at 4:30 AM. He should be home by 5:00 AM. So remember to be quiet next week so he can get the sleep he needs."

"Okay, I'll remember. I know he needs his rest."

"Get dressed now and hurry. Your father went down to the store, and we'll be leaving after he gets home."

"All right, I'll get dressed."

I went back into my bedroom to dress. Great, what about Rich? I needed to get to him, but what would I do after I got there? I still didn't have a plan. Church started at 10:00 AM and was over at 11:00 AM. I knew that I would be forced to stay at home for at least an hour so we could have lunch together. It would be at least twelve thirty or one o'clock before I could leave to see Rich. I dressed quickly and went back into the living room where James and Marie now sat waiting for me.

"Are you ready to go, Zeke?" James asked.

"Yep, I'm ready."

We got into the car and began the drive to church. The church was a ten-minute drive, so I used the time to think of a plan. But my thoughts drifted back to my dream about Nicole drifting up from the bottom of the quarry. What if that were true? What if she really had slipped out of the tarp and drifted to the surface? She would surely be found, and everybody in the area would be questioned. No, that was not possible. I had tied the tarp tightly and weighed it down with rocks. She couldn't break free from the tarp, or could she? I needed to be sure. I needed to go back to the quarry and see for myself. I could not risk her being found.

We arrived at church and went inside to be seated for the sermon. It was different now; I sat with the adults, not in the Sunday school class with kids. I laughed inside. Other kids now fear me as much as I feared the older kids at church years ago. I gave out the punishment now, and everyone knew it. Even the adults at the church stayed clear of me. They whispered to one another as I passed by them. It actually made me feel good because they showed respect for me—not for who I am, but for what I have grown up to be.

The preacher was his normal self. Every good person was going to heaven, and every bad person would suffer hell and damnation. The country was now involved in the Vietnam War, and he rambled about the evils of war and the destruction that came with it. His sermons always focused on the eternal damnation that nonbelievers would endure. Fire and brimstone continued to spew with each word he spoke. The congregation was mesmerized by his sermon.

They sat totally silent as their eyes remained fixed on him behind the podium. It was as though he were actually God himself.

The sermon finally ended, and everyone began to exit the church. My father stopped to talk with some of his friends who were standing near the entrance of the church. It wasn't long before we were in the car headed home. I looked at my watch; it was now eleven fifteen. Time was rapidly running away from me, and I still have not decided on a plan regarding Rich. We arrived home, and Marie began to make lunch.

Lucky for me that lunch consisted of soup and sandwich, which wouldn't take long to make or eat. I changed clothes and went into the living room to wait for lunch. Marie came out of the kitchen and began to set the table. I know it was only minutes, but it seemed like an eternity before lunch was finally on the table. I wolfed the food down as quickly as I could. James looked over at me and said, "Zeke, you ate your lunch so fast I don't understand how you could taste it."

"Sorry, Dad, I was just hungry because we didn't have breakfast this morning."

"That's okay, Zeke. I was just teasing you. Why don't you go out and ride your bike for a while. Just be back in time for dinner."

"Okay, Dad, thanks. I'll see you at dinner."

"Okay, Zeke. Be careful when you ride in traffic."

"I'll see you later, Dad."

With that I was out the door and on my bike. I rode as fast as I could to get to my hideout. I desperately needed a plan. I guess the only thing I can do at this point is see if Rich brought the straw stack down on top of himself. Then all my problems would be over, or would they? If Rich had pulled the four-by-four loose and the straw stack collapsed on him, he would be dead. But what about when the paper-mill workers removed the bales from that stack so paper could be made? They would surely find the body. After that, police would scour the neighborhood questioning everyone. What about all the things I had stashed there—the handcuffs, tools, starting fluid, and the rag I used for a gag? That stuff could be traced back to my dad and my home. Not good. No, not good at all.

I arrived in the weeds just prior to the opening in the fence and stashed my bike. I listened for a couple of minutes to see if I could hear anything. Not a sound came from the straw stacks that surrounded my hideout. I looked at my watch. It was nearing one o'clock. No need to worry about the watchman; his round was made at noon.

I slipped through the hole in the fence and walked in the high weeds to the edge of the straw stack. I heard moaning as I removed the half bale blocking the tunnel entrance. I entered the tunnel, grabbed the flashlight, and turned it on so I could see my way into the hideout. I was shocked by what I saw when I put the flashlight beam on Rich. He was bleeding from several places on his arms and head. The four-by-four center post was still in position. I lit the lantern and turned again to look at Rich. He was a mess. I went over to him. I first checked the cuffs to make sure they were secured; I then checked the parachute cord that secured his feet. Both the cuffs and the parachute cord were securely in place. I then removed the gag from his mouth.

"The rats, the rats!" he screamed. His voice was very hoarse, probably from trying to scream for help all night through the gag.

My god, I had forgotten about the rats I had seen a couple of days ago.

"What do you mean the rats?"

"Zeke, the rats were all over me, there were dozens of them. I couldn't keep them all away. Please don't leave me here again, please, Zeke!"

I looked at his arms, head, fingers, and ears. There had to be at least thirty rat bites on him. A couple of small pieces of his ears were missing; chunks of skin were missing from his arms and fingers. I decided that Rich had suffered enough. I couldn't imagine what it was like trying to fight the rats off without moving the four-by-four. He was at least able to kick his feet to keep the rats away from his feet and legs. It really must have been brutal. But what would I do with Rich?

"Please let me go, Zeke, please!"

"Shut up and be quiet so I can think!"

I thought for a moment, and the idea rushed to my head. I would leave him here with the flashlight.

He could use his hands enough to shine the light on the rats. They would then run away as they had when I saw them earlier last week.

I would then slip back after dark and light the straw stack on fire in the area of the hideout. By the time the flames were visible from the outside, the entire straw stack would be consumed by flames. Rich wouldn't need to worry about the rats after that! He would burn alive. He would know what pain was before he died.

But wait, I'm not thinking clearly. I need to make sure I take the cuffs, screwdriver, parachute cord, screws, washers, and the can of starting fluid back home. I can't take the risk that the fire will get hot enough to render everything completely to ashes. Then it hit me. Make Rich unconscious again with the starting fluid, then take the cuffs off, the screws out, and put everything back in the saddlebag of my bike. I will need to do this when I return after dark. I need to return in the early hours of the morning so I am completely concealed. If I were lucky, the fire would go undetected until it was far too late to get the fire under control.

"Rich, I will leave you the flashlight so you can shine it on the rats. They will run from the light so they won't bother you tonight."

"No, Zeke, please let me go. I won't tell anyone anything, I promise."

What, I'm supposed to believe that? He was chewed up all over, and he won't tell anyone what happened? Not a chance.

"Shut your mouth or I'll take the flashlight with me, and the rats will return to chew on you again."

"Okay, Zeke, I'll be quiet. But can't you just light the lantern so the rats will stay away?"

Not a bad idea—just light the lantern and all the rats will stay out of the area. But wait; if the lantern is lit, the flicker of light after dark may appear like the stack is on fire to the night watchman making his rounds. I'm glad Rich said something. It was obvious I wasn't thinking.

The flashlight could appear the same way if I did not completely seal the tunnel opening with the half bale of straw. It really was not necessary to make sure that Rich had sufficient air inside my hideout or not; he was going to die anyway.

"Okay, Rich, I'll light the lantern and put the flashlight at the entrance of the tunnel so I can light the way in when I return."

"I'm begging you, Zeke, don't leave me here!"

"Look, you idiot, either stop whining or I'll leave you here without any light at all to keep the rats away!"

Rich buried his head in the straw and began to sob uncontrollably. His sobbing did not have any affect on me at all. After all, he was the one who chose to piss me off. I wasn't going to let anyone piss me off and get away with it!

I put the gag back on Rich and crawled over to the lantern and checked the fuel. There was more than enough fuel to keep it lit until I returned after midnight. I lit the lantern, grabbed the flashlight, and headed down the tunnel to go outside. I could hear Rich continue to sob as I went down the tunnel. I reached the entrance and quickly sealed it closed with the half bale of straw that I used as a door. I quickly worked my way back to the opening in the fence and jumped on my bike to return home.

I thought about my return to the straw fields tonight. James would be at home this evening and would not leave for work until four o'clock tomorrow afternoon. I would really need to be quiet when I slipped out my bedroom window tonight. I would need to make sure that both he and Marie were sleeping soundly before I made a move.

I turned onto Michigan Avenue, and my thoughts immediately changed to focus on what was in front of me. Two cop cars were stopped on the street.

One of the cops was walking to one of our neighbor's house. He walked up the sidewalk to the front door and began knocking. My God, were they looking for Rich? Why else would they be here?

I turned into our driveway and put my bike in the garage. I walked out of the garage toward the house and saw my old enemy Sergeant Murray begin to walk up the sidewalk toward our house.

"Hi, Zeke, remember me?"

"Yeah, I remember you."

"Do you know Rich Wagner?"

"Yeah, I know him from school. Why?"

"Well, Rich has been reported missing by his parents, and we are going through all the neighborhoods adjacent to his to see if anyone has seen him. Have you been in contact with Rich recently?"

James opened the front door of our house just as I was about to answer Sergeant Murray's question.

"What's the problem, Officer?" he asked.

"Well, Mr. Baker, we're looking for a missing boy from the area."

"What's my boy got to do with it?"

"We don't know if Zeke has anything to do with the boy's disappearance. We're just going from neighborhood to neighborhood looking for leads in the case."

James looked over at me with a questioning look on his face.

"Zeke, do you know anything about this missing boy?"

I thought back to the time that the idiot Rich had come over to my house when I was working in the yard a few days ago. I remember Marie yelling out the window for me to get rid of that kid and get back to work in the yard. Rich's stupidity was going to get me caught if I wasn't careful. I also remember that Rich's back was to Marie when he was talking to me. No way did she see his face; it would be impossible for her to identify him.

I could not let Sergeant Murray know that I had seen Rich recently. He would start asking too many questions around the neighborhood about Rich and me. I just couldn't take a chance.

"No, I don't. I do know him from school, but I haven't seen him since the end of the school year."

Sergeant Murray quickly replied to my comment. "Is that right, Zeke?"

"Yeah, that's right!"

"That's strange, Zeke. His parents said that he told them that he was with you the day before his disappearance. Why do you suppose he told them that?"

I knew I couldn't trust that idiot to keep his mouth shut. I must keep my composure. I could not display any nervousness, anxiety, or fear.

"I don't know why he would say that. I haven't seen Rich at all since the end of the school year."

Now Marie bursts out the door. "What did Zeke do now?"

Sergeant Murray quickly responded, "Why would you think that Zeke did anything, Mrs. Baker?"

"That boy is always a problem. He's constantly fighting at school and everywhere else he goes. Zeke's a real problem child."

I could see the pain come across James's face. He could not cover the internal anguish that he was feeling because of Marie's comment.

"Well, Mrs. Baker, that's interesting to know. I'll make a note of it on my report so we can investigate this further. Is there anything else you would like to say, Zeke?"

"No, I've told you everything I know about Rich. There is nothing else to tell."

"Okay, Zeke. It's been very nice talking with you today, Mrs. Baker. I'm sure I'll be back in touch with you soon. You folks have a good day."

"Thanks, Sergeant Murray," Marie responded.

God, she pisses me off. Why the hell did she say that anyway? She has no idea what I do or what I've done.

James and Marie walked into the house, and I followed. Marie was on James immediately.

"Well, James, I know in my heart that Zeke is involved in this. He is pure evil, and you know it."

"I don't know anything of the kind, Marie. I have never seen Zeke do anything evil. Yeah, he gets in fights, but so do many of the other kids his age. Zeke's only problem is that he's tough and wins his fights, so everyone is afraid of him. That's why people talk bad about him. It's not because he's evil, it's because they're all afraid of him."

Now the screaming starts. "You just can't see it, can you, James? Zeke is a problem, and it's past time to get him under control. I think it's time to put him in military school so he can get some discipline!"

A disgusted look came across James's face, and without saying a word, he stormed out the door toward his car in the driveway. I heard the car door slam, and the car sped off down the street.

"Well, Zeke, are you happy now? Your father would rather leave than deal with you. You have been a problem to him all your life!"

I didn't say a word. I just went to my bedroom for the evening. I didn't even come out for dinner.

I heard James come back home about nine o'clock. I could again hear Marie attack him in the living room. I know she hates me. I don't know why, but she has hated me as long as I can remember. I can't worry about that now; I must focus on staying awake so I can handle my real problem, Rich.

Chapter 25

Damn it! I fell asleep. My eyes raced to the clock next to my bed. It was almost one o'clock. I needed to get ready to go to the straw fields! I listened for any sounds of Marie and James. The house was totally silent. It was obviously a full moon tonight because my room was lit up like an early-morning sunrise. I slipped out of bed and put on my clothes, still no sound from Marie or James. I eased over very carefully to the window so as not to make a sound. Now for the real problem, I needed to open the window and screen without making a sound. The window proved to be no problem, but the screen was aluminum, and every inch I moved it resulted in a slight screeching noise. I think it took me five minutes to get the screen fully opened.

I slipped through the window and onto the ground. I reached back inside the window and pulled it down to within a couple of inches from its fully closed position. I walked to the front corner of the house and looked out into the street. I could clearly see every car in the street because of the streetlights along the road. I accounted for all the neighbor's cars parked in driveways and on the street. No unknown cars were around. I walked to the back corner of the yard and looked across the back lot toward Maple Boulevard to assure everything was clear there also. Good, no strange vehicles there either.

God, I wished this moon wasn't so bright. Maybe it was just me, but everything seemed very bright as I slipped across the yard to the garage. I quietly slipped into the garage and got my bike. I checked to make sure that everything I needed for the trip was in my saddlebags. The starting fluid, rag, screwdriver, and matches were all there. It was time to go. I looked out the garage door toward the street. Everything was clear. No sign of any traffic coming down the street. I eased out of the garage down the driveway toward the street. I turned south on Michigan Avenue. The streets were completely clear of traffic; so far so good. I reached the dirt lane along Mason Run without any difficulty and without being detected by anyone. I was now glad that the moon was full tonight. It would have been difficult to navigate this lane without the light provided by the full moon.

I finally reached the opening in the fence. I looked down at my watch, one forty already; time is flying. I opened my saddlebag and retrieved the starting fluid, rag, matches, and screwdriver. I took a moment to think and look around before I made another move.

The watchman would make his round through the straw fields at two o'clock. I must wait until he finishes his round in the straw stack field to execute my plan. I must make sure that he works his way back toward the paper-mill before I do anything else. This is the only way that I will be sure that the fire will go undetected until it is totally out of control. I slipped through the opening in the fence and waited next to the edge of the straw stack for the watchman to appear. I was surprised that not one ray of light escaped from the entrance to the straw stack. That was good; I was worried that a strange light would draw the attention of either the watchman or a snoopy neighbor from the other side of Mason Run.

I looked down at my watch, one fifty now. Now time is really dragging. I listened to see if I could hear anything out of Rich. Not a sound came from the straw stack. Good, maybe he was dead already. At least that would save me time. I would only need to remove the cuffs and the screws, gather up everything else, light the match, and head for home.

I was snapped out of my trance by the watchman's flashlight beam as it danced across the field toward the key hanging at the fire shack. I watched as he stopped at the shack and punched the clock with the key. I noticed the glow of a cigarette hanging out of his mouth. He stood next to the shack and puffed on his cigarette for a few moments. This was even better than I expected. I remember my father telling me a few years back that management forbids any straw field worker from smoking while in the straw fields. I could just see the cops questioning the watchman tomorrow. I'm sure they would ask him if he was smoking while he made his rounds. Would he lie to save his ass? Yeah, I'm sure he would.

The watchman finally began his walk back toward the paper-mill. I waited a full fifteen minutes to assure he was back across Noble Avenue and on his way to his rounds within the paper-mill. I moved to the center of the straw stack and removed the half bale from the tunnel entrance.

Light immediately poured out of the tunnel into the darkness of the field. I jumped into the tunnel and pulled the bale back into place so the light could not be detected.

I crawled into the hideout; Rich was sound asleep. He never moved as I crawled near him. I stopped and listened for a moment to see if he was still breathing. Yep, he was still breathing, probably exhausted from his previous night of horror with the rats. Well, it really didn't matter to me. It was time for me to finish Rich off.

I doused the rag with starting fluid, grabbed his head, and placed the rag over his nose and mouth. He began to kick violently, so violent that the four-by-four center post began to move. I held tightly to Rich so that he wouldn't pull the center post totally out of position. Finally his body became limp, and I released my grip on him. His face fell down directly into the straw. He lay motionless in the straw. I untied the parachute cord that was binding Rich's feet and removed the handcuffs. I then quickly removed the screws that held the handcuffs to the four-by-four. I searched for anything I may have left behind that may not completely vaporize in the heat of the intense fire, which would be soon to follow. The only thing left was the small toolbox, flashlight, and the lantern. I turned on the flashlight and put the lantern out. Darkness fell around me. I grabbed everything and crawled out of the hideout into the tunnel toward the straw stack entrance. I pushed the half bale out into the field and pointed the flashlight down the tunnel toward the hideout.

I had to be sure the area was clear for my escape. I stepped out of the straw stack and into the field. I looked around and listened for any sounds nearby. It was totally silent with the exception of the crickets chirping all over the field. I grabbed everything except the flashlight and starting-fluid-soaked rag. I ran toward the opening in the fence to my bike. I put the screwdriver, handcuffs, screws, parachute cord, and starting fluid in my saddlebag. I put the toolbox and the lantern on the ground. What would I do with this stuff? I couldn't take it home; my father would find it and surely know where it came from. Wait a minute, why don't I just put it back where I got it? I grabbed the toolbox and lantern and crawled back through the fence toward the straw stack.

I must hurry now. I don't want Rich to wake up before I light the straw stack on fire.

I grabbed the pitchfork and shovel that I had stashed in the loose straw around the base of the stack and the flashlight from the tunnel. I began the walk to the fire shack where I had taken the items earlier. I opened the door; I am startled by the loud creak of the hinges. Damn, slow down, Zeke. You're starting to be careless. I carefully closed the door behind me as I entered the shack. I turned the flashlight on and sat the toolbox back on the self; I hung the lantern back on the hook and placed the pitchfork and shovel back in the corner behind the door. Everything was now returned to its proper place within the shack. I turned out the flashlight and exited the fire shack carefully so the hinges would be as silent as possible.

I stop and lean against the fire shack to catch my breath and relax for a moment. I am relieved that it is almost over. All I need to do now is walk back to the straw stack and flip a match down the tunnel toward the opening of my hideout. I was kind of sad that I was about to destroy my hideout. It was a place where I could go and get away from everything and everybody. I will miss it.

I walked back to the straw stack and looked down the tunnel with the flashlight; no sounds came from the hideout. I was just about to light the match to ignite the straw when it hit me. What if Rich had awakened and crawled out when I was at the fire shack? I couldn't take the chance; I had to make sure he was still inside. I crawled into the tunnel to the entrance of the hideout. I turned the flashlight beam toward the area where I had left Rich. Yep, he was still there, passed out from the starting fluid. I crawled back into the tunnel and stepped out into the field. I turned the flashlight out and laid it on the ground beside the straw stack. I then threw the starting fluid rag into the tunnel and took the box of Ohio Blue Tip matches out of my pocket. With a quick flip of my wrist, I struck a match on the side of the box. The light from the flame jumped across the walls of the tunnel like shadow men endlessly running down toward the hideout. I tossed the match down the tunnel, and it landed exactly at the entrance of the hideout. The straw immediately erupted into flames. It was almost as if it were soaked with gasoline. The fire raced down the tunnel toward me and inside the hideout out of sight.

I grabbed the flashlight. No need to put the half bale back in place; the fire would need all the oxygen it could get to burn as hot as possible.

I ran back to the fence, crawled through the opening, and grabbed my bike. I looked back toward the straw stack. The north side of the stack was entirely covered by flames.

This was not a good thing. The stack was burning much faster than I thought it would. I needed to hurry and get out of the area. I jumped on my bike and rode as fast as I could down the dirt lane toward Noble Avenue. No traffic, great. I turned on Noble toward Michigan and pedaled faster. I pulled up into a yard on Michigan Avenue because I saw the headlights of a car coming up the street. The car stopped at the stop sign and continued on Michigan toward the river. I could not waste any more time. The straw stack was surely completely engulfed in flames by now. I raced toward home, slid up the driveway quietly and into the garage.

I was completely covered in sweat now. I think it was a combination of nervous sweat as well as the physical stress of the ride back home. I quietly stepped out of the garage and looked toward the straw stack fields. The sky was a total glow now. I could see flames leap high into the air above the houses that were across the street from my house. What's that? Crap, sirens. Someone had already called the fire department. I looked down at my watch in the moonlight. Three o'clock already! I needed to get back in the house and in bed before all the excitement started. I quickly crossed the backyard toward my window. I stopped just outside my window to listen for any sounds from my parents. Everything was silent. I opened the window and climbed into my room as quietly as possible. I again waited in silence as I listened for any sounds coming from my parents' room. Still total silence, that's good. I didn't need them to know that I left my room. Marie would surely believe that I started the fire if she knew I was out of my room. She would probably call the police and turn me in just to get rid of me for good.

I slipped off my clothes and put on my pajamas. I was calm now, not nervous at all. I slid under the covers and listened as the sounds of the sirens traveled down Noble Avenue toward the straw stack fields. It would be far too late for them to save Rich now. He was more than likely just a pile of ashes. I could hardly wait to read about it in the afternoon newspaper tomorrow. I know that the fire department will investigate the fire to try and determine a cause.

But in this case, I think that's impossible. The straw stack will be a pile of ash before they can ever get the fire out. It's time for me to get some sleep now. I'm exhausted.

Chapter 26

What the hell? "James, James," Marie is screaming.

"What's wrong, Marie?" I heard James respond.

"One of the straw stacks in the field is on fire!"

I looked over at the clock on my nightstand; it's a little after five o'clock. Wow, it's still blazing. That means the fire department is probably just letting it burn while they wet down the stacks near it so they don't have the whole field ablaze. I decided to play along with Marie. I opened the door to my bedroom and walked out toward the living room where Marie and now James stood looking out the window at the straw stack fields. I could still see flames shooting over the neighbors' houses as the fire raged. I faked rubbing sleep from my eyes and said, "What's wrong, Mom?"

Marie turned around and glared at me.

"What are you doing out of bed?"

"I woke up when you were yelling at Dad."

"Well, at least one of the straw stacks in the field is on fire. The fire department and the police are there, but it looks as if the fire is out of control."

"Wow, I wonder how the straw stack caught on fire?"

"I don't know, but I'm sure the police and fire department will investigate the fire and determine the cause. I just hope we don't have a firebug around setting fires for the fun of it. Now get back to bed and go to sleep!"

"Okay."

I turned around and walked toward my bedroom. I was somewhat intrigued by Marie's firebug comment. Why didn't I set more than one straw stack on fire? It would have been easy to do. I probably could have set at least three on fire without any difficulty. After all, it was just a flick of a match. That would have kept the fire department investigation team busy for a while.

I went back to my bedroom to lie down in bed and immediately fell asleep. My mind drifted to Rich in my dreams. What a picture. I saw Rich covered with rats gnawing at his body, blood spurting from every bite, screams of pain and agony spewed from his mouth. Then my dreams shifted to the fire. Rich lay there surrounded by flames; the fire inched closer and closer. He finally awakes and stands with the flames surrounding him. He has nowhere to go. The flames inch closer, the heat becomes more intense, his skin begins to blister from the heat. Gut-wrenching screams come from deep within him. He drops to his knees as his skin begins to melt from his body. Flames engulf him entirely, and life leaves him as the inferno rages around him.

I snap back to reality from my dreams. I am totally covered in sweat and breathing very hard. I guess the dreams have taken their toll on me. I can hear Marie and James talking in the living room. I listen closely, but I can't understand everything that they're saying. Well, I guess it's time to get out of bed. It's almost eight o'clock anyway. I sat on the edge of the bed for a few minutes still trying to make out what Marie and James were talking about. This is strange. They are definitely trying to keep their voices quiet.

I dressed quickly and walked out into the living room where Marie and James sat having coffee. It appeared that James was upset because the paper-mill cancelled all work shifts today because of the fire. I could understand why he would be upset. He would have to spend the day with Marie, and I'm sure he'd rather be at work than spend the day with her.

"Hey, Dad, did the fire department ever get the straw stack fire under control?"

"I don't think so. Smoke is still pouring into the air, and the police and fire department are still there."

"Maybe I'll ride my bike over there and see what's going on."

"No, you stay away from the straw stack fields! They'll think you had something to do with the fire. I don't want the police over here bothering us," James said glaring at me.

James had a very stern look on his face, and I wasn't about to question his judgment.

"Okay, Dad, I won't go anywhere near the straw stack fields today. But can I just walk over to the neighbor's house across the street so I can see what everyone is doing?"

"I guess so, but don't cross the Mason Run boundary fence. Just look from there. You'll be able to see the fire from there if it is still burning."

"Okay, thanks, Dad."

I walked across the street to a vacant lot that is directly across the street from our house. I stopped at the Mason Run boundary fence and looked toward the straw stack that served as Rich's tomb. The firefighters had leveled all the brush near the fence that surrounded the straw stack field and the brush within the field near the straw stack that had housed my hideout. No way could you enter the straw stack fields now without being detected by one of the snoopy neighbors whose property bordered the Mason Run.

The straw stack no longer was ninety feet tall. It was now a mound of glowing embers. Occasionally a flame would jump into the air as if it were trying to escape from the pile of hot ashes. The firefighters were busy dousing the surrounding area with water just as I figured they would be. They couldn't risk the fire spreading to the entire straw stack field. Kind of funny, their water hoses were connected to the fire hydrant at the fire shack where the tools, lantern, shovel, and pitchfork were stored. Of course, the cops were all over the place.

But that was okay with me. The way I figured it, the firefighters were all over the area around the fire shack, and any remains of my footprints would be gone. I laughed inside and thought, sorry about their luck. I wondered how long it would take my old friend Sergeant Murray to look me up again. I knew that my name was probably already on his list of people to interrogate.

Wow, a gust of wind came through, and the pile of ashes rose to full flame again. Good, I need to make sure that Rich is cooked beyond recognition. With any luck, he will just blend into the pile of ashes.

I turned away from the fence and started to walk back home deep in thought about the events of the prior night. I was snapped back to reality by our neighbor Ray Morrow.

"It was quite a fire last night, wasn't it, Zeke?"

Ray was an elderly gentleman who was known throughout the neighborhood for his kindness. He often worked with local charities, helping them get donations for various worthy causes. He was always friendly toward me. I thought he was basically a good guy.

"Well, I guess so. I really didn't know anything about the fire until my mother woke me up about five o'clock this morning."

"Yeah, I guess I was lucky to see it in full blaze. I'm the one who called the fire department about three o'clock this morning."

Great, I wonder if he saw me or not. I can't act nervous. I must keep calm.

"What were you doing awake at three o'clock in the morning?"

"Well, Zeke, when you get my age, you use the bathroom often during the night. I had just come out of the bathroom when I saw the straw stack on fire. The flames were already leaping high into the air. I called the fire department immediately, and then I went to the fence at the Mason Run to watch them arrive."

"Have the police talked with you about the fire yet?"

"No, not yet, but I'm sure they will before long."

I needed to be careful here with my next question. I didn't want to raise any suspicions in his mind. I really had to watch what I said while talking with him. He was a very smart person, and I knew it.

"Well, Mr. Morrow, I really hope they catch whoever set the fire. My father has already lost one day of work because of the fire, and he may even lose more than that. We really can't afford for him to miss many days of pay."

"I know, Zeke. I'm just sorry that I don't have any information for the police. I didn't see anything except the flames when I came out of the bathroom. I didn't have my glasses on, and without them, I am almost blind. I went into the bedroom, put my glasses on, and immediately called the fire department. I really wish I had put my glasses on and taken a moment to look over the area before I put the call into the fire department. There was a full moon last night, and I may have been able to see someone if they were in the area of the straw stacks. The few moments it would have taken to do that would not have made any difference. The fire was already out of control."

"Maybe the police and the fire department investigators will find something that will give them some clues about how the fire started."

"I hope so, Zeke. We can't have folks going around the neighborhood setting fires. I mean whoever started this fire may decide to start setting houses on fire while we sleep. That would not be good, lives would be lost."

"You're right, Mr. Morrow, we don't need anyone like that around."

"Good talking with you, Zeke, have a good day."

"You too, Mr. Morrow, see you later."

"Bye, Zeke."

Good, Mr. Morrow didn't see me or anyone else in the area. That's great news. I don't need to worry now. I'm in the clear. It is impossible to put me at the scene of the crime. But wait a minute, what about my fingerprints on the shovel, pitchfork, toolbox, and the lantern? Damn, another mistake on my part. I forgot about fingerprints. I guess I won't worry too much about that.

I'm sure the firefighters touched many areas within the fire shack when they hooked up their water hoses to the hydrant. Anyway, why would the police look in the fire shack for clues? Surely that would be the last place they would look.

I was only home for about thirty minutes before there was a knock on the front door. I went to the door to see who was there. Of course, it was my old friend Sergeant Murray.

"Hi, Sergeant Murray, how are you?"

"I'm okay, Zeke. Are your parents at home?"

"Yes, I'll get them."

I turned around to get them only to find Marie walking toward me.

"It's Sergeant Murray. He wants to talk with you and Dad."

"Come on in, Sergeant Murray, I don't know where that boy's manners are. He should have invited you inside."

"No problem, Mrs. Baker. The boy just probably didn't want me in the house without first asking you or your husband if it was okay."

James now enters the room and looks at Sergeant Murray and then looks at me with questioning eyes.

"How can we help you, Sergeant Murray?" James asked.

"Well, Mr. Baker, as you are probably aware, this fire in the straw stack fields is under investigation as a possible arson."

"Yeah, I thought that the police and the fire department would be looking into the cause of the fire."

“We’re going door-to-door in the area to see if anyone has seen anything. We started with Mr. Morrow across the road. He’s the one who put the call in to the fire department.”

“Did he see who started the fire?”

“No, he really didn’t see anything except for the flames from the fire. Did you happen to see anyone in or around the straw stack fields or a stranger in the area?”

“No, my wife and I were asleep until all the commotion from the fire department and the police woke us.”

“I’ll tell you, Mr. Baker, this whole thing has me puzzled. Somehow I think this has something to do with that missing boy, Rich. You know, your son’s friend.”

This really pissed me off. I couldn’t just stand there and say nothing.

“I told you before, he’s not my friend.”

“Zeke, be respectful to Sergeant Murray. He’s a police officer!” James snapped.

“Okay, I’m sorry, Sergeant Murray.”

“That’s okay, Zeke. It was my mistake. I thought he was a friend of yours.”

Sergeant Murray handed James one of his cards and said, “Please call me immediately if you find out anything about the fire or the missing boy.”

“Don’t worry, Sergeant Murray, I will call you if I have any information at all. I hope you find the boy and the person who started the fire.”

“Have a good day, Mr. and Mrs. Baker. Try to stay out of trouble, Zeke.”

With that, Sergeant Murray went out the door and down the steps toward the street.

Stay out of trouble, Zeke. What a jerk. He doesn't know me. He can't just assume I'm bad. I remember what Marie told him earlier. Yeah, just like everyone else, he believes what he is told about me by her. Damn her!

The news crews have pictures of the fire on the front page of the newspaper. Wow, the flames must have been another hundred feet above the top of the straw stack. I would have loved to have been able to see the fire when it was at its peak.

There were not many details in the newspaper about the fire. The article just stated that the fire was of a suspicious nature and that police and fire department personnel were handling the investigation.

Firefighters finally turned their hoses on the pile of burning embers toward evening. I guess they now felt that the area was safe and it was time to water down the ashes of the straw stack. I knew the investigation would begin soon. Over the next few days, I would always take time to walk across the vacant lot to the Mason Run boundary fence so I could watch the investigation team work. They actually raked the ashes apart a section at a time, looking for clues related to the origin of the fire. I was amazed how meticulous they were when they did this. I laughed to myself, kind of like looking for a needle in a haystack.

During the next week, the search intensified for Rich. It was all over the newspaper and television news. The boy was missing, and they were asking everyone to help assist in the search for him. Little did they know that he was vaporized now, not just missing but gone forever.

Weeks have now passed since the fire and the disappearance of Rich. Sergeant Murray has questioned everyone about both the fire and Rich. The nightly local newspaper continues to say that no further clues have been found in either case. I was riding my bike down the street one day, kind of thinking about nothing yet about everything. I was just passing Mr. Morrow's house when I heard him shout, "Zeke!"

I turned around and rode into Mr. Morrow's driveway.

"Hi, Mr. Morrow, how are you?"

"I'm fine, Zeke, how about you?"

"Oh, I'm okay. What did you want?"

"Well, Zeke, Sergeant Murray has stopped and talked with me several times over the last few weeks."

"Yeah, I know. I have seen him on your front porch a couple of times. I'm sure he's working hard to find the person who started the fire."

"Yes, yes, he is. But he continues to ask me questions about you, and that bothers me. He really believes that you had something to do with the fire and the missing boy."

"Why does he think that?"

"I don't know, Zeke, but he brings up your name every time he stops here. He really thinks you're a very bad kid. He believes that you are capable of setting the fire and hurting the boy. Are you? I mean did you have anything to do with the fire or the boy?"

"Of course, I didn't, Mr. Morrow. I didn't have anything to do with the straw stack fire or Rich's disappearance. I don't know why Sergeant Murray thinks that I was involved. The fire started during the night, and I was in bed asleep. As for Rich, I have not seen him since the end of the school year. I have no idea where he is."

"I know, Zeke. I told Sergeant Murray that I could not believe that you would have anything to do with either case. I also told him that you stay around the house a great deal of the time doing chores for your father and mother. But I don't think I was able to change his mind about you, he seems to be obsessed with you."

"I don't know what else I can do to make him believe me. It seems like everyone thinks the worst of me. I just wish everyone would leave me alone."

"I understand, Zeke, but don't let it bother you. Sometimes the police just get frustrated when they're working on a case and focus on something or someone who has nothing to do with the case at all. Just relax and enjoy yourself, Zeke. Sooner or later, they will forget all about you."

"Thanks, Mr. Morrow, I'm glad that you talked with me."

"You're welcome, Zeke. Go on now and ride your bike. Forget about Sergeant Murray, and he'll forget about you."

"Okay, thanks again, Mr. Morrow."

I rode out his driveway and down the street. Sergeant Murray was becoming a real problem to me. I needed to be very careful. I'm sure he was watching me every chance he got. He might even be watching me now. Marie was the one who put me in his mind. She was the one who planted the seed in his tiny brain. Damn her.

It was very near dinnertime, so I headed home. I parked my bike at the front steps in full view so everyone would know that Zeke was home. I picked up the nightly newspaper from the steps and went into the house. I threw the paper on the couch, and it unfolded and opened up to the front page. The headline read, INVESTIGATORS DETERMINE THE CAUSE OF THE PAPER-MILL STRAW STACK FIRE. I quickly sat down on the couch and began to read the article. It seems that the fire marshal determined that the cause of the fire was spontaneous combustion. It seems that per the fire marshal, the weather conditions were perfect for a spontaneous combustion event to happen within the straw stack fields. Amazing, the thought had never crossed my mind. I know that we had studied spontaneous combustion in science class in school, but I never thought about that being a possibility with the straw stack. It was a lengthy article that went into depth about spontaneous combustion and the facts around their final determination regarding the cause of the fire.

"Zeke, is that you?"

"Yeah, Mom, it's me."

I hear her coming down the hall from the kitchen toward me. I really didn't want to talk to her or even see her.

"What are you doing?"

"I was just reading the paper. The fire marshal finally determined how the fire started in the straw stack fields."

"Well, it's about time. What did they say caused the fire?"

"They say it was caused by spontaneous combustion within the straw stack. The article goes on to say that all weather conditions were perfect for a spontaneous combustion event to happen in the straw stack fields."

"Well, it's never happened before, and I hope it never happens again. Now get washed up for dinner."

I walked into the bathroom almost exploding with laughter inside. Rich is gone, Nicole is gone, the fire has been investigated, and Zeke is in the clear again. Again a rush of excitement came over my body. Zeke, the dumb kid, the kid who will never make anything out of himself, has outsmarted them all again. Even Sergeant Murray was unable to pin anything on me. If I stay smart and careful, none of the Sergeant Murrays of the world will ever outwit me. I will never be caught. I will stay in control. The world awaits Zeke, and Zeke awaits the world.

Chapter 27

I went back to school in the fall of 1966, back to deal with arrogant teachers, back to deal with kids who thought they were tough, but quickly found out they weren't. I was really getting sick of being in this town and very tired of the people who lived here. I guess that I am just very tired of life itself. Imagine that I am approaching my eighteenth birthday, and I'm already sick of life. I wonder how many other kids think the same way I do. I bet not many.

The next seven months passed quickly, but not without many, many nightmares for me. Someone was chasing me in my dreams. Chasing me and screaming that they were going to kill me. He always carried a knife that was dripping with blood. He was faceless to me. For some reason, I could not make out his face even when he was standing in front of me. He never quite caught me even though I could see the knife clearly. I could even see the bright redness of the blood on the blade. I watched as droplets of blood dripped off the blade and spattered on the ground. Everything was very clear in the dream except for the face of my pursuer. No matter how hard I focused to see his face, my eyes would continually blur, making it impossible to identify him. I would lurch forward in bed and awake every time my pursuer would get near me and raise the blade to kill me. This dream was recurring and happened at least twice a week for the last two years since the beginning of my sophomore year in high school. Every detail was exactly the same in every dream. It was driving me crazy. I needed to know who he was and why he wanted to kill me.

Marie continued her hatred toward me. She screamed more now at James when he was home. It was as if she was preparing for me to leave, and she wanted to make sure that she was in charge of at least one person's life. I felt sorry for James. When I was gone, he would have to suffer the wrath of Marie alone. Right now I was there, and she could always focus her constant anger toward me. Not for long though; no, not for long at all.

The talk about Rich on the news and in the newspaper faded, and only on the anniversary of his disappearance was there any mention of his existence. His parents would always make a pleading statement for his safe return on one of the local TV stations.

I would watch as his mother would cry uncontrollably when his father delivered their annual plea for the return of their son. It didn't bother me at all. I kind of liked watching them cry their eyes out. Rich deserved what he got. I was not sorry at all for killing him. In fact, I was glad he was dead. Rich, Nicole, and Whitey deserved what they got. I will never feel sad for any of them.

It's only a couple of months before high school graduation. I can't wait to graduate and get out of this hell I live in daily. I need to be out in the world on my own. Life will be much better for me soon.

I'm thinking about my future as I walk home from school today. I really don't know what kind of work I want to pursue, but jobs are plentiful, and I can take any job for a short period until I decide what I really want to do. I have no intention of attending college. I can't stand school now, and I sure won't spend money to attend college. Anyway, I don't have any money to spend, and I know that James can't afford to send me to college. I'll do fine; I'm really not worried about it, and I can take care of myself.

I reached home, and I noticed that James was standing near the garage in the driveway. Funny, I thought that he was working twelve hours today, from seven in the morning until seven in the evening. No matter, I was kind of glad to see him.

"Hi, Dad, what are you doing home?"

"I decided to work eight hours today instead of twelve. Come on in the garage, I want to talk to you."

In the garage to talk? I wondered what he wanted. Where was Marie? She wouldn't let us talk in the garage. She would need to know what we were talking about. No, she would not tolerate this.

I entered the garage with a confused look on my face and said, "Where's Mom?"

"She's at Jenny's beauty parlor getting her hair cut and styled."

"Oh, okay. What did you want, Dad?"

Without saying a word, James walked over to an old cupboard that my grandfather had made years ago. I watched as he opened the bottom door of the cupboard and reached for a screwdriver that was in his back pocket. He laid the screwdriver on the shelf and removed everything else from the shelf and placed it on the floor. He then picked up the screwdriver and began to unscrew a board from the back of the cupboard just above the shelf. He removed the board and laid it on the floor next to him. He reached in the opening and pulled out a small metal box that had a lock on it. He reached in his pocket and took out a ring of keys. He selected a key and unlocked the box and opened it. He reached inside and pulled out two envelopes. He turned and handed them to me. I looked at him, and he said, "Go ahead and open one of them."

I opened the first envelope and looked inside. I was shocked, totally shocked. There was a stack of fifty-dollar bills inside the envelope.

"Go ahead, count them, Zeke."

I began to count them. I could feel sweat bead out on my forehead. I counted, fifty, one hundred, one hundred fifty, two hundred, all the way to twenty-five hundred dollars. The first envelope contained a total of twenty-five hundred dollars! I was severely confused now. My father never had any money. Where did this come from?

"Dad, I don't understand, where did all this money come from?"

"I've been saving it for years,"

"But why, Dad, why did you save all this money?"

"For you, Zeke, the money was saved for you. The other envelope has another twenty-five hundred dollars in it. It's a total of five thousand dollars for you, Zeke, for your future. I want you to go on the senior trip this year with all the other kids at school. You deserve to go and have fun for a change."

"Does Mom know about the money?"

"No, and she must never know about the money. She will take it away from you, and it's not hers. It's your money because I saved it for you."

My senior trip was to Florida. I wanted to go just to see what it's like in Florida. I have read about it, and it seems like a great place to go, especially in April.

"I don't know what to say, Dad, except thank you. I will only need two hundred dollars for the senior trip."

"I know, Zeke, but you can use the rest of the money after you get out of school to get started in life. You will be able to get some furniture, an apartment, a car, pretty much everything you need to get started on your own."

I thought for a moment. I had recently completed driver's training and got my driver's license. But Marie was not about to let me drive the family car. No, in her words, I was far too careless to drive a car.

"But wait, Dad, how will I explain where I got the money for the trip to Mom?"

"I've already taken care of that. You know Mr. Morrow across the road very well, don't you?"

"Yes, yes, I do. He's a good person."

"Well, I've known Mr. Morrow since I was very young, and he is a good friend. Mr. Morrow and I have worked up a plan where he will tell Marie that he is paying for you to go on the senior trip because he likes you and wants to see you have the opportunity to go."

"Mr. Morrow would do that for me?"

"Yes, Zeke, he thinks a great deal of you, and he wants to help."

"Well, that's great. I'm glad he likes me, but how is he going to convince Mom that it's okay for me to take his money and go on the senior trip? She will never agree to that!"

"Oh yes, she will, Zeke. Mr. Morrow has known your mother for a long time, and Marie and all her family have great respect for Mr. Morrow. You see, Mr. Morrow is a longtime friend of your mother's family. He helped Marie's family get through the Great Depression by buying them groceries and clothing when they needed it. When the roof of your grandfather's home needed repair, Mr. Morrow paid a contractor to fix it. He never asked for anything in return for his kindness and generosity. So when he comes over to talk with Marie, she will listen. She will not disrespect Mr. Morrow by questioning his decision to give you the money that you need for your senior trip. No, she will never question Mr. Morrow because her family owes him a great deal for his kindness."

Wow, this is all new to me. People are being kind to me, giving me money, lying to Marie so I can go on a trip. I was stunned. I was really going to have a chance to enjoy some time away from home. Better than that, I would have money after graduation to leave this hell and finally be out on my own.

"Look, Zeke, we will put all the money except for the two hundred dollars back in the box and put the box back in its hiding place. I will give the two hundred dollars to Mr. Morrow so he can come over and give it to you for the trip. Here's the spare key for the lock on the box. All I ask of you, Zeke, is to wait until you graduate before you take the money and leave."

"Don't worry, Dad, I will wait. I've waited this long, I can wait a couple of months more."

James put two hundred dollars in his pocket, placed the other money back in the box, and put the box back in its place of safety. I thought for a moment. If Marie ever knew that James had done this for me, she would go ballistic. I would never tell her. This proved to me that James cared about me, and in my heart, I knew she was the evil one in the family.

A couple of days later Mr. Morrow came over to our house and pitched the senior-trip scam to Marie. He told Marie that I had helped him several times over the years when he needed groceries carried into the house, shoveled snow for him, and helped him with other chores when he needed help. I was amazed. He was very calm and relaxed as he sat and lied about everything to Marie. Marie had a very confused look on her face. I guess she wondered why anyone would care enough about me to pay for my senior trip.

"It was good talking with you, Mrs. Baker. I hope it's okay with you if I give Zeke two hundred dollars for his senior trip. Of course, I have checked with the school, and this amount will include enough money so he has available spending money while he is there. Florida is such a lovely place, and I know that Zeke will enjoy spending a week there."

"Well, I guess it's okay with me, Ray, but this is quite a bit of money. Don't you think that a hundred and fifty dollars would be sufficient?"

Great! Now she's trying to cut money out of my pocket that is already mine anyway. Why can't she just keep her mouth shut and let him give me the money? I suppose it would be all right if he were giving the two hundred dollars to her.

"Nonsense, Marie, I won't hear of it. Zeke deserves to have the money available to him so he can do what he wants in Florida. I don't want him to worry about running short of cash."

Mr. Morrow stood up and took four fifty-dollar bills out of his wallet and handed them to me. These were the same fifty-dollar bills that I recognized from a few days before.

"Here, Zeke, please take this and enjoy your trip. I hope you have a great time and enjoy the sunshine."

"Thanks, Mr. Morrow. I really appreciate the money for the trip. I will enjoy the fun and the sunshine. I'll even pick up a souvenir from Florida for you."

"Now don't go wasting your money on souvenirs on me. I've pretty much got everything that I need already in my house. You just take the money and have fun."

"Okay, Mr. Morrow, I will have fun on the trip and spend the money wisely. Thanks again, Mr. Morrow, thanks for everything."

I guess Dad was right. Mr. Morrow was a good friend to him, Marie, and me. I can't wait to make the trip to Florida!

Chapter 28

Finally, senior-trip day is here! I packed everything I needed for the trip last night, and I'm ready to go to the airport. It's a cool morning, and James just went outside to start the car so it can warm up for the trip to the airport. The plane is scheduled to depart at ten o'clock. It's almost seven o'clock now, so we have plenty of time. The Detroit Metropolitan airport is only thirty miles from our house, and most of it is expressway driving, so it won't take long to get there.

I walked out into the dining room where Marie has just put breakfast on the table.

"Well, boy, you'd better eat some breakfast before you go to the airport."

I looked at the table; great, mush again. She must get a deal on this stuff at the store. I can understand why—it's only fit for dogs to eat. God, I hate this stuff! No matter, I sat down and ate the disgusting breakfast anyway. There was no reason for me to start anything with her now. After all, I was on my way to the airport and away from her for a week. Seven days without having to listen to her bitch at my dad or me. I finally had a chance to have a good time by myself without her around. Yeah, I know, all the jerks from school will be there too. But that really doesn't matter; I don't have to hang around with them.

James came inside from putting my luggage in the car and said, "Zeke, it's time to hit the road."

"I know, Dad, let's go. I'm ready!"

We both jumped in the car at the same time and headed toward the airport. I was anxious to get to the airport and board the plane. I had never flown anywhere before, and I couldn't wait. James had told me about his experience with flying. He had flown several places during the war. He said it was fun to fly, and he was sure that I would enjoy it. Just the thought of getting away from home excited me.

"Zeke, what do you plan to do after you graduate from school?"

"I was thinking about getting a job at Ford Motor Company. I read in the newspaper that the Monroe plant was going to be hiring two hundred new employees in mid-June. That would be perfect timing because graduation is June ninth this year. I know the pay will be good because they have an employees' union. I'll probably get an apartment on Elm Avenue. The house on the corner of Elm and Michigan has a room for rent right now."

"Sounds like a good plan, Zeke. You're right, the pay will be good, and I know the workers there work a lot of overtime. Most of them work twelve hours per day, seven days a week."

"Dad, I want you to know that I plan to pay the money back to you. I know that it took you a long time to save that much money, and I want to make sure I give it all back to you."

"No, Zeke, I don't want the money back. I started saving the money for you the day you were born. The money has always been for you, not for me. You keep it and make sure you save money for yourself so you can have a good life. Also, Zeke, I don't want you to rush into marriage. Take your time, and you'll find the right woman for you."

"Don't worry, Dad, I have no plans on marrying anyone in the near future. I don't have any girlfriends, and I don't want any. I'm fine by myself. I don't need anyone else in my life right now."

"Okay, Zeke, but I want you to make good decisions in your life. I want you to be able to enjoy life to its fullest because you have not been allowed to enjoy life as a kid."

"Don't worry about me, Dad. I'll be fine."

We pulled into the departure lane at the airport and slowly made our way to the first set of entry doors to the airport terminal.

"Got your ticket, Zeke?"

"Yep, I've got it right here," I said as I pulled the ticket from my pocket.

"Okay, Zeke, have a good time. I'll pick you up at four o'clock next Saturday."

"Okay, Dad, I'll see you then. Thanks again for giving me the money to go."

"I didn't give you the money, Mr. Morrow did!"

We both had a good laugh, and I turned around and went through the entry doors of the airport terminal. The place was alive with people. Everyone seemed to be in a hurry to get to their destination. I walked up to the ticket counter to check my suitcase. I was greeted with a very pretty smile from the airline attendant on the other side of the counter. She was beautiful and a very pleasant person. She looked at my ticket and said, "Tampa Florida, what a great place to go this time of year."

"I hope so. I've never been there before. I'm going on our senior trip, and we're all supposed to meet at the Holiday Inn near Clearwater Beach."

"Be careful, Mr. Baker, lots of very pretty girls hang out at Clearwater Beach. You can get in a lot of trouble there."

"Don't worry, I'll be careful. I just want to get away and have a good time."

"What seat would you like, Mr. Baker?"

"I would like an aisle seat at the rear of plane."

"Okay, let's see what I have. You're in luck, I have seat 29C available."

"That's perfect. Please reserve the seat for me."

"Okay, Mr. Baker, 29C is reserved for you. Have a good time at the beach, and have a safe trip."

"Thanks!"

She handed me my ticket and boarding pass. She then took my suitcase and placed it on the conveyor belt, where it quickly disappeared behind a small door covered by clear strips of plastic.

I walked quickly toward my departure gate. I wanted to make sure I was there in plenty of time to board the plane. I did not want to be left behind. I walked faster as I thought about being left behind. I actually started to jog for the gate now. No wonder all those other people were in such a hurry. They probably didn't want to be left behind either. I finally reached the gate one full hour before the flight was scheduled to depart. I was somewhat relieved now. I can just sit and wait for the attendant to call for boarding the plane.

This is my first experience in an airport, but all you really have to do is follow the signs, and you can move through the airport rather easily. It really wasn't difficult at all. I'd heard before about people who had a lot of difficulty finding their way in an airport, but you'd have to be a complete idiot not to find your way easily in this airport.

Many of the seniors who were taking the trip began to congregate in the area of the gate. None bothered to talk with me or even sit close to me. I think they were amazed that I was actually taking the trip. Screw them! I don't really care what they think. Their opinion did not mean anything to me. I laughed inside when I saw their parents fussing over them. They had to bring Mommy and Daddy along so they could be sure they would be safe at the airport. What a joke. They should know that nothing is safe in life. There is always somebody waiting in the shadows to take life away from you.

"Attention, all passengers. Flight 486 to Tampa, Florida, is now ready for boarding. We will start boarding with the tail section of the plane first. Passengers seated in rows twenty-two through thirty, please step up to the podium for boarding."

I had purposely requested a seat in the rear of the plane because of a newspaper article that I read recently. It said that most people flying don't like to sit in the rear of the plane. It seems that it's noisy in the rear of the plane, and in a crash, the rear of the plane would suffer the most damage.

What the hell; if the plane crashed, everyone would most likely be killed anyway. Why would you care if you were killed first or last? You'd still be dead, wouldn't you? Well, that was fine with me if all the people sat forward in the plane. I would be by myself in the back of the plane, and that would be great.

It was finally my turn at the podium, so I handed the attendant my ticket and boarding pass. She looked it over and smiled at me and said, "Have a nice trip, Mr. Baker."

I thanked her and walked down the ramp toward the plane. The captain and flight crew greeted me at the entrance to the plane. They seemed like nice people. I walked down the aisle to my seat. Several people in front of me had carry-on bags, so I had to wait until they were out of the way so I could sit down. Finally I was in my seat and buckled in for the flight. So far I was the only passenger sitting in the entire row 29. I really hoped it would stay that way.

Crap, here comes a guy in a nice three-piece suit looking at the row-seat identification panel above the seats. Yep, he's headed for row 29. He sat down in the aisle seat directly across from me. He looks like he's about thirty years old and very well built. I start to turn my head away, but our eyes make contact.

"Hi, my name's Jeff Pierce, what's yours?"

"Hi, I'm Zeke Baker."

"Do you live in Tampa, Zeke?"

"No, I'm flying to Tampa with members of my high school class for our senior trip."

"Why are you all the way in the back here? Why aren't you up front with the rest of your class?"

"I'm kind of a loner. I tend to stick by myself. I like it that way."

"That's funny. I'm the same way. To tell you the truth, I thought you were older than a high school student. How old are you anyway?"

"I'm a few months from my eighteenth birthday."

"I would have guessed you for twenty-one. You look older than seventeen, and you look like you're a strong guy."

"I can hold my own. I don't like people to push me, and I always stand my ground. I've been in many fights during my life, and the only one I remember losing was when some dopes decided to gang up on me. It took a while, but I eventually got even with all of them."

"Unbelievable, you sound just like me when I was growing up. I felt the same way you do. I think I'm going to like you, Zeke. What are you going to do after you graduate from high school?"

A screech came over the intercom system, and a commanding voice said, "Good morning, passengers. This is the captain speaking. At this point, I would like you to please take a moment to listen to the stewardess for in-flight safety instructions."

The stewardess explained the seat belt use, emergency exits, flotation devices, oxygen use, etc. It was apparent that she had done this several times in the past. She knew this routine by heart.

"This is your captain. All stewardesses and passengers, please prepare for flight departure."

I made sure my seat belt was fastened and my seat was upright for takeoff. The plane began to move down the runway with increasing speed. I glanced out the window toward the runway. The markers on the runway were now flying past. The plane lifted off the ground and rapidly rose into the air. Wow, this was fun!

I looked back at Jeff and said, “I’m sorry, this is my first flight, and I’m really amazed how easy it was for the plane to get off the ground. I even forgot the question you asked before we were interrupted by the captain.”

“That’s okay, Zeke, I understand fully. I can still remember my first flight. I asked what you planned to do after you graduate from high school.”

“Oh yeah, that’s right. Well, I was thinking about getting a job at Ford Motor Company in Monroe, Michigan. They plan to hire a couple of hundred people around the middle of June. My graduation day is June ninth, so it would work out perfectly for me.”

“That’s too bad, Zeke. I’m a project manager for a construction firm based in Tampa. We do work all over the country, including Florida. We have a couple of big road projects going in the Tampa area that will last for around four years without any add-ons, and there are always adds to every construction project. I was hoping that I could get you to hire into the construction firm where I work.

The pay is far better than you can get at Ford. You could learn to be a heavy equipment operator and be licensed to use heavy equipment in any state.”

“That sounds like a great job.”

“It is a great job. Look at me. I worked for the company for eight years, and I am now a project manager making fifty thousand dollars a year. The work is hard, and most guys who aren’t tough won’t last. But I think you have what it takes to make it. I’ll tell you what, you don’t have to make a decision now. I’ll give you my business card, and you can call me if you want the job. The company trusts my judgment. If I tell company management to hire you, they will hire you.”

He reached into the vest pocket of his suit coat and handed me a business card. It read, Jeff Pierce, Project Manager, Tampa Bay Area Construction. Very impressive, this entire conversation was very impressive to me.

“Thanks for the card. I’ll think it over when I’m in Florida. I will call you and let you know whether I will take the job or not. I really appreciate the offer.”

"Okay, Zeke, I'll wait for the call. I know you will like the work if you just give it a chance. I'm going to take a short snooze before the flight lands in Tampa, relax and enjoy the flight"

This is great; only Jeff and I were seated in row 29. How was I lucky enough to get seated next to a person who would offer me a job in Tampa? This is probably the luckiest day of my life. Think about it, a job where the weather is always warm, and a job outdoors in the sun. It was all too much for me to comprehend.

Should I accept his offer and leave Michigan? What about James? I wondered how he would feel about me leaving the state. I needed to make sure that he would be okay with it. I owed it to him. He wasn't a bad guy. All the beatings I took from him were driven by Marie. I know that he hated it there as much as I did. He just didn't have a way to escape. I leaned my seat back so I would be more comfortable. I needed to think about Jeff's offer. It was important for me to make the right decision. I wanted to be able to enjoy life for a change.

Damn, I fell asleep. I'm startled awake by the captain's booming voice, "Welcome to Tampa, passengers. The temperature is seventy-five degrees with bright sunshine."

I looked across the aisle, and Jeff is rubbing his eyes trying to come back to reality from dreamland just like me.

The plane was in its final descent to the runway. My ears were popping with the altitude changes. I could hear the landing gear lower and lock into place. The plane made a slight hop as the wheels touched the runway. We were finally on the ground. The intercom clicked on again. "This is the captain again, folks. On behalf of myself and the flight crew, I'd like to thank you for flying with us today. We hope you enjoy your stay in Tampa."

The plane taxied to the gate. Once we were at the gate, people began to busily retrieve their carry-on baggage from the overheads.

"Hey, Zeke, don't forget to call me about the job."

I looked up at Jeff. He was already out of his seat waiting to exit the plane. I was in no hurry. A lot of people had to get off the plane before I could get off.

I guess that was one drawback about sitting in the back of the plane. Yeah, you were first on the plane, but you were last off the plane.

"Don't worry, Jeff. I will call you and let you know whether I want the job or not. I owe it to my father to discuss it with him before I make a final decision."

"That's okay, Zeke. I fully understand that you would need to talk it over with your father. You should respect his advice. Have a great time this week, and enjoy the sunshine!"

"I will, Jeff, thanks."

Jeff hustled off down the aisle as the nearest passenger was now at least fifty feet in front of him. I got out of my seat and began my walk to the exit door. I was finally on the ground in Tampa, twelve hundred miles away from home and loving it already.

Chapter 29

We arrived at the hotel and checked in at the front desk at one o'clock. The clerk told us that our rooms would not be ready for us until three o'clock. She seemed like a nice lady and told us just to leave our bags at the front desk, and we could pick them up later to take to our room. Our trip chaperone, Ms. Stafford, told us to all gather in the lobby so she could explain the events scheduled for the day. I noticed that everyone stayed their distance from me. I didn't care. I wasn't there to be with them anyway. I was there to enjoy Florida and have fun. I didn't need anyone to have fun. I had learned a long time ago that I could have fun by myself.

We all listened while Ms. Stafford explained that we were going to hang around the pool at the hotel today. Lunch and dinner would be provided in the hotel restaurant. She finally ended with, "Please feel free to ask questions, but please state your name as I am not familiar with everyone in the group."

"Yes, my name is Zeke Baker, when are we going to Clearwater Beach?"

"Good question, Mr. Baker, we will be going to Clearwater Beach every day of our stay starting tomorrow. Our plans are to have a cookout and bonfire at the beach on the evening of the third night of our stay. I'm sure everyone will enjoy their stay and the terrific weather that is forecasted."

We had lunch, and the food was great. I sat at a table by myself, which was fine with me. After lunch Ms. Stafford stood in the center of the tables and said, "Okay, we need to pick room partners for our stay, but we have one problem, we do not have an even number of boys. So for this trip, one of you will be lucky enough to have a room by yourself."

I quickly said, "I'll stay by myself if it's okay with the rest of the boys in the crowd."

"Well, okay, Mr. Baker, but I think we should see if any of the other boys would like a room alone before we make a final decision. Now, is there any other boy who would like to have a room alone?"

I looked around the crowd to see if anyone had the nerve to challenge my request to be alone. No, none of these fools would have the nerve to challenge me, and I knew it. Not a soul spoke a word.

"Well, Mr. Baker, I guess you're the lucky winner of the room-alone contest. I hope you enjoy your stay in Florida."

"Thanks, Ms. Stafford, I'm sure I will enjoy my stay in Florida."

"Okay, everyone, it's time to grab your bags and get to your rooms, so let's go to the front desk and get our keys."

There were a total of twenty-six of us, including Ms. Stafford, so we needed fourteen rooms—six for the girls, six for the boys, one for me, and one for Ms. Stafford. We all gathered our keys and raced to our rooms to put on our swimsuits.

My room number was 128, about halfway down the hall on the first floor. I opened the door and was in awe. I had never been in a hotel room before. The linens on the bed were crisp and neat. The bathroom was spotless with a nice, shiny ceramic tile floor. Small bottles of shampoo and lotion stood next to tiny bars of soap on the bathroom sink. Fresh-smelling white towels and washcloths hung neatly on the towel bar. My feet gently sank into the carpet with each step as I walked across the bedroom. I pulled back the curtain on the patio door and was amazed that my room was exactly at the center of the end of the pool where the diving board was located. This is perfect, just put on my suit and walk out the patio door to the pool. Wow, it can't get any better than this.

I quickly changed and stepped out into the pool area. The pool was great. A bar area with tables sat at one end of the pool, kind of tucked in the corner out of the way. It was a place where you could have a Coke, chips, hot dog, and a candy bar. The entire pool area was very nice. I sat down in one of the lounge chairs near the entrance of the pool. The temperature was about eighty degrees now with cloudless sunshine. What a great day!

I lay back in the lounge chair and closed my eyes. I could feel the warmth of the sun soak into every pore in my body. Relaxation overcame me, and I drifted off to sleep.

Dreams quickly came to me in my sleep. The image of the burning straw stack raced into my mind. I imagined what the expression on Rich's face would look like if he awoke just before the flames overtook him. I could see his eyes clearly in my dreams. It was sheer horror in his eyes as the flames quickly approached him. He was choking on the smoke that filled the straw chamber. He was like a caged animal unable to escape, unable to save himself. I could hear his muffled screams, his attempted cries for help. I could see flames leaping from his clothes as he dropped off into unconsciousness. I imagined the tremendous pain and torture that Rich experienced during his last seconds of life. It was as if I were in the straw chamber with him.

A chill came across my body, and I slowly came out of my dreams and back to reality. I sensed a presence close to me, too close. I opened my eyes, and there sat Ms. Stafford next to me in a bathing suit, reading a book.

"You were kind of restless in your sleep, weren't you, Mr. Baker?"

"Yeah, I guess I was dreaming. By the way, call me Zeke, not Mr. Baker."

"Okay. Zeke it is. What were you dreaming about?"

"Oh, nothing. You know, just normal stuff that you think about every day."

"I know that I dream of falling sometimes, and I almost jump out of bed."

"Yeah, I've had those dreams."

We talked for a long time. She actually seemed like a very nice lady. During our conversation, I found out that she was twenty-nine years old and had moved to the Monroe area at the beginning of the school year to become an English teacher at the local high school. She was not married, but was engaged to be married to a man named Brad, who remained back in her home state of Wisconsin.

Brad was a physical education teacher at the high school in Rhinelander and was trying to land a teaching job in the Monroe area so he could be with her.

"Well, Ms. Stafford—"

"Wait a minute, Zeke! If I have to call you Zeke, you have to call me Mary when the other kids aren't around."

"Okay, I will call you Mary when nobody's around. I think I'll go for a swim now."

"That sounds like a great idea, Zeke," she replied.

I then stood up and began to walk to the edge of the pool. I turned back to look at Ms. Stafford for a moment. She had this funny look on her face. It almost appeared to be a look of intrigue. It was like I had piqued her interest, and she was suddenly unsure of herself. She quickly looked away as our eyes met.

I jumped in the pool and swam around for a while. After a few minutes, I looked back at her chair. She was gone and nowhere to be seen at the pool. I thought about our conversation for a moment and the look in her eyes. I just shrugged it off, got out of the pool, grabbed a towel, and headed toward the patio door and entered my room to change clothes.

I sat on the edge of my bed for a while thinking about the events of the day. This is going to be a great vacation. None of my classmates on the trip will bother me; they know better. I will be able to relax at the beach or at poolside, eat when I want, and sleep when I want. I knew that everyone had to be in their room for the night at ten o'clock. That was fine with me, because if I wanted to go out for the night after bed check, all I needed to do was slip out the patio door into the pool area and circle back to the lobby and out the front door of the hotel.

It was time for dinner, and I was hungry, so I headed to the dining room at the hotel. The dining room was rather large, and our tables were reserved in the back right corner of the room. Many of my classmates were already seated.

I sat down at the far end of the table away from everyone else. Others began to take their seats, and the last one to arrive at the table was Ms. Stafford.

At this point, the only seat left was next to me. She looked over at me and said, "Well, Zeke, it looks like I have to sit next to you tonight."

"Yeah, I guess so. It's the only seat left."

Ms. Stafford spent a great deal of time talking with Lucy, one of my classmates who sat directly across the table from her. I just listened and responded back only when someone spoke directly to me, which wasn't very often. I sat and ate dinner quietly. The food was great. I had baked grouper, which was delicious. I knew that I liked to eat fish, but I had never had fish that tasted this good.

After dinner I returned to the pool side café. I sat alone and ordered a Coke from a waitress named Gina. She seemed to be very happy with her job and had a huge smile on her face when she greeted me. I sat and watched as some of the other students swam and played around the pool. Some of my female classmates looked very attractive in their swimsuits. A couple of them wore two-piece suits that seemed to draw boys into the pool area like magnets to steel. I kind of laughed inside. I'd bet that none of these dopes have had sex with a girl yet. I had already been with two girls, and I really didn't have any interest in being with one right now. Every time I got close to a girl, I got hurt, and I was really tired of it.

I thought back to my father and the kindness that he held within his heart toward me. He wasn't a bad person; he just had to do what Marie said or there would be hell to pay. I really couldn't blame him for his anger toward me at times. I could understand his frustration. He didn't want to be mean to me, but he was caught in the middle with no place to go. I don't know how he could stand to live with her at all. When she wasn't yelling at me, she was yelling at him. It seemed like most of the time she was yelling just to be yelling.

I looked down at my watch and was shocked to see that it was nearing nine o'clock. I got up from the table and made my way to my room to relax and watch television.

Tomorrow would be an entire day at Clearwater Beach. I was ready to enjoy a full day at the beach.

I opened my door and turned the television on and lay down on my bed. The next thing I remember was opening my eyes and seeing daylight peer through my patio window. I had fallen asleep almost as soon as my head hit the pillow. No dreams at all tonight, finally a peaceful full night of sleep. I felt great. I looked at the clock on the nightstand. It was 7:10 AM already. That was good. We were leaving the hotel for the beach at nine o'clock, so I had plenty of time to take a shower, get my stuff together for the beach, and have breakfast at eight o'clock in the dining room.

We all met at the hotel lobby at 8:45 AM to wait for the bus to take us to the beach. The bus was on time, and the ride to the beach was less than fifteen minutes. We all raced off the bus to lay claim to our portion of the beach with our beach towels. I wandered off fifty yards from the rest of my classmates and laid my towel on the far side of a stone wall that was approximately three feet high and extended out from the shore toward the ocean. The stone wall tapered as it proceeded out toward the ocean and disappeared in the sand about fifty feet from the water's edge. This would be great. I could lie here on my towel and enjoy another day of perfect warm weather and sunshine

I lay peacefully for a while, and then I heard people talking. They were moving in my direction, closer to me. I lay still and listened. I knew they couldn't see me unless they crossed over the stone wall to where I lay. As the voices got closer, I could tell that one voice was Beth, a girl in my class who was one of the football cheerleaders. She was really a beautiful girl, and in her two-piece suit, she was sure to draw a lot of attention from the other boys. The other voices were Dennis and Chuck. They were two guys who I knew from school. Football jocks who thought all girls at school should fall at their feet. They sat down just on the other side of the stone wall. They were discussing the upcoming prom at school.

Dinner for prom night was going to be held at the local Howard Johnson's just outside of the city of Monroe. The prom dance after dinner was scheduled to be held in the gymnasium at the high school. I hadn't decided whether I would attend the prom or not. I really had no desire to attend.

I sat quietly and listened to their conversation. Dennis and Chuck were talking about how good the food was going to be as they had apparently eaten at the restaurant before. Beth cut them off in mid sentence and said, "So the food's good, so what! Don't you guys want to have a good time on prom night this year? We already went to the junior prom last year. It was kind of a waste of time for all of us. All you guys do is stand around and talk to each other, and the girls stand around all night and wait for one of you guys to ask them to dance. It's our last chance to have fun before we go off to college. I'm going to State, Chuck, you're going to Northern, and Dennis is going to Eastern. We may never see each other again. We need to plan to have a blast. It will probably be our last chance ever."

Chuck spoke next and said, "Okay, Beth, what do you think we should do on prom night?"

"I think we should go to dinner and then skip the dance and go out to the beach on Lake Erie at the state park and party. You guys can get some beer somewhere, can't you?"

"Yeah, I have a buddy who can get some beer for us," Dennis replied.

Beth giggled like a small child. "Great, then it's a plan!"

Chuck now took over the conversation. "Let's think about this a minute. The park closes at 12:00 AM every night, dinner is at 5:00 PM, and the dance starts at 7:00 PM. If we leave right after dinner, we should be at the beach no later than 6:30 PM. That will be perfect. There's one problem, how are we going to have the beer on the beach with the DNR constantly patrolling the area?"

"That's easy, stupid," Beth replied. "We'll park the car at the last beach parking lot where the fishermen park their cars and walk to the end of the beach where the channel to the lake separates the state park from Ford Motor Company property. The beach is closed at this end of the park because of storm damage.

I read in the paper where it will remain closed because the state does not want to spend the money that it will take to restore the beach."

"The DNR has no reason to patrol there. We will be out of sight, and after dark, we will be the only ones on the beach anyway."

"What about the car? They'll see the car, won't they?" Dennis replied.

Beth, now frustration in her voice, said, "Yeah, they'll see the car and think it's some fisherman's car who's fishing in the channel. Hey, if you guys don't want to do this, then I'll find somebody who will!"

Both Dennis and Chuck immediately responded with, "No, no, it's okay with us. It sounds like a great idea. We just need to make sure we leave the park before 12:00 AM because they lock the gates when they close."

"Don't worry, boys. We'll leave the park by 12:00 AM so you can check in with your mommies!"

"No, it's not that. We'll go somewhere else and party with you. Our parents don't expect us home until the next morning anyway," Chuck responded.

"Great, then it's a plan. You guys get the beer. We'll have a small campfire, drink, and have fun! Let's go for a swim now!"

I heard them race off toward the ocean together. I was familiar with the area that they were talking about. I fished there with my father a couple of times. It is about a half-mile walk from the parking lot to where the lake meets the channel. A marsh lies directly across the channel from the state park. It is part of the property of the Monroe Ford plant. My uncle was the head of security at the Monroe plant.

He told me that the Ford big shots used the marsh for duck hunting, and nobody else was allowed in there. His security guards drove the perimeter road of the property every two hours to make sure that no trespassers were on the property.

Beth never spoke to me at school or anywhere else. She always turned away from me when she saw me. She acted like so many other people who thought they were better than I am.

Her father worked at the Monroe Auto Equipment and held a management position. They had a nice home on Hollywood Drive, the most expensive area to live in Monroe.

She knew that my family was poor, and she didn't want anything to do with a person like me who didn't have the money to buy her nice things.

I really didn't have any plans to attend the prom, but I had a reason for my parents to think so now. The Howard Johnson's was only one mile from my house, and the state park was another two miles past that. All I had to do was skip the dinner, hide in the brush next to the channel, and wait for them to arrive. After they arrive, I will sneak close enough to them so I can see and hear everything they say. It will be interesting to see what happens when these dopes get drunk.

I swam a little in the ocean and returned to my beach towel and lay down. I noticed that Beth looked at me when I walked back from the ocean to my towel. I could tell by the look on her face that she wondered if I had been next to the wall all the time. She was probably wondering if I had overheard her conversation with Dennis and Chuck. Let her wonder; I don't care.

Chapter 30

The next few days of the trip went by very quickly. It was about noon on our final day in Florida. We were staying at the hotel today because it was raining and forecasted to rain all day. I decided to go down to the hotel gift shop and see if I could find a gift for Mr. Morrow. He, like my father, had told me not to get him a gift, but I felt I at least owed him something for his kindness and help. I went out into the hall from my room, and Ms. Stafford was just coming out of her room. She was directly across the hall from my room. She had on a very nice light blue blouse and a pair of jeans that were probably a little tighter than they should be.

"Hi, Zeke, have you enjoyed the trip?"

"Yes, I have enjoyed the trip. I've had a great time!"

"Good, Zeke, I'm glad that you had the opportunity to enjoy yourself. Where are you going?"

"I'm going down to the hotel gift shop to look around."

"Okay, remember lunch is at noon in the dining room."

"Yeah, I remember. I'll be there."

Ms. Stafford has been very nice to me the entire trip, I thought. She has gone out of her way to talk to me and often sits next to me in the dining room and at the pool. She really is a very nice person.

The gift shop was empty except for the clerk who was sitting behind the counter reading a magazine. She glanced up at me when I walked in the door. She didn't even bother to ask if I needed any help; she just went back to reading her magazine. I looked around for a while and decided to buy a small polished ocean seashell and a can that was labeled Canned Florida Sunshine. I think Mr. Morrow will get a big laugh out of that.

I really would like to buy something for James. After all, without him I would have never been able to go on the trip. But I knew that if I bought him something, I would have to buy something for Marie.

She didn't deserve anything, and I was not about to buy her anything! I knew that she would get pissed off if I bought something for James. She'd yell at him for weeks because of it. I was tired of her yelling at him, and I'm sure that he was tired of it too.

I went up to the counter to pay for the items. The clerk was so focused on her magazine that she didn't even realize that I was there. I probably could have stolen the items, and she would have never known. After a few minutes, I said, "Excuse me." This seemed to startle her, and she looked up and glared at me and said, "What do you want?"

"I'd like to pay for these items."

I thought for a moment that in another place, at another time, I would have taught her a lesson. I would have knocked that glare off her face.

"That'll be five dollars and thirty-six cents," she barked.

I handed her a ten-dollar bill, and she gave me the change and immediately went back to reading her magazine.

I dropped the gifts off at my room and went to lunch with the rest of the crowd. Ms. Stafford sat next to me again. She was a friendly person, not like other teachers. She really seemed to be interested in me as a person, not just as a student.

Beth sat directly across the table from me with Dennis next to her and Chuck sitting next to me. I thought this to be a little odd. All these guys avoid me. Why are they sitting near me now?

I ordered my food as Ms. Stafford made small talk with Beth and Dennis. They talked about the football season and Beth's four-year career as a cheerleader. I just sat and listened. Ms. Stafford excused herself to go to the bathroom just as my food arrived. I had just begun to eat my lunch when Beth said, "Zeke."

I looked over at her and thought, *Why the hell is she talking to me? She never talks to me.*

"What?"

"Are you planning on going to the prom this year?"

"I don't know, it's none of your business anyway."

"Just answer her question, Zeke," Chuck said.

I turned and looked at Chuck with anger in my eyes.

"What the hell are you going to do if I don't answer her question?"

He slumped in his chair. He knew he was no match for me, and I could tell he was already sorry for what he had said. I had to be careful here. I didn't want them to cancel their plans because of me.

"Don't get mad, Zeke. We just thought you might like to hang out with us at the prom," Chuck replied in a sheepish voice.

I thought for a moment before I answered him. I really didn't want to screw this up.

"I don't know why you guys would want to hang out with me. None of you have ever gone out of your way to talk to me or even made an attempt to be my friend. But that doesn't matter. I'm not going to the prom anyway. I plan on going to the teen club that night and enjoy myself. You guys go and have a good time."

"Okay, Zeke, we just thought that you might like to hang out with us and have some fun. It would be kind of a last hurrah before we go off to college."

"Well, I'm not going to college, Chuck, so I don't need any last hurrah or any new friends."

All three of them got up and left the table at the same time. I really hope that they don't change their plans. After all, I was looking forward to watching them at the park. It would be kind of a last hurrah for me.

Ms. Stafford returned to the table and said, "What happened to Beth, Dennis, and Chuck?"

"Oh, they said they weren't hungry, so they left to go to the pool since it has now stopped raining. I guess you can't trust the Florida weatherman."

Mary chuckled and said, "Okay, they'll probably get a hot dog or something to snack on at the poolside café."

"Yeah, they probably will."

I finished my lunch and went to my room. I sat on the bed staring out the patio door toward the pool area. Many of my classmates had started gathering at the pool. The sun was out now, and it was about eighty degrees. It was developing into a perfect afternoon. I saw Beth, Dennis, and Chuck sitting at the far end of the pool laughing and carrying on. I hated people like them. They had a sense of self-worth that was far beyond reality. They really needed to be knocked down to their proper level in life. I just sat there watching everyone for a while. They were all having a great time. This was probably one of the many great times that they have had over their life. Funny, this was the first good time that I can remember since my grandfather held me so many years ago.

I put on my swimsuit and walked out to the poolside. It was 3:00 PM, so I had plenty of time to enjoy the sun before dinner. I went down near the end of the pool where Beth, Dennis, and Chuck sat. I lay down in a lounge chair directly across the pool from them. They didn't even notice I was there. They were having too much fun. It wasn't long before Ms. Stafford came over and sat down next to me.

"Enjoying the final hours of your last day here, Zeke?"

"Yep, the weather sure won't be like this when we get back to Michigan."

"No, it's still pretty cold there. Zeke, I've noticed that you don't really interact with any of your other classmates. Is there a reason for that?"

"No reason, I just like to be by myself. I like it better that way. Nobody expects anything from you if you don't expect anything from them. I'm kind of a lone wolf."

"I guess it makes sense, Zeke, but don't you think you would have more fun if you at least spent some time with your classmates?"

"No, I don't think so. When I was growing up, I tried being friends with other kids, and it only led to problems."

"I know your past, Zeke. Many of the other teachers speak of you, and none of them like you. As I understand it, you have been labeled as a problem child for a long time. I don't quite understand it. I don't even look at you as a child. I have talked with you numerous times during this trip, and you have always been nothing but a gentleman. I think you somehow got a bad rap years ago. I think your reputation has just followed you through the years. It's really a shame."

"Well, sometimes things happen for a reason. Maybe I really am a bad guy. Maybe you only see the good in me, and everyone else sees the bad."

"I don't think so, Zeke. I'm a pretty good judge of character, and I think deep down inside you're a good person."

I was thinking about telling her just how wrong she was when one of the girls at the end of the pool called her over to take a picture with them. She got up out of the chair and smiled at me as she walked away.

I went back to my room and watched television for a while and then got dressed and went to the dining room for dinner. I had stuffed flounder for dinner. God, was it good! I had never had food so delicious in my life. After dinner I went back to my room and changed into my other swimsuit that was dry so I could lie on the bed and watch television for a while before I went out to the pool. I closed all the curtains so no one could look in the room to see what I was doing. I did not want to be bothered. The hotel attendant locked the gate to the pool at 10:00 PM every night. I had plenty of time to relax before taking a quick swim in the pool.

I was laughing at the *Three Stooges* on television when I heard a knock on my door. I looked over at the clock on the nightstand. It was 7:55 PM. Who could that be? I hoped it wasn't Beth, Dennis, and Chuck. If it were, there was sure to be trouble.

I opened the door, and standing there in her robe was Ms. Stafford. She had a tall glass half filled with some amber-colored liquid and ice in her right hand. I looked at her and said, "Hi, Ms. Stafford. What do you want?"

"It's Mary, remember? Is it okay if I come in, Zeke?"

"Sure, it's okay, Mary."

I opened the door, and she entered the room. I could smell liquor on her breath as she walked past me. She walked into the bathroom and then looked in the closet.

"Is there something that you're looking for, Mary?"

"No, I just wanted to make sure that we're alone, Zeke. I wanted to continue our conversation from this afternoon. We got interrupted when the girls called me over for a picture."

"Yeah, I know. But I really don't want to talk about my past. I'm enjoying myself, and I want to keep it that way."

Wow, it was very obvious that Ms. Stafford had quite a bit to drink. She was having trouble walking straight, and she had a slight slur to her words when she talked.

"Okay, okay, Zeke. We can talk about anything you want to talk about."

I sat down on my bed and looked up at her. I didn't have anything to talk to her about. I couldn't think of anything to say. Maybe I could talk to her about things she liked to do when she was growing up, or maybe I could talk to her about her home state of Wisconsin. Yeah, I'll do that.

Before I could say anything, she sat down on the bed next to me. The top to her robe opened slightly and exposed her bare breasts to me. God, they were perfect! She looked over at me and glanced down to see what I was looking at. She gently put her hand under my chin and raised my eyes to hers.

"Do you like what you see, Zeke?"

"Yes, Mary, you are beautiful."

"Thank you, Zeke. I hoped that you would like me."

She leaned over to kiss me. Our lips met, and her tongue entered my mouth. I was immediately aroused. Her hands clawed at my trunks. She pulled them off and threw them on the floor. She then slipped her robe off her shoulders, and I watched as it gently fell to the floor. My God, her body was beautiful. I was immediately filled with desire. She climbed on top of me, and in less than a second, we were having sex. She was incredible! I reached up and grabbed her breasts. She leaned her head back and screamed with passion. I was a little nervous that someone in the adjoining room would hear us, but that thought quickly left me as I rose to an explosive orgasm. She fell down on my chest, and both of our bodies trembled for several minutes.

"God, Zeke, that was really terrific. I'm glad that you wanted me. I have wanted you ever since we got here, and I didn't know how to ask you."

"I'm really glad you came to my room tonight, Mary. You are beautiful, and I never thought that you would want me to make love to you."

"I don't know why you would think that, Zeke. You're a very handsome young man, and I think a lot of women my age would want you."

"What about your fiancé, Brad?"

"What about him? He'll never find out that we made love unless you tell him."

"Well, I guess you don't need to worry about that because I don't even know him."

She smiled at me and began to kiss me again. We had sex that night in every position imaginable until we were both exhausted and drifted off to sleep.

When I woke up, she was lying next to me with her arms around me. I looked over at the clock on the nightstand. It was 6:15 AM. I needed to wake her up. We were scheduled to leave for the airport at 8:30 AM. I kissed her on the forehead while I gently caressed her right breast. She woke up, and a huge grin came across her face.

"Wow, it was quite a night, wasn't it, Zeke?"

"Yeah, it was a night I'll never forget."

"Zeke, please don't tell anyone about this. I would lose my job, and I can't afford that."

"Don't worry, I won't tell anyone. Remember, I don't have any friends anyway, so I really don't have anyone to tell."

"Thanks, Zeke. Wow, 6:30 AM already. I was hoping that we would have time to make love again this morning, but I guess not. We have to get moving so we can get to the airport."

She jumped out of bed and quickly put her robe on and tied the belt and started to walk to the door.

"Mary."

"Yes, Zeke."

"I would like it if you would sit with me on the plane. Can you do that?"

"Sure, Zeke, I'd be glad to sit with you."

"Let me check the hallway to make sure it's clear so you can get to your room without anyone seeing you."

"Good idea, Zeke."

I got out of bed and looked at my swimsuit lying on the floor where she had tossed it the night before. The entire night flashed through my mind again. God, I wanted her! I put my swimsuit on and cracked the door open to check the hallway.

"The coast is clear, Mary."

She slipped through the doorway and kissed me as she exited the room toward hers.

I jumped into the shower. I couldn't get the events of the evening out of my mind. I was really lucky to have slept with her. In my mind, she was really out of my league.

We all met at the front of the lobby to board the bus for the airport. Mary smiled at me as she entered the lobby area. She was dressed much more reserved now than she had been during our stay. She had on a business suit and a blouse that buttoned at the neck. It didn't matter. She was still beautiful.

Mary stood next to the bus as everyone boarded. I was the last to board. She stopped me as I started to board.

"Give me your airline ticket, Zeke, so I can get us seated together."

"Okay, here."

I handed her my ticket and boarded the bus. The driver pulled the lever to close the door, and the bus lurched forward toward the hotel exit. It took about twenty minutes to get to the Tampa airport. Everyone piled off the bus and headed inside the terminal for our departure. Ms. Stafford walked up to the ticket agent with my ticket and had our seats assigned together just as she promised. We boarded the plane on schedule.

Our seats were at the back of the plane, so I went and sat down while Ms. Stafford made sure that all students were on board. When all students were seated, she came and sat down next to me.

The seat directly across from us was vacant, so I put my hand on her leg, and she immediately put her hand on mine. This made the trip home far less painful than it would have been.

James was waiting for me at the gate when I got off the plane. I introduced Ms. Stafford to James and told her good-bye. Inside I wanted to go with her. I couldn't wait to make love to her again.

"Well, Zeke, did you have a good time?"

"It was better than I ever imagined that it would be, Dad. It was really a perfect trip, and I'm glad that you made it possible for me to go."

"You deserved it, Zeke. I'm glad that I saved the money for you. There's enough left for you to get out of town if you want to and make a new life for yourself. It's really up to you now. You'll be out of school for good in six weeks. All the decisions for your life after that will be made by you and you alone.

I looked out the side window of the car and watched the cars stream by as we entered I-94 eastbound toward home. I thought about James's words to me. Decisions made by you and you alone. He had no idea that Zeke had made plenty of his own decisions already. Zeke has already decided that he was in charge and will never be controlled by anyone again.

Chapter 31

The remaining days of school dragged past as I waited for prom night. Beth, Chuck, and Dennis were keeping their distance from me as most people do. That was fine with me. I didn't want them asking any more stupid questions. I wanted them to keep their party plans for prom night. After all, this was their last hurrah, wasn't it?

I wanted to be with Ms. Stafford again. She was on my mind all the time. I tried to talk with her a couple of times, but someone always came along and interrupted us. I was going crazy with passion for her. Three weeks had passed since our fantastic night of sex in Florida. I decided that the only way to talk with her alone was to wait for her after school. I knew where she parked her car in the parking lot at the back of the high school. It would be difficult to meet her there because many other teachers parked in the same lot. How the hell was I going to talk to her alone?

I thought about it all day and finally decided to put a note under her windshield-wiper blade. I slipped out into the parking lot at lunchtime and placed the note under her wiper. The note read,

"Please meet me at the Macomb Street riverfront parking lot after school tonight, [signed] Zeke."

I walked quickly to the Macomb Street parking lot after school that night. It was a cool, clear afternoon. Seagulls glided past across the river just inches from the water, then up and over the Macomb Street Bridge. They were really very graceful birds. The parking lot sat about fifteen feet above the level of the river. I became very nervous when I approached the parking lot, as this was very near the place where Whitey attacked me several years before. I walked over to the edge of the guardrail above the river and looked across to the spot where Whitey held me captive. Anger grew inside me. My mind raced through the sequences of events that surrounded Whitey's demise. Blood rushed through my veins and roared to my brain. My head began to pound. I again blacked out with anger as I had so many times in the past.

"Zeke, Zeke," I heard faintly in my pounding head.

I snapped out of my rage coma and turned around to face the intruder speaking my name. It was Ms. Stafford sitting in her car. I didn't even hear her drive into the parking lot. Before I could say anything, she said, "Quick, get in the car before someone sees you!"

I ran around to the passenger side of the car, jumped in, and closed the door. She immediately drove the car to the very back of the parking lot in the northeast corner facing the river. She put the car in park and turned the engine off. I looked at her and said, "God, Mary, I've missed you so much."

"I know you have, Zeke. I could tell it in your eyes every time I saw you at school. But we really need to talk."

"Okay, what do you want to talk about?"

"Well, Zeke, we need to talk about us."

"What about us?"

"Zeke, the night we had in Florida was terrific, and I will never forget that. But I am a teacher, and I need this job. I can't afford to lose my job because of an affair with a student. I hope you understand, Zeke. I mean, I have a fiancée, a career, and a future right now. I just can't continue to see you. I've lain awake at night thinking how to tell you. I don't want to hurt you, Zeke. You are really a good person inside, and I do care about you. You are nothing like the person who was described to me by the teachers who think they know you. You need to believe me when I tell you that they don't know you at all."

What a fool I am! When am I going to learn that girls and women are nothing but trouble, heartache, and pain? My God, I am really stupid! I must have been out of my mind to think that someone like her would care about someone like me. She's a beautiful lady with a future. She doesn't want a punk like me to hang around and ruin her future. All she wanted was to use me when she needed me and throw me aside when she was done. Just like Nicole and Polly before her. I was nothing to them.

Anger filled every inch of my body now. Rage was taking control of me, and I couldn't stop it. I looked over at her and said, "You really don't understand, do you?"

"What do you mean, Zeke? What don't I understand?"

"You don't understand me at all. I am not a good person, everyone knows that, and you're too stupid to understand it. You're just like every other female who I've been with. All you care about is yourself. You could care less about me. I should really teach you a lesson, a lesson you'll remember for the rest of your life. In fact, maybe I will."

My eyes burned into hers, and a look of intense fear crossed her face.

"My God, Zeke, you're scaring me!"

"Don't worry, Mary. I'm not going to hurt you now, but think of me when you go to your car in the parking lot after school, or when you lie down to go to sleep at night, or maybe when you're in the shower. Yes, think of me because I'll be there when you least expect it. That sound that goes *bang* in the night just might be me. Of course, you could leave here and report this conversation to the police, and no doubt they would come after me. But before you do that, you might consider what I would tell them about Florida. Yeah, that's right. Let's see, a teacher and a student together in bed. You would be ruined for life. It would be impossible for you to get a teaching job again. The scandal would end your relationship with Brad, and you would be alone. You would probably be homeless living on the street, sleeping in a heap of cardboard boxes. Not a pretty sight, not pretty at all. But what the hell, maybe I'll just tell them anyway. I've got nothing to lose. In fact if this got out, the other students would even have a greater respect for me."

"No, Zeke, please don't do that. Please don't tell anyone about us. You really are the monster that they told me about. You are a mean and evil person deep down inside. I misjudged you. You are not the person I knew just a few weeks ago in Florida."

"You aren't the person you were in Florida either, Mary. You judged me wrong then, and you're judging me wrong now! I am really worse than you think. I am your worst nightmare. I am the fear that lives and grows inside you, fear that you cannot escape. The things you heard about me are far from the truth. The truth is that I am far more evil than you or anyone else can comprehend. But I'm willing to give you a break and not tell anyone our secret. Unfortunately, my silence has certain conditions.

"Conditions, what conditions, Zeke?"

I laughed. "Well, I guess you could really call them rules, rules you must live by. You simply follow my instructions, kind of like an assignment that you would give to your class at school. Your assignment is easy, Mary. It should come natural to you, and the instructions are very simple to follow. You must have sex with me when I tell you, where I tell you, and whenever I ask you."

Now the fear was replaced on her face with total panic. "No, Zeke, we can't. We'll get caught. It's too much of a risk."

"Really. Well, okay, Mary. I'll see you around, or I'll read about you in the newspaper."

I opened the car door and began to get out of the car. She grabbed my arm and pulled me back in the car.

"Wait, Zeke, I'll do what you want, but we need to be careful."

"Careful? Why, I have nothing to lose. No, I have nothing to lose at all. In fact, I want you now!"

"Now, right here in the car, Zeke?"

"Yes, right here in the car, unless you'd rather do it on the riverbank where everyone driving over the bridge can see us."

"No, the car is okay. We'll do it in the car."

"Great, get in the backseat, bitch."

She looked sternly at me, but she knew not to bother talking back to me. She knew that I controlled the situation now. She also knew that I would make good on my threat if necessary. God, the feeling of control came over me, and it was great. I was in total control of the situation, and I loved it!

Mary got out of the front seat and quickly entered the backseat of the car. I just jumped over the front seat into the backseat. She was wearing a nice navy blue skirt with a long-sleeve white blouse that buttoned up the front. It had a ruffled front with a lace collar. She took off her shoes, then her nylons, and finally her panties. I was tearing off my clothes rapidly. I was more than ready for her.

"Okay, Zeke. I'm ready, please hurry. I don't want anyone to see us."

"You're not ready yet. When you're ready, we'll do it."

"I am ready, Zeke. Please hurry, I want you."

"Nice try. I know that you really don't want me. You're just saying that to please me. We'll start when you take the rest of your clothes off."

"No, Zeke, I can't be totally naked here in the car. It would take me too long to get my clothes on if someone came near us."

"Quit talking and take them off now!"

"Okay, okay, please quit raising your voice. Someone will hear you."

Mary took off her remaining clothes and laid them on the floor of the car. She now lay naked in front of me. I could faintly see her bathing suit tan lines from our Florida trip. The tan lines were much like the memories of our trip to Florida. They, much like our Florida memories, were also fading. She was really beautiful, but that really didn't matter to me now. She was just something for me to use now. Any feelings that I had for her were gone, and any respect that I had for her was gone also.

I looked into her eyes and said, "Get up so I can lie down on the seat because you're getting on top."

She didn't even question me this time; she just moved aside so I could lie down. As soon as I was in position, she got on top of me. The sex was great. I didn't know if she liked it or not, nor did I care. It was really all about me now.

When I finished, I started to put my clothes back on so I could leave. She reached for her clothes, and I blocked her hand.

"No, you're not putting your clothes on until after I leave. I still want to look at you."

"Zeke, please let me put my clothes on, I see a man walking toward us. His car may be parked near us, Zeke. He'll see me here with you."

"So what? I like seeing you naked, maybe he will too."

I looked around to see who was coming. It was an elderly man who looked to be around eighty years old, and he was walking very slowly. He stopped about fifty feet from Mary's car and got into an old Dodge sedan. Too bad, I was starting to get excited about him getting a look at her. I wanted her humiliated; she deserved it.

I finished dressing and opened the car door to get out. I looked back at her. She sat there trying to cover her breasts with her hands.

"Hey, take your hands off them. I want to see them again before I leave!"

She slowly pulled her hands away so I could take one last look.

"Don't try to avoid me, Mary. Remember, when I want you, you need to be where I tell you, when I tell you. Trust me, I will spill my guts if you decide not do what I want."

"Okay, Zeke, I will do what you want. Just don't hurt me. I don't want to be afraid all the time. I really need to be able to keep my thoughts straight so I can teach classes."

"If you behave, you won't need to worry. But if you don't, then I'll have to deal with you. The choice is yours."

"I'll be good, Zeke, you don't have to worry."

With that I slammed the car door and walked toward the street. I thought about what she said. *I'll be good, Zeke, and you don't have to worry.* What a bunch of crap! I have been lied to by every girl or woman I trusted, and I wasn't about to trust her. When the time comes, when I don't need her anymore, I will make sure that she can be trusted. I will make sure that she never talks to anyone about me.

Chapter 32

Senior prom night is tomorrow. I have been with Ms. Stafford several times since our meeting at the Macomb Street parking lot. She is behaving very well and knows her place with me now. She never complains anymore, and she always does everything that I ask of her. I've even had sex with her one evening on her backyard picnic table. She was extremely nervous about it, but it excited the hell out of me. I imagined her neighbors watching us in the darkness through their windows. It was really a rush for me.

Marie is dead set against me going to the prom. I lay in my room tonight and listened to her scream at James.

"That boy has been a problem his entire life. He has caused us nothing but trouble, and you continue to protect him and let him do what he wants. He'll be the death of you yet!"

"Now, Marie, that boy has worked hard to make it through school, and he deserves to enjoy himself and attend the prom. It's his last chance to be with his friends at high school. It will be a night that he will remember forever."

They argued on and on into the night. I really didn't care what Marie said; I was going to the prom, and she wasn't about to stop me. James worked hard and kept defending me, and she kept tearing me down. He was fighting a losing battle with Marie. But he wasn't about to give up. I drifted off to sleep thinking about what James had said. *It will be a night that he will remember forever.* Funny, that's exactly the way I looked at it too.

When I awoke the next morning, James was sitting at the kitchen table drinking coffee. I walked into the kitchen, and he greeted me with a huge grin on his face.

"Good morning, Zeke! Are you ready for the big day?"

"Good morning, Dad. I'm ready, but I don't think Mom wants me to go to the prom. I overheard you guys talking last night."

"Don't worry about that, Zeke. You're going to the prom, and that's final. In fact, I'm going to let you use the car."

I had taken a driver's education class at school last year and passed the driving test at the sheriff's office. After I got my driver's license, James took the opportunity to let me get some driving experience on our local country roads. He would ride in the passenger seat and correct me when I made any false moves or errors during these driving exercises. He was really a good teacher and very patient.

I knew that James had probably sold his soul to Marie so that she would agree with this. No way could I turn him down on his offer. I couldn't disappoint him by telling him I didn't want the car, but this presented a problem to me. I had planned on riding my bike out to Waterworks Street, near the state park, and hiding it in the brush while I walked the final two miles to the site where Beth, Dennis, and Chuck planned to party. What the heck am I going to do with the car? I can't tell James that I don't want it. He would be disappointed because this was probably something that he fought for desperately with Marie. Thoughts and ideas raced through my mind. Wait a minute! I could drive the car out near the area and park it in the parking lot of the Waterworks Bar. The Waterworks Bar was a small bar located on the corner of Waterworks Street and Dixie Highway. They were famous for their bar burgers and fries. James had taken me there for a burger one day after we had fished at the state park. The burgers were really good.

"That will be great, Dad! I don't know how you got Mom to agree to that, but I really appreciate your trust in me."

"That's okay, Zeke. You really deserve this, and I want you to enjoy your night."

"Thanks, Dad."

I walked back into my room and sat on the edge of the bed for several minutes going through my prom night plan in my mind. I needed to be sure that I was undetected on that night. I had to make certain that I was not seen by anyone. The only thing I can do is park in the back of the bar and walk through the fields of weeds and brush that grow from the bar parking lot to the edge of Waterworks Street.

It was only a couple of hundred yards and much more concealed than walking up Dixie Highway from the parking lot to Waterworks Street. This is really the best place to leave the car and enter the state park without being detected.

School was only a half-day session today, but the time dragged for me. I wanted to get out and get to my hiding place along the channel near the lake. I couldn't wait to spy on those dopes. I watched as the clock slowly ticked its way to noon. I had decided to walk to school today. It was really a beautiful spring day, sunny and the temperature was nearing eighty degrees already. It will be a great night for a stroll near the lake.

James was at home when I arrived. He was putting the finishing touches on cleaning the car when I walked up the sidewalk. He didn't have to leave for work until 3:30 PM. James planned to walk to work today so that I could have the car for the prom. He often walked to work, even in the winter. The paper factory was about one-half mile from home. The main reason that he walked to work was because of Marie's constant bitching about wasting his money on gas for the car. She bitched so much about it that James walked to work even on the coldest evenings during the winter months. Sometimes I believed that James would do anything just to shut her up.

James grinned again when he saw me and said, "Well, Zeke, just a few more hours and the fun begins!"

"I'm sure it will be a good time, Dad. Everybody's talking about how good the food is at Howard Johnson's and how great the band is that will be playing at the dance. I can't wait until five o'clock gets here so I can enjoy the dinner before the dance begins."

"I hope you have a good time, son."

"I plan on having a great time!"

I left James and went into the house. Marie must be in her bedroom, and that's fine with me. At least she'll leave me alone for a little while longer. I need to get my clothes together for tonight.

I plan on wearing a suit to dinner, and I need to have jeans, tennis shoes, and a shirt for after the dance. Of course, I was not going to the dinner or the dance, but I was the only one who knew that. My plan was to change clothes in the parking lot of the bar and then begin my walk to the lake. I placed my after-dance clothes, along with my flashlight, in a small suitcase and carried it out to the car. James threw me the keys as I walked up to the car.

"Okay, Zeke. I put the finishing touches on her, she's all yours now."

"Thanks again, Dad!"

James went over to the house and began to roll the hose up. I stood there and looked at the car. It was shining brightly in the sunlight, and it really looked nice. It was a 1961 Plymouth Belvedere, robin's egg blue in color. Under the hood was a 383 cubic inch motor that was very fast on the road. I was in the car one time with James a couple of years ago. We were on the expressway when he said, "It's time to blow the carbon out of this thing." He punched the pedal to the floor, we both lurched back into the seat, and the speedometer jumped to one hundred miles per hour almost instantly. It was really a beautiful and fast car.

I opened the trunk and put my suitcase inside. I tried to think of anything else that I may need for my adventure tonight. No, I had my flashlight; nothing else was really necessary. How would I know, anyway? I really didn't know if they were going to show up or not, and what could I possibly need even if they did?

I slammed the trunk closed and walked over to the house where James was finishing with the hose.

"Hey, Dad, I could really use a little cash for tonight if you can spare some."

"Sorry, Zeke, I almost forgot about that. Here, here's forty dollars. That should be enough. You won't need any gas for the car, I already filled it up."

"Forty dollars is more than enough, thanks!"

"That's okay, Zeke. Why don't you go cruise around town. I know that kids your age like to hang out at the Dixie Drive Inn Restaurant. Why don't you take the car and hang out there and talk with your friends?"

Poor James, he didn't know that Zeke really had no friends. I never really told him that I didn't make friends. No, I only made enemies. No need for him to know that. I just kept letting him think that I had friends like everybody else.

"Thanks, Dad, I'll go for a ride. I'm sure that some of the guys are at the Dixie right now."

"Be careful, Zeke. That car has a lot of power."

"I know, Dad. I'll be careful."

I backed the car out of the driveway and headed toward town. It was great to be behind the wheel of the car. It was even better that I didn't have to deal with Marie today. I didn't know where the hell she was, and I didn't care.

I cruised through the Dixie Drive Inn and then headed north on Monroe Street to the Park 'N' Snack. The Park 'N' Snack was another teen hangout that had burgers, fries, and drinks. The Dixie was at the south end of town, and the Park 'N' Snack was at the north end of town. The local teenagers cruised both of these locations to see their friends and meet girls. I noticed Beth leaning against a car at Park 'N' Snack as I started my cruise around the building. There was no sign of Dennis and Chuck. I began to wonder if I missed them at the Dixie. Both places were packed with seniors, and it was difficult to watch my driving and the activity of the people in the parking lot. When I drove around the building and circled back to the front parking lot, I heard someone yell, "Zeke, Zeke." I stopped the car and looked in the direction of the voice. It was

Beth. She was running over to my car. She had a huge smile on her face. My window was down, and she put her forearms on the side of the door, placing her face inches from mine, and said, “Hi, Zeke, what’s with the suit? Did you decide to go to the prom?”

I could smell beer on her breath already. I guess she planned on making an early start of it.

“No, I’m not going to the prom. I just put the suit on so I could get out of the house without any questions. My other clothes are in the trunk so I can change later. Right now I’m just out cruising through town and enjoying myself. What are you doing?”

“Oh, I’m just hanging out here. Chuck and Dennis just left in Dennis’s car to cruise the Dixie. I decided to stay here with my friends. Hey, Zeke, I’ve got a case of cold beer in the trunk of Chuck’s car, do you want one?”

“No, I’m good, but thanks anyway.”

“Come on, Zeke, it’s really good beer, one won’t hurt you.”

I knew that I needed to keep my senses about me, and I didn’t need beer; I needed to stay sharp.

“No, I don’t want any. I don’t want to take a chance on the cops picking me up. They don’t like me, and I don’t need to give them a reason to arrest me.”

“All right, Zeke, but you’re missing a good time. Won’t you change your mind about the prom?”

“Nope, there’s nothing at the prom that I want. You guys go and have a good time.”

“Okay, Zeke, maybe you’ll change your mind and come anyway.”

“Yeah, maybe, but I don’t think so.”

She turned back to her circle of friends, and I drove away. It was three o'clock now. I decided that I would go to Howard Johnson's and have a late lunch. After all, I wasn't going to be able to get dinner anyway, and I was hungry already.

The food was great, just as Dennis and Chuck had said it would be. I had a sixteen-ounce porterhouse steak with baked potato, corn, and a tossed salad. It was a perfect meal and very delicious.

The waitress brought the check, and I looked down at my watch. It was 4:15 PM already. I needed to get out of here before everybody started to arrive for dinner. I paid the bill and got into my car and drove out of the parking lot in the direction of the state park. It was still warm, and the sun was still shining brightly as it began its descent into the western skyline. It would be dark in a few hours, and I needed to get to the lake.

I pulled into the bar and drove to the back and parked under the limbs of a shaggy weeping willow tree. The limbs hung low to the ground almost concealing the car where I parked it. This is a perfect place to leave the car. Very few cars were in the front parking lot. I knew that anyone who came now would park in the front so they wouldn't have to walk so far to enter the bar. This made me feel somewhat safer with my plan.

I quickly changed into my jeans, shirt, and shoes. I tucked my flashlight into my back pocket and looked around very carefully to see if anyone was watching me. There were no houses near here. The rear of the bar had a solid-steel exit door from the kitchen to the parking lot. The bar had windows in the front and side of the building, but no windows were on the rear of the building. All the cars were in front of the building, so I would not be visible to anyone who exited the bar and went to their car.

I quickly slipped into the weeds and began my walk to Waterworks Street. I jumped across the roadside ditch and walked along the edge of the road toward the park. Waterworks Street was a gravel road that was seldom traveled. The road bordered the state park property on the east side and acres of farmland on the west side. The main entrance to the state park was about one-half mile from Waterworks Street, and most people visiting the park used that road because it was paved and well maintained.

I reached the side entrance to the park a little after five o'clock.

All seniors attending the prom would be eating dinner now at the restaurant. I hoped that Beth, Chuck, and Dennis were there. I was a little worried about Beth. If she kept drinking, she'd be passed out and wouldn't make the trip to the park. I hoped that wasn't the case.

I looked toward the check station where the DNR officer is normally stationed to sell daily or annual passes to the park. The shack where they normally sit is empty. This is normal for this time of day. I've been here before, and the officer always leaves for the day at 5:00 PM. I still have not seen any vehicles at all on the road. I turned and walked down the park entrance road toward the lake. I decided to walk directly down the road to a path that goes through a small wooded area to the lakeshore. From there I would walk down the beach south to the channel. I still had approximately one mile to walk after I reached the lakeshore. But I wasn't worried. I had plenty of time to make the trip before they finished dinner and drove to the parking lot nearest the channel.

When I reached the lake, I stopped for a moment to look out across the water. Seagulls swooped down from the sky occasionally to grab an unsuspecting fish for dinner. A few fishing boats bobbed up and down in the water. The wind was blowing slightly out of the west, so the lake was calmer than normal. But there was enough wind to make waves about a foot high. A few seagulls were sitting on the water, and with every wave, they would disappear on the down slope of the wave and reappear on the up slope. The entire beach was vacant of people. It was not quite the time of the year for people to be at the beach yet. The weather had been cool prior to the beginning of the week, so the water temperature was still cold.

I continued my walk on the beach toward the channel. I did not see a sign of anyone until I reached the parking lot nearest the channel. There sat two cars; both were empty. They were probably cars of fishermen fishing in the channel. This didn't bother me because I knew they would leave before darkness set in for the night. I was about a quarter mile from the channel now. I walked away from the shoreline toward the picnic area to see if the fishermen were fishing on the point where the lagoon meets the channel.

This is a place where the fishing is good, and most people fish here. I walked up behind a big sycamore tree and peered out toward the point. Yep, there they were fishing off the point. This was good because I would be hidden from them for the remainder of my walk, and I would be at least a half mile away from them when I reached my destination.

I turned back toward the lake and continued my journey. I finally reached the channel. I could only guess where they would set up their party site, but I figured they would want to be near the channel and the lake so they would go undetected. I found a great location to hide. One of the giant cottonwood trees had been blown down by the storm that went through here. It was at least four feet in diameter and made a perfect place for me to hide. I could sit on the limbs and look directly toward the lake, or I could just sit on the ground behind the trunk and peer over the trunk toward the lake. The limbs from the other side of the tree would camouflage me. This was a perfect spot. It was 5:45 PM now. It wouldn't be long before they arrived.

I lay back against the tree trunk and thought back about Whitey, Nicole, and Rich. They really deserved what they got. I wasn't sorry about killing them. They tried to control and hurt me, and I was tired of being hurt. They all should have stayed away from me. My mind drifted to many thoughts of the past, and it wasn't long before sleep overtook my body.

Chapter 33

I was snapped awake by the sound of voices. I lay motionless for several minutes, listening. I heard the familiar voice of Dennis yelling at Chuck, telling him to gather some wood so they could start a fire. Damn, I hear him breaking brush very near me. It sounds as if he is just on the other side of the tree where I'm hiding. I listen as he works his way toward the channel. It sounds like he has made at least three trips back to where Beth and Dennis are setting up camp. He was probably carrying firewood back to their campsite. I can hear them laughing and clowning around. I looked down at my watch and saw it was 6:30 PM. They actually arrived about the time I expected. I heard them all talking and laughing together now. No more brush breaking, no sounds of footsteps anywhere near me.

I just started to turn around and edge up the side of the tree trunk to look in their direction when I saw a movement in front of me. I peered through the brush and saw the two fishermen in the distance making their way to their cars. I needed to stay still for a while longer to make sure they didn't see me. They were soon out of sight. I edged up the side of the tree trunk and looked in the direction of where Beth, Dennis, and Chuck were partying. There they were, Chuck sitting on a red cooler and Dennis sitting on a green cooler. Beth lay in a webbed lounge chair that she had apparently brought from home. They were about a hundred feet from my hiding spot. All of them had a beer in their hand, and it appeared they were all on their way to a drunken stupor. I continued to watch as they talked and laughed together. I heard them talking about the dinner, their friends, and how much fun they were going to have at college.

They paused and gazed out toward the lake for a moment as a large crane flew from the edge of the lake off into the fading daylight toward the Ford marsh. The bird left the ground and made several deep-throated screams, apparently disgusted that it had been disturbed by the loud intruders. I watched the bird as it disappeared into the marsh.

Chuck stood up and got each of them another beer out of the cooler. Beth stood up and took off her blouse and slacks. Underneath was a very skimpy bikini. God, she looked good.

Dennis and Chuck followed her lead and dropped their pants and shirts. Both were wearing swimming trunks under their clothes. The fire was blazing now, and I wondered if the park DNR officers would be able to see the fire on their rounds. I really kind of doubted it as this was a remote area that was only frequented by fishermen now.

They were really pouring down the beer now. Chuck then made a mistake. In fact his conversation was to lead them all to a big mistake. Chuck said, "What about that creep, Zeke. He is really a piece of work, isn't he?"

Dennis replies, "Yeah, he thinks he's a tough guy. That jerk actually thinks he is the meanest guy in school. Well, I'll tell you what he is, he is the stupidest jerk that I have ever met, and he needs a real ass kicking."

Beth now with a drunken laugh says, "Yeah, he gives me creepy looks every time he sees me. I think he's psycho. He always stays to himself and never talks with anyone. He's really probably retarded."

They continued their conversation about me, and my blood began to boil. Stupid, retarded, psycho! I'll show them stupid; I'll fix these idiots. I sat back down on the ground and shut their conversation out completely as I thought of a plan. It only felt like minutes that I sat there, but it must have been an hour because when I looked at my watch, it was 8:00 PM. They were really getting loud now and laughing hysterically.

I eased up the tree trunk again and looked toward the glow of the fire. It was getting dark, and the flames jumped up into the darkness pushing sparks high into the night air. Beth was really loud and slurring her words. I was shocked when I heard her say to Dennis and Chuck, "Do you guys want me?" There was total silence. Then Dennis said, "What do you mean?"

"I mean do you both want to do me? Because I will let you both if you want me. I'll make you guys like it."

Wow, she must really be drunk. But then I thought, no, here's another bitch that just cares about herself and no one else. I know that she has a boyfriend who is a freshman in college at Northern Michigan University. She has been dating him for at least two years. Another tramp like Nicole, another person like Polly and Mary; they're all alike. They get what they want out of people and don't care who they hurt along the way. This is really pissing me off. Anger grows rapidly inside me, I can barely contain myself. "All bitches are the same," I said quietly to myself.

Chuck and Dennis sat there looking dumbfounded at each other. Then Beth stood up and unfastened her bikini top and let it fall to the ground.

She turned toward the guys with her hands cupped under her breasts and said, "Well, boys, do these look good?"

Both of them together slurred out, "Wow!"

She slipped off the rest of her suit and lay back on a beach towel that was positioned next to her lounge chair. Dennis and Chuck stripped off their suits rapidly like it was a race to see who could get to her first.

Dennis won the race and was on top of her in a flash. Chuck sat on the edge of the lounge chair watching them. Beth reached up and starting stroking Chuck, getting him ready for his turn. Everybody was moaning and carrying on. It was actually turning me on to watch them. Dennis finished, and Chuck climbed on immediately. Chuck was much larger than Dennis, and Beth obviously enjoyed him much more. Chuck finished and rolled off Beth leaving her lying there naked. They all lay motionless for several minutes. Finally Beth said, "Does anyone want more?"

Dennis didn't say a word; he got on top of Beth again, and she moaned with delight. Then it was Chuck's turn. Chuck finished again and lay next to Beth. He looked over at her and said, "Wow, Beth, that was terrific!"

"I told you guys you'd like it."

Dennis lit up a cigarette and looked over at her and said, "Don't you and Doug date anymore?"

"Sure, he's still my boyfriend. I make love to him when he's around, and when he's not, I make love with whomever I choose."

"Well, I'm really glad you chose us today!" Chuck said with almost a giggle in his voice.

They continued to lie and sit around naked, and the fire continued to roar. The beer flowed even freer now. Beth was really getting loaded. She moved her towel closer to the fire and lay down. Dennis and Chuck moved the coolers and lounge chair next to her. They each took turns stroking her breasts and ass. They couldn't keep their hands off her. It was like a little kid with a new toy.

Beth sat up for a while drinking more beer and letting the guys touch her freely. They spoke very little now. They mostly sat there touching one another. The guys were getting aroused again, and I thought round 3 was about to begin when Beth said, "Wait, guys, let me rest a little while. Then we'll do it again."

"Okay," they both said in a dejected voice.

Beth lay down on her towel facing the fire. Chuck and Dennis sat talking and continued to pour down the beer. I listened to them talk about Beth and how glad they were that they came with her tonight. They talked about going to college in the fall and actually became sad when they thought about not seeing one another daily like they have since the beginning of high school. I looked down at my watch. It was ten o'clock now. If they were going to have sex with her, they needed to do it soon because they had to get out of the park by midnight or the DNR would come looking for them. It really wouldn't be too hard to find them if they walked near here. The blaze of the fire had died somewhat, but would still be visible if the officer walked close enough.

Chuck finally gets up and moves over next to Beth who is motionless. He touches her, and she does not move.

"This is great, Dennis, she is sound asleep."

Dennis walks over and shakes Beth gently. She still does not move. Now he begins to shake her harder and yell her name. Unfortunately, the full day of alcohol has taken its toll. She is totally passed out and not responding.

Dennis looks at Chuck and says with frustration in his voice, "What the hell are we going to do with her?"

"It's only a little after ten o'clock. Maybe she'll wake up by ten thirty or so. That'll give us plenty of time to get out of here before the DNR comes looking for us."

Dennis continues to try and wake her without any success. Frustrated, he sits back and drinks another beer.

He looks over at Chuck and says, "Well, if the bitch doesn't wake up by eleven o'clock, I'm leaving her here."

"We can't do that!" Chuck replies.

"The hell we can't. What do you want to do? The car's a half mile away, and we can't carry her and all our stuff. Do you want to wait for the DNR to find us half drunk with beer in our possession and a naked girl?"

"No, but I don't want to leave her here alone."

"Why not, nobody will find her here. The park opens at 7:00 AM, and we can come back to pick her up then. She will probably still be asleep anyway."

"Damn, I really wanted her again."

"Yeah, so did I. Maybe she'll let us have her again in the morning."

"I hope so."

I watched as they sat drinking another beer and smoking cigarettes. It would be fine with me if they left her.

I remembered what she said about me just a few hours ago. I remembered what they all said about me.

After several minutes, Dennis kneels down next to Beth and shakes her while yelling her name. She moves slightly, but does not wake up. She just mumbled a few words that were not recognizable and then lay motionless.

Dennis and Chuck both begin to get dressed. They put all the empty beer bottles back in the coolers, picked up their towels, and folded up the lounge chair. Chuck put some more logs on the fire, and it blazed to life again. Dennis looked down at Beth and said, "That should keep you warm for a while. Thanks for everything, baby, we'll be back for you in the morning."

They grabbed their coolers, towels, and the lounge chair and began their walk to the car. It was 11:30 PM. They barely had enough time to get to their car and get out the gate before the DNR did their final check of the parking lots.

I watched them disappear into the darkness. I wanted to make sure that they were gone. I couldn't take the chance that they would return for something they forgot. They may even change their mind and come back after her, but that was not likely. So I sat there and waited patiently until it was 12:15 AM. I figured they weren't coming back if they had not returned by then.

I slipped out from behind the tree and looked over at Beth. She lay there naked with her back toward me. The shadows created by the fire danced around her. I walked over and kneeled next to her. Her body trembled a little; she must have been dreaming. I just kneeled there and watched her for several minutes. She was a beautiful young lady with a perfect body. I touched her hair. It was soft and full. The scent of her perfume entered my nostrils, and the fragrance overcame me. She was perfect in every way. I wanted her, and I was going to have her. Then I was going to teach her a lesson about not being faithful to her boyfriend and also a lesson of respect. Yes, she would learn that I didn't like being called names, especially by tramps like her.

I began to touch her and stroke her much like Dennis and Chuck did earlier. In about another thirty minutes, she began to move a little. I caressed her right breast, and she sighed softly. She was slowly coming out of her beer-induced coma and back to life.

She finally awoke and turned over, her eyes still closed.

"Hmmm, that feels really good."

I kept rubbing her breast without saying a word. Slowly her eyes opened, and she looked up at me.

"Zeke, what the hell are you doing here?"

She pulled away from me and tried to cover herself with the beach towel she was lying on.

"Well, it's pretty obvious, isn't it?"

"Where are Dennis and Chuck?"

"They left. You were too drunk to wake up, so they left you."

"No, they wouldn't leave me here with you."

I laughed loudly. "They didn't even know I was here."

"How long were you here?"

"Oh, long enough to see everything that went on. Yep, I saw everything and heard everything that you guys said. Remember, I'm the psycho."

"Well, I'd better get dressed and start walking to the park entrance. Maybe someone will give me a ride home. What time is it anyway?"

I looked down at my watch. It was one o'clock.

"It's one o'clock, sweetheart, and you're not going anywhere. I want some of what the other guys got, I want it now, and you'd better be good at it."

"No, Zeke, not you."

She clutched the towel close to her now and began to move away from me.

"Why not, you don't seem to care who you give it to. Poor Doug doesn't have a clue, and you don't even care about him."

"It's not like that, Zeke. I do care about Doug. I just need to have some fun once in a while. He's probably doing somebody at college anyway."

"Get over here and lay down. I don't want to hear anymore lies out of you. You'd be smart to do what I say, Beth, unless you'd like to be smacked around a little. The choice is yours."

She slowly started to move over in my direction. She had the look of a scared caged animal on her face. You could see the fear in her eyes.

"Kiss me," I commanded.

She leaned over and started to kiss me. I could feel her lips tremble. I grabbed both her breasts and squeezed hard. She jumped away.

"Don't, Zeke, that hurt!"

"Get back here!"

She moved back toward me very slowly. Her entire body was trembling now. Our lips met again, and I pushed her back on the towel. I stood up and took my clothes off as she watched.

"Please be gentle, Zeke. I'll make sure you like it, just don't hurt me."

"Oh, I'll like it all right."

"I jumped on top of her and began what was the roughest sex that I had ever had with anyone. She screamed out at one point, and I put my hand over her mouth. I looked down at her and said, "I'll give you creepy, psycho, and retarded, you bitch."

I finally finished after about ten minutes. I rolled off her and lay next to her. She turned her back to me and began to sob. After a few minutes, I got up and turned her over and got on top of her, cupping her breasts in my hands. I squeezed them hard again, and she began to wince in pain.

"You know, Beth, you really shouldn't call people names. It really pisses them off."

She began to sob harder. I entered her again and began to pump hard inside her. Thoughts of Polly, Nicole, and Mary entered my mind. Anger overtook my thoughts, my body, and my actions. My eyes closed tightly. I went harder and faster. No sounds came from Beth. I squeezed her harder and tighter. Beth began to quiver violently, and I finally exploded inside her. Wow, this was the best sex I ever had; it was really tremendous.

I opened my eyes and looked down at her. My hands were not on her breasts as they were before. They were around her throat. Her eyes were open and glazed, much like Whitey when he lay on the riverbank several years before. She was dead, and I didn't even have the pleasure of realizing I killed her until it was over. Damn, I hadn't really planned on this. I needed to think, but time was limited.

Flashes of lightning now jumped across the sky in the west. I could hear the distant rumble of thunder. Great, this is just what I need, a thunderstorm along with a dead body.

What the hell can I do with her body? I can't leave it here. The cops may be able to trace me to her. Then what would I do? It would be impossible to lie my way out of this one. Then it struck me. The Ford marsh would be a perfect place to hide her body.

I knew from my experience in the Port of Monroe marsh that many boggy places existed in marshy areas. All I needed to do was to carry Beth to the lake and walk about thirty feet out in the lake to a point where a large sandbar went in a half-moon shape across the mouth of the channel. This is the only place you could cross the channel; anywhere else would be far too deep, and the undercurrents were dangerous. James had talked to me about it when we fished in this area years ago.

I put my sneakers on to make sure I didn't cut myself on any broken glass. I picked up Beth's clothes and tied them in her towel, making a loop on the end so I could put my arm through it for easy carrying. I reached in my pants pocket and got my small flashlight. It would be impossible for me to find my way after I got to the marsh without the flashlight. Still naked, I bent over and picked up the lifeless body of Beth. I walked to the water's edge and began to work my way out to the sandbar. Damn, the water is cold this time of year. The claps of thunder are now getting closer, and the wind is starting to blow. I hope the wind doesn't cause sparks from the campfire to start a grass fire. I would get caught for sure then.

I reached the sandbar and began my walk toward the Ford property. I had to be careful here; I didn't want to risk slipping off into deep water. It would be impossible to hang on to Beth and swim also. I finally reached the other shore and the Ford property. The wind was really howling now, and the storm appeared to be a fierce one with plenty of lightning and thunder.

I laid Beth down on the shore so I could rest. She probably only weighs 110 pounds, but it seems heavy to me now. I rested for only a moment before picking her up and continuing.

I wondered what Dennis and Chuck were going to do because of the storm. They can't drive back here to get Beth with their car until 7:00 AM. I guess they could drive to the gate and walk in to get her. It's only about a mile and a half walk, but I doubt they are smart enough to do that.

I turned on my flashlight and put it in my mouth to light the way as I eased up the marshy shoreline. I sank deeply into the muck with every step. God, this mucky crap stinks.

Damn, headlights are coming down the service road that runs along the edge of the marsh. It's probably the Ford security guards that patrol the area. I quickly place Beth on the ground and turn out my flashlight. I watch as the car gets closer. Spotlights from the car dance across the cattails and water. I am only about thirty yards from the service road hidden in a brushy area. I can only hope they don't see me.

The car is directly beside me now, still casting the beam of the spotlight into the marsh. I can see the Ford security logo on the driver's door of the car.

The car stops for a moment, and I see the flame from a cigarette lighter as the driver lights a cigarette. He turns the spotlight off and now sits thirty yards from me, smoking his cigarette with the radio blaring Elvis Presley's "Hound Dog." I was so nervous I almost forgot to breathe. The lightning was now so fierce that at times the marsh was lit up like daylight. I thought sure he'd see me.

The car lurched forward when the song finished, and he continued on his way without ever turning the spotlight on again. That was a close one, too close. I continued on with Beth. After I had covered about another hundred yards, I turned and walked toward the center of the marsh. I found an especially mucky area about fifty yards in the marsh. I laid Beth down into the muck and cast the flashlight on her. Her eyes had that death stare that I had seen before—cold, glazed eyes of emptiness.

The rain started to pour down now as the storm intensified. I need to get out of here. I step on top of Beth's stomach and feel her sink into the muck. I jumped up and down on her until her ass was sunk deeply into the muck. I jumped on her chest, legs, and face until she was completely covered with muck. I then pushed her towel and clothes into the muck until they were completely sucked under. I scanned the flashlight across the area where I had laid Beth. Neither she nor her clothes were visible. "Good-bye, bitch," I said as I walked away.

It was much easier traveling through the muck without the weight of Beth upon me. I was a total mess by the time I got to the lake.

Muck covered most of my body, and I had several scratches from the brush along the way. The rain was falling so hard now that it stung when it hit my skin. I dove into the lake and started rubbing the muck off my body. It was really hard to get all the muck off my shoes. But I finally managed to get all the crap off me. I was very cold and tired now. The temperature must have dropped fifteen degrees since the storm started. I really needed to get out of here and get home.

I walked from the beach to the spot where I'd left my clothes. It was still pouring down rain, and all my clothes were drenched. The fire was completely out now, and wisps of smoke streamed up into the beam of my flashlight.

I quickly put my clothes on and started walking as fast as I could toward the parking lot and the road that exited the park. I looked down at my watch along the way. It was 3:30 AM. Damn! I wanted to be at the bar no later than 3:30 AM.

I didn't want James's car at the bar after closing time. Someone might see it sitting there and wonder why. Even worse, someone might break into the car or steal it. Nothing I could do now. It was impossible to get there before 4:00 AM. Even so, I needed to hurry.

I turned out my flashlight as I got to the road that exited the park. I couldn't risk being spotted by anyone. Only a mile left to the park exit gate now. The rain had let up a little, and that made the walk more bearable. I was still cold, but I knew that I had dry clothes and a jacket back at the car. I had only walked a few hundred feet more when I saw what appeared to be a person carrying a flashlight coming up the road in my direction. I knew they couldn't see me, so I stepped into the brush and waited.

I heard muffled voices. It must be at least two people. I wondered what the hell they were looking for at this hour of the night. They were soon near me, and I realized by the voices it was those two jerks, Dennis and Chuck. I listened to them as they approached me. I heard Chuck say, "Boy, she is really going to be pissed off at us for leaving her out here alone."

"Yeah, well, she shouldn't have gotten so drunk that we couldn't wake her up. It's her fault, not ours," Dennis replied.

Their voices drowned out as they passed me because the rain started to come down hard again. I waited until they were a few hundred yards from me before I continued to my car.

I reached the exit gate, and Dennis's car was parked a couple of feet from it. I stopped and looked at Dennis's car. I remembered it was a nice '57 Chevy Impala, cherry red in color. It was really a beautiful car. I thought for a moment. I wanted to break some windows out, or put some dents and scratches in the nice finish on the car. But I didn't want to draw any attention to the fact that someone else might have been here tonight. So I just kept walking toward Waterworks Street and my car.

The rain had fallen hard enough to wash any sign of me being at the campsite. How were these two guys going to explain that they couldn't find Beth? Nobody would believe them. I laughed out loud. These two guys were going to go down for the disappearance of Beth sure as hell. I hadn't planned it, but without thinking, I'd really gotten back at all of them by killing one of them. I was laughing hysterically now, and I couldn't stop.

It was 4:15 AM and still raining when I reached the car. I stood in silence for a moment to make sure that the area around the bar was clear. Good, nobody around. I got into the trunk of the car to get my clothes. James had an old blanket in the trunk for emergency reasons. I stood next to the car and took off my clothes. I wrapped myself in the blanket and sat down in the backseat of the car. I was really chilled and needed to warm up. I reached up front to the ignition, put the keys in, started the car, and turned on the heat.

After about fifteen minutes, I dressed and jumped in the front seat of the car so I could drive home. I put the car in the garage and hung my wet clothes and shoes on a ladder in front of the car. They would dry there, and Marie would never have any idea they were wet.

I unlocked the back door of the house and very quietly went into my room. A lot of excitement had happened this evening. I was completely drained and exhausted.

I took off my clothes and lay down in bed. Sleep and dreams were upon me immediately. The dreams turned into nightmares, and the nightmares into horror. My enemy with the blood-dripping knife chased me through the marsh and into the woods in my nightmares. I couldn't let him catch me. I could never let him catch me.

Chapter 34

Sun beamed through my bedroom window. I looked over at the clock on my nightstand. It was almost one o'clock. I was amazed that Marie had not rousted me out of bed yet. It wasn't like her to let me sleep. I got up and went into the bathroom and took a shower.

When I came out of the bathroom, I heard Marie call "Zeke" from the living room. I walked toward the living room to see what she wanted.

"What do you want?"

"One of your classmates went missing last night."

"Really, how do you know?"

"It's all over the news this morning."

"Who was it?"

"Beth Carter."

"What happened?"

"The reporters say that she, Dennis Johnson, and Chuck Mann went to the state park after prom dinner. It seems they went there to make a campfire, have a party, and drink beer. I figured that you kids drink alcohol all the time. You can't fool me. You're probably as bad as the rest of them."

"Look, I told you before. I don't drink alcohol. I know all these kids. What do they think happened to Beth?"

"They don't know, but I think your two friends are in real trouble. The police are interrogating them right now. It seems they were the last ones to see her. They claim that she was drunk and they couldn't wake her up, so they left her there at the park. They planned to come back and get her in the morning when the park opened. They told police that they came back at about 3:30 AM to get her because of the storm. They said they parked their car at the gate and walked in to where they left her, but she was gone."

"She's probably just mad at them and hiding at a friend's house. I know her. She'd do something like that just to get even with them."

"Well, I hope so for her sake. But if that's what she's doing, she'll be in real trouble because the police have helicopters, dogs, and volunteers searching the area for her right now."

"She'll turn up somewhere, you just wait and see."

I turned and walked to my room and lay down on the bed. I began to wonder about death. I had already killed four people. The cops had only found one body. The others would probably never be found. I guess it's possible for Nicole and Beth to be found, but it's really not very likely.

My thoughts turned to Mary for a moment. I wasn't sure what I was going to do with her. So far she had played by all the rules, and I was having fun with her. I had no plans to screw that up. The sex was great, and I only saw her when I wanted her. She would never tell anyone. If she did, she'd lose her job and her fiancé. It would destroy her.

But death itself was beginning to interest me. What really happens when you die? Is there really a heaven and hell like the old Baptist minister preached all these years? Or is it all a bunch of crap they feed us just to get everybody to give them money every Sunday? I didn't know, but I did know that death really doesn't change anything. I mean, when you die, the grass keeps growing, the clouds keep moving in the sky, the sun still comes up in the morning—nothing really changes. You just aren't there anymore. After a few years, everyone forgets that you were ever there at all. So what does it all mean, anyway? I guess I'm not smart enough to figure it out. But I do know that I don't fear death. What's to fear? Beth just went to sleep and stayed that way. I thought about it for a moment. She'll never feel sadness or pain anymore. Maybe I should have died a long time ago.

I turned my thoughts to Chuck and Dennis. They were going to go down for Beth's disappearance, and I knew it.

Beth wasn't going to come home from a friend's house; she would never come home. I wonder what they will do with them. How would they be able to prove any case against them? The body will never be found; I'm pretty sure of that. The only way that would happen is if it popped up through the muck when one of the big shots was there hunting. That would be pretty funny. The guy would probably shit himself. I imaged it for a moment and laughed out loud. Not likely though. Duck season is closed now and won't open until the fall. Nobody will be in the marsh until then, and by that time, she'll be a pile of bones and nothing else.

Only a couple of days more of school left until graduation. We will be practicing for graduation night for most of the remaining time at school. The principal is a real fanatic about making sure that everything goes right. He doesn't want any mistakes. Everybody must be seated in alphabetical order so they are in line correctly when their names are called to receive their diplomas. What a bunch of crap. Just give me the diploma at school or mail it to me. I don't need to sit in a crowd of people who I don't like just to get a piece of paper that doesn't mean anything to me.

I can't wait to get out of this hellhole that I live in. I stay away from home as much as possible. I don't need to talk with Marie at all. It always leads to trouble, and I'm tired of it. I have already decided that I will never come back home again after I leave. I will miss James, but I think that his life will be much better without me. But sometimes I wonder about that. Marie always takes her anger out on me now. If I'm not here to scream at, she may decide to focus her anger on James. I hope not for his sake.

Maybe James should just leave with me. If I decide to stay in the area, he can keep his job, and we could rent a house somewhere and live together. I know that he would never do that, but it made me feel good to think it was possible.

I decided to get dressed and ride my bike out to the state park. After all, maybe they need help searching for Beth. I wasn't doing anything anyway. I could join in with the search team, and maybe I'd be the one to find her. I laughed hysterically. Yeah, that would be great, wouldn't it?

On the way to the park I stopped at the Big Boy restaurant on North Dixie Highway. The restaurant was near Howard Johnson's, about a half mile from the park entrance. It was nearly three o'clock, and I was really hungry. I knew they had really good burgers here, and it normally wasn't crowded. I walked inside and sat at the counter. This is a good place for me to sit because nobody else was sitting at the counter. A real cute waitress with a name tag that read "June" waited on me. I ordered a burger, fries, and a Coke. I grabbed a newspaper that was lying on the counter to read while I was waiting for my food.

I heard a commotion at the door, and I looked around to see six cops coming into the restaurant. I could tell by their uniforms that they were from the sheriff's office. They took all but one of the remaining stools at the counter. The only stool left vacant was the one next to me. That was fine with me; I don't like cops too close to me. I returned to reading the paper, and June went over to them with menus in her hand. I focused on the paper while June got coffee for all of them.

"Hey, kid, kid. What the hell, are you deaf?" I heard one of the cops shout.

I turned toward the cop. "Are you talking to me?"

"Yeah, pass the sugar, will ya?"

"Sure."

I slid the sugar down the counter toward him.

"Thanks," he replied.

I returned to the newspaper and started to read an article about fly-fishing. The cops started talking together about the missing girl. My interest piqued. I needed to listen carefully to hear what they were saying because they were talking very softly to one another. My eyes remained focused on the newspaper with my ears focused on the cops' conversation.

I heard the fat cop who was sitting second from the end say that he thought the two boys had probably raped her, then killed her, and hid the body. He thought they had taken the body in their car and dumped it somewhere out in the woods, somewhere away from the park. All of them had theories about what happened to Beth that night. One of them had a picture of Beth that he showed to the other cops. They all looked it over to make sure they knew exactly what she looked like. The cop closest to me said, "Wow, she is really a pretty girl, isn't she?" Every cop at the counter agreed with him.

June brought my burger, fries, and Coke. I wolfed down the food and left the restaurant for the park. I rode into the park and was stopped at the little DNR shack by an officer.

"Hey, kid, what brings you to the park today?"

"I'm just out for a ride, and I like the trails here."

"Well, the southeast end of the park is closed to all visitors right now."

"Why?"

"We have a girl that went missing here last night, and we have a team of people searching for her."

"Oh, I hope she's okay. But don't worry, I'm going to the northeast side of the park anyway."

"Okay, but make sure you keep away from the search area. Some of the boys have daughters of their own, and they are really upset about this missing girl. They may cuff you and throw you in a car if they see you in the area."

"Okay, I'll make sure I stay away."

I rode off toward the northeast side of the park. I looked down the road toward the southeast end of the park when I passed by it. I could see the cop cars with their flashing red lights rotating. They were parked in the middle of the road so no cars could pass.

I continued my ride toward the northeast corner of the park. When I got to the beach, I parked my bike and walked up to the water's edge. You could see large crevices in the sand. The pounding rain from the night before had created small rivers that cut through the sand on their way to the lake beyond. Everything was still soaked. The sun was bright now and warm. It was far different from last night when I was freezing cold and the wind was howling.

I began walking up the beach toward the southeast corner of the park. It was at least a mile walk to get near enough to see what was going on. I had to be careful. I could not been seen; otherwise, the cops would surely question me about being there. I didn't want to draw any attention to myself, but I just couldn't stay away.

I could sneak along the shoreline without being seen from the grassy fields that extended from the road to the picnic area. The shoreline ground level was much lower than the picnic area and the grassy fields that lay beyond. I was still very cautious. The shoreline jutted out eastward about a half mile from where the channel met the lake. A big sycamore tree stood at the farthest point east. I stopped by the tree and peered down the lakeshore. I saw what appeared to be four divers in wet suits in the lake. One of them was only about three hundred yards from me. It looked like they were working their way in my direction. I looked up and saw people walking on a knoll in the grassy field that led to the road. I had no idea how many people were searching, but I knew that I had to get back to the other end of the park. I turned and hurried down the shoreline back to the northeast corner of the park.

I sat down on a swing near where I parked my bike. I never thought about the sheriff's office having a search this intense. In fact I never thought about them even looking for her. I am really getting careless, and careless will get you caught. If they were intensely searching the area, wouldn't they look in the Ford marsh also? I hoped not. But then again, if they find her body, they would blame Chuck and Dennis for her death, not me. They were the ones who left her there alone. Nobody knew that I was there, and they never would.

I rode back toward the little DNR shack. I saw a channel 4 news truck turn the corner and drive in the direction of the cop cars that were blocking the road on the way to the southeast corner of the park. They were probably there for a press conference with the Monroe County Sheriff. I wish I could be there during the conference. It would be interesting to hear what they had discovered. I figured that they would search the lake, channel, and lagoon area with divers to see if Beth had staggered off and drowned while she was drunk. They would probably search the entire park for her. That would take a lot of time. The park covered five square miles with a marsh at the west and north. It would take a lot of people and some intense planning to assure that all these places were searched properly.

It was nearing 6:00 PM when I arrived home. I went directly into my room and lay across the bed. I thought about Mary and wondered what she was doing tonight. Maybe I'd slip over to her house and have some fun with her. Then I thought, no, not tonight. I had scrapes and scratches all over me. This would only lead to questions that I couldn't answer. I'd better wait until I heal up before I see her again.

I went out into the living room and picked up the evening newspaper off the couch. The headlines read, LOCAL GIRL MISSING. I began to read the article. It said that two local youths were being held for questioning related to her disappearance. The sheriff's office was certain that they would find her. Her parents were pleading for anyone who knew the whereabouts of their daughter to come forward and speak with the sheriff's office.

I thought about Chuck and Dennis. They must be really basket cases by now. The cops had questioned them all day after a night with no sleep. They must be ready to collapse. Well, it's their fault. I was not the one who started it. Maybe if they had been nice to me, this never would have happened. But they were involved with Beth, making fun of me, calling me a creep, psycho, and retard. Well, I don't feel sorry for them at all. I hope they rot in jail.

Chapter 35

I sat on my bed thinking about events since prom night. Three weeks have passed now since the disappearance of Beth. They never found any trace of her, and as I suspected, they searched the entire park area. Her parents have been on television pleading for help and offering a thousand-dollar reward for information leading to the return of their daughter. A thousand dollars! That's a lot of money. I could return her to them, but I don't think that's what they had in mind.

The graduation ceremony went well. The principal was happy because everyone was seated properly, in line when their names were called to pick up their diplomas.

Poor Chuck and Dennis, the Monroe County Sheriff announced today that they were going to be charged in the disappearance of Beth. The prosecutor made a statement in the paper that said they would be tried as adults. He made the decision based on the fact that they could not provide an alibi for the time they left Beth until the time they returned to the area and called police. They told the cops they were sleeping in their car in the Howard Johnson's parking lot waiting for morning to go back and get her. The detectives said that Chuck and Dennis both admitted to having sex with Beth that night. They figured that the boys raped Beth, killed her, and drove to a remote area to dump the body. They then returned to the area pretending to look for her. The detectives wouldn't give any further details, but they said that the boys gave conflicting stories about the events of the night.

Conflicting stories? What the hell, these dopes are stupider than I thought they were. I could remember the events of the night. They sure as hell should be able to tell the same story. They were both there. What the hell, it doesn't matter to me.

I decided last week that I was going to take Jeff up on his offer and go to Florida. I liked the Tampa area when I was there, and I needed to get away from Monroe.

I had taken the opportunity to visit Mary yesterday evening. I made her make love to me on the hood of her car in her driveway. Even though it was dark, I saw some guy walking his dog down the street as he passed a streetlight in front of Mary's home.

Mary didn't see him because she was faced the other way, but I saw him clearly, and I know he saw us. He actually stopped for a few moments and watched us. Then he just walked away down the street with his dog. I was sure that he could only see our bodies moving in the darkness. It was impossible for him to see exactly who we were from the sidewalk. But this excited the hell out of me. For a moment, I actually thought of calling him over and letting him join in the fun. But I decided that it might not be a good idea. I might decide to get rid of Mary like the others, and I didn't want anyone to know who I was or that we were together.

James walked into my room and snatched me away from my thoughts. My suitcase lay open next to me on the bed. I was going to start packing for my trip.

He looked down at me and said, "Here, son, take this."

He handed me an envelope.

"What's this, Dad?"

"The rest of your money, you're going to need it, son. I wish you would stay here and get a job. There are plenty of jobs in the area. You can go get an apartment in town somewhere so you can get out of here and away from Marie. I just think Tampa is a long ways away, and I don't like you being that far from home alone."

"Don't worry, Dad, I'll be fine. I thought about hanging around town, but I don't really like it here. I need to go somewhere and make a new start for myself. I need a place where nobody knows me."

"I know how you feel, son, and I can't blame you. I just hope you stay safe. When are you leaving?"

"I'm leaving in three days. I'm taking the 5:00 AM bus to Tampa on Friday. The bus switches drivers in Knoxville, Tennessee, and that driver takes us on to Tampa. I should arrive in Tampa late Saturday afternoon."

"I'm going to miss you, son."

"I'm going to miss you too, Dad. Thanks again for the money. I will use it to buy a car and get an apartment when I get to Tampa. I should have more than enough leftover to get me through until I start getting regular paychecks. I already talked to Jeff in Florida, and he has a job waiting for me."

"Okay, son. I'll see you before you leave, won't I?"

"Sure you will, Dad."

James looked tired and sad when he walked out the door. I hoped that he continued to work long-hour days seven days a week so he could stay away from Marie. He deserved better. He worked hard, and he never was allowed to have any good times. I know his life will be worse than ever now. The only way he could fix it would be to leave home for good. I wouldn't blame him at all if he did exactly that.

Friday, June 26, 4:15 AM, it was finally time to leave for Florida. I was going to walk to the bus station, but James insisted on taking me. The bus station was only about a mile from home. James had the car running and was waiting for me. I grabbed my suitcase and walked out the front door to the driveway where the car was parked. I hoped that this would be the last time I ever saw this house again. Far too much pain and bad memories were stored here, memories that I longed to forget. I didn't even bother to say good-bye to Marie. She was still in bed, and I had no reason to see her anyway.

James and I were both silent during the drive to the bus station. Once we reached the station, I got my suitcase out of the trunk and walked over to James's side of the car.

"Good-bye, Dad, and thanks for everything," I said as I reached out to shake his hand.

"Good-bye, son," he said as our hands met.

I looked into James's eyes. I saw a loneliness there that I had not seen before. It was a look of uncertainty and total despair. This saddened me deeply inside. But there was really nothing that I could do to help him. He was lost within himself.

I turned and walked into the bus station. I never looked back at James. I didn't want to see his sad eyes anymore. I wanted to remember him in happier times. Funny, I couldn't even think of any happier times that I had experienced with him. My childhood had been lost to him, and I think that's what bothered him the most. He had worked so hard and so long that he didn't really know anything else.

"Sir, sir, you're next in line, how can I help you?"

I looked up, and the ticket clerk was looking directly at me.

"Sorry, I guess I was daydreaming. I need a one-way ticket to Tampa, Florida."

"That'll be sixty dollars, sir."

I reached in my pocket and peeled off three twenties and handed them to the clerk.

"Okay, sir, here's your ticket. You'll be taking bus number 5 today, and you will switch drivers at Knoxville, Tennessee. Take your bag with you to the bus, and the driver will stow it in the luggage area for you. We have magazines and snacks for sale at the counter on the right, and the restroom is through the door on your left. Thank you for choosing Greyhound for your travel today."

I thanked him for the information and walked over to the lobby to sit down and wait for the driver to pull the bus up in position.

I thought some more about James. I decided that I would save a few dollars from my paycheck each week so I could pay to fly him down for a visit. He could stay with me for a couple of weeks and relax. I knew that I would need some time to get situated in my new apartment, but I decided that it was something that I wanted to do. It would give us a chance to get to know each other better.

The bus finally pulled into position for departure. I went out and handed the driver my suitcase, and he stowed it in the baggage compartment. I boarded the bus.

My seat was number 13D, a window seat in the middle of the bus. I sat down and watched as people filtered in and out of the bus station. People continued to board the bus. A very tiny old lady sat down next to me and said, "Hi, sonny, how are you today?"

I grinned at her and said, "I'm fine. Are you going all the way to Florida?"

"Yes, I'm going there to stay with my daughter for a while. She thinks I need her help, but I really think she needs my help."

We both laughed, and I agreed with her. All the passengers were on board now and seated. The driver put the bus in gear, and it lurched forward beginning our journey to Florida. I lay back in the seat and drifted off to sleep.

I woke up when the driver announced a stop for breakfast at Dayton, Ohio. People scrambled off the bus and entered a little hole-in-the-wall restaurant to eat.

After breakfast we continued our journey toward Florida. The old lady sitting next to me was quietly knitting and humming a tune. I just sat back in the seat and thought about finally escaping from my life at home.

I didn't tell Mary that I was leaving. Why should I? I don't owe her anything. Anyway, moving to Florida will start a new life for me. I would meet new people, work a new job, buy a car, and rent an apartment. Life will finally be good.

Our next stop was Knoxville. We ate while the new driver cleaned and fueled the bus. I listened to all the people talking while we were eating. Everybody was excited about their trip. Some of the folks were only going as far as Atlanta, Georgia, and other drop points along the way farther south. Most of the passengers were going to Tampa to enjoy the sunny weather and beaches. It sounded to me as if I was the only one going to start a new life.

The bus rumbled along through Georgia. We ran into miles of construction along the way and some very rough sections of road.

It was hard to sleep with all the starts and stops, but somehow I managed to get a few hours of sleep.

We arrived in Tampa at 6:00 PM on Saturday, June 27. The sun was shining brightly, and it was very warm and humid. The driver said that it was eighty-nine degrees as he stopped the bus at the Tampa terminal. Everybody piled off the bus and waited as the driver unloaded the baggage.

Several cabs waited in line for potential customers. I grabbed my bag and went over to the first cab in line and got in the backseat.

"Where ya headed today, kid?" the driver asked.

"I'm going to the Tarpon Inn on U.S. 19," I replied.

"That's about a twenty-five-dollar fare, kid. Are you okay with that?"

"Sure, let's go, and stop calling me kid."

I was really tired and wanted to get to the motel and get some sleep. The driver jabbered on about the various night hot spots to visit in Tampa. He just kept talking on and on, most of the time I didn't bother to listen to what he was saying. I just laid my head back, closed my eyes, and listened to the traffic zoom past.

We finally pulled in the motel parking lot. The driver looked up in his mirror and said, "That'll be twenty-three dollars."

I reached in my pocket and handed him a twenty and a five and told him to keep the change. He thanked me and drove away. I walked inside the lobby to the motel desk. A young man was bent down behind the counter working on something very feverishly. He smacked his head hard on the counter when he stood up to greet me.

"Ouch, damn, that hurt!"

"Yeah, I bet it did," I replied.

"Do you have a reservation?"

"Yeah, it's under Zeke Baker."

He shuffled through a file that had the letters *A* through *Z* across the top.

"Yep, here it is. How long are you going to be staying with us, Zeke?"

"I'll be here for at least two weeks."

"Okay, the room charge is twenty dollars per night plus tax. I'll need one week paid in advance for your stay. So with tax included, I'll need $145.60. You'll be staying in room 110, which is right in front of the pool there."

I looked through the window in the direction he pointed. It looked like a good location with a great view of the pool. I handed him $160, and he handed me back my change. We talked for a moment about nearby restaurants, which ones were good and which ones weren't. I thanked him and went off to my room.

I opened the door, and the air conditioning was doing a great job. The room was cool and perfect for sleeping. A small stove and refrigerator sat in one corner with a sink across from them. The cupboard was filled with dishes and everything I needed to make meals at home. The only thing I needed to do was get groceries. I would do that another day, not tonight. I didn't even bother to get anything for dinner; I was just too tired.

I laid my suitcase on a small table under the clothes rack at the far end of the room. I took off my clothes and flopped on the bed in hopes of a good night's sleep.

I woke up and rolled over to look at the clock on the nightstand. It was 8:00 AM already. I had slept around twelve hours without waking up and, more importantly, without a dream. Well, it was time to get out of bed now. I had to get something to eat and buy a car. I was scheduled to meet Jeff in two days so I could find out where I was going to be working.

I walked down the street from the hotel to a small restaurant for breakfast. The food was great, and I relaxed and chatted with the waitress for a while before I began my journey to buy a car.

I didn't have to look far for a car dealer. Tarpon Ford was directly across Highway 19 from the restaurant. I finished my coffee and ran across the highway. You can't really walk across the highway here; traffic is crazy. If you don't run, you'll never make it to the other side.

I walked around the used-car lot and looked at what they had to offer. I found a very nice-looking white 1960 Ford Fairlane coupé that was tagged at seven hundred fifty dollars. The tires were new, and the engine was a six cylinder. The odometer had seventeen thousand miles on it. I sat down in the vehicle to see what it felt like in the driver's seat. It was great. I really liked the car, and I already decided that I was going to buy it. Just then a loud knock rang out on the window.

"Hey, kid, get out of the car!"

I looked up to see a short stocky salesman glaring at me through the window of the driver's door. I opened the door of the car and stood up and faced him. He looked up at me and said, "What the hell are you doing in there anyway?"

"I want to buy this car."

The salesman laughed hysterically and said, "Yeah, okay, kid. I'm sure that you just happen to have $750 in your pocket."

I immediately reached in my pocket and peeled off $750 from my roll of bills. The salesman stepped back a couple of paces and said, "Well, I see you're serious, son. Let's step inside and close the deal."

It only took about thirty minutes for me to be the proud owner of my first new car. I sat down in the driver's seat and started the engine. The feeling was unbelievable. I put the car in gear and pulled out onto Highway 19 and drove back to the hotel.

I sat on the bed and counted the money that I had left. It was a little under four thousand dollars. I was in good shape, with a car, a place to stay, money, and a job waiting for me.

I cruised around town the next couple of days just enjoying myself. It was finally time to meet with Jeff. His office was just north of Tampa in a small town named Odessa. I walked in at 9:00 AM, and he was sitting at his desk waiting for me. He looked up at me, and a big smile crossed his face.

"Hi, Zeke, I'm glad you decided to come and work for me. I think you'll fit in well with my crew, and I know you can take the punishment that goes along with the job. I'm going to start you out as a mason tender."

"What the heck is a mason tender?"

"Well, a mason is a cement block and brick layer. He puts mortar on the block and sets the block in place. Each time he does this, he makes sure each block remains level, in a straight row. Completing this over and over again until the job is finished. Your job is to mix the mortar for him and make sure that he always has enough blocks or bricks at his side so he can do his job. It's hard work, but you won't have a problem handling it."

"Sounds like a good job to me, Jeff. When do I start?"

"Tomorrow at 7:00 AM. We're building a huge shopping complex off Sheldon Road, and when we're done with that, we have another complex to build on Tampa Road. I have enough work laid out in front of me for the next five years."

"What's the pay for the job, Jeff?"

"You'll be getting three forty per hour with time and a half for overtime."

I thought for a moment, three forty per hour. That was fifteen cents per hour more than James made at the paper company.

"Great, Jeff, I'll be there on time every day. You can count on me."

Jeff jotted down the address and handed it to me. He shook my hand and said, "Your site boss will be Joe. He's a good man, you'll like him. Good luck, Zeke, let's plan to have dinner in a couple of weeks. You can let me know what you think of the job."

"Okay, Jeff. I'll talk with you then."

I walked out the door and thought about my new life. I was alone now in a new city, and I was finally at peace inside. But is it possible that life will really stay this way?

Chapter 36

I arrived at the job site about fifteen minutes early. Many of the workers were standing around talking, smoking, and drinking coffee. I walked up to a short thin man who was wearing a hard hat and said, “I’m here to work, and I’m looking for Joe.”

“I’m Joe,” I heard from a voice behind me.

The words were spoken in a very deep voice, and I turned to face a giant of a man. He was at least six feet six inches tall with very wide shoulders. I would guess his weight at 275 pounds.

“Are you Zeke?” he snarled.

“Yep, I’m Zeke, and I’m ready to work.”

He reached out and shook my hand. My hand barely reached across his outstretched hand, and he clamped down like a vise when he pumped his arm up and down. His hands were thick with calluses, the hands of a workingman.

“Okay, Zeke, you’ve got a tough job. Old Nate over there is the mason, and your job is to keep him busy.”

I looked over toward where he pointed, and there stood a black man who looked to be in his late fifties wearing bib overalls. He had a thick gray beard, and he broke into a smile when I looked at him.

"Come on, boy, it's time to get to work," Nate said.

Work it was for me. The blocks were heavy; the bags of mortar weighed eighty pounds. I'd get the mortar mixed as he told me. Then I would move the wheelbarrow over to him so he could reach the mud. By then he would need more blocks, then more mud. This cycle went on all day. I was totally worn-out at the end of the day. I had never worked so hard in my life. When it was time to leave, Nate took me aside to talk with me.

"Hey, boy, I want you to know that no mason tender has ever kept up with me like you did. You are the best rookie that I've ever seen since I've been working in the business."

"Thanks, Nate, I worked as hard as I could. I just hope I won't be too sore to work tomorrow."

"Ah, don't worry, in a couple of days, your muscles will get in shape, and the job will be easy for you. Where are you living, anyway?"

"I'm staying at the Tarpon Inn until I can find an apartment."

"That's too far from the job site. You'll burn all your money up in gas traveling back and forth. I'll tell you what I can do for you, boy. I have an extra room at my house that you can rent from me. It'll only cost you twenty dollars a week, and that includes food if you can stand my wife's cooking."

"Really, do you mean it?"

"Of course, I mean it. Now you go back to your room and get your stuff. Here's my address."

He handed me a crumpled piece of paper with his address scrawled across it. I looked down at it, 12958 Gunn Highway.

"Thanks, Nate, I really appreciate your helping me out with a place to stay. I'll help around the house with anything that you need."

"Oh, I know that's right. Don't worry, between me and the missus you'll keep busy."

I moved in that very evening. I met Nate's wife, Millie. She was a very nice person, just like Nate. They didn't have any children, but it was clear they were very happy.

Weeks went by, then months, then a year. I didn't have any contact with Marie at all. I had taken the time to send James a couple of postcards with pictures of various beaches on the front of them. I knew he would want to know that I was doing okay.

I had also talked with him on the phone a few times. He was always glad to hear my voice. I tried to get him to come to Tampa for a visit, but he said that he just couldn't afford to take the time off work. Yeah, I really didn't believe that. He knew that Marie wouldn't let him take the time off just to see me. Why would she let him waste money just to visit me? That would be totally wasted money in her mind, and she would never let that happen. So after a couple of times of asking, I just gave up on the idea.

I was now a seasoned mason tender, and old Nate even let me lay brick from time to time. He was really a good man. I enjoyed staying with them. Millie's cooking was terrific.

The first thing I'd ask her each morning when Nate and I were leaving for work was, "What's for dinner tonight?"

Both Nate and her would look at each other, laugh, and say, "Wow, you'd think this boy was starving to death."

We all burst out in laughter. I was really growing close to them. They were good folks, and they treated me like their own child.

I was getting along with everybody at work, and I was putting money in the bank every week. I didn't need very much money each week. Millie packed us lunch every day, and I had breakfast and dinner with her and Nate. I didn't smoke or drink, so I really only had to spend money for clothes and gas for the car. Life was good.

Then it happened. I went into work one morning as usual with Nate. We were sitting drinking coffee before we started for the day when Joe walked up to us with another person following him.

"Hey, boys, I want you to meet your new boss. I've been transferred to a different job site. Hank here will be your new boss. It's been good working with you, boys."

Both Nate and I said good-bye to Joe, and he turned and walked away. Hank reached his hand out toward mine. I don't know why, but I didn't like this guy, and I didn't even know him yet. I raised my hand to his and shook it.

He had a weak grip. I hate men with sissy handshakes. He looked me in the eye and said, "So you're Zeke."

"Yep, I'm Zeke, and this is my friend, Nate."

"I'm not interested in talking with Nate right now. I want to talk with you. I've been around the company for a while, and I know the business backward and forward. I know who my friends are, and I know who my enemies are. You're pals with Jeff in the front office, aren't you?"

"Well, Jeff's the one who hired me, if that's what you mean."

"Yeah, and rumor has it that you have dinner with him once in a while. Is that right?"

"Sure, we have dinner together once in a while."

"Well, I don't like the front-office people, and I don't like people who complain to them about what's going on in the field. So I'd keep my mouth shut and get to work if I were you."

I began to boil with anger, and Nate sensed it. He grabbed me by the arm and started dragging me toward the job site.

"Come on, boy, let's get to work. There's no sense causing trouble with the boss. Let's just do the job we're paid for, that's what we're supposed to do."

"That's right, kid, let that old man pull you away from here because you don't want to mess with me. I'll hurt you like you've never been hurt before."

"Let me go, Nate, so I can go back there and beat his ass. He deserves it. You and I work hard, and he's got no right talking to me that way."

"No, boy, that'll be more trouble than you need. Besides, he's the boss now."

We worked hard the rest of the day and spoke little of the incident. Nate and I continued to work together every day for the next six months. The jerk Hank would come over at least three times a week to hassle us and tell us that we weren't going fast enough. He wanted more block laid, and we needed to speed it up. I knew that Nate was not as fast as some of the other masons on the job, but his work was better. I grew to hate Hank very quickly. I kept hoping that he would get moved to another job site so we'd get a new boss. Hopefully one who understood the meaning of good work and one who appreciated the people for doing a good job.

I had dinner with Jeff several times over the next few months, but I never mentioned anything about work or the problems with Hank.

We mostly talked about sports and fishing. Jeff really enjoyed those topics. Besides, I didn't want any trouble. I just wanted Hank to leave us alone so we could do the job.

I was just beginning my third year with the company. Nate and I talked about celebrating my second full year with the company that evening at home. He said that Millie was making my favorite dinner along with a pecan pie for dessert.

"Nate, I want you to know that you and Millie have been good to me. You folks have treated me far better than anybody else has during my entire life. I could not ask for better people than you and Millie."

"Thanks, Zeke, you're a great kid. Millie and I both like having you around the house. You've been a great help to us, and we hope you stay with us for a long time."

"I don't have any plans on leaving unless you throw me out."

"Well, you don't have to worry about that."

Just as we were about to start work for the day, Hank drove up in the company truck.

"I need to talk with you, Nate," he said.

We both started to walk over to Hank as we normally would. Hank glared at me and said, "Is your name Nate?"

"Stay put, boy," Nate said.

I waited while Hank and Nate talked. I saw Nate's shoulders slouch and his head drop. I wondered what the hell was going on. I couldn't hear a word. Hank jumped back in the truck and drove away toward the other end of the complex. Nate turned around and walked back over to me.

"What's wrong, Nate?"

"Hank fired me."

"Fired you? What the hell, you're the best mason here!"

"You know that, and I know that, but Hank thinks I'm too old and slow to do the job. Can you give me your car keys so I can go back home and let Millie know?"

"Damn it, Nate, he can't fire you."

"Yes, he can, Zeke. There's nothing that we can do about it. He's the job site boss, and what he says goes. Just give me the keys, and don't cause yourself any trouble because of me. I'll be back to pick you up at quitting time."

I handed Nate the keys and walked over to the job site where my new mason was standing. He spoke something to me, but I didn't hear him, nor did I speak with him at all. He was no Nate, and he never would be.

My anger built inside me every minute that I worked. I hated Hank, and I wanted him dead. He would pay for what he did to Nate. You just don't treat good people like that.

Nate came back at five o'clock to pick me up. We rode back to the house in silence. I was exploding inside; my head was pounding. I had to fix this, and I had to fix it quick.

I walked into the house, and Millie was sitting at the kitchen table. I could see the sadness in her face, and I could tell that she had been crying.

"Don't worry, Millie, everything will be okay. I'll make sure of it."

"Zeke, you don't understand, we'll lose our house. We can't afford to live here if Nate doesn't have a job. We just don't have the money."

"Don't worry, Millie, I'll pay the bills. I make enough money to pay for everything. You and Nate fix things up around the house. I know that you've wanted him to put a new vanity in the bathroom and paint your bedroom. This will be a good time for him to do all those things."

Nate was standing next to Millie holding her. He said, "The boy is right, Millie. You've got a bunch of things you want fixed around here, and this will give me time to do it. Anyway, after I get everything done, I'll find a job with another company and pay Zeke back for helping us out of this mess."

"No, you're not going to pay me back a dime. You folks took me in when I needed help, and now it's my time to help you."

"That boy is pretty hardheaded, Millie. I don't think that we'd better argue with him. Let's have that special dinner that we promised him for his two-year anniversary."

We sat down to a terrific dinner and talked about the years that had passed. My mind was on Hank all the time I talked with them. He had hurt someone who I actually cared about, and I had to fix that.

After dinner I said good night to Nate and Millie and went to my room. I sat on the bed thinking of how to deal with Hank. I couldn't just talk with Jeff to get Nate hired back. That wouldn't work. Hank would make life miserable for both of us after that. Besides, he made Millie cry. I had never seen sadness or pain in her eyes before. I wanted that happy Millie back. I wanted her eyes to sparkle like they had when I met her. But I needed a way to deal with Hank.

Hours went by as I sat on the bed. Finally it hit me. They were going to do a twenty-five-thousand-square-foot cement pour next Friday at our job site. That would be perfect. Hank always worked late the last Thursday of every month in the construction trailer getting job status up-to-date for the front office. Friday was the last day of the month, so he would be working late next Thursday for sure.

I would park my car in the hotel parking lot down the street and walk to the construction trailer where he would be working. I would kill him and bury the body where the cement pour was going to be the next day. But how do I kill him? Hank is a strong guy, and I need to be careful to get the drop on him before he suspects anything. That was going to be difficult because he knew that I didn't like him, and I knew he didn't like me. I needed to think and plan this out now.

I thought for what seemed like an eternity, and then I had it. I would come into the trailer and tell Hank that the mason tender who worked with one of the other masons had not mixed the mortar properly for the blocks on the interior walls where the cement pour was going to be the next day. Hank couldn't risk having a wall fall down during the pour and injure a worker or inspector. He would have to check out the mortar joints for himself. I would walk with him to the site to show him the wall in question and kill him there away from the office. I would bury him next to the exterior wall foundation and use the hand compactor to compact the sand back in place so it would look natural and ready for the cement pour the next day. The only personnel around would be a security guard who worked in a fenced area at the far end of the complex guarding the tools and equipment that the workers used daily. His security trailer was at least three quarters of a mile from the site where I planned to kill Hank. I knew for a fact that this guard spent most of his time listening to the radio during the evening, so he would be no threat to me.

The days drifted past slowly. Nate worked daily on the projects that he wanted to complete around the house. Millie seemed to be somewhat happy with Nate being around the house. They were really in love, and the pain of Nate losing his job didn't seem to bother them as much as it did last week. I knew inside that Nate wanted to go back to work. He didn't want to depend on me to pay the bills.

After all, he and Millie had only known me for two years. For all they knew, I would leave tomorrow, and they would never hear from me again. I knew that Nate was a good person who really cared about me, but I also knew that I would never be a true friend to anyone again. My ties with friendship had ended long ago.

It's finally the end of the day on Thursday. The job site whistle sounds, and it's time to quit for most people, but action time for me. I went home on time and sat down for dinner at the dining table with Nate and Millie. Nate seemed unusually quiet tonight.

"What's bothering you, Nate?"

"Ah, it's nothing, Zeke."

"Nate, I've known you too long. I can tell when something's bothering you, now what is it?"

"Well, Zeke, I went to two job sites today to apply for a job, and both of them told me they were looking for someone younger. The one guy told me that I should just retire because no construction site today will hire someone as old as I am."

I could see in his eyes that this bothered him deeply. His spirit was broken. Broken by a man who was much less of a man than Nate, a heartless man who would be dealt with this evening.

"Don't worry, Nate. Things will get better for you. I can feel it deep inside. You're a good man, and good things will happen to you."

"I hope so, Zeke. I want to make sure that Millie is provided for after I'm gone."

"Gone, a mean old buzzard like you will never die. You're just too damn ornery to die."

We all busted out into laughter. Nate got a big grin on his face, and his whole attitude changed for the remainder of the evening. I helped Millie with the dishes while Nate sat reading a book in the living room. Millie thanked me for helping them pay the bills, and I thanked her for being the person she was to Nate and me. I wished many times that Millie would have been my mother. Life could have been much different for me.

After the dishes were done, I went to my room for a while to concentrate on the planned events for the evening. I needed to make sure I had thought through everything. I looked at my watch. It was 7:30 PM now and time for me to get moving.

I went out into the living room and told Nate and Millie that I was going out for a drive and that I may even take in a movie while I was out. They seemed happy that I was going out to enjoy myself.

I drove down the road toward the motel to park my car. My anger grew toward Hank. He had no reason to fire Nate. I knew that he didn't like me, but why didn't he fire me instead of Nate?

Then it struck me. He didn't fire me because he knew if he did, Jeff would be asking questions. Hank knew that job site bosses had full control of the labor, and he knew that Jeff wouldn't question his judgment of firing an old black mason who he didn't even know. The only way he could get to me was by firing Nate. He was trying to get to me by hurting someone I cared about. Hank was just another person who was trying to control me, just another person who would pay for it.

I got to the hotel and parked my car out of sight in the back. It was a short walk to the construction site from here, so it wouldn't take me long to be face-to-face with Hank. I reached the site and knocked on the trailer door.

"Who is it?" Hank yelled.

"It's me, Zeke," I replied.

“Come on in.”

I opened the door and walked into the trailer. Hank was sitting behind the desk with a pile of papers in front of him. He looked both pissed off and confused to see me.

“What the hell do you want, kid?”

Kid, I thought. I was at least four inches taller than him, and I knew I was stronger. The last two years of lifting twelve-inch blocks and eighty-pound bags of mortar had strengthened every muscle in my body. He was just trying to piss me off.

“I wanted to talk to you about the cement pour tomorrow.”

“What about it?”

“Well, you know the mason tender, Ralph, who tends for Ron?”

“Yeah, of course, I know him. What about him?”

“I know that he mixed the batches of mortar wrong for one of the interior walls of the building, and it might fall during the pour and hurt somebody.”

“Why would he do that, and how the hell would you know anyway?”

“He told me he did it to get back at you. He said you docked his pay a few weeks back for taking long breaks. He was really pissed off about it, so he figured he’d screw up the mortar mix so the wall would fall. He told me because he knew that I was working the pour, and he wanted to make sure that I stayed clear of the wall.”

I knew that it would hit home when I mentioned the docked pay. I remembered that Hank and Ralph were screaming at each other because of his shorted paycheck a few weeks back.

“Well, that son-of-a-bitch, I’ll fire his ass for this! He’ll learn not to mess with me. What wall is the bad one?”

"I'll have to go with you over to the site and show you."

It was pitch-dark out now, so Hank grabbed a flashlight, and we headed out the door to the job site. Hank never spoke a word along the way, and all I thought about was Nate and Millie. I knew I could talk with Jeff and get Nate's job back if Hank was out of the picture.

We reached the job site, and we entered the building through one of the truck-dock doors. The flashlight beam danced across the interior of the building, and I noticed that a half-dozen shovels and rakes leaned in the corner against the wall directly in front of us. That was good. The only thing I would need to find was a hand compactor so I could compact the dirt after I buried him.

"Okay, kid, which wall is it?"

"It's the wall directly in front of us. If you take your finger and rub it along the mortar joint, you will see that the mortar will crumble and fall out of the joint."

Hank walked over to the wall and raised his hand to the mortar joint. Just as his hand was about to touch the joint, I put my forearm around his throat and squeezed hard. The flashlight fell to the sandy floor, and he began to kick and struggle wildly. I actually felt his larynx pop as I increased pressure on my hold. I could feel drool running down my arm from his mouth. Suddenly I heard a loud snap, and his body became limp. I held on for a little longer just to make sure he was dead. I released my hold and let him fall to the ground. I grabbed the flashlight from the ground and cast the beam toward his face. Yeah, he was dead. His eyes were just like Whitey's, glazed and lifeless looking up to nowhere. Bubbles of foam trickled from his mouth and down the side of his face.

I grabbed a shovel and began to dig a final resting place for this piece of trash. I dug the hole about four feet deep and rolled him into it. He hit the bottom with a thud. I quickly shoveled dirt on top of him and grabbed a rake to smooth out the area. I looked around for a hand compactor. I knew that several would have to be here for the pour tomorrow. I found a compactor along the far wall and thoroughly hand-compacted the gravesite. I put the shovel and rake back in place and compacted the sand on the way out to eliminate my footprints.

I went outside and walked back to the construction trailer. I went inside to put the flashlight back on the wall. I wiped all traces of my fingerprints from the flashlight and the construction trailer.

I hung the flashlight back on a hook on the wall where Hank had taken it from earlier. I stood for a moment and thought about everything. Was I forgetting anything?

I knew that Hank lived alone, so I didn't need to worry about anyone missing him at home. I looked around the room for anything out of place. I noticed a set of car keys lying on the edge of Hank's desk. Damn, I forgot about his truck parked outside. How was I going to get rid of his truck and still get back to my car without being seen? There was only one thing I could do. I needed to drive Hank's truck back to the hotel and leave it there. It would probably take them a couple of days to find it, and by then the cement job would be done, and Hank would never be found. I made sure my fingerprints were wiped clean when I shut the trailer door.

I jumped into Hank's truck and drove back to the motel. I parked his truck in the back corner of the hotel parking lot next to the fence. I wiped everything down so I could be sure my prints were not to be found.

I looked around to see if anyone noticed me drive into the parking lot. The lot was empty. I jumped into my car and drove back to Nate's house. All the lights were off when I got home, so I went quietly to my room for the evening. I lay back on the bed and relaxed. I felt good about what I had done. Guys like Hank need to be killed. They have no good purpose in life; they are only evil, and evil needs to die.

Chapter 37

We finished the final sections of the pour job on Saturday. I made sure that we started where Hank was buried so I knew that area would be completed first. Some of the guys asked about Hank, but most of them were happy that he didn't bother to show up for work. We didn't need him here anyway. Every worker knew his job and worked hard to finish the cement pour. Believe me, I was glad they did.

I went to Jeff's apartment on Sunday to talk with him about Nate. I knew that he would be home. He was always home on Sunday. He had told me once that it was the only time he had to himself. He liked to relax, watch sports on television, and drink a couple of cold beers. I rang the bell on the door, and I was just about to ring it again when the door swung open.

"Hey, Zeke, come on in," he said with a big grin on his face.

"Hi, Jeff, do you have a couple of minutes to talk?"

"Sure, sit down. Do you want a beer?"

"No, I'm good."

"Okay, suit yourself, but I'm going to have one. What can I do for you, Zeke?"

"Well, I don't know if you were aware that Hank fired Nate a couple of weeks ago. Nate is the mason who I've worked for since you hired me."

"No, I can't say as I ever heard of him firing Nate. I really don't know all the workers at every site. I'm sorry, but I don't think I know Nate. Why did he fire him?"

"Well, I didn't really want to say anything, but I think that he fired him because of me."

"Because of you, I don't understand. Why would he fire him because of you?"

"Hank didn't like it because you and I are friends, and he did everything he could to make it hard for me at the job site."

"What the hell is wrong with that guy? He's causing problems with you, and all I ever heard about your work from Joe before he left was that you were the best worker on the crew. Now the damn fool hasn't shown up for work for a couple of days. I should have the construction manager fire him."

"No, Jeff, that's not necessary. I would like you to get Nate his job back if that is possible. He is the best mason at the job site, and he makes sure his work is done right. I hate to see him lose his job because of me."

"That's not a problem, Zeke. Your word is good, and if you say Nate's a good man, I believe you. I'll get him back on the job next week."

"Thanks, Jeff, I really appreciate your helping Nate, he deserves the job."

"No thanks necessary, Zeke. You've done the job, and I know it from the reports that Joe gave me during your first six months at the site."

"Jeff, I have one more favor to ask."

"What do you need, Zeke?"

"I don't want Nate to know that I had anything to do with him getting his job back."

"Okay, Zeke, if that's what you want, that's how it will be. Nate will never know that you made it happen. Now let's sit back and watch the football game. It's just about time for kickoff."

I sat there the rest of the afternoon and watched the game with Jeff. He was really a great guy. I was glad that I had taken him up on his job offer.

I went into work on Monday as normal. Still no sign of Hank, and the police had now been called in to investigate his disappearance. They came around and talked to all the workers to see if they had any idea where Hank could be.

I told them that I only knew Hank from the job site, and I had no idea what he did when he left the job. That was pretty much what everybody told them. None of them knew anything of his personal life. He was a loner.

I went home that evening, and Millie was all smiles.

"Why the heck are you so happy, Millie?"

"The construction manager called Nate today and gave him his job back. He starts back to work at the same job site tomorrow."

"That's great, Millie. I knew they would hire him back. He was too good a man to let go."

Nate walked in the room beaming with happiness.

"Hey, Zeke, looks like the team is back together again tomorrow."

"Yeah, Millie just told me the good news."

"I just can't help but wonder if you had something to do with this, Zeke. I know that you know that Jeff guy in the front office, and I know that you go to dinner with him sometimes. He carries a lot of weight with the decisions made at the company. He had to be the one to make the call to the construction manager to get my job back."

"Well, I think you're wrong, Nate. I think they finally figured out what they lost when they let you go."

"Maybe, maybe you're right. Hey, did they ever find Hank yet?"

"No, the cops were nosing around today asking a lot of questions. Nobody seems to know where the hell he is or what happened to him. Maybe he just decided to leave. Who knows?"

"Well, I hope he stays gone. He was nothing but trouble for you and me the whole time he was there."

"Yeah, I know. It'll be great to be working with you again. Just as you said, the team is back together."

We all laughed together, and Nate and Millie put their arms around me and gave me a big hug.

After dinner I went to bed. I was exhausted both mentally and physically. It was only seven o'clock, but it didn't matter. I needed the rest. I drifted off to sleep immediately, and then the dreams came.

The death faces of Whitey, Nicole, Rich, Beth, and Hank all drifted in front of me. Their dead, glazed eyes, the cold stares, and Whitey's insane laughter rang out in my ears. I couldn't get away from them. Everywhere I went, they followed. I began to run frantically through a plowed field toward a house at the edge of the field. I recognized the house as I got near it. It was the home of my grandfather who was long since dead. It would be safe there; I knew it would. Nothing could harm me in that house. The only real happiness that I had ever felt was within those walls.

I raced toward the house as fast as my legs would carry me. I turned to see if they were catching me, but wait. There was only one person chasing me now. A familiar sight, it was the blood-dripping, knife-carrying demon that had chased me so many, many nights before. I was never able to see his face. It was always a clouded image even when he was close to me. I could not let him catch me. I knew that if he caught me, I would be dead for sure. I must reach the safety of my grandfather's house before he catches me.

I dodged around the old hickory tree that borders his property. I raced through the walnut trees near the creek bed. I leapt into the air jumping the creek with ease. I'm almost there, almost to safety. I raced up the steps to the screened porch and opened the door and hooked and locked the latch behind me.

I looked through the screen from the porch and watched as he crossed the creek bed and turned toward the house. But wait, he's walking now. He's not running as he was before.

He's just walking up the path to the house. My eyes are fixed toward him as he approaches the house. Only the screen separates us now. I can see the blood dripping from the dagger in his hand. He has his head down watching each drop of blood as it falls from the dagger to the ground. I am frozen in position; I can't move even though I try. Slowly his eyes begin to rise from the drops of blood falling from the dagger. He turns and faces away from me now. I can clearly see his hair moving as the breeze rushes past him. Will I be able to see his face this time? Do I really want to see his face? I still can't move; my feet are glued to the floor of the porch. Just then his head snaps around, and I'm looking eye to eye with me. The demon that has chased me so many times over the years is me! I alone have caused myself the horrific nightmares. I alone am the only one who can end the nightmares.

"Zeke, Zeke, wake up, what the hell's wrong with you?" Nate said as he flipped the light on in my room.

I looked up, and Nate was standing over me with a concerned look on his face. I am completely covered in sweat, and I am shaking.

"I guess I was dreaming, Nate."

"I guess you were, Zeke. You were screaming about demons and blood dripping from a dagger. What the hell were you dreaming about?"

"I don't remember, Nate. I don't remember anything."

"Well, I can tell you that you scared the hell out of Millie."

"I'm sorry, Nate. I'll try not to let it happen again. I don't know why I would be screaming in my sleep. I haven't been sleeping very well lately, and maybe I was just overly tired. I had nightmares years ago when I was a kid, but they stopped a long time ago." I hated to lie to Nate, but in this case, it was necessary.

"All right, Zeke, we were just worried about you. Now get back to sleep, and get some rest this time. No more screaming."

"Okay, Nate, tell Millie I'm sorry I scared her."

"Okay, Zeke, I'll see you in the morning."

Nate left the room, and I lay there thinking about what just happened. All this time, it was me in my dreams. I was the one who drove my thoughts to this dream so many times over the years. Marie must be right. My inner self believes that I am evil. So much so that I haunt myself during my dreams.

Nate and I went to work the next day, and nothing more was said of the incident. The cops continued to question us about Hank. The questions and newspaper articles about the missing construction supervisor stopped after a few months. Life went on without Hank, just like it had with the others.

Nate and I continued to work together at different sites for the next four years. Nate and Millie were good to me, and we never argued about anything. We got along as families should.

Nate and I got to the job site one morning during early January. It was unusually cold in Tampa. The temperature had dropped to thirty-two degrees overnight. I had on a heavy coat and gloves. I had just poured a cup of coffee for Nate and me when the construction supervisor's truck drove up.

"Hey, Bobby, how are you doing today?"

Bobby Moline was our construction supervisor on this job. He was a great guy. He was always clowning around with the guys and telling them jokes. I know all the guys worked harder because they liked him.

"I'm okay, Zeke, but I have some bad news for you."

I thought it was another one of Bobby's jokes. But then I looked at his face, and I could tell it was no joke.

"What's the problem, Bobby?"

"It's your father, Zeke. It seems he was walking to work last night during a heavy snow and ice storm. He started to cross Noble Avenue toward his place of work when he slipped on the road and fell. The message I got from the police said it appeared that he hit his head on the road and was knocked out. While he lay there on the road, a car hit and killed him. The driver of the car said he couldn't see him until it was too late."

I felt Nate's hand touch my shoulder. He said something to me, but I never heard the words. I felt a tear slowly falling down my cheek. I hadn't shed a tear in years. I had no reason to cry until now. James had given everything to me. He had made a new life for me, and now he's gone. I had just talked with him on the phone last week. He sounded tired. He was sixty-four now, and he was still working all the hours he could. I knew he never had any fun; he never had the opportunity to enjoy life.

I looked up at Bobby and said, "I'm going to need some time off, Bobby."

"I figured as much, Zeke. You take all the time you need. Just call me when you're ready to come back to work."

"Okay, Bobby, thanks."

Nate looked at me and said, "Zeke, why don't you go home and get packed to leave. I'll have one of the boys take me home after work."

"Yeah, Nate, I guess I'd better get packed and start the trip back. It's almost a twelve-hundred-mile drive and probably with some bad road conditions along the way."

"Okay, Zeke. I'm sorry about your dad. I know you thought a great deal of him."

"He was a good man, Nate."

I left the job site and went home to pack. Millie met me at the door with tears in her eyes.

Nate had called her and told her about my father. She hugged me and told me she was sorry. I thanked her for her kindness. She told me to go pack and that she would make me a couple of sandwiches so I could have something to eat while I was on the road.

I packed everything I needed for the trip, grabbed the sandwiches, and told Millie good-bye.

"Please make sure you are real careful on the road, Zeke," she said.

"I will, Millie. You take good care of Nate while I'm gone."

I started my car and pulled out of the driveway and began my journey home. Funny, home was here now, and I didn't even think of Monroe as home anymore. In fact, my stomach turned over as I thought about seeing Marie again. I had not seen her in six years, and I never really wanted to see her again.

I pulled into a hotel at Knoxville, Tennessee, to spend the night. It was a small hotel, but the clerk was nice, and so were the rooms. I unlocked my room and put my suitcase on a chair in the corner. I looked over at the phone on the nightstand. I didn't plan on calling Marie to let her know I was coming home. I had no reason to call her. The thought of speaking to her turned my stomach.

I sat on the edge of the bed and thought about James. I tried to understand how this could have happened to him. He was always so careful. Why didn't he drive the car to work if the weather was bad? Why would he walk and risk falling at his age? It just didn't make sense to me.

Then it hit me like a ton of bricks. I remembered the nights that Marie would scream at him when he wanted to drive the car to work. I can remember those nights vividly. She'd scream, "You don't need to waste gas to drive to work. Gas costs us money, and we don't have money to waste. You need to get off your ass and walk to work. The exercise will do you good."

Yeah, the exercise will do you good. What the hell did she do for exercise? She didn't do a damn thing for exercise. James worked seven days a week all the time, and she still bitched at him every day.

I sat there staring at the wall. My mind went back to the days of my childhood. Back to the days, weeks, and months of relentless verbal and physical abuse that I took at her hands. Back to the times when she would force James to beat me just so she could control me. She used James as a tool to try and destroy my spirit. He really had no choice. She had brainwashed him over the years. His spirit was broken years before mine. He deserved better. He was really a good person, and good people deserve good things.

My trance on my childhood deepened. I went to a place in my mind that I seldom was driven to. A place where all my childhood fears surrounded me. I could hear Marie screaming at me. It was as if she were standing next to me. I relived every word that Marie ever said to me in anger, every beating she gave me. I relived the nights that I lay in bed and listened while she screamed at James for his perceived shortcomings. I was in a mental meltdown that deepened with each minute that passed.

I sat in my hotel room for three days in a self-induced depression coma. I only came out of my trance when the maid would knock on the door. I would yell through the door to come back tomorrow, and she would be gone. On the third day, the desk clerk who checked me in came to the door and demanded to see me. I opened the door, and he looked shocked at what he saw. I was unshaven, my face was drawn from days without sleep, and I still wore the same clothes of three days prior.

"Uh, I'm sorry to bother you, Zeke. But when you checked in, you said you were only staying for one night. Tonight will be your third night with us, and my boss is getting a little nervous about collecting the daily fee for your stay."

I reached in my pocket and handed the man two fifty-dollar bills and told him, "I'll be leaving in the morning. This should handle the charges. Just keep the change."

"But, Zeke, one of these bills is more than enough to cover the charges for your stay."

"Yeah, I know, but I really won't need the money anymore, so you keep it."

I didn't wait for his response. I just closed the door and went back to sit on the bed. I know what I need to do now. I need to deal with the person who made me the animal I am. I need to end her reign of terror for good. I remembered an old saying by Confucius that I had heard in school during history class one day. "Before you embark on a *journey of revenge*, dig two graves."

I knew that I would also be destroyed with Marie's demise, but it was something that I should have done a long, long time ago. I thought about Nate and Millie. I wondered what they would think of me when the news reached them. It really didn't matter. I would never see them again anyway. They would forget about me as time passed.

I lay back in the bed and passed out from fatigue. I didn't wake up until 8:45 AM. I finally had a good night's sleep, and I was ready to continue my journey. I threw my suitcase in the car and drove north on I-75 toward Michigan. It was past time to settle the score with Marie. I wondered why it had taken so long for me to figure out my real enemy.

Chapter 38

I knew that James would already be buried by the time I got home. It really didn't matter to me. He was dead, and I couldn't do anything about that. I could remember him and see him clearly in my mind. I remembered when he had shown me the money that he saved for me. His eyes gleamed when he handed me those two envelopes. It was the happiest that I had ever seen him. He was proud to have been able to help me start a new life. I felt sadness inside because I had only spoken with James a couple of dozen times over the years since I left home. He always sounded happy to hear from me. The main reason why I had called him so few times was because of Marie. She always seemed to answer the phone the last couple of years, and I didn't want to hear her voice anymore. I didn't care if I never spoke with Marie again, and she knew it.

My mind focused on my childhood while I drove up I-75 north. No child should have been treated the way that I was. No child should suffer the abuse of a parent. My blood boiled at times when I thought of the years of abuse at Marie's hands. She was the one who taught me hate. She was the one who taught me evil. I couldn't stop thinking about her.

I stopped in a small restaurant near Dayton, Ohio, to get something to eat. I was starving. All those days without food were finally catching up to me. I walked in, and a long counter of stools was on one side of the dining area, and a row of booths and tables was on the other side. I picked a stool near the middle of the counter and sat down. You could see the grill cook busily flipping burgers and dropping fries in the deep fryer. He was a burly guy who appeared to have forgotten to shave today. The waitress was a tiny thin old lady scurrying around behind the counter, getting coffee and other drinks for a booth of people in the far corner. She had sandy gray hair that was put up in a bun. She looked like she had worked hard all her life, but she still managed to smile politely to the customers. I grabbed a menu out of a rack that hung on the edge of the counter while I waited for her. After a while, she worked her way over to me. She placed that polite smile on her face and said, "What'll you have, young man?"

"Everything looks good to me, and I'm really hungry. I think I'll have two cheeseburgers with fries and a bowl of chili."

"I guess you are hungry, son. You won't be able to get off the stool after you finish this meal. What'll you have to drink?"

"How about one of those thick chocolate malts that you have a picture of on the front of the menu?"

"Okay, that's a good choice. The malts here are the best in town. I'll turn this ticket in and start making your malt."

"Thanks."

I was still angry inside. I was always angry inside. Funny, when I stayed with Millie and Nate, I never thought about being angry until Hank came around. They were good people who loved life. I can't say as I ever loved life.

My thoughts were interrupted by the door of the diner opening. In walked a man, woman, and a small boy. They looked like they were in their midthirties, and the boy looked to be around four or five years old. They picked the table directly behind me to sit down. I looked at the boy's face while they walked to the table. He didn't smile; in fact he looked sad. I wondered what was wrong with him. Maybe he was tired or just bored today. I didn't know. The boy sat with his back toward me, and the man and woman sat facing each other at the ends of the table. The boy was a cute little guy with blond hair. He was dressed in a little sailor's suit, including the hat.

I turned back toward the counter just as my malt arrived. The waitress set the malt in front of me and scurried away to attend to other tables. I took a sip of the malt, and she was right; it was the best malt I had ever tasted. I sat for a while enjoying my malt, and it wasn't long before my food was in front of me. Wow, the cheeseburgers looked to be a half pound each, the fries covered a full plate, and the chili was in a very large bowl. The waitress looked at me and cracked a smile and said, "Well, boy, do you think that will hold you until dinner?"

"Yeah, I think this should be enough food for the rest of the day. Maybe my next meal will be breakfast tomorrow morning."

We both laughed, and she rushed away to attend to other customers.

The food was really good. I wolfed down the first cheeseburger and half the fries in no time. I was just starting the chili when I overheard a conversation at the table behind me. The woman was yelling at the little boy because he'd got ketchup on his sailor outfit. His name was Billie. She continued yelling at the boy, telling him he never did anything right. "Why can't you be like other kids? You're always causing trouble. I can't ever enjoy a meal without you ruining it."

The little boy started to cry, and my blood pressure began to rise. I sat quietly hoping that she would stop her tirade on the boy. The boy was sobbing uncontrollably now, and she said, "Michael, take this brat to the car and lock him in so I can enjoy my food for once. You're the one who wanted him, and you can take care of him."

The guy didn't even say a word to her; he just got up from the chair and picked the boy up and walked to the door. I couldn't believe it. This kid was only four or five years old, and they were going to lock him in the car alone.

All the years of control and abuse came back to me again. I watched as the boy and his father went out the door. I pushed my other cheeseburger to the back of the counter and laid a fifty-dollar bill under my half-empty malt glass to pay for my meal. I stood up and went over to the table where the woman sat alone eating her food. She looked up at me standing over her, and I said, "Don't even say a word, lady. It wouldn't take much right now for me to shove that food down your throat and leave you choking on the floor. Let me help save your life someday by giving you a piece of advice. Let that child be a child because he deserves it. He is allowed to make mistakes along the way, he's a kid. You're the adult, and you should act like one. Someday that boy will grow up, and he will hate you for what you have done to him. His hatred for you may go deep enough that he can't control it, and that's when he will come for you. He will seek you out and destroy you as you destroyed him."

A look of panic and fear crossed her face. She jumped up from the table and ran out the door without looking back at me. I grabbed my coat off the chair and walked toward the door.

"Hey, boy, don't forget your change," the waitress yelled.

"Keep it, I won't need it anymore."

"Hey, boy, come here a minute."

I walked over to where she was standing next to the cash register and said, "What do you want?"

"I heard what you said to that woman. You're right, she seems like she doesn't care about that boy. She only cares about herself."

"Yeah, sometimes you need to care about yourself, but not at the expense of others, especially a little kid."

I turned and walked toward the door leaving her standing there with a puzzled look on her face. I went out the door, and the woman and her husband were standing next to their car. The man looked over at me while she whispered something into his ear. I just looked back at them and said, "Not today, I don't believe I'd try anything stupid if I were you, Michael. Lady, for your sake, I hope you listened real well to what I said. There are already enough guys like me in the world. So treat that kid good so he will grow up and be able to enjoy life along the way."

I turned and walked to my car and drove away. I knew she wouldn't change, but it was worth it for me to tell her what I thought. Maybe she will remember what I said the next time she starts yelling at the boy.

Dayton was about a 2½ hour drive from my parents' home. My mind was racing again, and I couldn't shut it down. That stupid lady in the restaurant had brought old memories back that I didn't want to think about. These were memories that would only die when I die, and not until then.

I pulled into the driveway and parked my car in front of the garage. I sat for a moment in the car just to collect my thoughts. I opened the car door and stepped out onto the driveway. I heard someone yelling my name. I looked across the street, and Mr. Morrow was standing there leaning on two canes. I walked over to him, and he said, "Zeke, I'm sorry about your father, he was a good man."

"Thanks, Mr. Morrow, he always spoke highly of you. I will miss him."

"I know you will, Zeke. Your father and I talked a lot about you. He was very proud of you. He spoke to me often about your job in Florida, he was very happy for you."

"Thanks, Mr. Morrow, for telling me that my father was proud of me. It means a great deal. I was very proud of him also."

I shook his hand and told him that I appreciated what he had done for me in the past. I watched him as he turned and walked back to the steps of his home. He looked much older now, and he wasn't as sturdy on his canes as he had been when I left home. I knew that he wouldn't be around much longer. It seems like death is just always around the corner waiting to suck the life out of you at the first opportunity.

I walked back across the street and up the steps of my childhood home. I stopped at the door. Just the thought of being back here gave me gut-wrenching pain. A cold chill consumed my entire body. But this had to be done, and I was the only one who could do it. I opened the front door and walked into the living room. Marie was sitting in the chair where James always sat. She looked up at me and said, "What the hell are you doing here? He's in the ground now, you weren't here when I needed you, and I don't need you here now!"

"I need to ask you something, Mom. I need you to tell me why you treated me the way you did?"

"I treated you the way you deserved to be treated. You were never any good, you were always in trouble. I know you had something to do with the disappearance of that boy Rich years ago. I know that he was here to see you a couple of days before he went missing. You told the police you hadn't seen him since school, but I know that you did."

"Well, for once you're right, Mom. I killed Rich, along with many others over the years that needed to be killed. I killed them all because of you, Mom. I killed them because nobody was going to control me anymore. I killed them because of all the hate and anger that you pounded into me day after day, week after week. You see, I did learn something from you. I learned how to hate from you, Mom, and I was good at it."

A look of horror came over her face. I could see little tiny beads of sweat begin to break out on her forehead. I think she now knew what I came home to do.

"I knew when you were little that you were evil. I should have sent you away then. I wished that you would have died when you were born. It would have been better for everyone. I blame your father. He should have been stronger with you. He should have beat some sense into to you."

I jumped up and smacked her across the face. She screamed in pain. I smacked her again and again. Each smack was followed by a loud scream.

"No, Mom, you're the one to blame. You created me from a helpless child. You created this monster that stands in front of you today. I should have killed you a long time ago."

I put my right hand on her throat and squeezed as hard as I could. I watched as her legs and arms flailed widely. Her eyes bulged out of her head. The room spun wildly around me. I felt the life leave her body, and she was limp in the chair. I released my grip and watched as her muscles twitched into death. I was suddenly at peace inside. I sat back on the couch and burst out in laughter. I had finally done what should have been done long ago. The real demon in my life was dead now. The real evil that I lived with all these years would never be able to hurt me again. It didn't matter what happened to me now; I had done the right thing. I had finally taken charge of my life.

I heard sirens in the distance. Marie's screams had probably been heard by a neighbor. But I didn't care. I just sat there and waited for their arrival. It was time for me to pay for my ways, but strangely enough, I was happy it was over.

Chapter 39

"Baker, get your ass up off the bed and come over here," I heard Sullivan bellow.

I broke away from my thoughts of the past and looked over at the cell door where Sullivan stood with guards, Burgess and Peters. His arm was in a sling. A cast protruded from the back of the sling and stopped about halfway up his bicep. I laughed inside. I bet that old boy was in a lot of pain from our little scuffle a couple of weeks ago.

"What happened to your arm, Sullivan? Did you slip and fall?"

"Shut your trap, Baker, or we'll take the clubs to you and beat some sense into you."

"Yeah, I'm really worried about that. What the hell do you want anyway? Can't a guy get a little peace and quiet around here?"

"It's that lawyer of yours, Welch. He's on his way here to talk with you. The warden wants me and the boys to make sure you're prettied up for him. I tried to tell the warden that was impossible, but he just wouldn't listen. I mean a big tough guy like you who kills his mama for fun. You just can't get that pretty no matter how you look at it."

"You really need to shut your mouth, Sullivan, before I break the other arm or maybe crush your skull and pop that little pea-sized brain out of your head."

"Don't think I'm not ready for you this time. The boys and I are trained on handling animals like you. The mistake we made the last time was we didn't chain you properly like an animal. The next time we take you out of the cell, we will chain you like the animal you are."

I just sat there and glared at him. I knew what he meant. Leg shackles, handcuffs, and a chain between them so I couldn't grab one of them. It really didn't matter what they did to me; I really didn't care. I wondered what Keith wanted now. He's done his job; he really worked hard during the trial.

My biggest problem was that I didn't have that cute-kid look for the jury. I didn't care how I looked to them. They knew that I killed Marie; I never denied it. I wasn't looking for their sympathy. Sure, when Keith put me on the stand, he took the jury through my childhood. He went through all the pain and suffering that I endured as a child. But I never gave the jury that feel-sorry-for-me look. Why would I? I wanted this over, and I was ready to accept whatever punishment they decided. No deals, lock me up, put a needle in my arm, do whatever you want, but don't put me back on the street. I can't trust myself among people anymore. I never know when the other person who lives inside me will jump out and kill again. I can't control him. I never have been able to control him.

Then I thought what if Keith and the jury knew about the others that I had killed? How likely would they be to feel sorry for me if they knew that? Even Keith, who thought he knew me, would shy away from the evil that lives inside me. He would have never taken the case if he knew everything about me. I laughed inside and thought to myself, if I really had wanted to beat this rap and get a mentally incompetent conviction, all I would have had to do is play the game. Play the game with the jury by looking like a lost, lonely soul who was scared of everything and everybody. Play the game with the psychologists and therapists who interviewed me. Just pretend that I really didn't know what I was doing, pretend that I heard voices in my head, pretend that I couldn't control my anger. That's all I really would have had to do, and they would have put me in a mental institution for a few years, and then I'd be back out in society to kill again. That's not what I wanted. I wanted it over.

I heard a message that came across the intercom for Sullivan. "Sullivan, lawyer Welch is coming through cell block A now. He should reach cell block C in five minutes. Prepare the prisoner for his arrival."

It was unusual for anyone to come to your cell to talk with you. I guess the guards and the warden thought this was the best way to handle it because of the problems they've had with me in the past.

I watched as Sullivan became nervous. He paced back and forth, speaking rapidly to Burgess and Peters about their duties to contain me. I laughed again inside. Because you see, it's really impossible for them to contain me. I've had eighteen months, twenty-four hours a day, seven days a week of thinking about how to destroy them. The guards don't plan like I do; they only think about containing me when the task is at hand and not before. I have the upper hand because I have all the time in the world to plan. These guys are thinking about getting off work, drinking a few beers, and screwing their wives or girlfriends. They're not spending their time worrying about me. Why should they? They only have to deal with me about once every thirty days. I've made a life out of dealing with people like them.

I hear the clang and rumble of the cell-block door being opened. I know that Keith is probably walking down the aisle toward my cell now. Sullivan nervously fondles the keys with his good hand. He is more nervous now than I have ever seen him. It's almost as if he is both certain there will be a problem and afraid of the consequences.

Keith finally reaches my cell and says, "Hi, Zeke, are they treating you okay?"

"I can't complain, Keith. The less I see of Sullivan and the boys, the better."

Keith turns to Sullivan and says, "Open the cell so I can go in and talk to my client."

"What the hell's wrong with you? Do you really want to go in the cage with this animal?"

"I told you before, don't harass my client! Now open the cell door."

"Okay, I'll open the door, but not before we shackle him."

"No, I don't want Zeke to be shackled. He doesn't deserve that kind of treatment."

Okay, it's your funeral. "Opening cell number 12," Sullivan screams down the aisle to the guard controlling the cell-block entrance gate.

Sullivan looks at me and says, "Sit on your bunk and don't move. I'm warning you, don't move a muscle. Burgess and Peters, you boys get your guns ready. If he makes a move from that bunk, shoot him!"

Sullivan puts the key in the cell door and eases it open for Keith to enter. Sullivan slams and locks the door behind him. Keith walks over and sits on my bunk next to me.

"How have you been, Zeke? I've been worried about you. That head guard, Sullivan, really has it in for you."

He was actually sincere with his words. He really was worried about my well-being. I'm glad that he didn't know the real me. It would have destroyed everything for him.

"I'm doing well. Don't worry about that dope, Sullivan. He's just a pain in the ass. He spends most of his time trying to piss me off, and he's not smart enough to do that."

Keith chuckles and says, "Well, I'm glad you're okay. A friend of yours called me the other day to see how you were doing. He is really worried about you. He told me that the Zeke he knew could never have done this."

"A friend of mine, how is that possible? I have no friends, you must be mistaken."

"He said his name was Nate, and he knew you from Florida."

Nate, I had forgotten about Nate and Millie. Why would they waste their time worrying about me? Did I really mean that much to them?

"Old Nate from Florida, yeah, I know Nate and his wife, Millie. I stayed with them for a few years when I was in Florida. Do me a favor, tell Nate that I'm really okay and not to worry about me."

"Okay, Zeke, I'll let him know. But I also wanted to let you know that I think the jury is on the verge of having a verdict in your case. It sounds like it may be a favorable verdict from what I'm hearing from one of the bailiffs who guards the deliberation chambers. He told me that he overheard them discussing your childhood abuse when the caterer was delivering lunch. It seems that most of them have a soft place in their heart for children who were abused."

I thought for a moment. I can't be put in a mental treatment facility. They'll put me back out on the street again in a few years. I couldn't let that happen; I wouldn't let that happen.

I was just about to address the problem with Keith when the intercom system started blaring again. "Keith Welch, pick up the cell-block phone," the speakers rattled.

Keith excused himself, and Sullivan opened the door so he could get to the phone. I could see his face from where I was sitting. I saw a big grin come across his face, and he had an excited pitch in his voice when he said thank you to the person on the other end. He hung the phone up and looked over at me. He walked quickly to the cell door and said, "Good news, Zeke, the jury has reached a verdict."

I couldn't risk it anymore. I had to do something.

"Sullivan, open the cell door. I want to walk with my client to the transportation van," I heard Keith say.

"Not without putting the shackles on him. He won't be leaving the cell without the shackles this time."

"Okay, do whatever you have to do. This will be the last time you deal with my client, anyway. He will be treated properly in the mental facility. He won't have to worry about taking any abuse while he is there."

Burgess and Peters were standing directly behind Sullivan.

Burgess held the leg shackles, Peters held the chain that went between the handcuffs and the leg shackles, and Sullivan held the handcuffs.

"Okay, boys, it's time to shackle this animal for transportation. Peters, you keep your gun drawn and shoot to kill if this animal tries anything."

"Yes, sir!" Peters responded.

Peters drew his gun and held it toward me. I could see the fear and nervousness in his eyes as he looked at me. Sullivan put the key in the lock and opened the cell door. It wasn't just Peters himself that was nervous; they all were nervous. I knew from experience that when you're nervous, you make mistakes. Mistakes always lead to trouble, and in this case, it could be fatal.

"Stand up!" Sullivan ordered.

I stood up in front of my bunk and outstretched my hands toward him. He approached me very cautiously.

"Keep that gun on him!" Sullivan barked.

"Yes, sir!" Peters responded.

Sullivan stepped toward me and clicked one side of the handcuffs on my left wrist while Burgess fumbled putting the leg shackle on my left ankle. Sullivan then snapped the other side of the handcuff closed on my right wrist. He again gave it an extra click just to inflict pain so I would know he was in charge. Keith stood watching and waiting patiently during the process.

Sullivan turned to get the final chain from Peters so he could lock the handcuffs and the leg shackles together. When he turned, it gave me my opportunity. I lunged forward and put the chain of the handcuffs around Sullivan's throat and pulled him back to me. Much like with Hank, I could hear his neck snap and feel his larynx crush. Burgess screamed, "Shoot him, shoot him."

I heard Keith scream, "Stop, Zeke, don't kill him!"

I looked over toward Peters just as he squeezed the trigger on his revolver. The shot rang clearly in my ears as the bullet drove its way into my right side.

I slumped back with Sullivan still in my grasp. It was too late for him, and I knew it. My first jerk on the chain of the handcuffs had snapped his neck. He was limp and lifeless now. Another shot rang out, and I felt a burning sensation in my chest. I released my grasp on Sullivan. I stumbled forward a couple of steps and fell to the floor.

Keith rushed over to my side, kneeled down next to me, and said, “Why, Zeke, why did you do it?”

I looked up at him and, with my last breaths, said, “Everybody has to die sometime, Keith. And besides, I already dug two graves.”

I saw a perplexed look come across his face as I faded into death and darkness.

Edwards Brothers,Inc!
Thorofare, NJ 08086
08 June, 2010
BA2010159

Journey Of Revenge